A NOVEL

ROBERT W. CHRISTIAN

www.ten16press.com - Waukesha, WI

Unholy Shepherd
Copyright © 2021 Robert W. Christian
ISBN 9781645382249
Second Edition

Unholy Shepherd
by Robert W. Christian

For information, please contact:

www.ten16press.com
Waukesha, WI

Cover design by Kaeley Dunteman

For my beautiful wife, Sarah.
Thank you for encouraging me to chase my dream.
"143".

"THEY SACRIFICED THEIR SONS AND DAUGHTERS
TO FALSE GODS.
THEY SHED INNOCENT BLOOD,
THE BLOOD OF THEIR SONS AND DAUGHTERS...
...AND THE LAND WAS DESECRATED
BY THEIR BLOOD."

Psalm 106:37-38

dUXBURY, 1981

The flashing blue and red lights of the police cars hit the peripheral of Maire's vision as she stood by the roadside, blanket wrapped, staring into the trees. The bustle of police, reporters, and locals hummed about her. She was aware of it all, yet there was no cohesion to any of it. She could not pick out a single voice through the haze in her mind. She simply stared, blinking now and then, but never shifting her gaze. If she tried hard enough, perhaps she could move her sight a mere three hundred yards down the bank, through the mass of greens, reds, yellows, and browns, and rest her eyes on her precious baby boy, who now lay on the forest floor.

"Mrs. Allerton? Mrs. Allerton?" a voice cut through the cone of silence she'd wrapped herself in. Maire felt herself blink twice before turning to find one of the policemen on the scene uncomfortably close to her. It seemed plain to her, now that she had returned from her private thoughts, that he had been trying to get her attention for some time. He was a short man, not more than an inch or two taller than Maire herself. *Dennis,* she thought to herself, *the short one is Officer Dennis.* He'd been one of the two men from the department to come tell her just a few short hours ago that they had found her

1

son. The other had been the captain, Alvin Lodge, who she could now see over Dennis' shoulder talking to the group of reporters that had flocked to the scene. *Vultures,* she thought sourly to herself. Shaking her head clear, she focused her attention back on Officer Dennis, who she could now see was holding a notepad in one hand and tapping a pen nervously upon it with the other.

"Keane!" she snapped, almost surprising herself with her sternness. She had not meant to round on the young man in such a fashion, but there was no way she was going to be called by her bastard of an ex-husband's name. Maire cleared her throat, took a breath, and tried to force a small, reassuring smile. "Apologies, Officer Dennis, but I prefer my maiden name, if you wouldn't mind. I'm no longer married." That wasn't technically true, but close enough for her.

"Of course," said the officer, though still clearly taken aback. "*Ms.* Keane," he continued, "I know this is a difficult time for you, but I need to ask you a few more questions."

A difficult time! Maire turned back toward the wood line and closed her eyes for a moment. The man had no idea what a difficult time meant. All the platitudes in the world wouldn't change what had happened. What could he know of her heartache? What could any of them know, these disingenuous charlatans, offering her their hollow sympathies and lip service prayers! Maire's eyes flung back open as she felt herself begin to shake. She must maintain some level of composure. The tears, the anger, none of it would bring back her darling boy. None of it would lift him from the hastily dug hole he was now lying in, covered only halfway with dirt and dead leaves, and carry him home safe and alive. He was in God's hands now. She at least, unlike all these other people, truly believed that. Maire brushed her hand over her eyes as subtly as she could. Still dry. *For now*, she thought.

"Go ahead, Officer," she said, not looking away from the trees and in a voice a bit less than a whisper. She half-expected to have to repeat herself, when, to her surprise, Dennis responded.

"Ms. Keane, I was looking over my notes from our first conversation back at your home, and I was hoping to go over it again. You see, the boys from Chelsea are going to take over the investigation and before they do that, they want us to construct a clearer timeline of events. They seem to think there's an inconsistency with your original statement and asked me to get a second one from you."

Maire sighed and turned around to look at Officer Dennis. "You think I don't know what Agent Mansfield is thinking right now?" she asked flatly. She was losing the strength to keep her composure. "Just because I wasn't born here, doesn't mean I don't know who the cops' prime suspect always is when a child goes missing!" Even in her own ears she could hear her native Cork accent begin to sharpen as she tried to hold back her agitation. In the twelve years since her marriage had brought her to this side of the ocean, her friends and family both here and back home had noted with a perverse delight how her speech had become muddled with the thick New England accents that surrounded her. They could always tell whenever she was losing her temper, however, when she slipped into her brogue. Her ex-husband in particular enjoyed seeing her get upset—just to "hear her Irish voice." *The pig.*

"Mrs. Aller— *Ms. Keane*," Officer Dennis corrected himself, "this is just standard procedure. There's no need to get upset. Between you and me, I don't think you're under serious consideration as a suspect for your son's murder. And we've also just received word that your husband—I'm sorry—your *ex*-husband's whereabouts for the past week have been confirmed as well. We have verification from our embassy that he has indeed been in Berlin on business since before your son's disappearance."

That didn't shock Maire. As much of a bastard as he'd been to her, the one thing she could say about Stanley Allerton was that he loved his children fiercely. Although the custody battle was going bitterly, and her lawyer assured her she would come out victorious, that didn't change the way he had doted on his son and daughter every chance he got. No. However much she might wish he was capable of something like this—just to give her another reason to hate him—Stanley could never harm their son. He'll be just as broken over this as she is. Maybe he'd just stay in Germany. That thought gave her little comfort.

"All right, Officer, what do you need from me?" Maire sighed. This was getting ridiculous, but she knew Officer Dennis wouldn't leave her alone to grieve until he had accomplished what he was supposed to.

"I just need you to give me your account as best as you can from the day your son disappeared until this morning. Maybe there's something you forgot to tell us, or remembered, since the last time we went over all this."

Four days for her to remember. Most people would find a task like that to be intimidating. But Maire had gone over every minute of each one of those days over and over in her mind, to the point that she couldn't think of one detail she had overlooked. She walked slowly over to the safety rail along the roadway and sat on it, hugging her blanket around her tighter. It would be easier for Officer Dennis to hear her there, away from the noise and confusion of the cameras. The last week was so vivid in her mind—the story so complete—that she was positive that she could nearly repeat her previous testimony verbatim, if she felt so inclined. There was still only one detail that she had kept to herself, a personal matter that may not even bear anything out on the actual case, yet still caused her to be uneasy. She would deal with it when she needed to.

The officer came slowly over. He seemed almost hesitant, as if sitting next to her violated some sensibility that he held. *Too professional*, she thought. *Poor kid just isn't ready for all of this.* She actually did feel a certain sense of pity for the young man. Anyone could see that he was in over his head. He clearly hadn't joined the department in their quiet little town thinking he'd be involved in a case like this. She glanced down at her watch. Twelve minutes to noon. The day felt like it was taking a lifetime. Maire could hardly believe that it was only six hours ago that she was at home holding out hope her boy was still alive.

Officer Dennis sat down on the rail next to her and looked at the ground in front of them. Maire got the impression that she would have to be the one to break the silence. She did not relish having to go over her statement again, but if it would help in finding the bastard responsible for her son's death, she could find the strength to keep herself together for another hour or so.

"Where would you like me to start?" she asked Officer Dennis.

Dennis looked at her, blinked a few times, and then quickly flipped open his notebook to sift through the pages. A sharp sigh of aggravation escaped Maire's lips before she could catch herself, but he seemed to take no notice.

"Let's start on Thursday evening and just go from there," he said after finding the page he was looking for in his notebook. She could tell by the way he had flipped back and forth through the book that his notes were in no particular order, and she anticipated having to stop several times while he caught up or added new information he'd missed. Or misplaced. Maire took a deep breath and began her account.

She took Officer Dennis through the four days, beginning with her son and daughter's arrival home from school on Thursday afternoon around three o'clock. Maire recalled how Braden had brought her a crayon-drawn picture of what was meant to be her and her children in front of their house. He had also included a yellow, stick-figure dog, which made her laugh. Braden had been asking for a dog for the last six months, but she had been resistant to the idea, knowing that she was going to be the one taking care of it. The picture was titled "MY FAMILY" in big, blocky child letters. She inquired where his father was, trying to be civil and point out that even though they were divorcing, daddy would still be part of the family. "Daddy's on the plane!" Braden had quickly answered, taking the picture back and pointing to the upper corner at what Maire had at first thought was a bird. The picture is still hanging on the refrigerator.

She remembered that her daughter had gone straight to her room. Maire noted how quiet she had been after coming in the house that day. She thought it a bit odd, even as of late. Maureen had always been a quiet child, and had been interacting even less since hearing the news about the divorce, but at the very least she'd come into the kitchen for an after-school snack before retreating upstairs to her homework or her book collection. That day though, she didn't say a word. All Maire had seen of her was when she took off her light blue windbreaker, hung it up on the hallway hook, picked up her backpack, and ran up the stairs. She barely even heard the bedroom door close from the kitchen. Maureen had the habit of door slamming, so that small detail stuck fast in Maire's mind. Of course, such minuscule details meant little to the police, so she hadn't mentioned it.

Maire recounted that it hadn't been until she had called the kids down to dinner that she first noticed Braden was missing. He had been playing and watching television in the living room for most of the afternoon. Maureen came down to the dinner table and sat down without saying a word. A minute or two passed and Braden still hadn't come to the table. Usually he'd run in as soon as she announced dinner was ready. Her boy loved to eat. She had walked into the living room, and it was then that she saw the sight that would haunt her for the rest of her life: the wide-open French doors leading to the backyard with her son nowhere to be seen.

She told him how the rest of the night was spent much like anyone would expect. She went door to door to see if any of the neighbors had seen him. She called all his friends' parents to see if he had shown up at any of their homes. No one had seen him. She then made the call to the police department to file the missing person report. They had asked if perhaps he was with his father, but she told them he had said he had some business overseas this week. She didn't know where he was staying but gave the police his secretary's number to call in the morning.

She recalled how the days leading up to this morning were a blur of police interviews, organized searches, and never-ending parades of friends, family, neighbors, and even strangers coming in and out of her house offering their condolences. *Meaningless condolences*, she thought. Through it all, only two things remained constant: no sign of her son was found, and her daughter had remained eerily detached. That second thought she kept to herself.

All of that continued until this morning. Her sister-in-law, Nancy, had taken it upon herself to come over after church the previous day, cook, and spend the night. Maire would have sooner had Lucifer himself over than the sister of her soon-to-be ex-husband, but she bore it as best she could. She had even managed a few hours of sleep before the police came to her door at just past seven. Nancy had answered and then came upstairs to find her. She had been sitting in the old rocking chair in Braden's room, thinking about all the times he had fallen asleep in her arms as a baby. It seemed an eternity ago now. When Nancy had appeared at the door and said the police were downstairs, Maire already knew what awaited her.

"Ms. Keane," Officer Dennis said when she had finished, "we need to ask you about your daughter."

She could tell he was nervous about something, and a cold chill ran down the back of her neck. Did they know what she had kept out of her statement? Maire kept all the composure she was capable of.

"What about her?" she asked as evenly as possible.

"Ms. Keane, the County Sheriff's Department received a call at around two in the morning on Saturday. The caller was a young child. She didn't identify herself and just began talking. She told the switchboard operator: 'North three mile twenty-five. Braden's lying down in the leaves. He's cold. Someone has to help him. He's not moving and he's too cold. Mommy won't listen. Mommy doesn't believe me.' The operator tried to get more from her, but she hung up right away. Ms. Keane," Officer Dennis sighed, "the FBI has a psychologist at your house right now speaking with your daughter. If that was her calling that night, they'll find out soon. Is there anything you'd like to add to your statement before that happens?"

Maire's legs went numb. It was all she could do to nod. Officer Dennis called the agents over, and Maire filled in what she had left out of her report. That Friday night, Maureen had wandered from her bedroom to where Maire was sitting on the couch. Her eyes were open, but she didn't blink, as if in a trance. Her words were clear though, if a little soft.

"Braden. Braden, wake up!" she said, standing beside the armrest of the couch. She stared straight ahead, but earnestly began patting Maire's arm. "Mommy!" She began to get more hysterical, but was still staring at the wall, unblinking. "Mommy, we have to go get Braden. He's cold! He's not moving! He was carried into the woods! I saw! I carried him! Mommy! North. Three. Mile. Two. Five. It wasn't me! I carried him, but it wasn't me! Please, Mommy, he's cold and he's not moving!"

Maire had stared at her daughter in horror. Finally, going against everything she'd ever been told about a sleepwalker, she shook her daughter awake. Maureen blinked and when her breathing returned to normal, she stared straight at Maire and asked if they were going to get Braden now. Maire was paralyzed, not knowing what to do. She told her daughter that she just had a bad dream and to go back to bed. Maureen had protested and began to cry, but Maire took hold of her daughter's arm and led her back to her room. When the police told her that morning that her son had been found on the side of Highway 3 near mile marker twenty-five, she finally understood what had happened to Maureen.

When Maire was a young girl in Ireland, her great-grandmother had told her stories about "The Demon Sight". She didn't remember much about it, but her great-grandmother had insisted that once every few generations, a daughter would be born and, marked as Satan's own, would see with the eyes of pure evil. Her grandmother and mother had told her it was all nonsense, just the ramblings of a superstitious old woman trying to scare her for her own amusement. Maire hadn't thought about those stories in years, but now she finally saw the truth in the old woman's yarns. She broke down in tears as she told all of this to the officers and agents now gathered around her. She looked from face to face, but none registered any sense of understanding. *Why should they understand*, she thought to herself. *No one could possibly comprehend what has happened to me!* Hers were burdens no mother should have to bear: her sweet, darling son was dead, and her daughter was the property of the Devil. Maire fell to the ground, hugged her knees to her chest, and continued to sob.

UNHOLY
SHEPHERD

ONE

Detective Manny Benitez took his last sip of beer and set the bottle on the bar. The crowd at Smokey's was changing over from the usual after-work crew to the after-dinner drinkers, and soon the air in the bar would reflect the bar's name. He wanted to be out before that happened. Smokey's was one of the few places in town that he actually liked to stop in to, as it was only a block south of Main Street and less than a five-minute walk from work, but he usually didn't stay past nine.

Manny got up from the bar, turned, and scanned the dining room. A small group of officers from the precinct had taken a table in a corner to his right and had begun their socializing. Manny didn't want to be spotted as he left if he could help it; the way he felt about his coworkers was complicated. They were all brothers-in-arms as civil servants, but he'd never really assimilated into the rest of the fraternity. He chose a longer path to the exit, around the tables to his left, hoping to get by unnoticed. He'd just reached the door and was about to push it open when a familiar, gravelly voice rose above the rest of the noise.

"Hey, Benny!" It rang out, and the rest of the patrons

15

seemed to lower their voices in response. "Where the hell d'ya think you're going?"

Manny tried to hide the cringe that came to his face as he turned. The voice had come from Sergeant Sam Wentworth, seated in the middle of a semi-circle of four other officers. Around him were the men who could usually be found with him when out on the town: Alan Scottsdale, Mike McKeegan, and the Henderson twins—Lance and Todd. These five had all been high school friends and came through the academy together. It was clear to all, even to the grade schoolers of the mid-80s like Manny, that Wentworth had always been the group's leader. Everyone knew the Wentworth Gang.

"Heading home, Sarge," he said, trying to sound as casual as possible. "I got an early morning."

"Yeah," Wentworth snickered, "huge day of pushing those six papers from one side of your desk to the other!" The entire table burst into laughter. Manny couldn't tell if it was sincere, or if they were just humoring their king. He figured it was probably fifty-fifty. He smiled along, gave a wave of his hand and, leaving them to their merriment, turned around and headed out into the night.

It felt strangely warm and muggy, even for the middle of August. Manny sighed as he walked to his car. Wentworth and the others weren't wrong. There was a reason that there was only one detective in the Sycamore Hills Police Department. It was a small town in the middle of nowhere, and there were very few crimes that were committed that needed much more investigation than talking to some of the locals or making a few phone calls. He sometimes thought about going back to school.

Manny reached his truck, and the driver's seat groaned

slightly as he sat down. The truck was nearly a decade and a half old, but it was the one thing in his life that he counted as a truly prized possession. He could still remember the day he bought it during his junior year of college. It had nearly one hundred thousand miles on it then, and its frame and body were starting to go, but he kept the engine running as well as ever. It was a point of pride for him to be able to work on his own vehicle; a little bit of his father rubbing off on him. He started the truck, rolled down his window to let in the night air, and drove off toward home.

It would take less than ten minutes to get from Smokey's to the house he rented on the northern end of town, and there were very few other cars out on the road after nine on a Wednesday. In a town of barely four thousand, the only ones out and about were civil servants and maybe some students from the local junior college. Manny switched on the truck's radio and turned right off Main Street onto the road that would take him home. He'd been listening to public radio on his way to work that morning, but switched to FM for his Top 40 for the ride home. With the strong bass beats of the latest release playing, he retreated into his thoughts.

Thus far, in his eighteen months on the force, his toughest case had been tracking down the culprits of a graffiti spree last fall. The only reason the department had even given it as much attention as they did was because the teens responsible had tagged the county courthouse, which stands within the municipal borders of Sycamore Hills. It had been a sneaker footprint preserved in mud that had confirmed what everyone already knew: the place to start shaking down potential suspects was the high school. Manny had a better rapport with the students, being much closer to their age than almost anyone else on the force. It only took him speaking to about a dozen of them before they took in the group of five boys, got their confessions, and sentenced them to probation until they turned eighteen.

It wasn't that he wanted more serious crimes in his hometown. The job simply hadn't fulfilled him from day one. As time went by, he found himself falling further into the trappings of self-analysis. Nights were the worst, when he had nothing but his television to keep him company. The more he allowed himself to delve into the depths of his soul, the more he became aware of some truths.

The most pervasive was his Latin American heritage. It opened the doors to Saint Anselm in New Hampshire, but it had never helped that he was constantly reminded that his college scholarship was one reserved specifically for minorities. Or that Wentworth, McKeegan, and the others insisted on Anglicizing his last name and calling him "Benny". He hated the name. Was it so hard to just call him "Manny"?

He'd had the opportunity to interview with the FBI during his senior year of college. His teachers assured him he was a sure thing, and that his skill set would lend itself well to the work. But what would have happened when he'd actually have to work? Would he really have passed the FBI entrance exams? Been a good agent in the field? Risen through the ranks? He would have failed eventually, and that would have proven everybody right. He was nothing more than a man who got his opportunities based on affirmative action. He decided not to take the interview and accepted an entry-level position at the New Hampshire State Department of Justice, working as an aide to one of the junior district attorneys. In the five years there, he had never even tried for one of the four promotions that became available. That's when he began to toy with the idea that he was afraid of failure and made the decision to move back to Sycamore Hills. He thought he was taking a big risk at the time, but now he knew it wasn't true. He was running back home and hiding where it was safe.

The headlights of the truck shone on his old burgundy mailbox, and the truck slowly climbed the gentle incline up to the garage. The garage door didn't work, and the garage itself was packed with stuff, so he parked out front and headed inside.

The house wasn't large, but it was functional and offered a nice view of the lake, which was fed by a small river that flowed through the county. Inside, he had three bedrooms, a full bath, and plenty of room in his living room to fit his sofa and recliner. His landlord had opened up the kitchen a few years before he'd moved in, giving the old mid-century home a more modern flow. Manny liked the house and felt very comfortable there. He was even considering talking to his landlord about purchasing it.

He tossed his keys on the end table and walked toward the couch. He grabbed the remote, turned on the TV, and scrolled through the channels to find the ball game. St. Louis was down a run in the seventh, and Manny scoffed as the announcer recounted the two-run lead they'd just given up in the top of the inning. They sure hadn't looked like the World Series champs of a year ago this season, and Manny suspected there would be no miracle run to the playoffs this year. Shaking his head, he tossed the remote onto the couch and circled around into the kitchen.

Manny opened the refrigerator and stood transfixed, not really looking for anything in particular. His dinner and drinks sat heavy in his stomach, so he wasn't hungry or thirsty. A cheer erupted from the TV, shaking him out of his thoughts. He closed the door to the refrigerator and peeked around the corner to see two Cardinals trotting around the bases. Manny smiled. That was more like it. Pulling himself back into the kitchen, he decided to go ahead and have a nightcap and went over to the cabinet that held the silver tequila. He filled a glass and swallowed the entire amount before filling it again and carrying it back into the living room.

After taking a tiny sip of the tequila, he placed the shot glass on the coffee table and sat back to enjoy the rest of the game. He was only half watching, though, as he retreated back into his thoughts. Why did he let Wentworth and the others continue to look down on him? Why couldn't he find satisfaction in what he was doing? Should he try to transfer to the County Sheriff's Department? Should he pack up and leave Sycamore Hills? He sat and sipped, but he couldn't see any of the answers, even when looking through the bottom of an empty glass.

Manny stood up, shut off the TV, and walked to the window. In the west, he could see clouds beginning to blot out the night's sky and dim flashes of heat lightning flaring up here and there. It wasn't enough to light up the night, and there were no accompanying rumbles of thunder to warn of any summer storm. It was almost as if nature itself was teasing him, promising a change that wasn't actually going to come.

Manny closed the curtains and slowly shuffled to his room, hoping a new day would bring some kind of change.

TWO

Through the streets of Sycamore Hills, in and out of the glow of the street lights, Ra'ah walked slowly. The air was hot and had a wet tinge to it, filled with the subtle smell of the farms and fields to the west of town. It smelled of change. It was time to begin his mission.

The world had become a vile cesspool, full of greed, war, and corruption. Even a just man hid secrets in his heart that spat in the face of the Creator. Ra'ah had lived in the slime with these creatures all his life and now, finally, had risen in his enlightenment to a plane that few others could reach. The muddy waters of existence were now as clear as glass, and their turbulence was no more. He had waited years, and now all was ready.

Turning north out of the downtown district, Ra'ah threw up his dark hood for protection against unfriendly eyes. Eyes that wouldn't see with the heart, nor with the soul, seeing only the flesh of the man and misunderstanding what was beginning here tonight. Ra'ah understood. He knew and did not fear any consequence, for the rewards far outweighed the punishment. He stopped for a moment and reached under his shirt to the hilt of his knife. It, like him, had been made for this purpose:

an instrument to serve in the great work ahead. He continued down the street, now lined with homes, silhouetted against the moonlight.

After a few minutes, Ra'ah stopped at his destination: a large two-story home in the heart of the little neighborhood. The sole source of light came from a lamp above the front porch. Everything else was dark and still, and somewhere inside, his first task awaited. He looked down at his watch. The face was barely visible, but there was just enough ambient light to read it. Three minutes until midnight. It was nearly time. Ra'ah looked up and down the street. All was silent. He crept along the fence line of the house and made his way into the rear corner of the backyard, next to a woodpile and under the shade of a small tree. He still had a few spare moments before he needed to spring into action.

And so, in the darkness before the new day struck, Ra'ah knelt and raised his eyes toward Heaven.

THREE

It was as if she was looking through two eye holes in a mask as she peered down at the sleeping boy. She could hear a muttered whisper, a low, hypnotic voice, speaking rhythmically, and though she couldn't understand the words, somehow she knew they were coming from her throat. A brown, unlabeled bottle in a gloved hand appeared in front of her, followed by another that lifted out of the darkness to uncork it. The second hand disappeared from her sight and then returned holding a white cloth. Delicately, the first hand poured some of the liquid onto the cloth and pressed it over the child's nose and mouth. Almost immediately, the young boy's eyes snapped open, and there was a moment of recognition in them before they rolled back in his head.

The eyes looked toward the half-open door for a moment, as if expecting someone to come rushing through. No one came, and the room spun with a blur back to the child on his bed, taking slow, shallow breaths. Her own will struggled to help him, which proved useless, and within seconds she could feel the weight of the child in the arms. Within moments, the hallway and staircase were rushing by, barely visible in the peripheral, and before she knew it, she felt the night's air rush onto the face. The arms laid the child down in the grass, and the eyes turned to look at the back of the house. Through the darkness, she thought she could just make out what looked like an upside down *U* above the back door. The eyes would not allow her to focus on anything else and turned back to the boy, lying peacefully in the grass. The arms appeared again to carry him a dozen steps further.

A pile of wood came into view, stacked about three feet high. On top, there were several longer pieces that formed a make-shift platform. She felt the weight in the arms lighten, and the eyes looked down at the young boy, now lying face down on top of the woodpile. Her own consciousness began to wrestle against the prison of the mask again as she felt the right hand grip the handle of something hidden under the shirt. The hand came back into view and she saw the knife: a long and curved blade with a carved wooden handle. She tried to shut the eyes but, though a gray veil began to fall over her sight, she could not shut out the image of the left hand grasping the boy's hair and raising his head while the knife was moved into position under his chin. The eyes looked to the night sky, and as her vision continued to fade, she heard those same low, muffled words. Just before the blackness finally took her, she felt the violent jerk of the right hand.

Maureen's eyes snapped open and she kicked the sheets off her legs as she leaped out of her bed. She could feel her breathing come in short gasps, and she felt dizzy from standing up too fast. She sat against the wall, closed her eyes, and took several deep breaths. Her heart was pumping in her ears, but ever so slowly, it began to slow and the thumping faded. She opened her eyes again to look over at her nightstand. The green numbers of her clock radio were the only thing showing in the darkness. 2:47. Maureen felt a slow churning in her stomach but managed to stand and creep back over to her bed. She reached down to find that her sheets were completely soaked. Balling them all up and raising them to her nose, she was grateful to find that it was just sweat. Still, it would be uncomfortable sleeping in her bed the rest of the night, especially since she found more sweat on her pillows. That, and the nausea which now began to build inside her, promised to keep sleep at a distance.

Maureen tossed the bedding back onto the bed and felt her way across the creaking wood floor to the small bathroom that stood on the opposite side of the tiny studio apartment that had only been home for three weeks. She knew the way should be clear, but her feet still hadn't memorized the path.

Her head still foggy from the nightmare, Maureen fumbled with the pull chain that hung along the wall next to the door. The harsh light from the single bulb disoriented her as she hunched over the sink. Staring at her reflection, she felt her knees buckle. She tried to steady herself using the sink, but it wasn't enough.

At that moment, she lost control of herself and fell to her knees. Her stomach convulsed violently, and she only just crawled over to the toilet before a torrent of vomit erupted from her mouth. The world went upside down for a few moments, and a grizzly slideshow of the images from her sleep rushed before her eyes, burning themselves into her memory, all punctuated by the inverted *U* above a white door. Another convulsion drove her forward, and she spilled more of her stomach's contents into the toilet—nothing but yellow bile and stomach acid.

The tempest continued in cycles until finally, stripped of nearly all her strength, Maureen lifted her hand one last time to the handle, flushed the last bits down the toilet, and gingerly pushed herself back into a seated position against the wall. It was only then, as she stared back through the door into the darkness of her apartment, that she became conscious of the tears slowly making their way down her cheeks. She raised a hand to her eyes and brushed away the moisture. It wasn't much, and she wasn't even sure why she was crying, but she felt somewhere deep inside of her a strange sense of disgust at her weakness. Her mother speaking.

Maureen quickly wiped her eyes one more time and, finding them dry again, struggled up to her feet and made her way back to the mirror. She examined her reflection. Her hair lay flat and stringy, still wet as if she had been caught out in the rain. Her eyes seemed slightly sunken in. She looked closer and saw that in her convulsions over the toilet, a blood vessel in her left eye had popped, and the white was now crisscrossed by ugly red spiderwebs. Frowning at her reflection, Maureen turned on the cold water tap and splashed her face. The water from the sink was usually cold, even when she turned on the hot water tap, but in that moment it felt as if a thousand icy needles hit her face all at once. It was both painful and exhilarating and cleared her senses so completely that she began to notice the dull throb in her temples. A headache had often accompanied the nightmares in the past, so it did not catch her by surprise. She knew just what to do if she wanted to ever get back to sleep.

Keeping the light on in the bathroom, Maureen plodded back to her bedside. She pulled the top drawer of her nightstand open and stuck her hand to the very back, searching for the familiar plastic bottle. She pulled it free and poured its contents into her hand. She turned slightly to allow the light to illuminate the dozen and a half little pink tablets until she found the half of one she was looking for. A half tablet of Darvocet, courtesy of Marie Adams, chased by a shot and a half of whiskey would get her back to sleep.

After putting the half pill into her mouth, she tipped the rest back into the bottle, and stuck it back where she had found it. She then shuffled over to the kitchen, which was really just some cabinets and a sink set on the wall with a refrigerator next to it. Maureen stooped as she reached the lower cabinets, searching for the bottle that she had taken from the bar where she spent her nights slinging drinks for the same half dozen people. In the three weeks since she started the job, she'd taken at least four bottles from the store room. It was the cheap stuff, not really fit for the consumption of decent individuals, and no one ever ordered it. Judging from the dust, she was fairly certain that Mr. Anderson had ordered the case more than ten years ago and was never going to reorder it. It might as well not go to waste, even if it did taste like lighter fluid. In truth, Maureen wasn't scared about losing her job over some pilfered liquor. A big, fake smile, a tight, white tank top, and her most flattering pair of jeans was all it took to have her boss and those slobs perched on the bar stools ready to hand over their car keys to her. To her dismay, though, the spot in the cabinet where the whiskey usually was was empty. She forgot she had finished the bottle before going to bed.

Shaking her head, she moved over to the refrigerator and grumbled as she pulled open the door. There was still a third of a bottle of the three-dollar chardonnay, sitting on the shelf in the door next to a bottle of ketchup and four cans of vegetable juice. It was sour, and she really hadn't liked it upon her first sip, but she'd take what she could get. There was no glassware in the apartment, and she really didn't care to pour it into a plastic cup, so Maureen simply took a sip of the offending white wine from the bottle and sauntered back toward the pale glow of the bathroom.

She knew she had about thirty to forty-five minutes before the combination of the wine and the pill would let her fall back asleep, and now that she was aware of her own body again, she felt dirty. Upon reaching the bathroom again, she went straight to the claw-footed tub and cranked the hot water knob as far to the left as she could.

Leaving the water running and setting the wine bottle next to the tub, Maureen returned to the mirror to scrutinize her reflection. The redness of the vessels in her eye had spread further into the white part, causing it to go completely pink. She frowned at herself and tugged the lower lid down to see how far the pink spread. To her surprise, there was still a bit of white visible, so hopefully there would be no concern at the bar that she had pink eye or something else that would force Mr. Anderson to send her home. She needed the shifts and the tips if she was going to be able to move on from Sycamore Hills within three months like she had always planned. After tonight, though, she might have to accelerate those plans. The wandering had become her safety net. Never staying in one place for too long had always been the best protection from the nightmares. But still, no matter how far she ran, or how many different people she became, they eventually found her, often forcing her to move on ahead of schedule.

She sighed and turned back to the bathtub and stuck her hand under the running water. It felt warm enough, so she plugged the stopper into the drain and allowed the tub to fill. She yanked off her T-shirt, pulled off her underwear, and turned again to look in the mirror. She frowned again as she stared at herself. Were her breasts starting to sag? Was that some new belly fat there? She turned around and took a quick look over her shoulder to examine her backside, sliding her hands down, grabbing and lifting up each cheek and letting go. They bounced once and settled back into place. Maureen allowed herself a quick half-smile. *At least that's all still in the right place. Must be the running*, she mused to herself.

Maureen did not allow her gaze to continue any further up though and quickly swung herself back around. She knew if she let her eyes wander, they would come to rest on the pale white scars that formed the innumerable *Xs* across her back. They were nearly invisible to most people's indifferent glances. In fact, no man she'd ever been with had mentioned them, even though she knew that they could be felt if he was paying attention and running his fingers over her back in a delicate way. She'd never been with a man who took the time to do that, as far as she could remember, and even if she had, she just assumed that no one cared.

Maureen pulled herself away from the mirror and returned to the tub. It was nearly half full, so she stepped in and lowered herself into the water, grabbing the bottle of wine as she did so. She propped herself up into a sitting position, with her legs straight, her back against the side of the tub, and her arms and head resting on the rim. It wasn't very comfortable, but it was the only way to get her entire body in the tub and not risk falling asleep. She took a sip and, now that the water had risen to a couple of inches shy of the rim, she lifted her foot to turn off the water. She quickly slid her toes back below the surface of the water; she hated to look at her feet. The big toes on each had never healed properly and were set at an unnatural angle. More battle scars to match those on her back.

Maureen pushed aside those memories and closed her eyes but still remained aware. The medication hadn't quite kicked in yet, and even the dim light of the bathroom intensified the pulsing behind her eyes. She balanced the wine bottle on her chest, not caring if the bath water warmed its contents, and sipped down another mouthful every few minutes. The stuff tasted the same warm or cold.

Eventually, her muscles relaxed, and she was able to focus on the warmth of the bath as her headache finally began to retreat. She set the now empty bottle beside the tub and slowly plunged her head below the surface. Sputtering slightly as she came up, she gathered her hair behind her neck and rubbed the water away from her eyes. Maureen let out a heavy sigh; the weight of her self-medication was beginning to press down on her shoulders. She unplugged the stopper and got out of the tub as the water began to swirl down the drain. Reaching over to the towel bar, Maureen grabbed the coarse, brown piece of cloth that usually served as her hand towel and began to pat herself dry. The fabric scratched at her skin, but she didn't care. All she wanted was to get dry and sink back into sleep without being harassed by more nightmares.

Maureen left the towel on the ground and picked up her clothes. She clicked the light off as she exited the bathroom, crossed the floor, and tossed the clothes onto the bed before moving to her dresser and putting on the first T-shirt and panties her hands could find. She looked back at the clock and found it was almost four. She reached down to make sure her alarm was set and added an extra hour. She didn't have to be at work until three in the afternoon and didn't see the point of waking up at an hour that was followed by AM, especially when she had a ten-hour shift to look forward to. Yawning, and not wanting to lie back down in her sweat-covered bed, she crossed the room over to the old, brown sofa, which she had found on a curb by the local community college on her second day in town. She had paid a couple of young men twenty bucks to bring it over and place it under the window, creating a living room of sorts.

She opened the curtains, flopped down, and peered through the window. From her angle, not much could be seen, only what few stars had dodged both the cloud cover and ambient light of the town, and then her eyelids fell. Had she adjusted her gaze slightly, though, Maureen may have seen the thin column of smoke beginning to rise in the northern sky.

FOUR

Manny pulled up to the pale gray colonial home, slammed his truck into park, and jumped out, pulling his sport coat on and tightening his tie. The call from the station had woken him up just before six, and he had hurried over as quickly as he could. His morning stubble itched his face, and he had to pop in two pieces of gum to cover up for not brushing his teeth. The sun was low on this usually quiet subdivision street, and the houses cast long shadows over the swarm of squad cars, fire trucks, and neighbors who had spilled from their homes. Hanson, Yancy, and Collins, he noted. Everyone on the force was there besides Wentworth and his gang. *Figures,* thought Manny. *Must be sleeping off last night.* Not that their absence mattered much to whatever was going on. Several of the deputies from County and the four fireman from Station One had swelled the ranks so that the Sycamore Hills Police Department only seemed to serve in the role of crowd control.

From what dispatch had told him, there had been a pretty significant fire spotted in the Parkside Ridge subdivision at a little after four in the morning, and the fire department had been dispatched to the scene. It was they who initiated the emergency tree out to the rest of law enforcement after discovering the body. The information had been hurriedly given to him, so, while he had a vague idea of what he might be walking into, he knew that much of details surrounding the previous night's occurrence would need to be gleaned from the firemen on scene and from the county crime scene investigator, who he was sure was called in before him. He was already scanning the crowd for Stacey. He'd never met her but, considering that she was likely going to be the only woman on the scene, he was certain he would spot her.

Manny caught the eye of Yancy as he weaved through the crowd and nodded to him. Yancy received it with a nod of his own and waved Manny over, lifting up the police tape to allow him through.

"Morning, Benitez," Yancy greeted him in his usual laconic way. Carl was one of those by-the-book officers, more interested in getting the job done than being likable. That wasn't to say he was outright hostile to others. He simply had a knack for keeping the personal out of the professional, used as few words as would do the trick, and was interested only in facts.

"Yancy," he returned, "what's the story on the ground?"

"Just like you see it. I've been here a little less than an hour. Arrived about the same time as County. The boys from the firehouse say they had the blaze out for only about twenty minutes, maybe half an hour, by the time we got here. CSI went in right away, and the boys from the sheriff's department had us all come out front so she could work."

Manny glanced up at the front of the house. "Doesn't look like there was really any damage out here," he said. "Was the fire in the back part of the house?"

"They didn't tell you?" Yancy seemed surprised. "The fire wasn't in the house period. Word is, it was a big blaze in the backyard. I didn't get a good look." Yancy turned for a moment to remind the crowd trying to press in for a closer look to remain back.

Manny glanced back at the house then around at the crowd that continued to swell in numbers on the street. "No idea about the body then?" he said, turning back to Yancy.

"That's your job, pal," Yancy returned, stiffly, his eyes still trained on the crowd.

"You're a picture of professionalism, Carl." Manny snatched a notepad out of his pocket and left Yancy to deal with the crowd. For some reason, he felt compelled to walk through the house and into the backyard rather than head around the outside. He pushed through the red door and into the front foyer. The walls were lined with at least a dozen and a half framed pictures. His eyes held one longer than the others: an 8" x 10" family portrait. Mother, father, a boy of about eight or nine, and a girl at least three years younger were posed under a large tree. Their smiles spilled out of the two dimensions of the photograph. They seemed truly happy. A woman's loud sob shook him from his spell and told Manny that the happiness of that day would be difficult for this family to ever remember again.

He followed the hallway back until the house opened up into a family room and kitchen. The family from the picture sat upon a white sofa, flanked on either side by two deputies from the sheriff's department. Most of the family members were there; the boy was absent from the gathering. A deep stab hit him in the pit of his stomach as he began to assume what the family already suspected. The body that he would soon face was their son's. The woman held a tissue to her nose and spoke through it, nodding occasionally to the questions one of the deputies posed to her. The daughter laid her head on her mother's lap, clearly confused by everything that was happening, while the husband sat with his arm around his wife, staring blankly and not speaking. Manny watched them for a moment and then caught the attention of the second deputy standing by and waved him over.

"Detective Manny Benitez, Sycamore Hills PD," he introduced himself quietly as the taller man came over. He offered his hand.

"Deputy Martin," he responded, grasping Manny's hand and giving it a quick shake. Whatever was being said over at the couch was clearly occupying his thoughts.

"Why don't we step into the kitchen for a second, and you can fill me in, Deputy," Manny suggested, moving away from the living room. They walked a few steps together before he turned around to face the man again. Manny lowered his voice. "Could you fill me in on the family, Deputy?" he said, flipping his notebook to a blank page. "Please," he added.

"Deputy Hargrove over there has been handling most of the questioning, but it seems that the husband, Tom Lowes, woke up a little before four this morning and went down to the kitchen for a drink of water. He spotted the blaze and called 9-1-1 immediately before going back upstairs to wake his wife and kids and get them somewhere safe, in case the fire spread to the house. That's when he noticed their son, Jacob, was missing from his bed. We just informed them of the body that was discovered in the fire. I only got a quick look at it, but Hargrove got a better one. It sure looks like a small child to us. Obviously, the parents believe it's their son. Hargrove is trying to assure them that we haven't confirmed that yet, so there's hope, but let's be real, right?" Martin shook his head. "It's a real son-of-a-bitch we got here, Detective."

"Clearly," Manny said, finishing his last note and looking up at the deputy. He was a few years older than Manny, but his eyes betrayed the fact that he hadn't seen much like this in his career. Likely enough, law enforcement hadn't been his original career choice. "Lowes," he thought out loud. "Why does the name Tom Lowes ring a bell?"

"Maybe you've seen him on those billboards just outside of town?" offered Martin.

"That's it. He owns that real estate brokerage. Supposed to be one of the best around."

"Yeah, he's all over. Helped my sister and brother-in-law with their home last fall," Martin said. "Funny thing is, I was thinking about calling him up and seeing about buying a home myself. Supposed to be a good time."

"So I've heard," said Manny. "What about the wife? Any idea what she does?"

"Consultant of some kind? She didn't really describe it. All I know is she mostly works from home so she can be around the kids. Do you think that's important?"

"You never know what might turn out to be important in an investigation like this," said Manny, placing a hand on the deputy's shoulder. "I like having all the details. Thanks for the information. I think I'll head out to the back and check in with the CSI. When you guys are done, though, I'd like to have a few words with the family myself, if that's all right."

"I'm sure Hargrove can get you a copy of his notes just as easily," replied Martin, "but if you want to make them go and repeat everything, I guess I can't stop you." He shrugged and nodded to Manny as he turned and headed back into the living room.

Manny nodded to the deputy's back and turned to the sliding glass door that led out to the backyard. Two more deputies from the sheriff's department were standing on either side of a large pile of burnt wood, behind which a slight, dark-haired woman crouched, gently picking through the debris with a pair of long tweezers. He pulled out his badge to show one of the deputies that he did indeed belong on site, but was waved in almost before he had opened it. They had obviously been expecting him.

"You must be Stacey," he said as he circled around the woodpile and stood behind her. He could just make out the blackened skull of the victim grinning at him over her right shoulder. The rest was obscured by her back. She didn't turn around and continued her work as if she hadn't heard him. "I've heard a lot of good things about your work," he continued awkwardly. "I'm Manny, Detective Manny Benitez, Sycamore Hills PD."

"You can call me Dr. Winherst," she said pointedly, without getting up, "and if you'd like to make small talk, at least make yourself useful and help me bag some of these samples. There's a box of gloves on the ground in front of you. Please use them."

"Why don't you take me through what you've found so far, before I step over there and mess up your process." Manny tried to sound as authoritative as possible in order to gain some semblance of control over the situation.

"Very well, Detective." He thought he caught a hint of sarcasm put on the last word and was almost positive he caught a roll of the eyes and a smirk as she rose to her feet. Despite the fact that she had to raise her head to a great degree to look into his eyes, Manny felt as if she were towering over him as she spoke. Her reputation for intensity had not been oversold.

"Your boys at the fire department did a satisfactory job putting out the blaze carefully, once they realized what they had, so I was able to get plenty of samples and get a good look at the body without having to move it. Early indications show a pre-pubescent male, maybe nine or ten years old."

"So you're thinking it's the Lowes' son?"

"Don't interrupt me, Detective! There isn't any scientific evidence to make that conclusion right now."

"It's called an intuitive leap, Doctor," he replied. "The family can't find their son, and we have a body that matches his in their own backyard. The facts fit the theory. But you're right, please continue."

She glared at him for a second and then resumed her professional tone. "It would seem that he was dead before the burning, as indicated by the lack of contortion of the body. There appears to be some salvageable lung tissue. I don't know if I'll be able to get anything definitive out of it, but I'll be able to analyze it better back at the county lab, and maybe at least confirm the lack of smoke inhalation. The fire obscured some evidence, but it seems pretty clear to me that the most likely cause of death was severe blood loss."

"How did you come to that conclusion?" asked Manny.

"The firefighters stated that when they arrived, the burning woodpile had the appearance of a three-foot-high log cabin.

They had just tamed down the flames to a manageable height when they noticed the body lying on top of the structure. So at that point, they set to work spreading the coals underneath and trying to preserve as much as they could. They did a decent enough job to where, even though the structure eventually collapsed down on itself, some of the larger pieces nearer to the body stayed relatively whole, if charred." She looked down at the pile.

"And how, exactly, does that help you conclude that the victim died of blood loss?" Manny questioned.

"Blood doesn't burn, Detective. Thanks to the firefighters, I can still see that there's blood all over the wood that was near the body. I also noticed what might be a small cut on the C1. I'll need to look at it harder under lab conditions, but yes, if you forced me to make a conjecture right now, I'd say the boy's throat was cut, and cut deeply. Death would have been very quick. The fire was most likely set to burn the evidence. There is one thing I find odd, though."

"And what might that be, Doctor?"

Rather than answer outright, Dr. Winherst lowered herself back down and directed a finger toward the body's feet. Manny squatted alongside her and let his eyes follow to where her finger was pointing. It looked like a large mound of burnt gelatin: a sickening pile of black, red and, purple mush.

"What am I looking at, Doctor?" Manny asked.

"Unless I'm mistaken, that's a burnt pile made up of the boy's entrails; stomach, liver, intestines, that sort of thing."

"And what's so strange about that?"

"The position," she retorted stiffly. "The woodpile collapsed, but slowly, according to the firefighters, and the body stayed in the same relative position that it is now. So if the body was laying on its right side, whatever entrails were left unconsumed by the fire should have spilled out down here." She pointed to the ground in front of the skeleton's torso. "There's no logical reason they should be down by the feet and behind the body."

"What about an illogical reason?" Manny mumbled under his breath. He didn't mean for anyone to hear, but Dr. Winherst's head snapped around toward him.

"What was that?" she said, less than kindly.

"Well, if there isn't a natural, physical reason that those organs should be there, would it make sense to say that someone removed them and intentionally put them there?"

"I suppose that could be one explanation. I'm pretty much wrapped up here. I'll be in touch with my report within the next twenty-four hours or so." She stood, stripped the glove off her right hand and offered it to Manny to shake. There was no discernible emotion in her eyes.

Manny nodded and grasped her hand. He turned away from the ash pile and looked toward the back of the yard. Along the fence line there was another firewood pile with row upon row of stacked logs. The pile was very neat and even, except for right at the end, under the branches of a lone tree at the fence's corner. Here, the wood had clearly been disturbed, and pieces had been hauled away, creating a stair effect that stood in stark contrast to the rest of the pile's neat symmetry. Manny paced the length of the stacked wood slowly. It was all the same wood, and he was certain that it would match the kind used to burn the body. *The only question is, did whoever did this know the wood would be here, or did they just get lucky?*

As he stood thinking about this, he noticed a yellowish

stain in the grass not two feet from him. He bent down for a closer look. It was evident by the patterns in the grass that whatever had been there had been raked up by hand, most likely the previous night. Manny bent down further and put his nose to the ground. The odor that he detected was faint, but what was there was sour smelling.

"Hey, Doc," he called before deciding against the informal. "Dr. Winherst, would you come over here for a second?"

Within moments, she came up behind him, and he indicated that she should squat down as he was.

"I don't seem to see any evidence markers over here," he said, feeling more confident now that he was certain he had found something she'd missed. The potential shift in the balance of power felt good, but he reminded himself to stay professional. He pointed to the pale yellow residue. "Does that look like vomit that someone maybe tried to clean up to you?"

The Doctor's dark brown eyes widened, and her face flashed with anger and frustration. "Emmsley, get over here!" she yelled over her shoulder toward the house. Within seconds, a thin, young man with sandy brown hair and glasses ran up to them. He had the expression of a student being called into the principal's office.

"Derrick Emmsley, my assistant," she said to Manny, gesturing at the boy. "Derrick, you were supposed to make a thorough sweep of the entire yard while I was examining the body. How is it, that Detective Benitez here found that?" Her voice hit its crescendo as her hand shot downward and pointed at the vomit.

"I, uh . . . I," Emmsley began to stutter, his face flushing crimson. It became clear almost immediately that he knew

41

there was no appropriate response. "I'm sorry, Dr. Winherst," he said and hung his head.

"Mark, photograph, bag, and tag," she snapped as she stood. "And fast. We need to get the body and the samples back to the lab. I'll be over by the vans. Find me when you're done so we can get out of here!"

She didn't even wait for the boy to nod a response before she turned around and began to stalk around the side of the house back toward the front yard. Manny stood and looked at the shell-shocked assistant as he proceeded with his instructions. *Poor kid,* he thought as he jogged the few paces needed to return to Dr. Winherst's side. The last piece of evidence had finally given him the beginning of an insight into the psyche of who could have done this. She seemed to sense his excitement.

"Is there something you'd like to discuss with me, Detective?" she asked blandly.

"Not really," he said as coolly as possible, "it's just, what kind of person has the mental makeup to murder a child and try to incinerate the body like that, yet has such a weak stomach that they'd throw up while committing the crime?"

"That vomit could have come from anywhere," she retorted. "It could have been from the dog for all we know. Let the science speak, and base your hypothesis on that, Detective."

"You might be right," Manny said in his friendliest voice. *Never mind that the family doesn't have any pets, Doctor.* They were nearly at the vans out front and the noise from the crowd was starting to make it hard to hear. He leaned in toward her a little. "One more thing."

"What?" she said curtly, clearly not wanting to spend any more time talking to him.

"You guys have the means to compare DNA over there at County, right?"

"We can compare one sample to another and see if there is a match, yes. But we're a small county, Detective. If we want to do anything more complicated than that, like compare it to the Federal Database or something, you're going to have to make a call up to St. Louis and turn the investigation over to the FBI."

"Well we wouldn't want that, would we?" When they reached the vans, Manny pulled open the passenger's side door for Dr. Winherst. She rolled her eyes and frowned, but hopped in nonetheless. "Let's keep that last part between us. Hopefully I'll have a suspect sooner, rather than later."

She nodded indifferently and grabbed the inside handle, pulling the door out of his grasp and closing it. She was such a cold woman, he was surprised he didn't get frostbitten shaking her hand. Manny shook his head again as he turned from the van and nearly slammed into Derrick Emmsley running breathlessly from the backyard, camera swinging from his neck, carrying the last evidence bag.

"Careful with that, pal," Manny said as cheerfully as he could. He certainly didn't want to add to the young man's agitation. He smiled and laid his hand on Derrick's shoulder. "Thanks for getting that last piece of evidence so quick. You're doing good work. Keep it up. Your boss will see it in due time." He gave the kid a quick pat on the shoulder and continued to head to the front door. There was more to be learned from the family, he just knew it. It would be a hard interview, but if he was going to get to the bottom of this, Detective Manny Benitez would have to harden himself and do what had to be done.

FIVE

Maureen's eyes opened of their own accord. She didn't want to wake up, but her mind betrayed her and wouldn't let her stay asleep. She raised her head off the couch cushions and looked around the room as the apartment slowly came into focus. She swung her legs around and felt the floor rise up to meet her feet. It seemed to sway underneath her for a moment. The effects of last night. Maureen laid her elbows on her thighs and rested her head in her hands, slowly rubbing her palms into her eyes. Last night's headache had abated, and now all that was left were the horrifying images from her nightmare. Front in her mind was the upside down *U*. Even going back to her childhood, letters and numbers would always be the things that stuck longer in her mind after the other visions and sensations had blended into little more than a swirl of impressions left on her psyche. Her mother and the nuns always told her that what she had locked in her head was the work of pure evil. The way she saw it, they were the ones who were evil; they were the ones who left visible scars. But since she couldn't change the past, she could only hope to outrun it for as long as possible.

She pushed herself to her feet, trudged across the room to her bedside, and groaned as she saw 9:33 on the clock radio.

44

There were still five more hours before she had to leave for work. She switched off her alarm and headed to the refrigerator, grabbing a can of vegetable juice from the door and drinking it down. She knew what she *should* do was run to the grocery store for some bread and maybe some milk and peanut butter, but that seemed like a chore today. It was going to be another night of french fries and a chicken sandwich behind the bar.

Maureen turned back to her bed and stooped down to pull out two dark-colored duffel bags from under it. They were filled with all of her clothes, her flip phone and charger, her IDs, and nearly $1900 in cash. She was ready to leave when need be, but she had intended to save up a few hundred more to get her car running properly again.

She'd only bought the old pile that spring. The doors were rusty, the air conditioning had never worked, and it was creeping up on two hundred thousand miles, but it had only cost her seven hundred bucks. She knew someone who could get hold of a retired West Virginia license plate for her, which cost five times what it would have cost to register the title, but Marie Adams was already supplying her with her medication, and Marianne Anderson had an eviction and three arrests on her record, so Maureen Allen had to keep her profile as low as possible, and therefore skipped the registration. The only reason she stopped in Sycamore Hills was the fact that the temperature gauge had indicated it was overheating, and she didn't want it to break down on the side of the highway. Within a day, she'd found a help wanted sign in a bar window and a for rent sign in an old building. She wasn't sure how long it would take to save cash and fix the car, so she had settled in.

But now that the nightmares had found her again, she prepared to pack up her life and run. The problem of her car remained, though. The grubby garage owner she had left it with was charging her an arm and a leg for the part he insisted was needed to fix it. Based on his quote, it would cost almost her entire cash reserve. Not that it mattered anyway. Though he swore the part was ordered over two weeks ago, it had yet to arrive. She wasn't going anywhere by car.

On her first day in town, she found out where the nearest coach station was in case she needed to make a quick exit. Unfortunately for her, the station was nearly twenty miles away with only the highway to take her there. None of the local buses went there. She'd have to walk, and a person walking on the highway, weighed down with two bags like she would be, would rouse quite a bit of suspicion or, at the very least, unwanted attention from handsy truck drivers. No, that wouldn't do either. Maureen knew she'd have to find a way out, and she would spend the next few days looking for it, but for now, circumstance had trapped her in this town with the nightmares.

As she calculated all of this in her mind, she grabbed a pair of running shorts, a T-shirt, and a sports bra and shoved the bags back into their place. She changed into her running attire and ran into the bathroom, grabbing her hair tie and pulling her honey-blonde tresses back into a ponytail. She spent only a moment in front of the mirror to mark the bags under her eyes and decided that she needed to buy a little tube of concealer before work tonight. She grabbed a five-dollar bill and her apartment key from the dresser, slipped on her socks and running shoes, tucking the cash into her left sock, and jogged out of the door, locking it and stashing the key behind the fire extinguisher in the stairwell. Then she raced down the stairs and out into the sunlight.

The air was damp and stifling. It was supposed to have rained the previous night but, since the humidity hung thick in the air, it seemed not a drop had fallen. Maureen picked up her speed until she found the pace she liked and settled into her rhythm. The old buildings of the town's former commerce area rushed past in her peripheral. At the height of post-war America, it would have provided the majority of the jobs to the local residents. But those were the grandparents of the current generation. The factories had closed, and those jobs had moved on and left the buildings standing. Small businesses on Main Street still provided a good living for some of the locals, but most commuted to the surrounding cities to ply their careers in cold office buildings. Still, it was more pleasant than a lot of towns in middle America that Maureen had lived in.

She hit Main Street and veered left at the courthouse to make her way over to the subdivision about a mile down the road. She had decided to run her usual route through town, and though she never measured it, she knew it should take her about half an hour. Half an hour to get lost in thought. Half an hour to run from the nightmares.

Her breath steadied into its rhythm, and the sound of her shoes on the concrete beat in time, hypnotizing her into that familiar state where she couldn't help but let her mind drift back through the years. Thoughts of the previous night awakened images of other nightmares, buried deep in her mind but never erased from her memory. She recalled the monster that would come in the night to her companions at the hospital when she was a girl: a lecherous ghoul overcome by desire, lifting the bed sheets and nightgowns to slither his hand up the warm young legs. She had watched through the eyes of a brute whose hands had held down the wrists of her schoolmate. She had seen every ounce of the fear reflected in the tears pouring from her eyes and had felt the violent thrusts as if it were her own hips doing the wretched deed. When the girl had wrenched a hand free and tore off the white collar from around her assailant's neck, it was Maureen's own hand that felt the sting of its strike on the young woman's cheek.

She kept running. The memory of a young black man tied to a chair flashed in her mind. His head was slumped, and the wall behind him was covered in blood and brain matter. It wasn't her own hand that had pulled the trigger, but she had again watched through the eyes of the man the hand belonged to. And then, of course, there was the first nightmare: arms that were not hers carrying the little boy and leaving him in the woods, buried under a pile of leaves. The picture of Braden's face—peaceful, as if asleep—was still an image that refused to fade, though it had been more than twenty-five years.

A daughter who sees with the eyes of evil. Her mother's voice snapped her back to the present. She had nearly reached the end of Main Street when she came to a stop. Her eyes were fixed on the subdivision sign no more than four hundred yards up the road. A prickle began to climb her spine as a dark foreboding hung in the atmosphere and held her in place. She turned around to look back down Main Street. Everything was silent. Main Street was never what one would call bustling but at that moment, there wasn't a soul to be seen, and not so much as a breath of wind broke the air. It was as if she were the only person in the world.

Maureen raced from the dead street toward the subdivision. When she passed the stone entry sign and turned down the first street, the silence that had followed her from Main Street was shattered. It was broken by the overlapping of dozens of voices singing a chorus of confusion. Maureen slowed her run as she approached the mass of people and vehicles. Her eyes moved from the county vans to the yellow police tape around the yard and to the white colonial home with the red door she had run past nearly every day for the past two weeks. The blue and red lights of the police cars were dancing on the side of the house. As Maureen continued to look on, her stomach dropped as another sight came into view.

From around the corner of the house came a stretcher with a black bag on it, pushed by two men in uniform. Maureen edged closer for a better look, while still keeping to the outer edge of the crowd. The officers loaded their cargo into the back of one of the vans as a young man in a jacket and tie came over from the house to speak to them. She watched as the man made a few gestures to the other two, who nodded back politely before closing the rear doors of the van and heading to the front seats. The man in the jacket and tie moved back toward the house, making a few notes in a small notebook he produced from his pocket. As he approached the front door of the house, his eyes raised to look out at the crowd. His gaze met her own.

Maureen broke eye contact within a second. Before she knew what she was doing, she began to back away. A cold sensation raised the hairs on her spine. The sickening suspicion that another of her nightmares had been brought to life struck her like a bolt of lightning. She had no choice; she was a slave to her feet and her instincts. She turned and ran.

Within moments, Maureen had left the subdivision and was racing back toward Main Street. All thought of completing her circuit was gone. The only thought in her mind was to head straight back to her apartment and take a pill to calm herself. Her eye contact with the man in the jacket replayed in her mind. His gaze held an intensity and determination that she was unfamiliar with in a man as young as he was. Did he see her turn and run the way she did? She had to admit, it was a mistake to have done so.

The sound of her feet moving from gravel to the pavement of Main Street hit her ears. The silence of the surrounding buildings made her footsteps echo all the louder. It drowned out all other ambient noise in her head and left her isolated from the world around her. Her eyes focused on nothing as she continued to run, trusting that her feet knew the way home.

Those feet brought her into a near collision, however, and a man's abrupt shout shook her awake. She managed to stop herself and reach out and grab him just in time to prevent them both from falling to the ground. She steadied them both and took a step back, wiping the sweat out of her eyes and tightening her ponytail. The man came into focus. He was tall and slender with a close-cropped, white beard and balding head. What hair he had left matched the color of his beard. He held a large, black plastic bag in one hand and was checking around the sidewalk to make sure nothing had fallen out during their near collision. His black, short-sleeved shirt was buttoned around the neck with a white collar. A priest.

"Close one!" he exclaimed in a cheerful tone. "I'm sorry,

I saw you coming down the street, but I thought you were far enough away for me to get the trash to the curb. You're faster than I anticipated." He smiled at her and tossed the bag into the garbage can.

"Yeah, well, sorry," she answered stiffly. She hated talking to priests, even ones that seemed nice. "Um, I hope I didn't hurt you or anything."

"Oh no harm, no harm," he sang out, laughing a little as he spoke.

"Well, that's, uh…that's good," Maureen stammered. She began to edge around him to continue on her way home, but the man didn't seem to notice.

"I've seen you running past the church before," he said as he nodded off to his right. She followed his silent direction and turned her head to face the red-brick building. Of course she had seen it several times before: St. Mary's Catholic Church. *There's always a St. Mary's*, she thought the first time she had passed it. So now, she wasn't only talking to a priest, but a Catholic one at that. She made a face as she looked at the church.

"Yes," he said thoughtfully, turning to stand next to her and looking up at the church as well, "if I recall correctly, I first saw you run past a few weeks ago. I took notice only because I'd never seen you before in the eight years I've been assigned here. 'You must be new in town,' I thought to myself."

"Yeah," she said, not bothering to look at him, "my car broke down three weeks ago."

"I see!" he returned, seemingly delighted at the information. "So you didn't intend to come here, but fate had other plans and now, here you and I are, having a nice little chat that we wouldn't have had otherwise. The small miracles of life!"

This was getting a bit too strange for her. Maureen turned to face him. "Yeah, well, not to be rude, uh . . . Father, but I kind of have some things on my mind, and I'd really like to get home." She tried again to get past him, but he stood fast.

"Oh, how rude of me," he replied. "Of course, of course." She nodded and began to leave once again when he stuck out his hand to shake. "I'm Father Patrick, Father Patrick McGill." The man was obviously not going to let her go until she acquiesced.

She shook his hand but remained silent.

"You seemed to be in a hurry," he continued, as if he didn't care that she didn't introduce herself. "I'd be remiss if I didn't inquire as to what was troubling you. As I've said, I've seen you run by the church a few times before, but never in such a rush. If I may be so bold, I should say that something has just happened that troubled you deeply."

"You haven't seen the crime scene over in the subdivision?" she asked, surprised by her own quick response.

"That would explain the flood of people I saw heading in that direction earlier this morning," he mused. His smiling face suddenly gave way to a more serious expression. "It is a sad thing that so many should want to be on hand to witness tragedy." He shook his head.

"I think someone's dead," Maureen found herself responding. Something about Father Patrick just drew it out of her.

"Tragic," he said, "simply tragic. I'm forced to ask, though, why is it that a scene like that, which made so many people flock to look on, made you run in the other direction?" He looked at her steadily, and it was as if he could see all her secrets.

She had no idea how she was going to answer, and her feet felt bolted to the ground.

"Father Patrick," a voice interrupted from the direction of the church, much to Maureen's relief. A younger, brown-haired man dressed much like Father Patrick came walking across the front lawn of the church and stopped a few feet away. "Father, I thought you were going to be in your office. I'd hoped to go over the parish budget for next quarter, as well as my sermon for this Sunday."

"Just taking out the garbage," he answered coolly.

"Is the custodian busy with something else, Father?"

"Father Preston Lane," Father Patrick said to Maureen gesturing to the young man. "My junior priest. A very devout man, a little too obsessed with propriety if you ask me, but surely that will be what raises him to Bishop before he turns forty." He smiled as he clapped the younger man on the shoulder and shook him like a man gently chastising a little brother. "What of our custodian, Preston? Haven't I always said that we're custodians ourselves? A priest shouldn't mind using his hands. After all, didn't our own Savior know His way around tools and labor? But, then, if it weren't for you, maybe I'd lose sight of the bureaucratic side of things that keeps the Church operating. Bless you for reminding me. I'll be there in just a moment to handle our business."

Father Preston nodded, turned, and headed back into the church. Father Patrick watched him go before turning back to Maureen, shaking his head and chuckling.

"What I said was true," he said to her. "St. Mary's might have gone bankrupt if it wasn't for him. It's likely why they sent him to me. The Diocese has always said that my flock adores me, but the accountants despise me." He paused to look at her for a moment, the smile on his lips amused and sad at the same time. "Well, I've detained you long enough. I'm sorry to hear about the tragedy you have witnessed, and more sorry that you can't stay to talk. If you ever need an ear, the church door is always open. Literally." He laughed. "I don't allow the doors to be locked, much to the chagrin of some. It was a pleasure to meet you, Ms...." He looked at her inquisitively and stuck out his hand for another shake.

"Allen," Maureen said, eyeing him carefully and shaking his hand one more time.

He tilted his head, beckoning her to offer just a little more.

"Maureen," she conceded.

"Maureen," he repeated, giving her hand a final shake and releasing her. "Until our next meeting, I'll pray for you and anyone who may have been hurt today." His eyes became grave despite the smile on his face. He nodded a farewell and turned to walk back toward the front door of the church, waving his hand back at her as he went.

Maureen stood frozen on the sidewalk until the church's door shut behind Father Patrick and exhaled with relief. She could not put her finger on what bolted down her feet, what made her legs inoperable, or what caused her to stay and talk to the man. She never talked to priests. It was a hard and fast rule ever since she had gone out on her own. No cops, no doctors, no priests. She could not afford to let her rules slip if she was going to get out of here and back ahead of the nightmares.

Maureen ran back to her apartment as fast as she could. She dashed up the steps, retrieved her key from its hiding place, and got inside, shutting the world outside with the slam of the door.

She went into the bathroom to wash her face. As she looked at her reflection in the mirror, the dark bags under her eyes reminded her that she had forgotten to buy some concealer. *No point in that now,* she thought sullenly. *Just throw on the push-up bra, and not a single one of those drunk bastards will even bother to look at my face.* With that notion in mind, she quickly splashed her face, dried it, and threw the towel on the ground.

There was only one thing she wanted to do now: shut off everything for a while. Maureen stalked across her apartment to her nightstand and ripped open the drawer. She grabbed the pill bottle and tipped one of the pink tablets into her mouth and swallowed, set her alarm to two, and flopped down on her sheetless bed with her knees tucked to her chest. She had her plan decided. She would let the pill help her sleep until the alarm went off, finish tonight's shift, and disappear.

By this time tomorrow, she'd be on a bus to anywhere else. By this time tomorrow, she wouldn't be Maureen Allen anymore.

SIX

Manny slouched on his bar stool, staring at his mug of beer and running over the day in his mind. He'd wandered into Anderson's and ordered his drink nearly an hour ago and had yet to take more than three sips. The honey-blonde bartender looked familiar, but he couldn't be sure, and he wasn't in the mood to begin speculation. If he had less on his mind, he might have been able to place her, but he was focused on other things at the moment.

During the interview, Mr. and Mrs. Lowes hadn't displayed any odd behavior, and both of them had readily agreed to a DNA swab. The samples were at the county crime lab now, and he'd have the comparison results to that vomit sample, along with the rest of the report, in the morning. He wouldn't have the report long, however, before he'd have to pass it along. This was what was weighing on him.

That afternoon, as he had been poring over the Lowes' personal information, Captain Wellner called him into his office. He knew the minute he saw Sheriff Taughten in the office that something was going to be shaken up in the investigation. And it was, in the manner that he had feared most.

"Detective Benitez," Captain Wellner had begun, using the

formal tone he always did when he had to deliver some bad news. "Please have a seat."

Manny had declined to sit, and the sheriff took over the conversation.

"Manny," he said, "we know that you'll do your best in the investigation, but we think we're going to need some help on this one."

"Okay," he said, knowing what was coming.

"We're going to need the FBI's resources to handle the DNA evidence," the sheriff went on, "and we just think that due to the sensitivity of the case, and its heinous nature, it's best to bring in folks with more experience in handling these types of situations."

"Are you pulling me from the case?" he asked harshly, not wanting to be put on the sidelines.

"You're the only detective in the department," Captain Wellner broke in. "We know that you're going to be an asset on this one. We've agreed that the department will offer support to the Feds, and you'll be our primary representative. Your ongoing investigation will come under their jurisdiction, and you'll be reporting directly to the agents that they send down. They'll be here within the next twenty-four hours."

"So do I have to stand down until my babysitters get here?" It just slipped out. Manny would have given a year's pay to take it back, but he just couldn't control his frustration. He knew the involvement of the Feds would relegate him to nothing more than an errand boy.

"Benitez, son," the sheriff scolded, "I think you'd do well to bite that tongue of yours when the Feds get here. Cooperate. Make sure you look like you know what you're doing. That way, we'll all get along a lot better and get those boys out of our hair all the quicker."

I do *know what I'm doing!* The bitter thought was still fresh in Manny's mind as he sat gazing at the three shelves of liquor bottles behind the bar. It was good that he'd decided not to head over to Smokey's after work. By now, he was sure, the gossip of the Feds becoming involved and his demotion to a supporting role in the investigation would have made its way around the station. He could only imagine the relentless ribbing he'd endure from Wentworth and the other cops if he were to show up at the usual hangout. Anderson's, on the other hand, was well known as the weekday establishment for the lower rung of drinkers who had nothing to go home to. It was a place where you went to be left alone; it was the perfect spot for him now. Manny lifted his mug and took a large swallow of beer. It had gotten warm during his silent vigil, and he could feel himself make a face as he swallowed.

"Sucks when it gets warm, doesn't it?" a woman's voice penetrated the haze that surrounded him. Manny looked up to see the bartender standing in front of him, hands on the bar, leaning over just enough to give him an eyeful of the cleavage poking out of her white tank top.

"Word of advice," she continued, "when you come in here to sit and drown your sorrows, it's usually more effective to drink more than half a beer in an hour. You'll never kill the right number of brain cells at your pace."

Despite himself, Manny broke into a half smile at her jab.

The woman grabbed his mug of warm liquid and dumped it into the sink behind the bar. She shot Manny a wink as she walked over to the tap and filled the mug with fresh beer and plopped it back in front of him. She then grabbed a bottle of tequila from the back shelf and filled a shot glass, set it on the bar next to the beer, and nodded at Manny to drink it. He took the glass in hand and took a small sip. It was some of the worst tequila he'd ever tasted, and he could feel the look of utter disgust twist his face as he swallowed. The woman let out a laugh as he set the remainder of the shot on the bar and pushed it away.

"Yeah, Mr. Anderson doesn't really spend much money on the liquor around here," she said.

"Clearly. I think I'll stick to the beer. Do I owe you for the shot?"

"Nah. Second beer's on me too." She grabbed the shot glass and raised it up. "Cheers."

Manny watched in awe as she downed the remainder of the nasty liquid, giving no visible hint whether it bothered her in the least. Almost unconsciously, he grabbed his beer mug and drained nearly half its contents in one gulp.

"That's more like it," she smiled as she slapped the bar with her hand, before turning her head to peer down to the men seated in the stools at the other end. "Better go check on the boys. You'll let me know if you need anything else?"

Manny gave a nod which she returned before sauntering over to stand in front of the three older, and somewhat unkempt, men. He watched as she filled each of their glasses with brown liquor and put her hand over her heart in thanks as one of the men handed her a large bill. They seemed familiar with each other, and he deduced that these men were probably regulars who she had been working her feminine charms on for a while.

Though she seemed totally committed to her act, Manny would catch her periodically rolling her eyes and, when the men weren't looking, allowing the phony smile to momentarily drop from her face before continuing with her flirtations. Here was a woman who was clearly not where she wanted to be. He wondered what her story was, and why he kept staring at her. She was attractive, to be sure: thin and lithe. And though she was a tad shorter than he usually liked and a few years older than he was, the curve of her backside pushing against her jeans as she leaned over the bar was an alluring sight.

Manny looked over at the television in the corner above the bar. He was hoping that the Cardinals game would be on, but he was confronted with the scene in front of the Sheriff's Department from a few hours prior. Sheriff Taughten was at the podium speaking to the assembled media. It was the part of the statement where he was going over the details of how the local authorities were going to be handing over control of the investigation to the FBI. Manny recalled the awkward feeling of being called to stand next to the Sheriff as he gave his statement and was relieved when Taughten hadn't asked him to say anything when he was finished.

"That's you, isn't it?" The bartender's voice made him jump. Manny marveled to himself at how he didn't hear her come up behind him.

"That's me," he managed to reply, his frustration with his bosses showing through. He looked at her, but she was staring intently, almost transfixed, at the screen.

"Young Boy Slain, Burned," she said, reading the caption at the bottom of the screen.

Manny eyed her carefully over the rim of his mug as

he took a slow sip. He watched as she walked over to the television, reached up, and turned up the volume. She seemed to ignore everything else in the bar. Manny knew that if the news channel ran the press conference in its entirety, she would remain like that for almost another five minutes.

Manny turned to scan the room. His eyes passed over the men that she had been flirting with and then beyond to a couple of younger men at a table in the corner. They were drinking quickly out of their glasses and laughing to each other, but their eyes were cast across the room. Manny followed their gaze and saw a group of three women who were just sitting down. They were in their early forties with too much makeup on and were dressed how they probably thought college girls dressed. They were clearly looking for a man to pay for their drinks and possibly take them home to make them feel as beautiful as they hoped they still were. It was enough of a scene to make Manny begin to regret his decision to walk in this world for the night.

"So you're a detective, then." Her voice brought him back to the moment.

Manny turned back around to face the woman, who was once again leaning over the bar and staring at him intently.

"Do you have any idea who did it?" she whispered, causing him to lean closer.

"I really can't discuss the case," Manny replied as official-sounding as he could.

"No, I get it. It's just odd, though. How could the person who did this get the kid out of the house and into the backyard with no one seeing him?"

Something about her was odd. It was human nature to be bizarrely fascinated with death. It was a coping mechanism of sorts. However, this woman had a different sort of look in her eyes. There was more to her question than mere curiosity. Manny decided to play along.

"We're working on several theories," Manny said matter-of-factly. "I'll admit, though, that detail is a tricky one."

"I'll bet the FBI will have some good insights," she said.

Manny thought he caught one of her eyebrows rise mischievously. Was she trying to tweak him? He simply smiled and nodded.

"I can't imagine the family would want to stay at the house tonight, after everything that's happened." She continued to probe.

Manny sat up a bit straighter at that. What was this woman driving at? "No, they're staying with family for a while."

It was the truth. The Lowes family was staying with Kristin's mom and dad for the next few days. He had a PI friend keeping an eye on them. He hadn't exactly cleared this with the captain and the sheriff, but he didn't want Tom and the family to skip town on him. And if they did anything suspicious, he wanted to be the first to know.

The woman nodded and paused for a moment before gathering up her hair into a tight ponytail. "It's just so sad," she said, almost to herself, "a kid that young having their throat cut like that and burned. It's almost too gruesome for words."

Manny had seen and heard everything he needed to. It was time to go. He drained his beer and got up off the stool, reaching into his pocket for his money clip. He pulled a twenty dollar bill out and laid it on the bar.

"I'd better get going," he said, trying to seem casual. "Big day with the Feds tomorrow. Will this cover my tab?"

She looked down and nodded, slowly taking the money before looking back up and flashing him a smile. "That's more than enough, thank you. By the way, I didn't catch your name." She stuck out her hand for him to shake.

"Manny Benitez," he said, taking her hand in his. "But, you knew that, didn't you, Ms....?"

"Allen," she laughed, "Maureen Allen. And, yeah, I caught it on the TV, but I just wanted to hear it from you."

"Well in that case," he smiled, "it was a pleasure talking to you, Ms. Allen."

Manny turned and made his way through the bar and out into the night air. He crossed the street to his truck and hopped in. He had no intention, however, of turning the key and driving home.

All evening, he'd sworn that he had seen that woman before. The moment she pulled her hair back, the answer came to him. She was there. After the body of the Lowes boy was loaded into the coroner's van, he had looked out at the crowd and caught eyes with a female dressed in running attire with honey-blonde hair tied back into a ponytail. At the time, he dismissed her turning and running back the way she came as no more than a neighbor out for a morning run who didn't wish to be part of the entourage around the house. But as he played out the scene in his mind, he recalled the strange look of horrified recognition on her face. He had no doubt that this was the same woman who had just poured him his beer.

He checked the time. There was still over two hours until the bar closed. Manny settled in for his long wait.

SEVEN

Maureen locked the front door of the bar and stuffed the key into the lock box beside it. It was well after midnight, and she had had a hell of a time getting the last of her regulars out of the bar. Stan was still sauntering off down the street toward home. She could just make out his round-shouldered form swaying in the streetlight at the end of the block.

The rest of the street was still, and only a couple of vehicles were parked. She thought she caught a flash of movement in the cab of an older-looking truck across the street from the bar, but when she looked again, she saw nothing. It seemed that the conversation with the detective had left phantoms in her head. She tried to shake them free, but their continued gnawing was almost impossible to ignore.

Anderson's bar stood on a side street about a block and a half south of Main Street. It was housed among several other storefronts in a turn-of-the-century building. Todd Anderson, the owner, had bought the building as an investment back in the eighties. Taking the money he earned from the dive bar and the rent from other tenants and adding it to the money he saved by paying his staff a paltry wage meant that he had never needed to find a real day job.

Maureen reached into her pocket and fingered the wad of bills that made up her tip money. Though she received mostly singles, her act with a couple of the regulars and that nice tip from the detective had raised the night's take to seventy-eight dollars. Thursday nights were usually her best nights, as the odd group of college kids usually stumbled in, looking to get their weekend off to an early start, but taking in over seventy bucks in this little town was rare. She couldn't help but smile just a little, happy that the cash in her pocket alone should cover the bus ticket. She wouldn't have to dip into the cash in her duffel bags, which now sat on her bed, packed and waiting for her to snatch them up and be on her way out of this mess. And away from the nightmares.

Maureen let out an unenthusiastic sigh at the prospect of her overnight trek to the bus station. She was more tired than usual after a bar shift despite being, happily, less drunk than she normally was. The weight of her nightmare, combined with the new knowledge that not only was a child dead but the body was also horribly burned, pressed down on her shoulders. No matter how many times she told herself that it wasn't her fault, seeing the things she saw in these terrible dreams and not being able to control them filled her with an enormous amount of shame. *Catholic guilt*, she thought to herself.

It was almost funny that she would use those words. The Catholic religion had never been anything but a source of unmitigated pain in her life. It was her mother's fervor and superstitious beliefs that had driven her to entrust Maureen into the hands of zealots—first at the hospital mere days after her brother's body was found, then for nearly eight years in that prison that masqueraded as a boarding school. In both places, the cross and rosary were front and center, and when simple prayer didn't work to drive the evil out of her, the priests and nuns would turn to more medieval practices. Still, the nightmares would come, and she would see into the depraved minds of those that made these places their playground. She would put on their faces in her sleep and wear them like the masks they themselves wore in the light of day, and she would understand how piety and holiness were just a cover for them—a shield to hide behind—while they acted on their deeper desires and lusts. She learned early that when you go head-on against an institution, it is you who suffer while the perpetrators get no justice. To this day, she has never forgotten the sound that a toe makes when it's broken.

And yet, even as Maureen stood alone on the sidewalk remembering all the lessons learned and the reasons that she tried to stay uninvolved, she felt her mind pull her feet in another direction. This unseen force, driven by the deep recesses of her subconsciousness, dragged her back toward Main Street. A desire to see the crime scene for herself took control of her body, and a subtle voice rang out in her head. *What if you're wrong? What if the nightmare didn't show you the death of that kid from the news?* She had to know. Biting her lip, Maureen looked up and down the dark street, searching for any movement, any set of eyes on her. She saw none. She closed her eyes, let out a deep breath, and began to briskly walk toward Main Street.

She mumbled to herself that this was a bad decision almost as soon as her feet hit the pavement of Main Street, and she moved more and more rapidly as she continued on her way toward the house with the red door. It wasn't really a snap decision, though, if she was being honest with herself. She thought of it during her conversation with the detective at the bar. It was the reason for her asking if the family was still staying in the house. Breaking into a crime scene was going to be one thing. Breaking into a crime scene with a victimized family still inside was going to be something else.

The crunch of gravel under her feet told Maureen that she was getting closer to the once idyllic subdivision. A pair of headlights appeared in the distance. She moved a few feet off the shoulder into the grass, slowing down as the car passed in the hopes that she would avoid detection. She flinched as another vehicle passed from the rear, going in the opposite direction. She watched the taillights head off down the road, stop several hundred meters away, and disappear. *Must have turned down a side street,* she thought.

The stone monument that marked the entrance to the subdivision came into view, and in a few moments, she was walking up the same street as that morning. The sound of a car pulling into the subdivision made her head whip back behind her. She saw nothing, though, and chalked it up to nerves. She turned back toward the lights and continued at a slow pace, as if she were dragging a weight behind her.

She came to a stop on the sidewalk just in front of the two-story home. Her eyes were fixed on the red door as she recalled with vivid detail the brief moment of eye contact with the young detective. The buzzing crowd from earlier had given way to the silence of the night, and the only sign that they had been there was the trampled grass of the front lawn and the pile of bouquets and stuffed animals near the front stoop. Maureen stared at the memorial, remembering another she had only been allowed to go to once before she was taken away. These homemade tributes to a dead child hadn't changed in a quarter of a century.

Out of the side of her eye, Maureen thought she saw a shadow blot out the light halfway down the block. Her head snapped around, trying to find the source of the movement. There was nothing to be seen. She silently cursed herself for allowing paranoia to get the better of her. She decided almost instantly that she was just making up phantoms to put in her path. It would be so easy to pretend she was being observed and to turn away at the last minute. She wanted to, of course, but she was determined to press on. She'd be damned if a shadow was going to be her undoing.

Creeping around the side of the house and heading into the backyard, Maureen had no idea what she would be looking for once she got into the house. Something that would ease her guilt or even prove the nightmare wrong, for sure, but she couldn't fathom what sort of thing that would be. The lights from the street dimly illuminated the grass, and she could now make out a patch of burned earth surrounded by more yellow tape. Small flags dotted the surrounding ground. She closed her eyes and tried to wish away her recognition of the obvious hallmarks of the crime scene from her dream. She still desperately sought to find something that could prove this wasn't what it clearly was.

Her hopes were dashed as soon as her eyes met the back of the house. As she approached, the darkness parted to reveal an upside-down horseshoe above the back door. A measured study of the object might have led another person to see it for what it was: a talisman for good luck and protection. To her, it was simply the upside-down *U* from her nightmare staring her in the face. Maureen felt a tingle run down her spine. She couldn't pretend any longer that this wasn't the house she had seen.

The battle within her raged as her mind tugged at her to back away, to not proceed, but the hypnotic allure of the home continued to beckon her closer. She crept to the door and placed her hand on the knob. Locked. Why she thought she would be afforded such easy access to a crime scene almost made her laugh out loud. After all, her vision had never revealed how the assailant had gotten into the house. The ludicrousness of what she was attempting hit her and shook her from her self-imposed trance. There was no need to push any further, and she resolved to turn and leave before she was seen. This resolve, however, only lasted for a moment.

The voice in the back of her mind whispered even more earnestly to her, insisting that there was something inside she had to see. Maureen's hand went to her scalp and pulled out the two bobby pins that kept the hair out of her face. A strand of her bangs slipped down into her vision as she knelt in front of the door. She brushed it aside, bent both pins, and inserted them into the lock. It had been a few years since she'd opened a door like this, but the muscle memory took over and before she knew it, she felt the familiar click of the door unlocking.

Maureen slowly pushed the door open and felt her stomach turn as she took her first step over the threshold. She closed the door quietly behind her and found herself in the home's darkened kitchen. She took one cautious step after another, slowly working her way further into the house. If her nightmare had really mapped out the home, somewhere up ahead there would be a staircase. She followed the hallway out of the kitchen. Its photograph-lined walls taunted her, making it more difficult to deny that she, at least in consciousness, had been there before.

She found the staircase exactly where she expected to find it. A sense of inevitability now gripped the majority of her being, yet that voice in the back of her brain rebelled to the end. As she climbed the stairs, her inner voices continued their quarrel, but by the time she reached the top, she was convinced that it was necessary to see it all through.

Maureen took a deep breath and blew it out loudly. The noise seemed to ricochet off the upstairs walls like a clap of thunder. She froze in her tracks and looked wildly around, expecting someone to come darting out of some hidden corner somewhere in response to the sound. Nothing happened, of course, but the sensation that it roused in her forced Maureen's breath to continue in short, shallow spurts, lest she make any more noise than she had to. She unglued her feet from the carpet and continued to pad along the hallway, her head peering from side to side looking for a certain doorway.

She found it, the second door on her right, covered by police tape. Maureen carefully took the tape down, allowing her to step into the room. The décor—cartoon robots, sports posters, and various other action figures—spoke to the fact that it clearly had been occupied by a young boy.

Maureen inched around the room, her eyes focusing on nothing, but the tips of her fingers lightly brushing along the walls and shelves, as if they knew better than her brain what they were searching for. She closed her eyes and continued to circle, her right hand serving as her only means of sensing. It grazed the shiny plastic of a poster and bounced along the spines of a row of books like a xylophone. She continued forward until her hand felt nothing but air while her legs were stopped by an impediment in her path.

As she opened her eyes, the sight of the child's bed filled Maureen's vision. It was a short twin, lying on a plain, wooden frame. The colorful sheets were reduced to hues of white, black, and various deep blues and purples in the dim room, lit only by the ambient light streaming in through the window. She could see that the blanket was still bunched up at the foot of the mattress, in the same position it would have been in after a young boy's legs had stopped kicking as he lost consciousness.

A brief glint of light next to the bed caught her eye. Maureen turned her head and settled her gaze on a small, round object, half hidden in shadow on the nightstand. She picked it up and, holding it in two hands, raised it close to her face. It was a child's alarm clock. Despite the darkness, she could pick out the twelve numbers that circled around the white face etched with two semi-circle stitches. The likeness of a baseball. Maureen peered closer to see that the hour hand and minute hand were two different-length bats. As she watched hypnotically, the hands of the clock wound themselves from their original position to reveal the time that it had read when the hands had grabbed the boy. The time that had been buried in her mind until that moment. 2:31.

A flurry of images passed in front of her eyes with blinding speed, yet she saw everything clearly. She could see through the eyes from her nightmare again. She could see the little boy asleep in the bed in front of her. She could feel him wiggle under the force of the hands holding a rag to his mouth.

71

She saw the hallway she had just crept down rushing by in the opposite direction. The woodpile in the backyard. The knife. And finally, the one moment of it all that wasn't in the nightmare, she saw her own clock radio reading the time. 2:47. Sixteen minutes later.

The horror of the realization spun Maureen's head in circles, and she threw the clock to the ground with a sharp cry. She finally realized what it was all about. For all these years, she'd accepted that the nightmares showed her what evil people were doing. She had even accepted that, somehow, she was seeing these things from the perspective of the people who were doing them. Now she realized that, all this time, in her sleep, she had been seeing them *as they happened*. Her heart rate climbed, and sweat broke out on her brow. Why, out of all the people in the world, would something like this happen to her: To see evil being done, but to be cursed to be unable to prevent it? To see through a killer's eyes, but to be unable to stop their hands? To see a young boy ripped from his bed, to feel his weight in her arms, but at that exact moment, to be miles away, trapped in slumber?

It was all too much. Telling someone never helped; a lesson she'd learned young. She had to get away. There was nothing she could do. She couldn't identify the killer, and no one would believe her anyway. *Run. Don't think, just run.* She still had time. Twenty miles to the bus station wouldn't be so hard, and it would still be dark for a few hours. What were the chances she'd be seen? She'd be gone, and by tomorrow, she wouldn't be Maureen Allen anymore. All she had to do was make it back to her apartment without anyone seeing her. She turned to go.

A white light hit her face, and the shadow of a pistol passed in front of it. She was blind to everything beyond the light, but a voice sounded from the doorway.

"Don't move, Ms. Allen," it said. She immediately recognized it as the young detective from the bar. "On your knees, please, hands behind your head."

His voice is oddly calm, she thought as she obeyed his order, slowly sinking to her knees and placing her hands behind her head.

EIGHT

Maureen had been sitting in the interview room for what seemed like days. He had hauled her straight in from the house, processed her, and shoved her into a holding cell. While there, she had resisted the urge to sleep for fear of more torment and took to pacing the three to four steps of the cell, stopping every few minutes to do some push-ups or use the low bed bolted to the wall to do a few dips. Anything to keep awake. The young detective had come back a few hours later, judging by the sunrise, looking as though he had only gone home to change clothes and shave. An attempt to look more formidable perhaps? It wasn't fooling her. She recognized the bags under his eyes all too well. They probably mirrored her own. In any case, he'd led her into the room she was currently sitting in and had left her to herself, most likely hoping that the time alone would bring her further discomfort and give him the edge he was looking for.

"Okay Ms. Allen," Detective Benitez said, slapping down his notebook and taking a seat at the steel table opposite her. "Let's just go over all of this again, shall we?"

The lamp that illuminated the room was behind his head, so she had to squint if she wanted to look at him. Once her eyes adjusted to the harshness of the glow, she was able to examine his face more closely. He was fairly attractive, she had to admit, with a strong jaw and dark, Latin features. Not necessarily her type, but his deep brown eyes were what caught her attention. They seemed as if they saw more than the average person. She was going to have to be exceedingly careful if she was going to explain her way out of this predicament, especially since the truth was so unbelievable.

"This isn't my first rodeo, Detective," she said. "I may not have the money for an attorney, but surely you have a public defender you can provide for me?"

"You haven't been charged with anything, Ms. Allen," he replied, allowing a grin to break on his face. "We're just talking. But if you insist, we can find someone to be with you during this interview and take you back to your cell for now. We're a small town, and the county courthouse doesn't have a whole lot of public defenders on staff. I'm sure we could get one here in a couple of days. Or you could confess to the murder of Jacob Lowes, and your cooperation will be rewarded. We can get you in front of a shrink, and you just might avoid the death penalty."

"Didn't know Missouri still had the death penalty," Maureen quipped, making no effort to hide her disdain.

"The death penalty isn't used often, it's true. It's reserved for the most heinous of crimes. I'm sure the murder of a child and desecration of the corpse would qualify." His tone raised slightly.

"Well, since I didn't kill that kid, I guess I got nothing to worry about." She wasn't going to let him intimidate her.

"I thought you wanted a lawyer. You're not doing yourself any favors making statements like that," he replied.

"What's the point?" She was getting tired of this already, and she knew she wasn't going anywhere for a while. "A public defender won't do me any good anyway."

"Because you're going to confess?" he smirked. "I'll need to bring in one of ours if that's what's going to happen."

"I'm not going to confess to anything, because I didn't do anything! And lawyers don't do anything but screw up just to line their own pockets."

Maureen watched as the detective slowly got out of his chair and strutted over to the single window. He shut the blinds, rubbed his eyes, and let out a loud sigh. Too loud in her opinion, all part of the act. She hated when cops did this, pouring on the melodrama, pretending that the answers they were receiving physically pained them, all to throw off their interviewee. This one's act wasn't very polished. He clearly hadn't interviewed anyone suspected of a serious crime before.

"Okay," he said, returning to his seat at the table, "you obviously have some experience in situations like this. So, since you're not going to cooperate, I'm just going to start talking, and you can feel free to correct me when I get something wrong."

Maureen shrugged. This was going to be good.

"I admit, I haven't had any time to really look into you," the detective continued in his self-important tone, "but, it's a pretty small town, and last night at the bar was the first time I've ever seen you." He paused and looked at her for an unwavering moment. "Or was it? Maybe the first time I saw you was yesterday morning running away from the crime scene."

She froze stiff. He *had* recognized her. She tried to hold his stare, but she blinked first.

"I thought so," he said triumphantly.

"It's not a crime to be out for a run," she retorted.

"Oh, not at all, but it *is* a crime to break into a closed crime scene in the middle of the night."

"Okay, so lock me up for that and go after the person who killed that kid." He wasn't going to run her over.

The detective softened. "All right," he said, "let's put a pin in that and get back to what we were talking about. How long have you been in town?"

"Three weeks or so. My car broke down, if that was going to be the next question."

"In fact, that *was* my next question," he smiled. "Thanks for the help. Now, you're living where exactly?"

"One of the loft studios in the old factory district on the south side of town. You want an exact address?"

"No, that won't be necessary. I suspect you don't have a legal lease or anything, knowing some of the guys that rent out those places. Where did you come to us from?"

"East." She wasn't lying, but she wasn't going to make his job easier.

"Can you be more specific?"

"Not really," she answered, doing her best to maintain her mask of indifference. "I move around a lot. Don't like to stay in one place for too long."

"How 'bout the last place you lived?"

"I stayed at a public house in Kentucky for a few months."

"They still have those?" He clearly didn't buy her answer.

"That's what they called it. I gave 'em seventy-five bucks a week and didn't ask any questions. As long as I got a bed and shower, I don't need much."

"A nomadic lifestyle like that might make someone think you're running from something." The way he said it sounded like an accusation. Maureen had no doubt it was intentional.

"Almost everybody is running from something." She could have sworn she saw the detective's face twitch as she said it. "Don't presume to know me. Whatever you're thinking, I can guarantee you're wrong." She sat back and crossed her arms.

"Whatever you say, Ms. Allen," he said, resuming his formal tone. Condescending, really, to her ears. "Why don't we go to the night of the murder. Tell me where you were."

"At home," she scoffed. "I remember I woke up around quarter to three. Nightmare." The memory of it sent a shiver down her spine. She tried her best to hide it. The detective was looking down at his notes, and didn't seem to notice, much to her relief.

"I'm assuming you were there alone," he said without looking up at her.

"Of course," she spat back. "It would be way too convenient for me to have been fucking someone and be able to give you his name, right? Not that I need a name as long as he's hard in all the right places." She was hoping to throw him off his game a bit. Unfortunately, she underestimated the detective's professionalism.

"It would certainly get you out of here and away from me sooner," he replied flatly, scribbling in his notebook. When he finished, he looked up at her again. "Saying that I believe that you were—in fact—at home alone during the murder, I'm curious as to why you just happened to be in the neighborhood the next morning when you're not a neighbor, why you know details about the case that weren't released to the public, and why you would want to break into the crime scene last night. Do you see how your story doesn't add up?"

"Something about the whole thing just seemed familiar," she relented. "I needed to be sure."

"Do you mean to tell me that you might have information about who did this?" His voice grew as he perked up in his chair.

"I…" she started, but thought better about it and decided to stop talking. She folded her hands on the table and made an effort to keep her lips pressed tightly together.

Just as the detective was about to speak, she heard the door open. Her eyes darted over as a black suit filled with a tall man sporting a close-cropped haircut entered the room. His face bore almost no expression as he strode straight up to the table and dropped a manila folder on it. He eyed Maureen briefly before turning to Detective Benitez.

"I'm Agent Howard Layton," he said in a smooth voice. His words carried the hint of a Southern accent. Maureen couldn't help but scoff. *He sounds like a self-righteous ass,* she thought to herself.

The agent shot her a look before addressing the detective. "I've taken control of this case, Detective, and I'll be finishing this interview. You can head out and speak to my partner, Agent Lorenzo. She's with your captain now getting up to speed. You can help with that."

Detective Benitez seemed to bristle at that and opened his mouth, most likely to protest.

"That'll be all, Detective," the agent said with a bite.

The detective seemed to have received the message and left the room, but not before he'd very deliberately slammed his

Robert W. Christian

notebook shut and shoved it into his pocket, staring at the
agent the whole time. The slamming of the door behind him
actually sent a jolt through her.

Agent Layton took the seat opposite her to make his formal
introduction. "I'm Agent Howard Layton," he repeated,
looking through the dozen or so sheets of paper that he had
brought into the room. "I'm the ASAC of the St. Louis branch
of the FBI. Do you understand what that means?"

"That you're trying to impress me with a fancy-sounding
acronym?" she retorted, settling back into her chair, trying to
appear as casual as possible.

"That fancy-sounding acronym means," he replied quietly,
folding his hands on the table and leaning toward her ever so
slightly, "that my title is Assistant Special Agent in Charge.
It means that there is only one person in this jurisdiction that
outranks me when it comes to law enforcement. And it means,
if I'm here in person, you should understand how seriously the
FBI is taking the murder of this child and the mutilation and
desecration of his body."

His tone did not change, but the intensity in his gaze told
the story. The years of care were written in the creases on his
face. His gray eyes had looked upon death and into the eyes of
those responsible for many years. Maureen had no doubt that
he would do what he could to pin this crime on her. She was a
convenient suspect with no alibi, a stranger to the town, and
a trespasser who broke into the crime scene. Well, at any rate,
she wasn't going down without a fight.

"You were fingerprinted before Detective Benitez began
his interview with you," Agent Layton continued, "and those
prints are now being sent to our analyzers."

Shit! This day had to come eventually. She did her best to keep her face as smooth as possible. *Just pretend it's poker,* she thought and blinked a few times but said nothing.

"You know, I've sat in front of a lot of killers, thieves, and rapists in my time, and so I like to think I've developed a sixth sense at being able to read people's stories." He stared hard at her and let his words hang in the air for a moment. "Now I've just met you, but I can tell that you have a lot of secrets that you'd prefer to stay buried. You've obviously had dealings with law enforcement before; anyone can see that. But I'd venture to guess that I'm not the first FBI agent you've spoken to."

Despite herself, Maureen felt her shoulders shrug and her head tilt to the side. It was as good as a confirmation for him.

"Yeah, I thought so." There was no sense of triumph in his voice. "I'll even go out on a limb and say it was a really long time ago, you may have even been a kid. The experience stayed with you didn't it?"

"What, have you been talking to my mother?" She couldn't stop the words. Her emotions were overloading; she slipped up and said too much to the detective, the FBI was running her prints, and now this agent was acting like he knew her. She immediately cursed herself for having allowed such a loss in control.

"I haven't, but it's interesting you'd think that, and it seems to prove me right." He allowed the smallest of grins to break through his face. "So let's focus on that for a minute. Tell me about the last time you spoke to an agent."

Maureen sat like a statue in her chair.

"Hmm, okay." Agent Layton shifted in his seat. "Look, Ms. Allen, I'm here to catch a killer. I haven't made up my mind about you yet. You may be who I'm looking for, you may not. In either case, you'll help yourself by cooperating and answering my questions, even if they seem totally unrelated. I assure you, I have my reasons for asking."

Maureen let out an exasperated sigh. "My brother was murdered when I was eight. They never found out who killed him."

"So that's why you don't trust cops."

"I don't trust cops," she fired back, "because even when I tell them the truth, they never believe me."

"Then give me a reason to believe you. That Detective Benitez has made some pretty strong accusations against you. There's a lot of circumstantial evidence that can make your life very difficult for quite some time." He folded his hands under his chin and rested his elbows on the table, trying to seem as though he was actually interested in helping her no doubt. He let his honeyed words hang in the air. It made her want to puke.

"You can all go to hell," she grumbled. There was nothing else to say.

Agent Layton sighed. "Have it your way, Ms. Allen. I guess we'll be getting to know each other very well. I don't have to charge you with anything to hold you as a person of interest. I won't have any trouble getting my petition approved to hold you for the maximum-allowable time." He stacked his papers but made no effort to leave. "That's ninety-six hours, in case you were wondering."

Maureen felt her jaw clench. She couldn't avoid jail time, even if she did tell them about her nightmares. The FBI's search would eventually uncover a lot of other things about her that would see her rotting in a cell anyway. Try as she might, there didn't seem to be a way to wriggle off the hook just yet.

And so, she readied herself for the staring contest she was about to have with Agent Layton.

nine

Manny paced the halls of the police station, deep in thought. Agent Layton had finished with Maureen Allen hours ago, and she'd been shown back to one of the holding cells. He hadn't gone to see her since then and really didn't have any other reason to still be at the station, but for some reason, he hadn't been able to head for home. Or maybe it was that he didn't want to. He was tired, but he couldn't shake the feeling that there was more to that woman than he had first suspected. Before their interview got interrupted, he was sure she was going to tell him something important.

It was well after midnight, and he was alone in the station save for Collins, who had drawn the overnight split since they had someone in holding. He decided to get to work digging into the background of Tom Lowes. The FBI had taken what was left of the vomit sample after the county lab had completed the basic genetic testing, proving it didn't come from anyone in the family. This weakened the case against either Tom or his wife being the actual killer, but it raised a whole new set of questions. Getting more information on the couple just might shake loose a possible suspect for him to focus on, while Layton had his people run the DNA through their database.

Manny found his way back to his desk and started looking over the Lowes family's phone records for the second time that day. He'd requested the last year's worth but so far, only the last four months had been delivered. Several numbers came up frequently, though they all had a reasonable explanation: several of Kristin's clients, Tom's office, and Kristin's brother's cell phone. There were no other numbers called in that time that raised any red flags for him.

The financials on the family hadn't come back yet. Manny had hoped they would have arrived that afternoon, but the county had indicated that the complete reports from the brokerage were still being put together. He couldn't help but wonder if they were stonewalling him and favoring the Feds. It was purely his inner pessimist talking. At least, he hoped so.

"Benny, you might want to get over here!"

The shout from the holding area shook him out of his thoughts. Without hesitation, he erupted from his desk and rushed toward the sound. As he rounded the corner leading to the cells, he nearly ran straight through Collins, who was standing at the hall's entrance.

"She's freaking out," whispered Collins in a hoarse tone. "She fell asleep a little while ago, but now she's tossing and turning all over the bunk and babbling some gibberish. I wouldn't have called, but I don't much feel like getting chewed out if she gets hurt on our watch."

"All right, Jack, thanks," Manny said, patting Collins on the shoulder. "Why don't you give me a minute?"

Collins hesitated.

"I'll call you if there's anything I can't handle," he insisted. Collins nodded, though it seemed with no great relish, and retreated around the corner. Manny turned his eyes back toward the hallway and edged toward the cell that held Maureen. He peered through the bars and was met with a strange, unsettling sight.

Maureen lay on the cot along the wall, facing the ceiling. Her back was arched, and her head snapped back and forth on the flat pillow. She was talking in her sleep. Collins had called it gibberish but, though he did not understand the words, Manny could detect language in the patterns of the syllables that came from her lips. The tone was unsettling, almost otherworldly. As he looked on, her movements seemed to take on a dance between two forces. Where at first she seemed to move in time with some unknown force, now it appeared as if she were struggling against it, wanting to move left but being dragged to the right. Her voice began to reach a crescendo, and Manny could clearly make out the final word she uttered before her eyes snapped open. She thrust herself upright and sprang away from the cot, her back crashing into the bars with a loud clatter. She snapped around and locked eyes with him. Though it was brief, he caught a wild, terrified look, like a cornered animal, before she shrank away to the opposite end of the cell and sat, hugging her knees and staring at the floor.

"Collins!" he called out over his shoulder, masking his disconcertment as best as he could. "I need you back here. Bring the keys to the cell!"

The other officer appeared moments later, keys jingling in his hand. He was composed as he stepped around the corner, but his mask of calm dropped away instantly when his eyes fell upon the slouching figure in the corner that was their prisoner.

He turned to Manny, his raised eyebrows and slacked jaw asking what they were supposed to do now.

"Open the cell door, Jack," Manny said as calmly as he could. "Then take a few steps back and let me speak with her alone before we decide what to do." He hoped it wasn't showing how upset he was at what he had just witnessed.

Collins nodded, clearly unable to find any words. He stepped forward and turned the key in the lock. The snap of the lock was the only other sound in the air apart from Maureen's breath coming in gasps. Manny pushed the door open slowly and looked back at Collins, jerking his head in the direction of the hallway entrance. Collins nodded at him again and backed up a dozen or so paces, far enough so that he could not be seen by anyone from inside the holding cell.

She didn't look at him as he slowly walked the five steps needed to put himself in front of her. Manny squatted down so that he could see her eye to eye. It was clear how frightened she was by whatever had just happened.

"Ms. Allen," he said softly, trying to sound as empathetic as possible, "are you all right?"

"Stay away from me!" Maureen shouted, turning ninety degrees to put a shoulder to the wall and hide her face in its bricks. Manny could see the single tear she was trying to cover.

He dutifully backed up a step but stayed crouched, hoping to make her feel more comfortable by not standing over her. He didn't really have much experience dealing with someone in this state. He sat back for a moment, trying to decide what to do.

He didn't have to wait long. With surprising suddenness, Maureen's body convulsed, and she shot forward toward the low metal toilet in the opposite corner of the cell. A torrent of vomit erupted from her before she could fully position herself above it, with some falling on the floor between her legs. She paused for a moment, panting, before a second wave burst from her. Manny could only watch as the disturbing scene unfolded. It was like watching a drunk girl at a frat party; that was the only other time he'd seen anything like this. The odor of it nearly made him gag.

He watched as Maureen let out a pained groan and flopped back against the wall, wiping her lips with the back of one hand before wiping her eyes with the palm of the other. She tilted her head back against the wall with her eyes closed and inhaled through her nose, apparently trying to get her breath under control. After a moment, she opened her eyes and stared at him. The pained smile that creased her lips stood in stark contrast to her weary eyes, and the short laugh that escaped her throat dripped with bitterness.

"I told you to stay away, Detective," she said weakly. "It wasn't a pretty sight, was it?" She let her chin fall to her chest and began to rub her temples. "Do you happen to have a handful of aspirin hanging around? Or better yet, something stronger? Maybe something you might have confiscated? Anything you got would be fine."

"Contraband is locked up at County."

"Remind me to get pinched by someone from County next time," she responded flatly as she pushed herself to her feet. "Can I at least get a drink of water to wash the vomit taste out of my mouth? Maybe splash my face a bit?"

Manny looked her up and down for a moment. She was clearly hurting from the experience and was trying to mask it with sarcasm and a spiteful demeanor. It could, of course, all have been an act designed to facilitate an escape, but judging by the way she was swaying unsteadily while she waited for his answer, he didn't think so. Still, he couldn't take any chances.

"Jack," he called, not moving his eyes from her, even as he heard Officer Collins' footsteps come up behind him. "Jack, take Ms. Allen to the bathroom and let her wash her face—don't take your eyes off her—and then take her into the interview room, lock the door, and wait outside for me. I'll meet you there in a few minutes."

Manny watched as Collins led Maureen by the arm around the corner before looking back at the vomit which had missed the toilet. He had plans for that. As quickly as he could, he dashed over to the supply locker, grabbed an evidence bag and gloves, and then ran back to the cell. He knelt down and scooped as much as he could into the bag and sealed it. This would either help his case against her, or completely blow a hole in it.

On his way to the interview room, he stopped into the break room and grabbed the bottle of aspirin from the first aid kit, stuffed it in his jacket pocket, and poured himself a cup of coffee. The coffee was only lukewarm, so he popped it in the microwave for a minute and was about to head back to Maureen, when he decided to grab a glass of water. No reason to make her suffer needlessly.

He had to carry the two cups in one hand while holding the evidence bag in the other, but the walk from the break room to the interview room was a short one. Collins was standing outside as requested, though he looked a little annoyed with his babysitting duties. It was understandable. Collins was the only member of the force younger than Manny, but had aced the academy and was known around the office as one of the most ambitious young officers to have come through in quite a while. Having been relegated to night shift guard duty must have seemed like a slap in the face to him, especially with a murder investigation going on. Manny could sympathize, but everyone had to pay their dues.

"Did she say anything to you?" Manny asked as he walked up to the young officer and looked through the half-blinded window into the interview room. Maureen was sitting at the table much as she had been earlier in the day, leaning back and slouching in the chair pretending to ignore everything around her.

"Not a word," returned Collins in a bored tone.

"Okay, I'll take another crack at her. Here, take this." Manny held out the evidence bag.

"What is that?" the young officer eyed the bag and its contents carefully.

"Her puke," said Manny matter-of-factly. He smiled as Collins made a face. "It's evidence, pal. I need you to call over to County and have someone come and pick it up. Let them know it's for the Lowes case. I know it's late, but the admin desk is staffed twenty-four hours. Someone will pick up. Ask them to see if the DNA they pull from this sample matches the DNA from the sample collected at the crime scene. When you're done, come back here and wait outside just in case I need you. I might be a while, so try to stay awake."

"What about the FBI?"

"I'm sure County will let them know what's going on," Manny said, maybe a little too sourly.

Collins rolled his eyes, but nodded and carefully took the evidence bag.

"All right, I'm heading in," said Manny. "Lock the door behind me and don't open it unless I knock."

Maureen's head raised as he shut the door behind him. He walked over to the table, put the aspirin bottle and water in front of her, and sat down in the chair on the opposite side of the table. She eyed him carefully as she reached for the bottle and poured out four tablets into her hand. She popped them into her mouth, took a sip of water, and tilted her head back to swallow. Manny nodded and tried his best to keep a pleasant look on his face as he took a sip of coffee. The flavor made it difficult, but its effect was more important than taste at the moment.

"Are you feeling better, Ms. Allen?" Better to keep it as light as possible. She had a lot of defenses up; he knew that all too well. If he was going to get her to open up, the last thing he needed to do was put her even further back on her heels.

"I've been worse," she replied. She had retaken her position, slouched back in her chair, rubbing her temples with one hand while the other draped over the back of the chair to support her weight.

"Well, I thought maybe we could talk about what happened back in the holding cell a few minutes ago?" He phrased it as a question intentionally, hoping the illusion of the choice to answer would make her think she's controlling the conversation.

"It was a nightmare, Detective."

"About what?"

She said nothing, so Manny decided to push a bit.

"It sure looked like more than a nightmare. You were thrashing around on the cot pretty hard. And you were mumbling something in some foreign language. When you woke up, there was fear in your eyes. Then, of course, there's the incident in the toilet." He tried to be delicate.

"You can just say I puked, Detective," she shot back. "Not like it hasn't happened before."

"Which part?" She wanted to talk; he could feel it. He just had to wait her out.

She sat still for what seemed like an eternity. It was so quiet that he could hear their breath.

"Ms. Allen—actually, can I please dispense with formality and call you Maureen?"

She shrugged.

"All right, we'll go with Maureen from now on, and you can call me Manny if it suits you."

She shrugged again.

"Okay, Maureen, this whole thing is starting to get a little weird. First, you ask me some pretty involved questions at the bar, then you mention details about the murder that were not public, and then I find you in Jacob Lowes' bedroom later that same night. You tell me that you were there because 'something about all this seemed familiar', but you decline to offer anything further. And now, I find you writhing around like you're possessed and vomiting like something out of a horror movie. What am I supposed to make of all this?"

"I have a condition." She shrugged, looking at the table. "I appreciate the water, *Manny*, but do you have something in the neighborhood of whiskey? It helps me medicate."

"Maureen, you act as if all this is a normal day for you.

Now either you killed that kid or you helped whoever did, or you know who did it and you're protecting them for some reason! Any way you slice it, you're going away, so just help yourself out and give me something I can work with!" Her defiance had pushed him over the edge.

"I already told you. I had nothing to do with it," she shot back, straightening in her chair and staring him dead in the eye for the first time since he walked into the room. Her breathing had become rapid, and her face was twisted into a pained look, as if his words had stabbed her in the heart. She sat frozen like that for a few agonizing moments before her expression fell, and she cast her eyes back down. "At least, I had nothing to do with it the way that you're thinking," she mumbled, almost inaudibly.

Manny unclenched his fists as he realized he had stood up in his frustration at her defiance. His back was arched and he was leaning over the table, looking at her. He composed himself and sat back down in his chair.

"All right Maureen, why don't you tell me what you're talking about?" He softened his tone one more time, hoping that he hadn't blown it. "Please," he added.

"You won't believe me anyway, so why bother?"

"Maureen, tell me!"

"You're going to find another kid dead!" she shouted, almost over the top of him. Her words hung in the air.

"Okay," Manny said slowly, after a moment. "Let's say that's true. How do you know?"

"My dreams," she said softly, staring at the table once again. "In the nightmare you saw me having, I was in a field. I'm not sure where, but it has to be close by. I'm looking through someone else's eyes, like I'm wearing a mask. I can see what they see, feel what they feel. They're chanting something in a language I don't know. I feel the words coming from my throat, but it's not my voice. In front of me, there is a large pile of wood, like a three-, maybe four-foot-tall log cabin. On top, there was a boy laid out. He was blonde, maybe a year or two younger than the other one, no clothes. I can see that his throat is cut, that he's already dead. The hands come into view, only they're not my hands. They're holding a knife with a carved, wooden handle and a long, curved blade. The knife starts cutting into the boy's stomach, but not in any violent way, more like he's being dissected. My own thoughts start to filter in, I can't stand to watch, and it's like I'm wrestling to pull myself away. The hands keep cutting him open, but everything starts go black. And the next thing I know, I'm awake and staring at you." Her hand shot out and grabbed the water. Manny could see that, as she lifted it to her lips, her hand was shaking.

"And did you have a similar nightmare the night that Jacob Lowes was killed?" This was all too incredible, but he had to make it seem that he was open to the possibility of all this being true. If he kept playing along with her, maybe she'd actually give him something that could break this case.

Maureen nodded. "In that one, I saw the hands put a rag over his mouth and take him right from his bedroom, through the house, and out the back door. There was the same type of a woodpile in the backyard. The same knife was used. It felt as if my own arm was jerking to cut the kid's throat before I woke up in my apartment."

"Where you were alone, with no one to corroborate your

story," Manny finished. He regretted saying that. He didn't believe for a second that this woman's dreams somehow predicted the future, or whatever she was driving at. Still, the misstep in his words might lead to her shutting down again.

"Told you you wouldn't believe me," she scoffed bitterly as she took another sip of water, popped another aspirin into her mouth, and swallowed them both together. "It's not like anyone has ever believed me." She went back to not looking at him. It was as if she were talking to the table, and he was just there to overhear her end of the conversation. "And why should they? Why would they? It's ridiculous." Her voice lowered until the last words were a whisper, and she sat, continuing to stare at the cold metal table, shaking her head.

A knock at the door broke Manny's concentration. A wall was breaking in her mind, and he was eager to take advantage of it. Irritated, he turned toward the door, but decided that it could wait. He had to make the most of this opportunity.

"Maureen—" he began, but another, louder knock at the door cut him off. Manny let out a grunt of frustration and stomped over to the door. "What?" he called out impatiently.

The door opened, and he was face to face with Officer Collins who jerked his head back and to the side, indicating that he wanted to talk to him out in the hall.

"A call just came in," Collins said once he had joined him out there. He opened his mouth to continue, but hesitated.

"Spit it out," Manny said impatiently.

"A fire was spotted in an empty field up on the north side of town. The fire department was dispatched about half an hour ago. They...," he paused again and lowered his voice. "There was a body in the flames."

Manny felt his eyes widen but made an effort to set his jaw and stay composed. Even so, a tingle shot up his spine, and he cast an eye back toward the room where Maureen sat.

"Come with me," he said, moving back toward the interview room. Collins followed.

Maureen raised her head as they entered the room. Their eyes met. They didn't speak, but even so, she began to shake her head again.

"Why?" she mumbled. "Why me?"

"Collins, get your cuffs out," he said.

"Want me to take her back to her cell?"

Maureen stopped mumbling and raised her eyes to meet his again.

"No," said Manny. "I'm going to the crime scene." He stared steadily back at Maureen. "And I'll be taking Ms. Allen here with me."

Ten

The detective's truck bumped along the single-lane road that ran past a stretch of farmland on the outskirts of town. Maureen sat in the passenger's seat, hands in her lap. The young cop at the station had closed the cold, steel handcuffs too tightly on her wrists. She kept looking down to see if her fingers were turning purple from a lack of circulation. So far, no. In any case, it's not like she could slip them, so she had no choice but to endure it all for the moment.

The truck was heading north, so the sun was on Maureen's side. Its rays, just starting to break over the tree line that formed the eastern boundary of the fields, poured into her eyes. As she looked at the fields, she felt she had been transported to another planet. She knew she was in small-town America, but the world always seemed so strange to her when homes and buildings were spread so far apart. She'd never gotten used to it in her years on the road; so much space for so few people. They couldn't have been driving for more than ten minutes, and already up the road about a quarter mile she could see the clustering of police vehicles at the crime scene.

The gravel on the side of the road crunched loudly under the truck's tires as the detective pulled to a stop in front of the

97

array of law enforcement vehicles. She sat still, staring out at the sight while he slammed the truck into park, pushed open his door, and stalked around to her side. The passenger's side door flew open and he unbuckled her seat belt before grasping her elbow to encourage her out of the car. Under any other circumstances, she would have been defiant, but it was as if she could feel the earnestness in his entire body, the nervous energy of a deep-seated fear, all concentrated in his grasp on her arm. Maureen almost felt sorry for the young detective and decided to just cooperate. For his sake.

They walked down a gentle slope for several yards until they were a few feet below the level of the road, out of the crowd of vehicles, looking out at the crime scene. No more than two hundred yards out into the field, she could see what looked like a heap of burned wood surrounded by a wide square of yellow police tape. A dark-haired woman paced around it, followed by a young man scribbling furiously on a notepad. Two officers were flanking them at two of the corners of the yellow square. The whole area was dotted with little orange flags.

As Maureen continued to scan the faces in the assembled mass, her eyes fell upon Agent Layton standing to one side, speaking closely with the female agent. She'd barely met the woman yesterday on her way back to her holding cell after Layton had finally ceased with his relentless questioning. The fact that he'd tried so hard—and failed—to break her made her smirk at seeing him again. She turned to glance to her side at Detective Benitez. To her surprise, he was looking at her, expectantly.

"What?" she asked, unnerved by his stare.

"Well, are you getting anything from the crime scene?"

You've got to be kidding me. That's *what I'm doing here?* Maureen thought to herself. She might have laughed if she hadn't been so annoyed and offended by his presumption. Did this man honestly think that she was some sort of a psychic? Did he think she was going to pick up on some aura of the scene and solve the whole case for him using only her mind? Clearly, he'd seen too many bad movies. She decided to mess with him, to give him what he deserved for the indignity.

Maureen closed her eyes, raised her handcuffed hands to her temples, and began a monotonic hum. She paced back and forth, acting as if she was a divining rod, changing direction as she pretended to narrow in on a supposed mystical force. It only took a few seconds, however, before she was tired of her little game, and she stopped in her tracks and gave the detective her best annoyed stare.

"It doesn't work like that, boss," she chided when it was clear he still didn't catch on to her teasing.

Detective Benitez let his chin fall to his chest. She could tell he felt foolish for even asking her to do something like that. "I should have known you wouldn't be any help."

"Hey, I'm not the one who brought me here, out of that nice comfy cell, to perform little tricks because he can't solve this case himself," she shot back. "I mean, what did you expect to happen?"

The detective opened his mouth, but no words came out. Fortunately for him, the approach of footsteps saved him from trying to stumble his way through something stupid. A tall, young man in a firefighter's uniform came up to meet them.

"Manny, I thought that was you," he said. "Can you believe this?"

"Hey, Ben," he greeted the fireman before turning toward Maureen. "Maureen, this is Ben Naismith. I went to high school with him and his wife."

"It's just like the scene on Thursday morning," the fireman told him.

"Why don't you give me the details."

"Well, we got the call around—"

"Hang on a second," the detective interrupted, looking around. He seemed to find what he was looking for and called out, "Yancy, can you come over here?"

Maureen had remembered seeing this man walking through the hallway of the police station once or twice while she was being herded back and forth from her cell to the interrogation room. As she recalled, he really didn't say much, and he only made brief eye contact with her once.

"Hey, Carl," the detective said as the officer came up to stand next to her, "can you please keep an eye on Ms. Allen here while I go talk to Mr. Naismith? Thanks." He and the young fireman walked away before an answer came.

As Yancy's eyes looked her up and down, Maureen could sense his indignation at having to babysit her. She didn't blame him. Where could she go? She looked at him and they exchanged shrugs, a silent pact to endure each other for a few minutes.

Maureen turned her head to watch the detective and the fireman speak in hushed tones next to a cadre of police vehicles. She could see two vans with the county name on them and three more behind these, which must have belonged to the Sycamore Hills Police Department. Further down the road, apart from the others, a plain, black sedan was parked. *The Feds' car*, she thought bitterly.

As her gaze continued to scan the field, Maureen felt a light tug on the hem of her shirt. She looked down to see a little boy, maybe three or four with sandy-colored hair and big, blue eyes, standing at her feet and staring up at her.

"What's that?" He was pointing at the handcuffs on her wrists.

Maureen didn't know what to do. She didn't have any experience dealing with children. Should she make something up? Tell the truth? Should she just ignore him?

"What's that?" the boy chirped louder, insistently pawing at her wrists. Clearly, he was not going to leave her alone until he got some sort of answer.

Maureen looked to her right at Officer Yancy and raised an eyebrow, silently asking what she was supposed to do. He just shrugged. Maureen sighed and crouched down to look the little boy in the eyes. Staring at him as menacingly as she could, she gave her answer. "They're called handcuffs," she whispered gruffly. "They put them on bad people to keep them from running away. I'm a bad person. So run along back to your mommy."

Rather than run, the little boy giggled and raised his tiny hand to her face, running his hand down her cheek.

"Benny, get away from her," a voice shouted. Maureen stood up to the sight of a young, dark-haired woman rushing down from the side of the road toward them. The moment she got to them, the woman scooped up the boy in her arms. "You know you're not supposed to talk to strangers," she chided the boy, holding her face nose to nose with his.

"Tasha, what are you guys doing here?" The voice of the detective came from up the hill.

Maureen turned to see him and the fireman jogging back toward them. The fireman came to their side and kissed the little boy on the top of the head.

"Hey, Manny," the woman replied after she put her free arm through the fireman's, who Maureen assumed was her husband. "We were coming back from staying at my parents' house. We had dinner there last night and, since Ben had the late shift and I don't have class until nine today, we decided to drive back down early instead of leaving late last night. When he saw the firetrucks, Benny insisted that Daddy had to be there, and he wanted to see him. I couldn't say no. What happened here?"

"We probably shouldn't talk about it in front of Benny," the fireman replied.

The woman nodded.

Maureen looked down at the little boy again. He was holding on to both of his father's hands but was facing her, smiling and rocking back and forth. His parents noticed.

"Weird, he's usually so shy around people he doesn't know," the young fireman said.

"I'm taking him home," the woman announced and gave the fireman a kiss on the cheek. "You'll be home Monday morning, right?" She received his nod before turning back to Maureen and shooting her a look.

Same to you, bitch, Maureen thought sourly.

The young woman turned and hoisted the boy up so that he was facing her. The little boy broke into a broad grin and raised his hand to wave at her. Maureen, not knowing what else to do, stuck out her tongue at him and made a face. He giggled and buried his head in his mother's shoulder. Maureen shook her head and then heard a brief sniffle of laughter come from her side. She snapped her head around to Officer Yancy, hoping to catch the crack in his serious facade, but he had mastered himself.

The detective shifted his head from side to side, eyeing Maureen and then the young woman and boy walking up the slope to their car. "What was that about?" he asked.

Maureen shrugged. "Kid just came up to me and started bothering me," she said. "Nothing more."

"Okay." He drew out the word, clearly skeptical of her explanation. He eyed her for a moment longer before turning his attention to the other officer. "Carl, I'm going to head down and speak with the Feds and Dr. Winherst. Can you please take Ms. Allen back up to my truck and keep a tight eye on her? I'll be taking her back to the station myself when I'm finished."

"Whatever you say," the officer returned in an even tone.

Maureen watched Detective Benitez stalk down the hill toward where Agent Layton and his partner were standing, silently watching over the crime scene. The agent's head turned at his approach, but his eyes looked past him and met her own. Maureen held his gaze, determined not to be the first to break contact. Layton cocked his head after a moment and turned back around to stare back across the field. *Small victories.*

"Well, Officer," she chimed as she turned toward the man the detective referred to as Carl, "shall we?"

The officer nodded, placed a hand on her elbow, and guided her back up the hill to await the detective. Maureen tried her best to keep her face even and ignore the queasy feeling creeping up in her stomach.

ELEVEN

"Why did you bring her here?" Agent Layton grumbled as Manny walked up next to him.

"I had a notion she might be useful," Manny shrugged, staring directly ahead at the smoldering remains of the fire. It all looked much like it had at the Lowes' residence. He could see Stacey Winherst kneeling down, sifting carefully through the ashes. The body was obscured from his view, but he knew that, before the day was out, he would come face to face with the charred remains of another child. It was not a sight he was looking forward to.

"She's a suspect, Detective," Agent Layton returned sharply. "Suspects belong in custody."

Manny turned and looked back at Maureen. She was leaning against his truck, a few feet away from Yancy, staring out at the field, as if transfixed by the sight of it all. A soft breeze tousled the few strands of her hair not contained by her ponytail as the morning sun lit her face. The image reminded him of how he'd found her attractive when he saw her at Anderson's less than two days ago. *She might even look better without makeup on,* he thought.

"Well, she obviously couldn't have done this from a jail

cell," Manny said, gesturing out at the crime scene. "I figured if she is involved somehow, it might help our case to bring her out here, under observation, and see if she does anything to tip us off."

It was a flimsy reason and he knew it, but at present, he was unsure if telling Agent Layton about the woman's supposed prophetic dream was wise. He himself didn't put it outside of the realm of possibility, but he was certain there had to be some other logical explanation for Maureen's episode in the cell last night.

Agent Layton paused for a moment, staring uncomfortably at Manny. Then, to his surprise, the agent leaned in and sniffed. "You haven't been home since yesterday, have you?"

Manny saw no point in lying. "No, I haven't."

"Uh-huh," the agent grunted out of the side of his mouth. "You wouldn't have happened to have stayed at the station all night, would you?"

Manny nodded carefully.

"And I assume that you spent at least some of that time talking to our suspect?"

Manny nodded again, defeated. He should have known better than to try and pass off bringing Maureen to the crime scene as some grand fit of inspiration. Any analytical mind could see that he had gleaned a fair bit of information from her that necessitated her presence.

"So, are you going to share what she told you with me, or am I going to have to file obstruction charges?"

Manny knew he had to be careful. Any sound-minded FBI agent wouldn't believe what he had witnessed, but he couldn't lie. He decided to massage the truth, for his own sake and for

Maureen's. "She had some kind of fit in her cell last night, maybe two in the morning or so. It was probably epileptic or something. She vomited pretty good. I collected some and sent it over to the county lab for comparison to the other sample from the first scene."

"What else?"

"She starts going on about having a dream about how another kid was going to get murdered," he continued. "Raving like a lunatic, really. It was all really bizarre. The way I figure it, if she's involved somehow, she had to know that her accomplice was going to do this tonight. Maybe she's a distraction. Or maybe her guilty conscience is starting to get the better of her. I don't know. Either way, I wasn't going to leave her in that holding cell with only Officer Collins to watch her. He's a good kid, and will be a good cop someday, but he doesn't have the experience right now."

Manny cast a look at Agent Layton from the side of his eye. Though an observer would think the agent wasn't paying attention, Manny suspected he was listening intently and scrutinizing his every word, so he decided to try to turn the focus back to the present. He wasn't going to earn the confidence of the Feds by spouting thin theories and unfounded suppositions.

Stacey Winherst was now making her way toward them, stripping off her plastic gloves as she climbed up the slope from the crime scene. Her dark hair was tied back and her boots were covered with footies. She wore her usual expression: the corners of her mouth ever so slightly turned down.

"The firefighters left this crime scene in even better condition than the last one," she said, speaking directly to Layton and not giving Manny a second look.

Manny rolled his eyes.

"I was able to get a very good look at the body," she continued in her measured tone. "The flesh is all but gone, but the skeleton is in as good a shape as I can hope for. I can say with full confidence that the victim was a pre-pubescent male, no more than nine or ten. There appears to be a nick on the C1, and I was able to observe a significant amount of blood on the wood under the victim's neck, indicating severe blood loss prior to death. As with the last body, I was able to find a pile of internal organs on a separate part of the woodpile."

"So in other words, the same perp is responsible," Agent Layton finished for her.

"I didn't say that," Dr. Winherst responded with a speed and earnestness that caught Manny completely off guard. "All I can say is that this crime scene follows the same MO as the last one."

"Of course," Layton replied with a subtle grin. "Is there anything else?"

"Actually, yes," she said. "I believe I may have identified an accelerant of some kind. There was an oily substance that was found on some of the unburnt wood."

"Do you have a sample?" Agent Layton asked. Stacey nodded. "Could you bring it over?"

Manny could hear in his voice that it wasn't really a question. He stood quietly, half expecting Dr. Winherst to object to the handling of evidence before she had a chance to take it to her lab. To his surprise, she immediately turned over her shoulder and called to Derrick Emmsley, who was walking away toward the road with an evidence box. He changed his direction at the sound of his name and strode up to the group.

Stacey pulled an extra glove out of her pocket and used it to pick up a test tube from the box.

"Go ahead and open it," Agent Layton said coolly.

Dr. Winherst hesitated for a moment, but obeyed.

Agent Layton bent forward and sniffed the contents of the tube. He nodded to Agent Lorenzo who leaned over and sniffed as well. He then turned to Manny and indicated that he should do the same. Stacey seemed to take offense, but allowed Manny to come over nonetheless. He took a deep breath, paused, and took a second one. The odor that overwhelmed his nostrils was the smell of burnt wood and smoke, but underneath was a second smell. It was equal parts spicy and sweet. Manny was sure he'd smelled something like this before, but couldn't place it.

"Well?" Agent Layton's voice came through the haze of his concentration.

Manny looked up to see that the agent was looking at him, no doubt expecting his assessment. "There's something familiar about the smell," Manny said slowly. "I'm just not quite sure what it is."

"I had the same thought," Agent Layton replied before turning to Dr. Winherst. "I'd pay really close attention to this sample, Doctor. I have a notion that finding out exactly what this substance is would go a long way to helping us in this case."

Dr. Winherst nodded, turned, placed the tube back in the box, and hurried up the hill with Derrick. Agent Layton leaned in and said something in Agent Lorenzo's ear. She nodded and followed the doctor and her assistant at a casual distance. Layton then turned to Manny and cocked his head in the direction of the burn pile. Manny nodded and they descended the gentle slope.

"I've never seen Stacey Winherst submit like that," Manny found himself saying, before he gave a thought as to whether it was appropriate.

"Well, we go back a while," Agent Layton replied, still facing forward, eyes fixed on their destination.

"Really?" Manny was surprised. He'd never really thought of it before, but he realized how little he actually knew Dr. Winherst. "She's not much older than I am. How can that be?"

"True, she's not much older than you, but she's had a longer career than you'd think. You don't think you're the only investigative mind to return to their hometown, do you?" he paused to let the new information sink in. "Stacey has always had a brilliant mind when it comes to crime scene investigation. She was one of the youngest CIs in St. Louis and was key in several murder cases that I myself was the lead investigator on. She helped me get several federal convictions. But she got emotional on one particular case about five years ago. It was a double murder of a young single mother and her daughter. They were beaten to death in their apartment on the east side of St. Louis. The prime suspect was the woman's estranged boyfriend. He had priors for drugs and battery, as well as a shaky alibi, but the evidence against him wasn't solid. The new DA was looking to establish his own credibility, so Stacey was able to convince him that she could prove the case against the boyfriend on the stand. The trial didn't go well. The boyfriend had backing from friends and could afford one of the better defense attorneys in the city. Once he had Stacey in cross-examination, he played her like a fiddle, got her to burst out in court, and was able to get much of her testimony thrown out. He managed to turn what was allowed into the record into nothing more than wild and vindictive speculation in the minds of the jury. The boyfriend was acquitted, and Stacey was asked to leave her job soon after."

"So, your point is she learned her lesson and became the iceberg she is?"

"I mean that once you learn a little more about a person's past, you can better understand their present."

"Do you think he did it?"

"What's that?"

"The boyfriend. Do you think he killed the woman and her daughter?"

"Most likely," said Agent Layton, his voice even and measured. "Fortunately, he wasn't that smart, and the trial made him believe he was untouchable." He turned to look at Manny again and smirked. "He tried to move eight hundred kilos of cocaine and seven dozen crates of illegal weaponry through St. Louis a year later. Last fall, I got him sent away for thirty-five years after some of his friends rolled on him for reduced sentences. In hindsight, I should really thank Stacey for putting him on my radar. He turned out to be the missing piece in a ring that I was trying to bust."

The two men had reached the burn pile. Manny followed behind Agent Layton as they circled around the exterior of the yellow police tape. He was waiting for the agent to lift the tape and let the two of them in, but he never did. Layton simply made a circuit around the outside, as if soaking up all the available information with his feet, and ended up in front of two men from the County Coroner's Office keeping vigil over a gurney with a black body bag on top of it.

"Gentlemen," Agent Layton greeted the men with a nod, which they returned silently as they moved apart a few paces to allow the agent and Manny room to stand by the body. Agent Layton slowly unzipped the bag to reveal the charred bones of the child. Manny felt himself shake his head sorrowfully as he took in the sight. He knew he must try and keep his emotions in check, but it was difficult while staring into the vacant eyeholes of a skull that hours ago would have stood atop a living, breathing boy with his whole life ahead of him. Someone had taken it upon themselves to gruesomely end that life, just like Jacob Lowes, and that thought filled him with a rage that could have burned a pile of wood ten times the size of the one they were standing by.

Manny turned his head toward the agent. Layton was staring down into the bag as well. He wondered if the older man felt the same as he did at that moment. He wondered, if he did, how he hid it so well. Or had the years he'd invested in this career simply numbed him to a sight like this?

"Let's load him up," Layton said quietly, zipping up the bag and glancing at the other two men who looked as though they were soldiers at attention in the presence of their commanding officer. Manny could understand the sentiment. Layton did command that sort of respect.

The men stepped in and began to wheel the gurney up toward the road. Its wheels bumped along the ground so the going was slowed in order to prevent the body from falling off. Manny walked alongside Layton a few steps behind.

"We gotta find this guy," Manny said as they went. It was

a silly and obvious thing to say, but he was uncomfortable walking beside the agent in silence. He felt like a puppy nipping at the heels of its owner and was beginning to believe that Layton saw him in much the same way.

"Guy?" said the agent, turning his head. "What about Ms. Allen? Do you think suddenly that she's no longer of any interest to us?"

"I, uh, well no, that's not it," Manny stammered, taken off guard. He'd forgotten about Maureen for a moment, and now he realized he wasn't sure at all anymore how she fit into all of this.

"Well, I'm actually thinking we should let her go."

"Really? Can I ask why?"

"I want to see what she does when she thinks she's free. I haven't made up my mind about her yet, but I do feel like this is one move that we can safely make."

Manny simply nodded and looked up the hill. They were nearly to the road. Manny's eyes quickly found Maureen where he had left her, still handcuffed and leaning on his truck. She wore a mask of indifference on her face. He couldn't tell if the experience was shaking her or not but somehow, he had a feeling that this wasn't the most stressful circumstance she'd faced in her life. At his side, he felt Layton's pace quicken and he lengthened his own stride to keep up, wondering what the man was going to do now.

They drew even with gurney and body bag as it began to pass in front of Maureen on its way to the coroner's van. Manny made it a point to not look directly at her and instead kept his eyes toward the road, focusing on nothing in particular. It was for this reason that he didn't notice Agent Layton stop the gurney in front of the handcuffed woman. Manny stopped and turned just in time to see the agent slowly, almost callously, unzip the body bag about a quarter of the way. Manny looked at Maureen. Her eyes were fixed on the bag's contents. He saw the golf-ball-sized lump forced back down her throat with a swallow and knew she was suppressing her gag reflex. He could almost taste the sour flavor of vomit in his own throat.

"Not a pretty sight, is it?" Agent Layton asked.

Maureen raised her head and stared at him, but then quickly slumped back into her pose of leaning on the car and reapplied her mask of disinterest and defiance. She didn't say a word. Manny caught himself before a smile of amusement broke out on his face. As serious and horrifying as the situation was, he felt a morbid sense of satisfaction at the sight of the veteran agent meeting his mental jousting match in the slight young woman. Layton seemed to know it, too.

"All right," he said, zipping up the body bag and nodding to the men to take it away. "I'm ordering your release, Ms. Allen. Detective Benitez will be taking you home, or wherever you want to go—within the city limits, of course. Get comfortable. You're not going anywhere for a while."

Layton nodded to him as a signal to take her away, pulling his phone out of his pocket as he walked toward his car. Manny stood next to Maureen and watched the agent go. As he opened the sedan's door, he turned and stared at them for a moment before disappearing into the front seat.

ᵼⱲELVE

"So how *does* it work?" Manny asked as he leaned over to the passenger's side and unlocked the handcuffs on Maureen's wrists.

"How does what work?" Maureen replied as she rubbed her wrists, glancing sourly at him.

"This magic power of yours. Obviously, I got it wrong back there when I thought you could read the omens in the air, or whatever. So help me understand what happens."

He cast one eye over to her as he began to drive off when he heard a sharp rapping on his window. Manny hit the brake and turned to see Captain Wellner standing alongside his truck, motioning that he wanted a word. Manny rolled down his window.

"Wanted to catch you before you sped away, Benitez," the captain said. It sounded to Manny as if he was just catching his breath. Most likely he'd run over to catch him.

"What can I do for you, sir?" he replied, eager to get on his way. Whatever he wanted, Manny was sure that it could wait.

"I saw you down by the crime scene talking to the agents. I just wanted to make sure you were being professional. You know, not getting in the way or anything."

"I was invited," Manny said curtly.

"Ah." Wellner nodded his head before leaning into the truck to look closer at Maureen, who was staring out the window, apparently pretending not to be listening. "Isn't she the one you brought into the station yesterday for breaking into the Lowes' house?"

"Yes."

"Oh." The captain seemed thrown by his short answer, seeming to wrestle with what to say next. After a beat, he leaned in close to Manny. "What's she doing here in your truck without any handcuffs?"

"Agent Layton ordered her release." Manny knew invoking the authority of the FBI would get this over with quickly. "I'm taking her home."

Wellner paused for a moment and began to back away from the car, nodding his head slowly. "Go ahead and head home yourself afterward. We'll make sure to call you when we get an ID on the body."

Manny nodded briskly and put his foot on the accelerator. When they were on their way again, he turned his attention back to Maureen. "So, you were saying?"

"I was saying what?"

"You were going to tell me how this power of yours works."

"Don't think I was."

Manny shook his head. In spite of all that was going on around her, she was sitting there and acting like nothing much had happened. A small part of him admired her fortitude. "All right, we can talk about something else. You haven't been here long, obviously. How did you end up working at Anderson's?"

Manny tried to sound cheerfully casual in the hopes that she would let her guard down and talk about her power later.

"Bartending is easy money when you're a chick," she said, still staring out of the window. "I needed cash to fix my car."

Interesting. "So, I take it you weren't planning on staying in town long?" he asked.

"Ding, ding, ding," she replied flatly. "Do I look like someone who would stick around a place like this?"

"It's not so bad."

"Why do you even care how long I was going to stay?" she shot back quickly.

"I don't," Manny smiled. He could feel he was starting to get to her. She seemed to respond more honestly when he annoyed her. "Just seems to me that you don't have any roots, which is atypical for a woman your age. You're not that young anymore."

"How the hell old do you think I am?!" Her indignity broke through her calm facade. Sometimes it was just as simple as finding a pressure point.

"Don't get me wrong, you look good for your age," Manny said, confident that he was getting under her skin and that she would let slip something he might find useful. "I don't usually go in for older women, but in another life, I may have asked you to a movie."

"If you wanna screw me, Detective," she spat, "just say so. You never know, I might let you."

Manny felt his jaw twitch. She'd won that round. He tried to say something clever in return but found no words.

"Yeah that's what I thought," Maureen said, shooting him a cruel smirk. "Shut the fuck up."

"That's no way to speak to an officer of the law."

Maureen didn't say anything. She simply rolled her eyes at him and turned back to the window.

"All right," he said after a moment, keeping up his casual demeanor the best he could. "I'm sorry for teasing. I'm just curious about you, that's all. You can't blame me. This is a pretty quiet small town, most everyone knows each other. Not a lot of people moving in and out around here, you know? Most people are boring. You're not."

"Yeah, well, thanks, Detective."

"You can call me Manny."

"Can, but won't."

"Avoiding attachments?"

"Something like that."

"Seems to me like that's been your life philosophy," Manny said, glancing over at her.

"I'm not the type of person that anyone would want to have around for a long time."

"Because you've done things?" he said, believing he knew where she was going with this. She was damaged goods, and most people carrying baggage would respond like this, hyperbolizing actions that were most likely the result of simple human nature and turning them into sensational deeds that damned them to a life of punishment. Of course, most of these people weren't actual murder suspects.

"You have no idea. I've done what I needed to do to survive. But I've never killed anyone." She spoke these last words with a firmness that took Manny aback.

Maybe she really didn't have anything to do with the actual killings. But whatever was going on, she was going to prove key to solving the crimes. *Good God, am I actually buying into this whole psychic thing?*

"So, I'm guessing you've got some warrants or something out there?" he prodded.

"You could say that."

"Been in jail?"

"Yep."

"More than once?"

"Sure."

"I've gotta ask, though," he said, "what makes a life on the road so appealing anyway? You running from something besides the law?"

"No," she said far too quickly, turning to look at him.

"That wasn't very convincing." Manny met her gaze. He could see her walls finally breaking down. Maybe she was tired of being the only one who knew her secret.

"You really don't want to know," she sighed.

"I really do."

"Your funeral," she said, shrugging her shoulders. In his peripheral, Manny could see her shifting herself so that her back was leaning against the window and she was facing him. She stared at him out of the tops of her eyes. "I keep moving to stay ahead of the nightmares, but they always find me. They found me here. How's that for honesty?"

"How long?" Whether or not her psychic visions were real, she genuinely believed them to be, and that fact seemed to inform her entire personality.

"Been on my own since I was seventeen. After running off from a reform school."

"How do you make your money? Just by bartending?"

"I don't sell myself, if that's what you're asking. Yeah, it's mostly bartending and waitressing. You don't need any education to do it, and most small businesses don't ask too many questions. And, yeah, sometimes I need to get creative to make rent or get a car or something. I sold some of the medications I was on when I was a teenager to other kids at school. I've obviously done other things that I'm sure your Fed buddies are going to dig up sooner or later. But that's life. That's survival."

"And you started having these dreams at that school?"

"Hell no! I was there *because* of them," she laughed bitterly and tapped her temple with her fingers. "Got a demon up here, they said. All the kids there had something like that. Some were thought to be possessed, some were addicted to sex at fourteen, some were gay. And one girl saw with the eyes of pure evil."

"And that's you, I'm guessing?"

"Yeah, well, at least that's what my mother always said. Some kind of old-country superstition. But she believed it, and so did the zealots running that place."

"So how did they handle that sort of stuff?" Manny asked. He turned again to Maureen to try and gauge the look on her face. It had turned hard and cold.

"Take a wild guess," she growled.

"I don't know," he replied uncomfortably. "Prayer?"

"Yeah," she scoffed, her voice soaked with angry sarcasm. "Prayer."

"So, if the dreams started before you went to that school, when exactly was it?"

"Eight, maybe earlier, but the first time I remember was when I was eight."

"Jesus!"

"I don't think he has much to do with it."

"I can't imagine how I'd handle something like that."

"Pain killers and whiskey seem to work."

The clustered homes and buildings of Sycamore Hills began to surround them. Main Street was still several blocks away, but the first traffic lights on the road into town were just ahead. Manny stopped his truck at the first red light, unsure of what to say next. Maureen's story, or rather the parts of it she was actually telling, sounded harrowing and seemed to explain a lot about her distrust and evasiveness. Yet, he still felt that somehow, he was going to need her in some way to bring the case to a conclusion. The light turned green.

"Where's your apartment?" he asked as he drove on.

Maureen glanced around quickly with the look of someone who could only figure out their location by using landmarks. Or at least she was trying to. "Actually, I'm just up here on the right," she insisted, pointing at the row of homes. "You can just let me off here."

"No," he said decisively, showing her that he had called her bluff. He returned her glare with an exaggerated grin.

"Four blocks south of Main," she sighed. "I got a studio in one of the old industrial buildings. I don't remember the name of the street."

"Branch Street," said Manny.

"Yeah, that's it. Should have known. All the street names around here have something to do with trees."

"Most of them, yeah."

"I think it's stupid."

"So do I."

Within minutes, Manny was heading south down Branch. Maureen, who'd been quiet, poked his arm with her hand and gestured ahead.

"Third one on the left," she said.

Manny pulled his truck over to the curb and put it in park before turning to her.

"Listen, Maureen," he said, trying to sound as calming as possible, "I'm sorry that you're involved in this. And I'm sorry I tried to use you as some kind of tool back there. But take some advice. You're going to need to be careful. I got a feeling this all might get worse before it gets better."

"I'm not stupid," she said as she pushed her door open. She hopped out of the truck and began to close the door before she stopped and leaned back into the cab. "Listen, I don't blame you for trying to do what you did. I might have done the same. But you should know something. The nightmares force me to look through the eyes of someone doing evil things. That much I figured out a long time ago. But I never put that into context until the other night. I always figured that there's evil that puts out—I don't know—imprints into the world, and when I'm around, they fill me up like a cup. When I was in the little boy's room, I found something that told me the truth: I see these things as they're actually happening. Not in the past, not in the future. Right then and there. So you see, I'm more cursed than I thought. There's nothing I can do to help you. Anyway, thanks for the ride, Detective." She stepped back and closed the door slowly.

Manny watched as she walked across the street, her eyes still down, arms wrapped around her. He had to say something, if only to indicate that he had heard and understood her, even if he didn't completely. He rolled down his window. "It's Manny!" he called to her.

"No, it isn't," she called back, not bothering to look. She reached the door to one of the buildings and disappeared inside.

THIRTEEN

Agent Layton stalked through the sheriff's department building toward his makeshift office. It was poorly ventilated and the summer heat made sitting in this interview room a trial, but at the moment, he didn't mind. He was eager to read the fax that he had just received. It had only taken a few hours for the information he was seeking to reach him, and that put him in a very good mood.

The conversation he had with the young detective about Maureen Allen's ability to predict a crime had shaken loose an old memory of some Bureau gossip regarding a case up in Massachusetts from when he was a young agent. He'd always thought that the veterans were just pulling his chain, that the FBI didn't really keep files on this sort of paranormal activity. In the intervening years, he personally had never worked any case that dealt with the kind of circumstances that a TV show could be built around, but the gossip still ran strong within the Bureau, and he'd heard his fair share of odd cases. He thanked his lucky stars that his best friend from those days held the same position in the Chelsea Field Office that he did out here. He might not have gotten a look at this otherwise.

Layton sat down at his desk and opened the folder to reveal case number 7-3919: the kidnapping and unsolved murder of Braden Allerton in the town of Duxbury. There were a few lines redacted from the document, but on the whole, it was pretty much intact. The reading was fascinating, but most intriguing was the collected notes from an FBI psychologist's examination of the victim's sister, eight-year-old Maureen.

Layton pored over the three pages of notes twice before closing the file and sitting in silence, pondering everything that he'd just read. A child's disappearance with no solid leads and a little girl named Maureen whose dreams had apparently led her to call the police, who in turn were able to discover the body. He needed to find out what happened to that little girl, who would be about thirty-four years old by now. If his suspicions were right, an ordeal like the one she'd been through would probably lead a person to change their name at the first chance they got.

FOURTEEN

Maureen was grateful for one thing as she paced back and forth between her bed and couch: she didn't have to go into work. Saturday nights at Anderson's was Angela and Shelly's night. Mr. Anderson used the two brunettes to make sure each Saturday drew in a horde of horny college boys. The two girls didn't even look old enough to be serving, and they spilled or gave away far too many drinks, but with the makeup they wore, and the tits-and-ass show they put on, Mr. Anderson couldn't care less if he had to spend most of Sunday cleaning the floor and massaging his books.

She didn't actually expect to keep her job much longer, anyway. She was pretty sure that news of her arrest had made the rounds in the small town and, even though she had been released, she was still a person of interest in the murder of two children now. She could just imagine the next time she stepped foot into that bar. Her weeknight regulars would look at her differently, though it might be a nice respite from their usual booze-soaked leers, and Mr. Anderson would call her into the back room and inform her of her termination. That would be fine, as she decided she had enough money to move on after all. The only problem was, now she was being watched not only by the local police but by the FBI as well.

She had seen the way Agent Layton looked at her at the crime scene that morning when he and Detective Benitez were having their little private conversation. She had hoped that the detective wasn't telling the agent about her latest nightmare and how it had predicted the discovery of the latest body, but she could tell by the man's look and body language that her hope was futile. Now, the FBI didn't just have a suspect but a freak on their hands. He must have sanctioned her release in order to bait her into something. What exactly, she didn't know, but she was positive that trying to get out of town would be just the excuse they were looking for to arrest her again.

"I'm screwed either way," she mumbled to her dim reflection in the front window. "They're going to find out about the rest of it. I'll be put away no matter what."

The anxiety of her comeuppance being so close behind her was starting to make the walls close in. Maureen pulled herself away from the window and walked to her nightstand. She pulled out the brown bottle, took out a pill, bit it in half, and swallowed it. The dulling effects of the pill should be just enough to calm her, but she didn't want to wait around in her apartment for them to take hold. She grabbed the flannel shirt off her bed and headed out into the deepening evening.

The breeze had freshened as the sun's last rays were now fully below the horizon, but it still was a warm night, so Maureen tied her long-sleeved shirt around her waist as she walked. She had no clear picture of where she wanted to go. Perhaps it was simply a case of wanting to take in as much fresh air as possible before she was thrown back into that stale cell at the police station; the impending loss of her freedom had triggered a desire to be outdoors.

She made her way north toward Main Street. She thought about stopping into one of the bars for a drink and a bite to eat, but she cast that notion aside quickly. The gossip of the small town would almost assuredly destroy her anonymity, and she didn't want to face the stares and whispers. Though, she admitted, she didn't know for sure that her name and photo had been released to the papers and news stations. She didn't have a TV at home nor did she read the paper, so much of her assumptions were completely created by her own imagination.

Doesn't mean they're not true, she thought sourly.

In truth, she would gladly get lost in a crowd if she didn't have to be around people to do it. She'd spent so much time alone that she didn't even think she still possessed the ability to hide among people. For years, she had believed that people could sense her scars, and the few that she had associated with over that time simply didn't possess the empathy to care about her baggage. In most cases, those individuals were men who were only after one thing.

Without realizing it, her feet had brought her to the sidewalk in front of St. Mary's. Maureen looked up at the red-brick building illuminated by lights in such a way that the church's name, spelled out in black metal letters, was easy to read from the street. There was very little light coming from behind the stained glass windows, which rose up on either side of the church's arched front door.

Maureen turned her head back down the street. Several groups of people were crisscrossing back and forth, some to cars, others ducking into bars. A large group of young men had clearly already begun their night's frivolities, and were hooting as they walked in the opposite direction of where she now stood. She watched as they turned down a side street in the distance, clearly heading over to throw their money at Shelly and Angela. No one seemed to give her a second look.

A force drew her away from Main Street and up the stairs of the church. Maureen recalled her conversation with the priest on the sidewalk two days back. The door was never locked, he'd said. She eased herself up to it, laid a hand on the wrought iron handle, and drew in a breath. She had no idea what she would do once inside, but she thought that maybe she could find some solitude within, even if she didn't find any spiritual fulfillment. She had long ago given up looking for anything of that sort in a building like this.

The door's hinges creaked as she pulled it open. She was surprised at how much the sound actually startled her, and it forced her to walk in slowly and ease the door shut behind her. Something about crossing the threshold of a church made her feel like an intruder, and she did not want to draw any attention to herself. Maureen inhaled deeply and walked further inside, swinging her head from side to side, scanning for anyone else.

The church was elegantly appointed. As she moved through the front welcome area and into the nave itself, she could see that the pews, divided into two sections by a center aisle, were made of richly stained wood and each contained a kneeler, thickly cushioned with red velvet. *Wouldn't want to hurt their knees,* she thought of the parishioners. Each side of the nave was adorned with a row of stained glass windows, much the same size and style as those at the front of the church. Maureen counted fourteen total, seven on each wall. They were dazzlingly colored, and each contained what she knew to be the image of a particular saint, though which ones, she hadn't the foggiest idea. Most of her childhood Catechism had left her.

The altar area was set a few feet above the congregation, on a stone platform of two concentric circles rising from the floor. The altar itself was draped in white linen and adorned with several tall candles in golden holders. The candles on the altar, as well as several smaller ones behind, were all lit and, along with a few of the dimly lit sconces hanging from the rafters, were the only source of light in the church. And, as in any Catholic church she had ever entered, a gaudy, golden statue of Jesus, arms spread on a mahogany cross, stood in the center of the altar, towering above the rest of the scene.

Maureen kept one eye on the statue of the crucified man as she took a seat in one of the pews in the middle of the church. She hadn't come to pray, of that she was certain. God had abandoned her long ago. And after the events of the last few days, all logic in her mind would scream against sitting in a Catholic church if one were looking for a place free of judgment where they could sit and be alone. She was relieved to see that St. Mary's was not one of those churches that hosted a Saturday night mass. Had anyone else been present when she entered, she would have turned right around and headed straight back to her apartment.

Maureen continued to stare at the crucifix. Even as a girl, she had always wondered, if what scripture said was true, why a person would allow themselves to be put through that much torment and misery. Did he have any idea beforehand what it would feel like? She had always been sure that if he did, he'd have never gone through with it all. Her mother and others like her had called it *The Passion*, meaning that their Lord willingly went through all that out of love for all mankind in order to forgive the world's sins. Given all that she had seen in her life of the worst in humanity, and what they were capable of inflicting on one another, she couldn't understand why God would forgive rather than punish. It definitely felt like He'd been punishing her for the last two decades.

"It's been a long time since anyone has come into the church at this hour on a Saturday night," a voice said behind her.

Maureen's head snapped around to see the old priest walking up the middle aisle toward the front of the church. As before, he was dressed in his black shirt and white collar, and his footsteps echoed on the bricks of the church's floor.

"It's Ms. Allen, right?" he asked, stopping alongside the pew.

Maureen nodded. The jovial smile that she remembered from their first meeting was nowhere to be found on his face, but his eyes were still relaxed, even kind.

"I saw you come in," he continued, casually looking about the church. "I didn't want to disturb you, but you look uneasy. And I must say you don't exactly seem comfortable sitting in that pew. Would I miss my guess if I surmised that you have not been to church very often in your life?" He chuckled at his own observation.

"Not since I was a kid," she found herself answering.

The old priest paused for a moment before sliding into the pew next to her. The two sat in uncomfortable silence, staring up toward the candlelit altar. Maureen clasped her hands and shifted in her seat, trying to anticipate what the man was going to say next. She wasn't used to any man, even a priest, showing her kindness without eventually exposing an ulterior motive. Her mind calculated all of the possibilities, and she turned her head slightly to make sure the front door was still where she left it. Yet, even though the desire to leave was strong in her mind, something held her fast to the church pew.

"I've never liked the decor in here myself," Father Patrick said, breaking the silence.

"What?" blurted Maureen, taken off guard at such a mundane comment.

"The decoration of the church," he said gesturing about. "I've never been a fan of stained glass, and the crucifix is very ostentatious. And grim too, don't you think? I've always favored ones that do a better job of conveying Christ's love as opposed to focusing on his suffering."

Maureen looked closer at the image of Jesus on the cross. She could now see that the artist had indeed taken extra care to ensure a look of utter pain and sorrow on the face of the crucified man.

"Would you have a different expression on your face if you were nailed up on a piece of wood?" she retorted. "I would think a Catholic priest would relish the idea of showing the flock that your Savior went through horrible pain for you. Isn't that what it's all about?"

Father Patrick let out a soft, sighing chuckle. "I can see that you had some much harsher church leadership in your youth. I admit that there are those within the church who harken back to the days of fire and brimstone teaching and focus more on repentance as a means to forgiveness."

Maureen saw a shadow cross his eyes.

"Not to say repentance doesn't have its place," he continued. "God knows, we've all got things we need to atone for." He turned and looked steadily at Maureen. "But the world isn't going to change based on admonishment alone. People need to look deeper into themselves than I feel the church asks them to sometimes. They need to find the light in the darkness as it were."

Maureen stared back into Father Patrick's unblinking eyes. "So, what? You're a 'light in the darkness'?"

The priest shook his head and turned to stare back up at the altar, leaning his head to the side as he spoke to her, as if he was a friend sharing an intimate secret. "I sometimes feel that I have more darkness than light inside of me," he confessed. "I've been a clergyman for three decades, and in that time, I've met and counseled hundreds—if not thousands—of people who have considered themselves consumed by it. And every single time, I could just as easily be counseling myself. I simply mean that it's up to each person to really look inside themselves and acknowledge that there is a deeper darkness but also a brighter light that can combat it."

"Ever met someone beyond hope?"

"I don't believe there is such a thing."

"You will if you keep talking to me." It just slipped out.

"It's kind of funny that we first met when you were running down the street, because I can see by looking at you that you've been running in a much different sense for most of your life," he replied in a cool tone. He still didn't turn his head to look at her, continuing to stare up at the altar. "It may surprise you that I have more insight into matters like this than one might think. But saying that, I can't imagine there's anything in your past or present that could make you a lost cause in the eyes of God."

"God doesn't want me," she said sullenly, looking down at her hands clasped tightly in her lap. She expected to hear Father Patrick instantly contradict her assertion, but he remained motionless in silent contemplation.

"There was a time in my life when I felt the same," he eventually said.

Maureen looked over at him. He was still staring up at the altar, but now his hands were clasped like hers. There was a forlorn look in his eyes, as if thinking of a memory that pained him. The absence of the friendly demeanor he had shown her up until now was staggering.

Father Patrick seemed to feel her staring at him and broke his eye contact with Jesus to turn his head and offer her a half smile and a subtle, dismissive chuckle. "Listen to the old man talking about himself when someone else is in need of aid."

"I don't want any help, Father, thanks," she replied.

"Most of the time what we want and what we need are two completely different things."

"Another kid was found murdered this morning," she whispered, barely audible even to herself. "He was killed and then burned on this big bonfire just like the other one." She hesitated, struggling with what she wanted to say next. The words felt as though they would die in her throat. "I . . . I was there. I saw the body." She turned her head to stare at Father Patrick.

He was facing the altar again, but his eyes were closed. After a moment, he made the sign of the cross and met her eyes. "A silent prayer for the child's soul," he explained. "Now, since you've seen fit to divulge this information to me, I have to ask what you were doing there."

"I was with the police."

"I wasn't accusing you of anything," he replied, apparently having caught her tone. "But why were you, a civilian, with the police at a murder scene?"

"I was in custody," she admitted quietly, her eyes falling to her shoes. "They—the cops—think I had something to do with the first kid. I was in jail being questioned by a detective when the call came in. He made me go with him to the scene."

"And did you have something to do with the first crime?"

"No! You know what, this is a bad idea." Maureen got up and turned to leave, but the old priest grabbed her hand and held tight.

"Please, sit down," he urged in a gentle tone, yet he firmly pulled her back into the pew. "We're just talking. I'm just a little confused about why you would be arrested on suspicion of a child's murder."

Maureen hesitated, not sure if she could afford to tell another person her secret.

"I assure you, you are quite safe talking to me."

"I . . . I had a nightmare where I saw the first child killed. The next morning, I went for a run and came across the crime scene. It reminded me of the dream, so I ran. I ran straight into you."

"That explains a lot," he said, nodding. "Please, go on."

Maureen recounted the rest of the events of the past few days. When she had finished, she waited for him to dismiss her as crazy.

"It's not the first time you've dreamed like that, is it?"

UNHOLY SHEPHERD

"No, it's—wait. You believe me?"

"I have no reason to doubt. Yes, Ms. Allen, I believe you."

"No one's ever believed me, just like that," she said mindlessly, almost to herself. She had no idea how to feel now that someone was taking her at her word. It almost scared her more. What kind of person was this okay with you being a freak?

"As a man of faith, I do believe that sometimes there are forces which connect people to the spiritual plain. There's no rational explanation and no choice really but to call it a miracle."

That word was too much for Maureen. "Okay, I can handle it if I'm just some freak, but miracles? Don't feed me that line of bull, Father!"

"Ms. Allen, if you really are seeing what you say, then I can think of no other explanation than that God has bigger plans for you than you might realize."

"Now you listen to me, Father," Maureen's voice echoed off the walls of the church as she emphasized every word. "God. Doesn't. Want. Me. God. Hates. Me. And if He's up there playing with my mind for some reason, then you know what? I hate Him too!"

She found herself standing over the priest shouting those last words into his face. He never blinked once. There was nothing else to do but leave.

"I'm sorry, Father," she said, quickly pushing past him and into the aisle. "Thanks for the chat, but I have to go. I shouldn't have come here." Maureen turned and ran down the aisle, out the front door, and into the night.

FIFTEEN

Father Patrick watched the young woman flee the church. He had resisted the urge to prevent her from leaving a second time. Once was enough. In his years as a man of the cloth, he had found that his greatest asset was getting people to talk to him frankly and freely. Eventually, he'd get through to Maureen Allen as well. He had no doubt of that.

The old priest turned himself back to the front of the nave and rose slowly to his feet. The weariness of his years always showed themselves in the creaking of his joints whenever he got up from a seated position. How much of that was from his age and how much was from his old life seemed less clear as time went on. He had been a soldier back then and in some ways, the ones that counted, he was a soldier still.

He walked slowly up to the altar, replaying their conversation. For a man with less faith, the idea of a person's nightmares coming true would seem inconceivable. For a person who had seen less darkness than he had, the notion would be almost too frightening to bear. He stared up at the image of his Savior on the cross and let out a long sigh. So many years, so many people he hoped he was helping in the name of Christ. The garb of a Catholic priest was one that he never thought would work with his mission, but it was the only faith he'd ever known and, though it had its faults, it was where he felt the most comfortable. The church hadn't fallen so far that it couldn't be used in his work. And there was still so much to do before he went to meet his Lord.

The priest crossed himself and turned to head toward his office. It was going to be a late night and reflecting on the enigma of the woman with sight was only going to push off finishing his notes on Preston's sermon.

SIXTEEN

Manny pulled a tissue out of the box and delicately handed it to Sandra Locke before taking his seat on the other side of the table. She dabbed it gently at her red eyes, puffy from crying for the last several hours. He knew how sensitive he'd have to be in interviewing her, but it was important he get things rolling and get some good information out of her. This was going to be a delicate balancing act.

The ID on the victim had come back late on Sunday. It would have been difficult to get, but fortune struck the investigation when Stacey Winherst had found a small tubular object in the pile of charred internal organs. It was labeled with a serial number that had given them the identity of the victim. It was a shunt to correct a congenital heart condition which Evan, Sandra's son, had been diagnosed with. The boy's ninth birthday was only three weeks away.

The revelation that the victim was the son of the county treasurer had piqued Manny's curiosity. The two boys were of the same age and were children of prominent figures in the community, both of whom had ties to the government. He knew that Tom Lowes had handled quite a few commercial building sales for the county over the years and Sandra, of course, handled all of the county's money. There had to be a connection.

"Ms. Locke," he said gently, taking out his notepad from his jacket, "I know this is going to be difficult for you, and I don't want to upset you, but I'm going to need to ask you some questions."

"I know," she said weakly. "I'll do my best."

Despite the redness and puffiness of her eyes, Manny could discern the dark bags under them. If he looked in the mirror himself, he probably would have seen the same. He had known that he'd be interviewing her today, but had only found out a few moments before entering the interview room that he was to be the *first* one to talk to Sandra. It was a responsibility that he wasn't expecting, but it sounded like the Feds were looking to use locals to interview locals.

"Can you please tell me about the shunt we found among the remains?" he asked as gently as he could.

"Evan was diagnosed with cardiomyopathy. Turns out it was genetic. We lost his father to the same condition while I was still pregnant. My OB thought it was a good idea to check out the baby at that point. I guess it was a good thing he did. Otherwise I would have lost him even before..." The recollection hurled her into another fit of crying.

Manny waited patiently for it to pass. He felt nothing but pity for her, losing both her husband and her child, but he hoped that he could get something useful out of her.

"I'm sorry," she said finally. "I just can't believe he's gone."

"It's okay. Please continue when you're ready."

"Thank you," she said. She paused for a moment, blew her nose, and looked back at him. "It wasn't easy. Evan was on the spectrum, you see. He'd wander off if you didn't keep a tight eye on him. I'm lucky that I found a job where I can work from home relatively often."

"Why don't you tell me anything you can remember about Evan's disappearance."

"It must have been around ten in the morning or so. We'd been out in our backyard playing in the sprinkler most of the morning. I went into the house for a few minutes to make some juice, and when I came back out, he wasn't in the yard. When he had run off in the past, he ended up at the park a few blocks from our house. He likes the sandbox. Obsessed with it really. It's one of the few things that can keep his attention for long periods of time. So I went over there to see if that's where he was."

"And when you found he wasn't there?"

"I ran around the neighborhood looking for him for a few hours. I checked some of his favorite restaurants, the library. I couldn't find him anywhere. I called a few of the neighbors to see if they'd seen him. No one had. I know you have to wait twenty-four hours to file a missing person's report, so I didn't know what else to do. I heard on Saturday morning about the fire and called to find out if it was Evan. I just waited and prayed until the Sheriff's Department called last night."

You're lying. "Ms. Locke, you know as well as I do, that thanks to the Amber Alert, you don't have to wait to report a missing child. I can't find one good reason why, with one child already murdered, you wouldn't call the authorities the second you couldn't find your son. How about you tell me the truth?"

Sandra's eyes widened and more tears welled up in them. She knew she was trapped. "I...I don't want to cause trouble in the department. I work with these people. You work with them. It's no one's fault!"

"Ms. Locke, Sandra, you don't have to worry about that. Just tell me."

"I did call the police. I called right away. They said that he was probably at the park, like usual, and that he would come home soon. I've called the police a lot in the past to go look for him. I think they're annoyed with me for calling so much over the years when it always turns out to be nothing."

He was sitting across from a woman who had been convinced by his own department that her fears were irrational, and that she was nothing more than an inconvenience to them. It was enough to make his blood begin to boil. "Who did you talk to?"

"Sergeant Wentworth."

Who else? It could have been any one of a number of the useless officers who polluted the police department, but everything always came back to that bulbous bastard. Manny tried to calm himself down. He would deal with that waste of space as soon as he finished with Sandra Locke.

"Ms. Locke, I'm so very sorry. None of this is your fault, and I promise that we'll do everything we can to see that those responsible for your son's death are held accountable. All of them. But for now, I just have a few more questions, if you'd be so patient. It's almost over."

Sandra nodded, wiped her eyes clear, and reached out to grasp his hand. Her grip was tight yet assured. It gave him hope.

"All right, good," he said, squeezing her hand back. "Now tell me, how well do you know the Lowes family?"

"I know them as well as most people in town," she said.

"We're not close friends, but the kids went to the same school, so I saw them around. Tom sold some property for the county a while back, so I knew him from that. We talk sometimes after church. His wife is nice, would even keep an eye on Evan from time to time when I did confession after Mass. You know, just your average casual acquaintances."

"Okay, and any information on that sale that you can give me? Anything relevant you can think of?"

"They were commercial buildings we weren't using anymore, over in Glenbrook. Some investor he knew bought them. I think they're going to redevelop and rent them out. I'm not really sure. I just did the books."

He made a mental note to look into the public record, asked Sandra to write down whatever names and contact info she had, and escorted her to the front door of the building.

"All right, Ms. Locke, I'm sure you'll be contacted by Agent Layton or Agent Lorenzo from the FBI as a follow up after I file your statement. Do you have someone you can speak to in the meantime? I mean, someone who can help you?"

"My sister is coming in from Illinois to stay with me for a while," she said. It seemed that she was drained of all her emotion. Her face had become blank.

As he walked her out of the building, all Manny could think of was the incompetence within the department that had allowed this little boy's abduction to fly under the radar in the first place. The sheer lack of care for this woman and her son by the slackers he called coworkers consumed his thoughts. His cordial, sad smile and small wave as Sandra walked toward her car was all he could muster while the eruption brewed inside, waiting to be released.

Manny bull-rushed his way back through the station doors and made a beeline directly toward Wentworth's desk. He found Sam sitting with his feet up, on the phone, laughing loudly at what was clearly a personal call. Manny swung his head from side to side. The captain wasn't in sight, and no other officers seemed to be paying attention to the sergeant's clear disregard for regulation. Fuming, Manny grabbed the receiver from Wentworth and slammed it down, severing the call.

"What the hell, Benny? That was my sister you just hung up on!"

Instead of apologizing, Manny knocked Wentworth's feet off the desk and spun his chair around to face him. He could feel the redness in his cheeks, and his heart was racing. "You stupid son-of-a-bitch!"

"What's up your butt?" Wentworth replied, attempting to turn his chair away.

Manny held firm. "Sandra Locke called in to report her son missing Friday afternoon, and you blew her off."

"You trying to say that kid's death is on me?"

"That's *exactly* what I'm saying!"

The station went quiet. Wentworth glanced from side to side, as if he was looking for his buddies to come to his aid. No one moved, so he raised himself slowly off the chair to make use of his frame. He looked down at Manny with cocky self-assurance.

"Now look here, you smug little asshole," he said, poking Manny in the chest with his sausage of an index finger. "We all know that kid was a little flipper. We've wasted a lot of time and manpower looking for him every time Sandra got scared after twenty minutes and called us. And what always happened? He'd find his way right back home. Every time. Safe and sound. So you tell me why I should've thought this time was any different?"

Manny clenched his fists in hatred for this blob of a man. Wentworth knew full well that dealing with a missing child, especially one the whole town knew was on the spectrum, should never be taken lightly. He had a thousand and more words for the man, but not a single one could get past his throat.

"Yeah, that's what I thought," Wentworth sneered. "So don't come at me like a big man when you got nothing on me, you spineless, self-righteous little spic!" He gave Manny a hard shove in the chest and turned to sit down.

Manny remembered nothing from the moment he lunged at Wentworth until the moment he felt the hands of the Henderson twins grab his arms and drag him off their ringleader. Manny blinked, and the face of the sergeant, awash in crimson, came into focus. As he regained some semblance of composure, he felt a throb in the knuckles of each hand that told him he'd landed some blows.

Captain Wellner had placed himself between the two men, and Wentworth was on one knee with his hand to his nose, trying to pinch off the flow of blood. "Jesus, Mary, and Joseph!" the captain shouted. "Benitez, my office. Now! Wentworth, get cleaned up. I'll deal with you in a minute."

Manny shrugged off the grip of the twins and stalked behind the captain. Captain Wellner shut the door behind them, shuttered the blinds, and took his place behind the desk.

"Sit down," he said, smoothing his tone.

Manny took a seat in front of the captain's desk. He knew he was about to face serious consequences for his actions and cursed himself for his lack of discipline. He was supposed to be there when this case was solved. He owed the victims' families that.

Captain Wellner heaved a sigh as he took his seat behind his desk, rubbing circles into his temples. "Detective," he began, looking up at Manny, "I have a lot of respect for your passion and commitment to your hometown and this department. I remember the day you came back and asked me for a job here at the station. I looked over your credentials and your performance reviews, and I thought you were nuts. I asked myself, 'Why would someone with your education want to sit at a desk and have so little to do?' I've watched you since then, and I've been proven right." The captain rose from his chair and moved around to sit on the front corner of the desk.

"This place is killing you," he continued, leaning in closer to Manny. "The monotony of the job has sucked you dry and turned your ambition into some kind of hot-headed ego trip. I mean for God's sake, Manny, we've got two dead children in a town that has never had a single homicide in my time as Captain, the FBI breathing down our necks, a department full of officers who are way out of their depths, and when I look at you, I almost feel like you're *enjoying* the chaos!"

Who could be happy when children are dying? "Listen, Arthur," he said, daring to use the captain's first name, "I'm not—"

"Let me stop you right there. I hate to do this, Benitez, but I'm taking you off the case."

"You're what?!" Manny shouted, erupting from his seat. "What for? 'Cuz I finally gave that piece of shit Wentworth what he deserved? He's the reason Evan Locke is dead, you know! He's the one who's been sliding by in this place for years!" He spat the last few words at the captain in disgust, figuring he had nothing to lose. He may as well get it all out.

"I'm not the one with the problem around here," he continued, pacing back and forth in front of the captain's desk. "This department is nothing but a boys club for the former high school kings. Everyone outside this room is half the officer they should be. You know Wentworth's a fat pile of useless crap. Scottsdale can barely read. McKeegan's only here 'cuz he likes to drive the police car and use his uniform to get laid. The Henderson twins do nothing but follow the other three around like little puppies! You know Yancy and Hanson are just here cashing a paycheck. Collins is the only one with any real drive, but that kid is so wet behind the ears, he's still learning the goddamn Miranda Rights! But no, I'm the one with the ego issue, and I'm the one you're tossing from the case."

"You're not giving me any choice, Benitez. I can't have officers getting into fist fights in the bullpen."

"He shoved me first, and you didn't hear what he called me. I won't repeat it, but I will say that I thought we had grown beyond that type of racial slur as a society." He gritted his teeth at the thought of the word. "I guess I was wrong."

"Look, I'm not suspending you. You can still come in and work on anything else we have for you. As for Sam, I do plan to put him on administrative leave while we have an internal investigation into the handling of the Locke situation."

"So he gets to sit at home and collect a paycheck?" Manny scoffed. "I'm sure he'll be heartbroken."

"You'd rather I just fire him?"

"I don't know, why don't you ask his daddy what you should do the next time you two play golf."

That was the sore spot. It was a well-known fact that the captain and Sam's father were longtime friends.

"Get out," Wellner hissed, his face turning a bright crimson and his body shaking.

Manny shoved open the captain's office door with a flourish and headed over to his desk without saying a word to anyone. Out of the corner of his eye, he saw Wentworth, tissue still in his nose, and T.J. heading in the direction of Wellner's office.

His desk was piled up with papers: notes on the Lowes family and Sandra Locke. A large cardboard box was on his chair. That was new. Manny leafed through the first few pages of its contents and realized it was the financial statements and other background information on both parties that he had requested late on Saturday. It looked as if whoever handled this at county had just printed out everything they could find and threw it all into the box. It was going to take an eternity to get it all in order.

"I hear there was a little excitement," a voice said over his shoulder. Manny spun around to see the unwelcome sight of Agent Layton. He was dressed in his usual neatly pressed black suit, and he had a dark green file folder in his hand.

"Which part?" Manny retorted, placing his case notes in the box.

"Why don't you run it all down for me?"

Manny shook his head and turned to face him. Agent Layton stood still, nodding his head, while Manny related the day's events.

"Well," Agent Layton puffed once Manny had finished, "it's a good thing I ran into you before you ran off and did something stupid. Let's take a walk out to your truck. You don't want to hang around here anymore."

Manny nodded slightly and hefted up the box of papers. The two men made their way out of the building to Manny's truck, and only then, did the agent break the silence.

"I'm going to need that box of material, Detective," he said formally.

"Can I ask why?" he asked, startled by the agent's demand.

"If you're not going to be part of the case, I can't allow you to drive away with evidence."

"Fine," Manny replied curtly, shoving the box into the agent's chest. "I've had enough of this!" He turned to unlock the driver's side door.

Agent Layton set the box on the ground and placed his palm on the door to stop him. "Hang on, son."

Manny blinked, unsure of why the agent was stopping him.

"Look," Agent Layton explained, "I can see you're invested in this case, but I have to keep up appearances. I'm not going to stop you from continuing to investigate on your own. In fact, I encourage it. So let's make a deal. You get to do whatever you need to figure out who this child-murdering bastard is—so long as you don't break any laws yourself—and I get periodic check-ins—no need for full disclosure. If you get any useful information, you tell me immediately. If local authorities harass you, I'll step in. The FBI's going to take credit for this case, but I'll be sure you get the recognition you deserve when it's all said and done. Sound fair?"

"I'll need that box of notes," he said after a moment of thought.

"No," Agent Layton said firmly.

"But you just said—"

"You didn't listen. I said I couldn't let you *drive away* with this box of evidence. I'm officially taking control of it on behalf of the FBI. I look forward to reading your notes and insights. But keep an eye on your front porch later today," he lowered his voice and leaned in. "A sealed brown box about the size of this one is scheduled to be delivered. There might even be one or two extra little goodies in there for you." Agent Layton winked and picked up the box.

"Do you know where I live?" Manny responded, taken slightly aback.

"Of course. I take the time to read up on anyone I'm working a case with. By the way, you were recruited to the FBI directly out of college, weren't you?"

Manny could tell it wasn't really a question. He gave the agent a measured nod.

"Why aren't you my partner on this right now instead of some local, hothead detective?"

"It wasn't a good fit." It was a lie, but it was better than the truth.

"Somehow I don't believe that." Agent Layton turned and headed back toward the station.

Manny pulled open the truck door and jumped into the driver's seat. The engine roared to life, and he headed to the first destination on the new path that his investigation was going to take. The moment Agent Layton had said that he didn't need to report everything, he knew exactly where he was going to begin.

He pulled onto Main Street, hoping his decision was the right one.

SEVENTEEN

Maureen gazed out of the mask that covered her face. Through the eyes, she could see a book. It was a large, leather-bound tome with yellowing pages. Red ink marked the pages with odd symbols and words in a language she didn't know. The field of her vision widened, and she could observe that she was seated or standing over an old, wooden desk. The light in the room was dim, with bright spots illuminating small halos about her. The light flickered irregularly. Candles.

The eyes moved to another book on the right. This book was marked with strange lettering. It was also in a language that she did not understand. A hand reached out of her view and returned with a foot-long baton. It was made of wood, and the fingers could feel a variety of bumps and crevasses. Carvings, she decided. The point of the baton was placed upon the book, underneath one of the strange letters. It traced a line across the page, from right to left before continuing on to the line below. A low voice came from the throat. She could feel the speaking. Not speaking, reading.

She felt her own consciousness begin to struggle for control, and the fog began to cover her sight. A snap of black gave way to Maureen's kitchen cabinets coming into focus across the room. She raised her head from the couch and sat up slowly, searching inside her skull for the familiar headache to come. None was yet apparent, so she decided to get up and check the time. She grumbled unhappily as she saw that she still had two hours before her alarm was due to go off.

Maureen felt grimy from the previous night's shift at the bar, and decided to jump into the shower. She was surprised to find she still had a job, but Mr. Anderson never brought up her arrest, if he knew about it at all. Maureen stepped in once the water was hot and inhaled the steam deeply, clearing the remaining fog from her mind. She almost regretted it. A lack of clarity would have been more than welcome, but nothing she'd tried so far could erase the imprints the nightmares left on her. She had to find a way out of her situation and this town.

Maureen dried herself off and threw on a pair of jeans and a white tank top, while grabbing a few dollars from her duffel bag. During her shower, she had felt her stomach rumble and decided to take a walk down to Main Street for a quick bite and grab some semblance of normalcy before the hammer fell on her. She stuffed her key and cash into her pocket and ventured out onto the street, shuffling her way north, scrutinizing her options as she went. Among the storefronts on and around Main Street, one finally caught her eye.

The Proper Cup was Sycamore Hills' only non-chain coffee house. It was a weekday hangout for many of the kids from the college and a midday fueling station for soccer moms and other Main Street business owners or employees. It was a quintessential coffee shop, featuring artisan-style pastries and baked goods along with fancy coffee drinks that the upper class liked. They prided themselves on roasting their own beans and only sourcing from local, organic purveyors, something they made certain to plaster all over the windows.

Maureen normally wouldn't go to a place like this, but she was hungry and didn't want to sit down at a restaurant. Given her limited knowledge of the town, it seemed like the best option. She never fancied herself a coffee drinker—she certainly never made any for herself—and when she did drink it, it was only ever the crummy, roadside-diner kind.

She was staring at the menu, trying to find just plain coffee, when a voice from behind startled her out of her thoughts.

"Maureen?" it said. "Ms. Allen, is that you?"

Maureen turned toward the door and saw that it was filled by the silhouette of Father Patrick, dressed in tennis shoes and jeans with his typical black shirt and priest's collar. His smile broadened as he closed the distance between them. She wasn't sure how she felt about being spotted in public, much less by a priest she'd yelled at a few days ago. Judging from the old man's beaming face, however, it seemed to be water under the bridge.

"So nice to run into you again," he said as he came up to her, tucking his newspaper under his arm. "I didn't know you were a customer here."

"Never been before," she said uncomfortably, scanning the room to see if his jovial greeting had caused any of the other patrons to take notice.

"Ah, well then, welcome. It's a favorite of mine. I admit, I have somewhat of an addiction to their caramel lattes. Isn't that right, Sophia?"

The young lady behind the counter nodded.

"One for me, please," he said.

"Medium, right?" confirmed Sophia.

"Absolutely. And for my friend here?" He gestured to Maureen, apparently indicating that she should order as well.

"Oh, uh, that's okay," she stammered. "You don't have to do that."

"I insist."

"Just a regular coffee, then." She looked over at him to find his eyebrows raised expectantly, as if he knew that she had intended to order something to eat as well. Maureen turned back to the lady at the counter. "And a raspberry Danish."

Father Patrick nodded in approval and handed Sophia money, telling her to keep the change.

"Come sit with me for a minute, won't you?" he said after they picked up their order. He led her over to a high-top table with two stools by the window, pulling out one for her before hopping up onto the other. He extended a hand toward the stool, inviting her to sit.

"Listen," Maureen said, trying to sound civil, "I appreciate you paying for my coffee, but I'm not really in the mood to talk. I got things I want to think about. Besides, don't you want to read your paper?"

"I've already read it," he said. He grinned, then pulled a pen out of his pocket and began to twirl it in his fingers. "I don't have much to do on Mondays so it's a good day to sit, have some coffee, and work on the crossword puzzle."

"See, you do have better things to do," she replied and turned to leave.

"You had another dream, didn't you?" His words froze her in her tracks.

How does he know? She sighed, turned back, and slowly

climbed atop the stool opposite him. Staring at the table top, she nodded, took a sip of her coffee, and immediately gagged.

"Something wrong with the coffee?"

"I wouldn't know, honestly. I don't drink it much." Maureen found a bowl of different colored sugar packets. She grabbed three of the pink ones and stirred them into her coffee. She took another sip and found it more tolerable now that it was sweetened up. She looked up at Father Patrick who was hiding his laughter underneath his hand.

"You don't have to be embarrassed," he said, raising his own coffee and taking a big sip. "Mine has much more sugar in it than that."

Despite herself, Maureen smiled and then added one more packet to her drink.

"So," Father Patrick said, lowering his voice and looking at her intently, "you had another dream. Does that mean this person has killed again?"

"No, it was different this time. I was reading books, by candlelight, in a language I didn't understand. And I was reading it out loud. There were symbols written in red ink on one of the books. That was basically it."

"I don't understand. *You* were reading?"

"When I go into these nightmares, it's like I'm putting on a mask. The person who's doing these things, I see through their eyes. If they touch something it feels like I'm touching it with my own hands or fingers. I can even feel what they feel, but most of the time, I can separate out my own consciousness. The scariest part is when I fight against it. It's like being a prisoner. Worse than that, I've only recently figured out that it's all happening in real time. I'm not seeing something that happened in the past or will happen in the future, so there's nothing I can do to help or stop it. I'm powerless."

The old man nodded as she explained. "And this is the only type of dream you have? Seeing through the eyes of other people?"

Maureen had never been asked that question before. She thought for a moment, trying to remember a time she'd dreamed anything else. She'd tried so hard to repress the nightmares that she wasn't sure she was even capable of having a pleasant dream.

"I think so," she said. "As far back as I can remember, when I do dream, it's only these types of nightmares. My mother called it 'The Demon Sight.'" At that, she stuffed a bite of Danish into her mouth.

"Hmmm," said Father Patrick, stroking the cropped hairs of his chin and taking a sip of his coffee. "As a man of faith, I can't help but question the name. What would make someone so sure that a gift like this is demonic and not divine?"

"I've never known anyone of faith to think otherwise," Maureen said sourly, pushing away the memories of years long past. "Besides, why would I only see through the eyes of people doing evil if I weren't filled with evil myself?" She allowed all the zealots' words to echo in hers.

"Perhaps it's meant as a tool to stop the evil?" he offered.

"I appreciate the vote of confidence, Father, but I'm far more sinner than saint. God, if He even exists, doesn't choose people like me."

"Of course He exists, Maureen. And of course He chooses people like us. What better way to show His love than to redeem the fallen?"

Us? The fallen?

Maureen was silently pondering these last words when she heard the sound of scampering feet running in her direction. She turned to see the little boy from the second crime scene running toward her. He stopped a few yards away from the table and stared at her for a moment before bouncing up and down, clapping, and giggling. Maureen furrowed her brow at him and tried to shoo him away. It was too late. The boy's mother was stalking over, carrying her to-go cup of coffee and frowning.

"Looks like they decided to let you go," she said, staring down her nose at Maureen. "I'd appreciate it if you wouldn't engage my son."

"Listen, lady, it's your kid who keeps bothering me. I can't help it that he finds me so fascinating."

"Whatever," she replied, rolling her eyes.

"Did I do something to you?" Maureen asked, doing all she could to stop herself from shooting out of her chair.

"Come on, Benny," she said, taking her son's hand and dragging him away. "We need to get you home for a nap."

"Home!" the little boy sang, oblivious to the tension between Maureen and his mother. He waved at her as they left the coffee shop. "Bye-bye!"

"Sorry about that," she said to Father Patrick. "I don't know what's with that kid—or his mother. His dad's one of the firefighters. They were at the second crime scene. I'm sure she thinks I've got something to do with all of this, and she's probably not alone."

Maureen stuffed the rest of her pastry into her mouth and chased it down with her coffee. To her surprise, she'd gone through her entire cup.

"The good book says that a little child shall lead us," mused the priest. "It's possible the innocence of that child can see something in you that others can't."

"Oh, Christ," grumbled Maureen. Now he was just serving her platitudes. Maureen grabbed the pen and newspaper from him and began to doodle in the margins.

"You know, Maureen, I think I'd like to have you over for dinner sometime and talk more about these dreams of yours. I'd like to learn more about them, maybe find a way to help."

"Uh, I don't know. Maybe." She continued to doodle.

Father Patrick was talking, but it began to sound like his voice was being swallowed up by water. The rest of the noise in the café followed suit. She was lost in an isolation chamber, staring at the newspaper, reading nothing, just seeing individual letters. They seemed to dance about the page, rearranging themselves into unreadable words. All the while she felt her right hand moving the pen throughout the margins.

"Maureen!" Father Patrick's voice cut through the fog and jolted her out of her trance. "Are you all right?"

She blinked and looked around. Father Patrick was staring at her with a look in his eye, as if she had been doing something very strange.

"Yeah, I'm fine," she said. "I was just thinking about—" She looked down and saw what she had drawn on the paper. A strange, four-letter word and three more letters followed by some numbers. She realized right away that they were from her latest dream. They must be some kind of clue, but at the moment she didn't want to think about it. She had to get out of there.

"I'm sorry, Father," she said quickly, tearing off the piece of the paper with the writing on it and stuffing it into her pocket. "I'm going to be late for work. Uh, dinner you said, right? Yeah, we'll have to do that some time. I've got to go, though. Bye."

Maureen left her garbage on the table and rushed out of the coffee shop and into the burning sunshine. She ran down the street and stopped in front of city hall. She looked up at the clock tower for the time. Twenty minutes until her shift started. She sat down on the steps to catch her breath and drew the piece of newspaper out of her pocket and stared at the letters and numbers, wondering what they meant. It looked like a code; it meant nothing to her.

Maureen crumpled up the paper in frustration and was about to throw it to the ground when she stopped. She didn't know why, but instead of doing that, she smoothed the paper back out, folded it tightly, and stuffed it back into her pocket. Then she got up and made for the bar.

EIGHTEEN

Maureen decided to go in through the alley door of Anderson's. She wasn't sneaking in, she just didn't feel like being seen until she was ready to put on her show at the bar. The episode at the coffee shop didn't let her make it back to her apartment, so she wasn't able to glamorize herself in the way that the regulars were used to seeing her. Equally unfortunately, she only had on her regular bra, which meant the girls wouldn't be out tonight. Without her usual cleavage, she'd have to work on her makeup a little more to make her tips. If she could even force her smile to the surface.

She moved quietly through the back storage area to the employee bathroom where she kept some emergency cosmetics hidden. She avoided detection and within seconds was rummaging through her makeup bag. She decided she would go with smoky eyes and just a little lipstick as her look for the night, and she was just getting out one of her brushes when the door flew open behind her.

"Maureen," Mr. Anderson said, walking through the door, "need you out front."

"Jesus, Todd!" she shouted back. "What if I was on the can?"

"Don't tease me," he replied sarcastically.

"I'll be there in a minute," she told him and turned back to the mirror.

"You don't need to do your makeup." He turned toward the door. "Hurry up."

Maureen stuck up her middle finger as the door closed. She decided to at least put on a little concealer to hide the bags under her eyes. Outside of them, the effects of the previous night's drinking were non-existent. She wasn't sure whether to be proud of that fact or concerned. Escaping into a bottle was nothing new for her, but the prevailing theory was that hangovers got worse the older you got, not better. She really didn't have time to think about that now. Mr. Anderson's strange tone had set her on edge, and she had no idea what she was walking into. She gave herself one last look in the mirror, drank a sip of water from the sink's faucet, and headed out to find out what was waiting for her.

She rounded the corner into the front of the house and was greeted by perhaps the least welcome sight she could have imagined. Sitting at the bar with Mr. Anderson, sipping a glass of water, was Detective Benitez. He and her boss were speaking in tones low enough that she couldn't hear anything other than dull murmurs, even in the empty bar. Their faces were serious, and she could only believe that whatever happened next, it wouldn't end well for her.

She cautiously approached, trying her best to keep her face even. They immediately broke off their conversation as soon as her footsteps echoed off the walls and turned to look at her. She caught a quick smirk flash across the detective's face, but it was wiped clear by the time she was standing next to him.

The three stood silently for a few beats too long for Maureen's liking, and so she decided to break the silence.

"Okay, gentleman," she said, making her best effort at a mocking tone, "what can I get you?"

"I'm actually going to excuse myself and let you two talk," Mr. Anderson said, got up from his stool, and disappeared into the back.

The detective watched him leave and then turned to Maureen. "I told him I was here on business for the FBI. Sure hope that little tidbit doesn't get back to Layton."

She moved behind the bar and filled a beer mug from the tap. She set it on the bar and pushed it toward the detective.

"Would love to, but can't," he said, pushing it back toward her. "We've got work to do."

The word *we* made her heart jump. What could he possibly mean by that? Maureen reached out, took the mug of beer, and drank down half its contents in a single gulp. She made sure to keep her eyes glued to the detective, trying to pick up any tell.

"Didn't think I came here to say that, did you?" he smirked.

She shook her head and continued to sip the beer.

"But you heard right. I said 'we'. I need your help. But, thanks to some excitement this morning at the department, I'm not, strictly speaking, part of the investigation anymore."

"And what sort of excitement is that?"

"I punched out a worthless, asshole sergeant," he said, shaking his head and stifling a laugh. He cast his eyes down and began caressing the knuckles of his right hand, as if massaging them after a job well done. Maureen could see the remnants of dried blood on them, not only confirming that he was telling the truth but confirming how proud he was of the badge of honor.

"I think I'm going to need some more context here."

He launched into a synopsis of what had happened to him that morning. "So," he concluded after a few minutes, "as you can imagine, I'm looking for a partner on this. And I'm going to need one that has a certain aptitude for working on the fringes of the law. The way I see it, you're still a person of interest in this whole business, so what better way for you to prove that you're innocent than by helping solve this thing?"

Maureen finished her beer and went back to the tap and refilled the mug halfway. "It sounds like you're giving me a choice, but you're really not, are you?"

"I think you pretty much ran yourself out of choices the moment you decided to break into the Lowes' house," he replied.

He may well have been right. She would have to go along for now, she decided. "Why me?"

"I think your abilities will give us some insights that the rest of the investigation can't uncover."

He's not even trying to be subtle. "So, you're going to use me?"

"Is that a problem?" he asked with annoying playfulness. "If you'd rather spend your time here with your lovely customers, by all means, do it."

Maureen rolled her eyes and took another sip of beer. "So what's the plan?"

"Well for starters, you're going to stay with me until this is all settled. We're going to start at my place by going through all the evidence I've collected so far. Maybe between that and your visions, we'll come up with something."

"Not much of a plan," she scoffed. "I've already told you that I don't see the future."

"Yeah, I know. I was listening. I'd be glad to hear any other suggestions."

Of course, Maureen didn't have any. She wasn't feeling particularly hopeful about the endeavor, but the detective was beginning to intrigue her. Plus, she wanted to see what he would do if they were to fail.

"Well then, Detective," she said, raising the mug and then draining the remainder, "I guess we're gonna go and catch us a murderer."

"It's Manny."

"No, it isn't."

Maureen set the beer mug in the sink and turned to head into the back to tell Mr. Anderson that she was leaving, likely never to be back. The detective got up and began to follow her.

"What are you doing?" she asked, rounding on him. "I'm only going in back to tell my boss what's going on."

"I've given him the broad strokes of the situation," he said. "Besides, I need to make sure you're not going to try and run."

"You don't trust me?"

"Not really."

Maureen threw up her arms, let out a sigh of frustration, and continued toward the back of the building with the young detective shuffling along behind her.

"Todd," she said upon stepping into her boss' cluttered office, "the detective is taking me out of here. I don't expect I'll be back."

"What?" he responded, clearly blindsided at the prospect of actually losing her as an employee.

"I won't be working here anymore," Maureen talked fast, hoping to fluster the man. "I'll take what I'm owed for the last week and get out of your hair."

"But, I . . . ," Mr. Anderson stammered, shuffling through his papers. "I haven't gone over the books yet. I thought I'd have more time."

"I'll take an even two hundred then," she said putting out her hand. "And I'll go ahead and help myself to a couple of bottles of whiskey from the back. Not the cheap crap you keep up front, either. And you drink tequila, right Detective?" She turned toward him.

Detective Benitez was leaning on the door frame watching the two of them. He perked up when she addressed him, as if being shaken awake. All he seemed to be able to do was nod.

"All right, and two bottles of tequila while we're at it," she said, turning back to her boss.

Mr. Anderson's face began to redden and he stood up, fists clenched. "You can't possibly think I'll let that happen."

"Why not?" Maureen replied. "I've been a good worker. Made you more money than I've cost you, that's for sure. But that's fine, keep the cash. I'll just help myself to the bottles. I'm sure you can figure out how to compensate yourself for the loss of inventory."

Anderson didn't say a word as she turned away, satisfied with her performance. She patted the detective on the shoulder and motioned with a jerk of her head that he should follow her. They made their way to the storeroom. Maureen grabbed an empty box from the hall and handed it to Detective Benitez. He began to protest, but she shushed him with a finger and set about filling the box with four bottles of some pretty decent bourbon, two of white tequila, and three six-packs of beer.

"What do you need all this for?" the detective managed to spit out as they entered the alley behind the bar and made their way toward his truck.

"Medication," she replied.

"Excuse me?"

"So where to next?" she asked, ignoring his question. "If I'm going to be pressed into the type of service you have in mind, I'll need to stop at my apartment and grab some of my things."

"Yeah that's fine," he replied. "And then we'll get some Chinese or something before we go back to my place."

The rest of the walk to the detective's truck and the drive to her apartment were completed in silence. Maureen could sense that the young man had absolutely no idea how to proceed. The tension seemed to grow in his body, and that made her more uncomfortable than the situation as a whole.

"I suppose you'll want to come up with me to make sure I don't jump out of the window or something," she mocked as the detective pulled up to her curb.

"That's the plan," he said stiffly, putting the truck into park.

Once inside the apartment, Maureen headed first into the bathroom to grab her toothbrush and then to the nightstand to grab her bottle of pills. She pulled a duffel bag out from under the bed and tossed the items in before hoisting it onto her shoulder.

"Uh, no," the detective said.

"What?"

"I'm thinking you should leave the bag and just take some clothes and whatever toiletries you need," he said. "You can just carry them loose."

"And why would I do a stupid thing like that?"

"Having all of your things in a bag ready to go makes it easier for you to run," he said.

Jackass. Maureen selected two pairs of jeans, one pair of cut-off shorts, three tank tops, a bra, and four pairs of panties. She removed a pillowcase from one of her pillows and tossed them in along with the toothbrush and pill bottle. She decided to leave her cash where it was. The detective could pay for everything.

"I don't suppose I'll be able to do wash if things take longer than you think, will I?"

"We can come back if you need fresh stuff."

Maureen gritted her teeth and slung her makeshift pack over her shoulder. Detective Benitez grinned at her. Maureen kicked her duffel bag back under the bed and stomped out of the room. She would make him pay for every snarky look he gave her.

Nineteen

"So, what exactly are we looking for?" Maureen said, shuffling through a stack of papers in front of her.

"Anything that could indicate a link between Tom Lowes and Sandra Locke," Manny said, exasperated that he had to keep reminding her.

The brown box was sitting on the front stoop of his house when he and Maureen had pulled up, just like Agent Layton had promised him it would be. Also as promised, the inside was neatly piled with photocopies of the notes that he had taken and all of the personal information that he'd received from the county that morning. There was also a full workup of each of their financials added in. The documents, however, were merely sorted into two piles, one for the Lowes family and one for Sandra Locke. His moo shoo pork had gone cold before Manny had managed to further categorize each document. More than a dozen piles now lay on his coffee table, and each one needed to be scrutinized. It was going to be a long night.

"I didn't think you'd be making me do busy work for you," Maureen grumbled, carelessly tossing the piece of paper she was holding onto the table and grabbing another egg roll.

"I don't know how to do any of this. I thought I was going to help you catch a killer."

"Most detective work is done just like this," he replied, trying to keep his patience. "In homicides like these that have the hallmarks of a serial killer, there's usually a reason that victims are chosen. Now in this case, both of the victims were small children. As far as I'm concerned, there's only two reasons to kill a child. The first reason is rooted in some kind of sexual desire. And that's not the case here, right?"

"Not that I've seen."

"Then we're most likely looking at someone who wants to hurt the parents by hurting their children," he said, picking up another paper from the Lowes' financial pile and holding it up. "Hence why we're looking for connections between the parents. So make yourself useful."

"I've already told you what the knife looks like. What else do you want?"

Manny sighed and massaged his temples. In the truck, she *had* described a knife with a twelve-inch, curved blade and dark wooden handle with some odd symbols carved into it. But she couldn't describe those symbols as anything except "not English" and said she could recognize it if she saw it again. She then handed him a piece of newspaper and told him that the words and numbers written on it were from another dream. It was a clue, but wouldn't be much help if they didn't have a perpetrator to search. Manny got up out of his armchair and went to the spare room that he used as an office. He picked up a yellow legal pad and pen from his desk, came back into the living room, and tossed them on Maureen's lap.

"Here," he said, sitting back down, "why don't you help me by writing down what I say. We'll make a chart of where these two families intersect."

"Don't detectives usually do this sort of thing on a big board or something?"

"Sure, we could," Manny shrugged back, "but I'm not exactly welcome at the precinct. So we'll just have to go low tech, okay?"

"Fine," she said, picking up the take-out box that held the egg rolls. There were only two left of the original order of eight, and he hadn't yet had one. Maureen grabbed both of the remaining rolls without looking in his direction and plopped them onto her plate.

"You're not even going to offer me one?" he teased, pointing at her plate.

"Why, do you want one?" Her mouth was full, and little flecks of pork and cabbage flew out as she talked.

He couldn't help but laugh and wave his hand in indication that she could eat the rest. Judging by the spartan nature of her apartment, he surmised that she didn't keep a lot of food around, and therefore it made sense that she was taking advantage of the big meal she had in front of her. He grabbed a napkin from the bag next to his feet and tossed it at her. She gave him a sour look as she snatched it off her lap and wiped her lips.

"Okay," he said, trying to get back to business. "Let's turn the pad on its side lengthwise and put Tom Lowes' name at the top of one side and Sandra Locke on the other. Locke's spelled with an 'e'. Okay, now for some common things. The kids went to the same school. They both went to St. Mary's Catholic Church."

"Where Father Patrick is," she said. The statement seemed to come out of nowhere.

"Uh, yeah, that's right," said Manny, puzzled. "I didn't know that you go there. You don't strike me as much of a churchgoer."

"I'm not," she said sharply. "I just met Father Patrick walking down the street one day. He likes to talk."

"My parents go to Mass every now and then. That seems to be what most people say about him. I don't know him personally, but I've heard good things."

"He's okay, I guess." She tapped the legal pad with the pen. "What else?"

"Oh, right. Well let's see, we can write down that they worked together on the sale of some county buildings recently."

"This is already a lot of ways they could be connected," Maureen sighed, as though writing down a few words had greatly taxed her. "How about a drink?"

"Really? Now?" Manny said, raising his eyebrows. *It's barely been two hours.* "Go ahead." He shook his head.

Maureen popped up and ran into the kitchen. She returned with a bottle of whiskey and two glasses. She put one glass in front of him and set about opening up the bottle.

Manny quickly grabbed it from her. "I'll pour," he insisted.

Maureen sat herself down on the floor in front of the coffee table with a loud sigh. She held out her own glass and Manny poured two fingers into the bottom before doing the same with his own.

"Kinda chintzy, don't you think?" she said, frowning at the amount of liquid.

"We got work to do," Manny replied. "Pace yourself."

He raised his glass to her, and she clinked her glass with his, though it seemed with no great relish.

"Mm, that's good stuff," Manny said before setting down his glass and picking up the pile of Sandra Locke's financial documents. "Okay let's see here. Church. School. Business. Most crimes have something to do with money, so let's start there."

Manny read through each document carefully, but nothing jumped off the page. Sandra's checking account balance hadn't varied by more than a few hundred dollars either way for years. She'd taken out a second mortgage on her home about a decade before, but her job at the county kept her paid well enough to manage. From what he could see on the statement, she wasn't in any dire financial straits. He was about to give up and move on when he saw a hospital bill on top of the pile.

The bill was for nearly $200,000 and was dated nine years ago. It looked to be a sum total of the hospital expenses for little Evan's care. There was the prenatal surgery, the NICU stay, and a follow-up surgery to replace the heart shunt. Manny grabbed the remainder of the pile and began to shuffle through it. A different picture started to emerge.

"I don't think Sandra told me the whole story," he said.

"How do you mean?" Maureen asked.

"Well, she told me all about her son's heart surgery, but not about how it just about broke her financially. It seems that her husband's life insurance policy paid off a hundred grand of the bills. But the insurance company deemed the surgery 'experimental and high risk', so they covered very little, leaving almost ninety grand to pay out of pocket. It was six months after this first bill that she took out a second mortgage on her home, I'm guessing to cover the rest. Thing is, now she's got two mortgages hanging over her. At first, I thought she was doing just fine, that she was making the payments and all. But it says here that the second mortgage was at a premium rate, and she was paying it out of a savings account from a different bank. And thanks to the interest, she ran through her money about nine months ago. She'd been paying off the original mortgage on the house, but that second mortgage had about forty-five thousand still outstanding.

"The bank had started foreclosure proceedings about six months ago. It looked pretty grim for her. But about three months ago, the whole mortgage was paid in full. Both mortgages. That's just over seventy thousand dollars. She was able to keep the house, and now has the chance to rebuild her savings."

"What are you thinking?" Maureen asked. She had refilled her whiskey and took a small sip.

"Isn't it obvious?" he said. "She's the county treasurer. I'm willing to bet on embezzlement or something like that. She could get away with it, if she had some help." *If she had help.* Manny threw down the papers in his hand and picked through the box on the table until he found what he was looking for.

"Papers on the sale of that county building," he explained to Maureen. "There's a work order for over one hundred fifty thousand dollars here. It looks like it's for lighting and drywall work. I don't know too much about contractor costs, but that seems incredibly high. For example, a five-pound box of drywall nails for one hundred sixty-nine dollars? I just bought a five-pound box at the hardware store last month for a tenth of that. And since when does the hourly labor charge for a crew of this size run into the triple digits? I think there was some money laundering going on here, and I think both Sandra Locke and Tom Lowes were in on it. Now, I scrubbed the Lowes' financials and didn't find anything, but he's a well-connected guy who can easily hide money in his business or in an offshore account or something, but Sandra? Well, it's pretty obvious she couldn't. Whatever the case, whatever they were into, it cost both of them their kids."

Manny jumped up off the couch and pulled out his phone. "What are you going to do?"

"I promised I'd give Agent Layton a call when I came up with something."

"Maybe that's not the best idea in the world."

"Why?" he asked her, perplexed.

"Oh, never mind," she said, turning on the television and scrolling through the channels. "It's just that, if it were me, I wouldn't want to call in with every little thing I found. Makes it seem like you're trying too hard to be liked. Like you want daddy's approval. I mean, what do you really have except a theory? Also, what do you think he'll say when you tell him you've got me hostage over here? I'm sure he'll just love that."

Manny paused for a minute and let her comments sink in. She made a point, though it wasn't one that gave him any real comfort. True, he had a theory about *why* the children were killed, but he didn't have any clear picture about *who* was doing it. Maybe it would be best to have a little more insight on that before going to the Feds. He wasn't officially part of the investigation after all, and they had access to the same information that he had in that box. More, probably, since they had greater resources and manpower.

He wasn't happy about Maureen being right, but he flopped down in his chair and tossed his phone on the coffee table. He sat back and glared at her for a few heartbeats. He thought he could see the barest hint of a smile form on her lips as she stared ahead at the TV.

†wen†y

Agent Layton took a long, slow sip out of his glass of water and adjusted the desk lamp to illuminate the contents of the folder he was just handed. Seated in that cramped, makeshift office, he began to trace in great detail the winding road that one Maureen Allerton had traveled since her brother's death.

After the eight-year-old girl had been examined by the FBI's psychologist, she vanished for a time into a boarding school in the northeast. All the file had was a name, but there were stories about this institution that he was at least nominally familiar with. The school had been shut down just before the turn of the century, but its reputation lived on, and it wasn't a good one. This was just the type of place that would create a guarded, untrusting type of person. Maureen Allen certainly fit the bill.

She cropped up again as an adult. The fingerprint analysis brought up a variety of misdemeanors and a felony, spread across four known aliases. And she wasn't overly sophisticated. They were all variations on her birth name and kept the same initials. He was puzzled by this at first, but after looking at the signature on a forged prescription for pain killers and a signature on an old car title registration, he understood the method to her madness. Despite representing two different names, the signatures were identical; the M and A letters of the first and last name were clearly legible, while the rest of the writing was no more than a couple of wavy lines. Layton found himself smiling at the fact that he didn't need to waste much time making connections between her identities.

So Maureen Allen, or Allerton, was a con artist and petty criminal. She had engaged in identity theft and forgery in her past. There was probably more that she hadn't been caught for, but what he had was enough for now. The only thing he still questioned was why she chose to live the way she did. His working theory was trauma from her childhood, and if she truly did have second sight, that might be another contributing factor. He'd need to know for sure, however, if he was going to follow through with his plan.

And of course, she'd be of no use to him if she was indeed capable of murder.

TWENTY-ONE

Maureen opened her eyes and stared up at an unfamiliar ceiling. Her arm, resting underneath her head, was numb and stiff, and the pillow she was lying on had an unfamiliar smell. She moved her legs and found that they were covered with a knitted quilt. Gradually, the fog of sleep wore off, and she realized she was lying on the couch in the young detective's living room. Her mouth was dry and as she turned her head, the half-full bottle of whiskey came into view. She had no headache, but she reached out for it all the same, sat up, and tipped a small amount into her mouth. She swished it around and swallowed.

"Well that's one way to start the morning," a voice behind her said.

Maureen turned around and saw Detective Benitez standing on the edge of the living room, holding a cup of coffee in one hand and several papers in the other. He was barefoot, dressed in an athletic T-shirt and mesh shorts, and his physique was more apparent to her than it had ever been. It was nice. He was certainly in shape but didn't seem obsessed with his body.

"What time is it?" she asked, rubbing the sleep out of her eyes and trying not to stare at him.

"It's about quarter to ten," he answered, coming over to the easy chair next to the couch and taking a seat.

"I don't do anything earlier than noon," she replied, laying back and covering her face with the blanket.

"There's coffee in the kitchen if you want."

"I'm not a coffee drinker."

"There's cereal and milk, too, if you're hungry."

"Didn't you hear what I said? I don't do anything this early."

"I'd think you'd be nice and rested after conking out the way you did last night."

His words made Maureen throw the blanket off her face and sit up abruptly. She could barely remember when she fell asleep, but she was certain it was only a few hours ago, like usual.

"What are you talking about?" she asked.

"You were out like a light pretty early," he said, setting the papers on the coffee table and taking a sip from his mug. "I was kind of surprised. You struck me as more of a night owl."

"What time was I out?" This was very confusing for her.

"Well, I was up until almost one," he said, cupping his coffee thoughtfully. "You'd been out for at least an hour. I remember because I looked over at you after Letterman's first guest, and you were slumped over and asleep. You didn't even wake up when I took your shoes off, lifted your feet up, and threw the blanket on you."

Maureen looked down at her feet. She hadn't even noticed that she wasn't wearing her shoes.

"I must have drunk more than I thought," she said, trying to rationalize what had made her sleep so easily in a strange place.

"Not really," the detective said. "We each had about the same amount. A couple of pours from the whiskey bottle. I don't suppose you had any dreams last night that might be useful?"

The question took Maureen off guard. She didn't recall any nightmares. She counted the hours in her head. If the detective was telling the truth, she'd been asleep for somewhere around ten uninterrupted hours. It almost didn't seem real.

"No, I didn't dream at all," she told him. "I was really out that long?"

The detective nodded his head and let his self-satisfied smirk take over his face. That seemed to be the only facial expression that he was capable of around her.

"That's not possible. I don't sleep like that."

"I guess you just really needed the rest then," he said. "Or you're just really comfortable here."

"I think I'll go ahead and take you up on that cereal," she said, reaching out and taking one more swig from the whiskey bottle to show him that she wasn't affected by anything he said. "Where do you keep it?"

"I can get it for you," he replied, setting his coffee on the table and rising from his chair.

"Not on your life," she said, jumping off the couch and shoving him back down. "Just tell me where the stuff is."

"Cereal is in the cupboard to the left of the sink," he said, shrugging and inclining his head in the direction of the kitchen. "Bowls are on the other side, third cupboard to the right from the corner. Milk's in the fridge, second shelf."

Maureen quickly walked into the kitchen. She wasn't sure that she was all that hungry, but she needed an excuse to get out of the living room for a few minutes. The young detective's patronizing way of speaking to her threatened to heat her up to a point where she would either slap him right in his face or shove her tongue down his throat. Neither option would do.

She stood staring at the cabinets for a moment before opening the one to the left of the sink. She scanned the shelves packed with the bachelor's survival kit of canned soup and boxed dinners and found a box of generic corn flakes. She pulled it off the shelf, hopped up onto the counter, and began to nibble the cereal straight out of the box. From her perch, Maureen could just make out the back of the detective's head poking out above the easy chair. She sat, wondering why she had allowed herself to get into the situation she found herself in. Getting involved with people went against every rule she'd lived by her entire life. She really didn't think that the detective needed her dreams to solve the case, unless the killer happened to be looking into a mirror. And the longer she stayed in town, the more sure she was that the Feds would force her to face her past sins. Of course, it may just happen that if her help really ended up being integral in finding a double murderer, she could find a way to leverage it into some sort of clemency. At the moment, though, the former seemed more likely than the latter.

Maureen sat in silence, continuing to nibble on the corn flakes and wrestle with her thoughts as they turned toward the detective. She still wasn't entirely sure what to make of him. On the one hand, that smug air of his trampled all over her last nerve and on the other, she almost felt a sense of pity for him. It was clear that he felt like he wasn't being afforded the respect he deserved from his fellow officers and his bosses.

She hadn't seen a whole lot of their interactions firsthand, but from what he said, it was probable that this was the case. The short time that she'd already spent with him taught her that he was tenacious at the very least. And he certainly seemed stubborn enough to become the kind of detective he wanted to be.

She hopped off the counter, leaving the cereal box behind, and slowly walked back into the living room. The detective was shuffling through several papers, frowning as he looked at them and mumbling something to himself that she couldn't quite understand.

"Something wrong?" she asked as she sat back on the couch.

"At the second crime scene, Stacey Winherst mentioned finding what she thought was some kind of accelerant used to set the fire," he said without looking up at her. "We've got a decent amount back from the crime lab from the scene, but nothing on that. I'd really like to have a look at it."

"How's that going to help?"

"If there's something unusual about it," he said, tossing the papers on the table and looking up at her, "then it might point us toward the person responsible. We can't afford not to have every piece of information, no matter how insignificant it might seem."

"So why don't we just go over to the crime lab and ask someone?"

It seemed like an obvious solution to Maureen, but the detective made a face that signaled to her that he didn't think much of her suggestion.

"It's going to be difficult to get anyone to talk to us," he said, thoughtfully. "But maybe we have no choice."

"Well then, I'm going to take a shower," she said, looking forward to taking advantage of a house with a proper water heater.

"Towels are in the linen closet in the hallway," the detective said. He was wrapped up in looking over his stack of papers for the fourteenth time, but as she got up and walked past him, Maureen caught him glance at her backside. She grinned and couldn't deny the flattery she felt.

That's right, she thought. *Look all you want. I know I have a nice ass.*

She grabbed a change of clothes out of the pillowcase and found the linen closet, pulling out two towels: one for her hair and one for her body. She mused about what a luxury it was to be able to dry different body parts with different towels as she stepped into the bathroom and stripped off her clothes. She turned on the shower, set the water to as hot as she could stand, and stepped in.

Maureen stood under the running water and tried to push the thoughts of the detective out of her head. Nevertheless, she couldn't help but wonder, if they had met under different circumstances, what they might be like together. The fact that she even entertained such an idea surprised her, as she rarely found herself thinking about a man in that way. All her life, she only sought them out when she needed a quick lay, and even then, she always made sure she was in charge of the encounter. Still, she suspected he might be different. Gentler. She imagined him kissing her neck, running his hands up her sides, laying her down—

"What the hell am I thinking!" Maureen said out loud, snapping herself out of her thoughts. She realized that her hand had begun to stray between her thighs, and she angrily pulled it away, cursing her weak, lustful thoughts. Maureen grabbed a bar of soap, scrubbed herself quickly, and rinsed off.

Maureen wiped off the steam-fogged mirror to reveal her rosy-skinned reflection staring back at her. She wasn't familiar with this woman. Despite all her efforts, she was becoming involved with matters that she knew she shouldn't. Maybe she wasn't running away as she normally would because this time, young boys only a few years older than Braden were involved. Maybe she enjoyed the company and attention of the detective, as abrasive and self-assured as he was. She searched herself for the cold, hard logic that would permit her to try once again to escape from her situation and found none. She could only stand there and stare, trying to bend her reflection back to the person she recognized.

The sound of the knob turning snapped her out of her thoughts. She threw the towel around herself as best she could as Detective Benitez's frame filled the doorway.

"Jesus!" she shouted at him as she retreated to the far end of the bathroom. "Don't you know how to knock?"

"I did knock!" he protested, turning his head and half covering his eyes. "I heard the shower turn off a while ago and then nothing. I just wanted to make sure you were okay. When I didn't hear an answer, I decided to let myself in. I didn't see much, honest."

"Well close the door!" she demanded.

He quickly complied.

Maureen unfolded the towel and wrapped it around herself, covering up her excited nipples. She felt embarrassed by her body's betrayal of her arousal at the idea of being seen the way she was. Maureen bundled up her hair in the second towel, picked up her pile of clothes, and walked out of the bathroom.

"All yours if you want it," she said, making sure to brush up against him as she passed. "And by that, I mean the bathroom, you perv."

Maureen smiled to herself as she strutted toward his bedroom to change. She hoped he was watching her walk away. She told herself it was because she wanted to show off what he couldn't have, but deep down, she wasn't sure that was one hundred percent true. She couldn't resist the urge to take a peek over her shoulder, and she just caught a look at his eyes as he closed the bathroom door. She felt a tiny pang of sadness as she heard the sound of the shower starting.

I'll bet he'll be glad I took such a hot shower, she thought to herself as she dropped her towel and began to dress.

TWENTY-TWO

"What are we waiting for?" Maureen asked Manny as they sat in his truck parked in the lot of the County Coroner's Office. "Why aren't we just going in?"

He pulled out his cell phone and checked the time. It was just after quarter to five.

"Just give it a few more minutes," he said to her, keeping his eyes on the front door.

Manny's plan was to wait until just before the office closed, feeling that it would give them the advantage of surprise. With luck, they'd run into a skeleton crew and few questions would be asked. He wasn't completely sure if the news of him being thrown off the case had reached the coroner's office, but he figured he would confront that issue if it came up. In any case, he'd find out very soon if Agent Layton was going to keep his promise to intervene if he got himself into any hot water.

What he was really hoping for was to see Stacey Winherst leave the building before he and Maureen made their entrance. She was the one person he didn't want to run into, not because she intimidated him, but because he wasn't in the mood for her attitude and their inevitable verbal jousting. He certainly began to think differently about the woman after his conversation with Layton. Manny could sympathize and maybe even empathize, but in the back of his mind, he still didn't understand why she couldn't just be polite sometimes.

"Maybe she's different away from work," he mumbled to himself, without realizing that he was vocalizing his thoughts.

"Huh?" Maureen said.

"Never mind," he said, looking back at his cell phone for the time. "Let's head in."

Manny led Maureen through the hallways of the office as confidently as he could. He had only ever been there once before when he had taken an orientation tour after being hired by the Police Department. He hadn't thought at the time he'd ever be back investigating a double homicide. Manny knew that the lab was at the rear of the building and down the stairs to the lower level. Their luck held out. No one stopped them or questioned their presence, and he was able to find the set of stairs that he was looking for, descending down into the basement.

At the bottom of the stairs, Manny found a sign pointing to the lab and followed the arrow to another sign and another hall before they were finally confronted by a pair of steel doors. He took a moment to gather himself. The reason for coming here was to find out about the missing accelerant report. That was what he had told Maureen. What he hadn't told her was that he also wanted to see if they had gotten DNA out of the vomit sample that he'd taken from the jail cell. And if so, if it was a match to the crime scene.

Manny took a deep breath and pushed through the doors as if he were an old west gunslinger walking into a saloon. In his mind, he felt like a fool, but he reasoned that if he looked confident enough walking in, someone would be more likely to talk to him and give up the information he was looking for.

The lab was quiet. The smell of alcohol mixed with other cleaning agents hit Manny's nose as he wandered among the tables of laboratory supplies toward the opposite end of the room.

"Hello?" Manny called out. Maureen stayed silent behind him.

After a moment, Dr. Winherst's young assistant came out of an office from somewhere in the back. He was carrying a box of neatly labeled samples in evidence bags, balancing it carefully.

"It's Derrick, right?" said Manny, hoping that a more gentle and familiar approach would loosen the young man's tongue.

"Yes, sir," answered Derrick as he placed the box on a table and dusted his hands on the side of the lab coat.

"I don't know if you remember me," Manny continued, pulling out his badge from his pocket and holding it up, "but I'm Detective Manny Benitez of the Sycamore Hills PD. We met briefly at the crime scene of the Lowes murder."

"Sure, I remember, Detective," he said, shifting his weight from foot to foot. He seemed nervous. Manny pegged the young man as the type who was likely a whiz in the lab but lacked the social skills to confidently speak to someone he thought of as his superior.

"I believe that Dr. Winherst brought back a sample of a supposed accelerant possibly used to start the fire at the second crime scene," Manny continued in his formal tone. "I was wondering if the tests on the substance had come back with anything."

"Well, yes, but . . . ," Derrick stammered uncomfortably.

"But, what?" Manny pressed him.

"Well, I'm not sure I'm supposed to discuss that with you," he said sheepishly. He leaned in to Manny and lowered his voice. "I heard that you weren't working the case anymore."

"And just who told you that?"

"Dr. Winherst."

Damn! Manny felt his face twist in frustration, and he turned away from Derrick, hoping to conceal his feelings. He found himself looking at Maureen, who was standing like a statue and observing the whole scene. Her face broke slowly into a sly smile as she roused herself and stepped past him, patting him on the shoulder as if she had interpreted his reaction as a silent plea for help.

"C'mon, kiddo," she said, stepping up to Derrick and tracing a finger down his chest. "Would we be here if we weren't helping with the case?"

The young man's tongue seemed to stick in his throat. Eventually, Derrick managed to pull his eyes off the woman in front of him and looked at Manny. "Who is she?" he asked.

"She's my partner," said Manny.

"That's right, we're partners. And we can't afford to wait. There's a sicko out there killing kids. So chop, chop! Let's see the info that the detective asked for."

Derrick hesitated for a second, clearly not sure what to do.

"Now!" Maureen shouted, helping to force his feet into action.

"Subtle," Manny whispered as they followed the young man over to a bank of computers.

"Hey, it's what you brought me for, isn't it?" She seemed very proud of herself.

"Just don't get carried away. We don't need to draw more attention to ourselves than necessary."

"Yes, Detective," she said, giving him a mocking salute.

"Manny," he said.

Maureen just rolled her eyes and turned around.

By the time they came up behind Derrick seated at one of the computers, he had already pulled up the report. Manny tried to read over his shoulder, but got lost almost instantly in the chemical formulas and CSI shorthand that littered the screen.

"So you said you guys figured out what the accelerant was," Manny said, flipping to a fresh page in his notebook. "What can you tell me about it?"

"It says here that the substance is comprised mostly of oleic and linoleic acids, with some other triglycerides and a very limited amount of diglycerides and monoglycerides," Derrick replied, reading off the screen. "Dr. Winherst notes that the concentration of each would tend to indicate a type of vegetable oil, most likely olive."

"Olive oil?" Manny said, puzzled.

"That's what the report says," Derrick said, pointing at the screen.

"Anything else?"

"Um, there does seem to be something else here," the young man said, punching a key to scroll down the page. "Dr. Winherst indicates an abnormal concentration of *Commiphora gileadensis.*"

"What is that?" Manny asked.

"I don't really know," Derrick said. "It's a scientific name for some kind of plant, that much I can recognize, but it's not really my area."

"Okay, how about you just spell it for me," Manny said, readying his pen.

Derrick spelled the two words for him once and then again when Manny couldn't keep up the first time.

"Okay, one more thing," Manny said. "You remember that vomit sample that Dr. Winherst had you collect from the first crime scene, right?"

Derrick nodded.

"What did you find out about that?" Manny asked. "You know, did you confirm that it wasn't from a dog or anything? Any hits from the FBI database?"

"Um, let me check," the young man replied. His fingers clicked on the keyboard for what seemed to Manny like an unnecessary amount of time to answer his question. "It doesn't look like the FBI came up with any match in the database," he said, turning around and facing them.

"But it is human, correct?"

"Yes."

So their perpetrator wasn't in the system. It certainly fit with Manny's theory that the pile of vomit at the first scene was the result of the uneasy stomach of a rookie killer. If that was the case, it told him that whoever was responsible wasn't a psychopath.

"Okay," he said to Derrick, "what about the second sample I sent in a few days ago for comparison? Did that DNA profile match the first one?"

Derrick clicked away again for several agonizing moments. Manny turned his head toward Maureen. She was watching everything with her arms folded across her chest. She looked stern, but still pretty in the bluish laboratory light. He found himself hoping with all of his heart that there would be no match, wincing inside at the thought of potentially having to handcuff her again.

"The data indicates no match." Derrick's voice brought him back to the moment.

Manny felt a smile of relief break across his face. "Good," he said, realizing that he was still looking at Maureen.

She tilted her head and furrowed her brow, as though she understood what he meant.

Manny turned back to Derrick and slapped the young man on the back. "That's good work. I think that's everything I need. Thanks, Derrick."

Manny stuffed his notebook back into his pocket and nodded to Maureen that it was time to leave. She turned and walked out of the room a step behind him. Manny could feel her eyes on him. They reached the double doors of the laboratory and walked through into the hallway.

"So vomit, huh?" Maureen's voice ricocheted off the wall and into his ear.

"What's that?" he said, hoping he could avoid answering any questions about the subject. Somehow, he knew he couldn't.

"You said you found a sample of vomit at the first crime scene," she pressed.

"Yeah," he replied.

"And you think that it came from the person who killed that kid?"

"Maybe. I was thinking that the person who killed Jacob Lowes had never killed someone before, and they got a little queasy at what they had done. I'm thinking it was the first time they'd killed anyone."

"And then you said you sent another sample for comparison."

"Did I?" he said.

They had reached the front doors of the building. Manny stopped to hold the door open for Maureen. She stared at him and stood a pace from the threshold, shaking her head. Manny rolled his eyes and walked through the door, propping it open for her to follow behind.

"I threw up in the jail cell after I had the nightmare about the second kid," she continued her suspicions.

Manny didn't say anything. Instead, he quickened his pace as they made their way to his truck.

"I was waiting in the interrogation room for you for a pretty long time after that." The volume of her voice had risen with the effort that she was exerting to keep up.

Manny reached his truck and quickly began to open the driver's side door, but Maureen had caught up and slammed it shut. She spun him around by the shoulder and slammed him in the chest with an open palm.

"That second sample you talked with that kid about was my puke, wasn't it?"

Manny took a deep breath and looked into her eyes. They burned with an odd look, neither furious nor dispassionate. "I figured it would either rule you out," he said, finding his voice after a moment, "or it would make the case against you. I needed to know." Manny hoped he didn't hurt her feelings too much.

"Okay," she said, almost cheerily, patting him on the shoulder and heading around the truck to the passenger's side door.

"What do you mean *okay?*" Manny called after her, stunned by her reaction.

"You said 'good' when that Derrick kid told you that my sample didn't match the other one," she called back over the roof of the truck. "That means you were hoping for that result. And now you might actually trust me. That's good for me. I know I didn't kill those kids. And now if I got another person on my side, so much the better when the rest of the shit crashes on me."

Manny couldn't believe what he was hearing. *The nerve of that woman!* he thought as he yanked his door open and jumped into the driver's seat. She followed suit as he turned the key and stepped on the accelerator.

"You know, I actually felt bad about doing that," he said to her as they drove down the road back toward Sycamore Hills proper.

"Don't. I don't blame you. You did what you had to do, so just forget about it."

"Yeah, but you're innocent. I just feel bad that I judged you as quickly as I did."

"You're just falling for my charms," she said dryly. "Better be careful, Detective. I'm not guilty of any murders, but that doesn't mean I'm innocent."

They drove for several minutes in silence while he tried to focus on the next destination and how to best divide the work between the two of them once they arrived.

"Isn't that the road to your place?" Maureen said as she pointed to her right.

"Yeah, but we're not going back there yet," he replied. "We got another stop to make."

"Where to?" she said, looking about her, as if trying to zero in on where they currently were. "The only thing thisway is the community college, isn't it?"

"That's exactly right," he said.

They had to research a couple of things and the library of the community college had much better internet connectivity than his place and, obviously, many more computers. He wanted to actually have some kind of breakthrough before he made any report to Agent Layton.

The look on Maureen's face told him she wasn't going to enjoy it very much.

ŧUEꞂŧY-ŧHREE

The library of the community college was about as busy as they expected for a Tuesday night a week before classes were to start. Relieved that they could work in privacy, Manny had little trouble finding two computers away from the others in the computer bank. He sat down in front of one machine and pulled out the chair in front of the other. Maureen sat, albeit with some hesitation. Manny slid the mouse across the pad to wake up the computer. Out of the side of his eye, he noted that Maureen was mimicking his movements with her own machine.

"All right," he said typing in the website he wanted on the keyboard, "I'll search for what this scientific name that Derrick gave us means; you see if you can make sense out of those numbers and letters you wrote down yesterday."

Maureen stared at him and didn't move. The look of confusion on her face told him that he may as well have been speaking Greek to her.

"Have you ever used a computer before?" he asked.

"Of course I have! It's just been a while."

"Well just jump on the internet," he replied, "and pull up the search engine."

"Which one is the internet?"

He leaned over to her computer and helped her. "That's the search engine," he said pointing at the screen. "Just type in what you're looking for in the bar there and hit *Enter*."

He watched as Maureen pulled out the piece of newspaper she'd written her scribbles and symbols on and laid it next to her on the desk. She then slowly, with only her index fingers, began to type. Manny couldn't help but grin as he turned his attention to his own computer.

"*Commiphora gileadensis*," he read off the screen. "Says here it's a tree that grows mainly in the Middle East. Used to make balsam or myrrh. Sometimes referred to as 'balm of gilead'. Why does that sound familiar?"

"Sounds almost biblical," Maureen said while her eyes were on her own screen.

"It does," agreed Manny as an idea sparked in his head. He vigorously typed on the keyboard, and what he found gave him the answer. "That's it! It's not an accelerant, it's chrism!"

Maureen stared at him with a furrowed brow and tilted her head.

"Olive oil plus myrrh," he said, "or balsam, if you want. It's chrism. What they call holy oil. This sicko is pouring holy oil on the kids."

"Why would he do something like that?"

"What did you come up with?"

"I don't know. I typed in what I wrote down and got a bunch of stuff in a list. Which one is what I'm supposed to be looking for?"

Manny slid over and scanned down the search results. It didn't take but a moment to find what he was looking for.

"Leviticus, chapter six," he said, clicking on the link and

reading, both to himself and out loud, the passage that it brought up, "'They must bring to the priest, that is, to the Lord, their guilt offering, a ram from the flock, one without defect and of the proper value.' Good God! 'The burnt offering must be kept on the hearth of the altar throughout the night, until morning, and the fire must be kept burning on the altar.' Guilt offering, burnt offering. The liver and kidneys shall be offered? What the hell?" The reading made Manny start to feel queasy as he pictured the bodies of the young boys burned and left on the stacks of wood. "This is almost like a full description of the crime scenes."

"Type in that other word you have written there," he told Maureen.

She slowly typed *Urim* into the search engine.

"Says here that Urim is generally accepted to mean 'light' in ancient Hebrew," he read. "It's starting to makes sense."

"So, the guy is an uber-religious nut?" Maureen said.

"Looks like it, but that's not entirely what I meant," he said. He decided it was time to tell Maureen. "When you were having your nightmare in the holding cell," he continued, turning her chair toward him so he could look at her straight on, "it was like you were speaking in tongues."

"Yeah, I know," she said impatiently. "But I already told you I don't know what I was saying, so what about it?"

"Maureen, I was able to understand one word. It was the last thing you said before you woke up. You said, 'Amen.'"

Maureen sat still for a moment, her eyes cast to the side, seemingly in deep thought. "So, I was saying a prayer before I killed those kids," she whispered. Her face began to redden and her eyes became glassy.

"You didn't do anything," Manny reminded her, placing his hand tenderly on her knee. He knew Maureen Allen wasn't a saint, that's for sure, but in that moment, she was just as much a victim. "This sick bastard is the one doing it. I'm just sorry that you have no choice but to watch."

"Wouldn't be how I'd choose to spend my nights," she said, giving out a morose laugh. She looked down and saw his hand on her knee. She picked it up and laid it in his own lap, giving him a warm smile as his consolation. "Thanks," she said and wiped her eyes, erasing every look of distress from her face. "So, what now? I mean, now we know we got a religious whack-job on our hands. How do we find him?"

"We can't assume anything," he said carefully. "This could all still be about money laundering. They could just be using the biblical imagery to send a message to Tom Lowes and Sandra Locke. In any case, we might as well pay a visit to St. Mary's."

"Why?"

"Nobody would know their flock better than a shepherd," he said, pleased with his eloquence. "Maybe the priest might be able to offer some insight."

"What about that *Urim* word?" she asked. "You said that was Hebrew. Should we be looking at Jewish people, too?"

"I'd say it's doubtful, but I'll bring it up when I give my report to Agent Layton."

"You still haven't told him you're working with me."

Manny shifted uncomfortably in his chair. "He doesn't need to know."

"He probably already knows."

She likely wasn't wrong, but he still wasn't in any hurry

to have the conversation. The longer he could put it off, the happier he'd be.

"I think we can head out," he said, changing the subject. "What are you in the mood for dinner-wise?"

Maureen shrugged.

She's retreating back inside herself, he noticed. He foresaw a night of her on the couch, hogging the remote and drinking whiskey until she fell asleep without saying more than a few sentences. And he'd miss another ballgame. If he wasn't so sure he'd lose her to the road, he'd drop her off at her place.

They headed out of the library and into the summer twilight. The heat of the day was still hanging in the air and hit Manny hard in the face as they left the air conditioning. He looked about, observing the small clusters of students who were just beginning to return to campus. For a moment, he found himself wishing he were back in school, sitting in a criminology class, before the real world had swallowed him up.

Maureen had gone ahead of him and was leaning on his truck with her arms folded. They didn't exchange any words as he unlocked the truck and opened the passenger's side door for her. She hopped up into the seat and closed the door before he had a chance to do the same. Manny couldn't help but smile to himself at her defiance as he walked to the other side and got behind the wheel.

"We'll go to St. Mary's tomorrow," he said to her as he backed the truck out of its parking space and headed out of the parking lot. "See how much they know about the families of the victims?"

He glanced over at Maureen, who simply shrugged and continued to stare out of the window with a faraway look in her eyes. He didn't see the need to press her further. She needed time with herself to process and stuff her feelings back into the corner of her mind where she kept things like this. He didn't blame her. She'd seen a lot, obviously, and with the nature of the person who had undertaken the killings coming into focus, anyone could be forgiven for being a little shaken. In his mind, it was still all about the money, but the twist of using Tom and Sandra's religious beliefs to send a message was a very disturbing one.

"I make a pretty good steak," he said to Maureen, trying to lighten the atmosphere of the truck's cab. "What do you say we pick up a couple, and I do some cooking for a change? I've got some dried chilies and limes. I could inject a little Latin flavor into the night."

"Keep it in your pants," Maureen replied, without the usual bite.

"I'll take that as a yes to steak," he said.

As they drove along, Manny wondered if the FBI's investigation was going along like theirs was. Surely by now, they had made the connection between the sale of the county building and Sandra's payoff of her son's medical bills. But had they understood the significance of the chrism at the crime scene and why the children were being burned? He would sure like to figure out for certain what language Maureen had spoken in her trance state on Saturday morning. There couldn't be many people in Sycamore Hills who could speak it, whatever it was.

†WEN†Y-FOUR

Maureen stared up at the cross atop the steeple of St. Mary's and frowned. Given all that she discovered about herself since the last time she was there, she wasn't exactly looking forward to setting foot inside again. Whispering prayers over young boys that were about to be murdered, even if it was in her sleep and it wasn't her literal hand on the knife, didn't inspire confidence that she wouldn't burst into flames upon entering. She knew the idea was outrageous, but she couldn't shake it. She wondered what part of hell was reserved for psychics.

A sharp jab into her back brought her out of her thoughts and made her jump. Detective Benitez smirked as he walked past, seemingly pleased with himself. She smacked him on the arm and watched as he stalked up the stairs toward the church's front door, trying to not let her eyes stray too far down his back. Admonishing herself for even considering it, Maureen shook her head and jogged up the steps to stand next to the detective.

The door swung open as he reached for the handle, almost as if they were expected. The smiling face of Father Patrick greeted them.

"Ms. Allen," he chimed, seeming to ignore the detective

completely. "I'm glad to see you again. Have you come to firm up our dinner plans?"

Detective Benitez turned and raised an eyebrow.

Maureen ignored the detective's look. "We've come to talk to you about something else, Father. This is Detective Benitez from the police department, but he'll probably try to insist that you call him 'Manny.'"

The detective held out his hand to shake the old man's and nodded his hello.

"I suppose you had better come in so that we can talk," the priest said.

The three of them moved into the entrance, allowing the door to shut behind them. Father Patrick seemed perfectly comfortable in the awkward situation, much more so than Maureen felt herself. She looked on uneasily as the two men held their conversation.

"Father Patrick," the detective began, putting on his investigative tone, "you may have heard about the double murder that is being investigated here in town. Two young boys, found three days apart, burned on large pyres."

"I have, sadly," the priest replied. "I've kept abreast of the local news. Though, actually, it was your companion, there, who first brought them to my attention."

Both men turned their heads to Maureen. She felt the color in her face drain and her feet back up one step.

"Don't judge her, Detective," Father Patrick said, reaching out and touching the detective on the shoulder. "I assure you, I just happened to run into her after each occurrence, and in my work, I've found that people are simply comfortable talking to me about things that are disturbing them."

Detective Benitez gazed at the old man, and it appeared to Maureen that he was trying to study the man, like a poker player looking for a tell. Father Patrick's face, however, betrayed nothing. He was going to keep their private conversations to himself it seemed.

"So, Detective," Father Patrick said, leaning himself casually on a nearby table, "I suspect you have found something in your investigation that you feel I may be able to help shed some light upon."

"What do you know about *Commiphora gileadensis?*"

"Though I am familiar with Latin, Detective, I'm afraid I'm not fluent."

"Balsam? Or, if you like, Balm of Gilead."

"Ah, of course," Father Patrick exclaimed with a muted laugh, "I suppose it is rather obvious when you think about the name. Yes, it's a plant from the Middle East, I believe. Balsam is the primary ingredient in chrism."

"Exactly," said Detective Benitez. "Thing is, we found quite a bit of the stuff on one of the bodies. The coroner's office originally thought it was an accelerant used to start the fire, but lab reports confirmed it was a mixture of balsam and olive oil. It seems that the murderer covered the body and wood in the stuff before lighting them on fire."

"Anointing them, you mean," the priest said, the joviality of his voice disappearing.

Manny nodded as he reached into his coat pocket and pulled out his notebook. "Father, the two boys were children of two of your parishioners. How well do you know Tom Lowes and Sandra Locke?"

"Lowes and Locke," the priest said thoughtfully. "Yes,

I'm familiar with both of them. They have attended St. Mary's as long as I've been here, and I'm sure even before that. They almost never missed a Sunday. Quite devout Catholics, both of them. Fixtures in the confessional, which I must say is relatively rare in this day and age. Mr. Lowes is a member of our lay council and the Knights of Columbus, if memory serves. And I'm mostly familiar with Mrs. Locke because of her son. One of the first things I learned about my congregation upon my arrival was of the surgery that saved his life. There were many prayers for that little one, I can assure you. Some people called him difficult, but the boy's soul was so gentle. I had no troubles with him in our First Communion classes."

"Was Jacob Lowes in those classes, too?"

"Yes, now that you mention it. In fact, they just celebrated their First Communion at Mass about a month ago."

"Father," said Manny, finishing his notes and looking back up at the priest. "It's come up in our investigation, that it appears Tom Lowes and Sandra Locke were involved in some sort of conspiracy to defraud the county of a substantial amount of money."

"How terrible."

"What would you say if I told you that it appears that the bodies of these two boys were staged in a manner suggesting an Old Testament sacrifice?"

"I would say that it's a horrifying thought. Though, now that you mention the holy oil, I could see why you would think that."

"Do you know of the reference in the Bible?"

"Of course I know it. Leviticus, chapter six. Though I

don't generally hold with the burning of sacrifices as the best method for atonement."

"We're working on the theory that there is someone else involved with the defrauding of the county," the detective continued, mirroring the priest's lean on the table, "and they are using both victims' beliefs to send a message through these murders. They might even be someone else in the congregation."

"I confess, Detective, I don't intimately know everyone in my congregation, but I consider myself a fairly good judge of character. And I can't think of anyone in my flock who could be capable of something like this."

"Well, not to disregard your analysis of people, but is there any way that someone from the church could steal a large quantity of holy oil from your stores?"

"We keep it locked up in the sacristy. Although, I'm not sure we keep enough on hand at any one time to cover a burning body in the way you've described. And truthfully, my junior priest, Father Preston, handles the ordering and stocking of things like that. He's in my office working on his sermon for this Sunday. I'll go grab him and have him take you into the back to discuss the inventory."

Father Patrick retreated around the corner to the side hallway. Detective Benitez blew out of his lips and paced back and forth in front of the door.

"Do you think Father Patrick had something to do with this?" she asked, surprised that she found herself even caring.

"I'm not sure," he said. "We're looking for a person with intimate knowledge of the Bible who might be tied to this church. But he's being more than helpful, and I don't want to think ill of a priest. Of course, I don't have to ask how you feel about him." The detective flashed his infuriating smirk at her.

She scrunched her nose in response.

"Oh, come on," he said, "it's pretty obvious that you like him. And what was that about dinner plans?"

"It's not like that. It's just talking."

"Hey, I'm not judging. Everyone needs someone to talk to."

The sound of a pair of footsteps coming around the corner prevented Maureen from replying, much to her relief.

"Detective," Father Patrick said as he came into view with the young priest, "this is Father Preston. He'll take you back to our sacristy and go over the inventory and the books. You'll be in better hands than mine."

"If you'll follow me, Detective," the young priest said, inclining his head and gesturing behind the detective. The two men headed off around the opposite corner, leaving Maureen and Father Patrick alone.

The silence that hung in the air was palpable. Maureen stared at the old priest and he stared back, his face even with the faintest twinkle in his eye. If the situation were different, she might have almost thought him amused by her presence. She wrapped her arms around herself, as though doing that would keep her nervous energy from erupting onto them both.

"Well, this has certainly been an interesting visit so far." Father Patrick smiled, sadly she thought, and slowly made his way into the nave of the church. Maureen followed behind.

"So, how did you become the detective's partner?" he asked her, after kneeling in the aisle briefly and sitting in one of the back pews.

"Detective Benitez came and got me at my work a couple of days ago," she replied, taking a seat next to him. "He seems to think that I can be helpful in solving the case, since the FBI has decided I'm not a suspect anymore. Or if they do, I guess they're waiting for me to off another kid."

"Ah," he said, nodding as if he understood completely.

"It's just messed up, you know?" she continued. "He thinks like you. That my dreams can be some sort of trump card against this guy."

"So you've told him."

"Yeah, I didn't have much of a choice," she confessed. "I guess I'm helping a little. Maybe. In my last dream, I was in a candlelit office or den or something, and I guess I was reading a Bible. That's why the detective asked you about Leviticus. That's what I was reading."

"I see. That's why you think the children might be burnt offerings," he affirmed.

"Yeah, pretty much. But there was something else in the dream, too. On the table next to the Bible, there was an old piece of paper—if you could call it paper. It had writing on it but it wasn't in English. I was definitely reading that too, but right to left instead of normal. Do you have any idea what that might be all about?"

"Could be the writing was in Arabic," he said, stroking his short beard in thought. "Or Urdu. Or Hebrew. Or even Aramaic. And that's just naming a few, but if the person responsible for these crimes is the type to use biblical imagery in staging the crime scenes, I'd bet on the last two."

"Can you speak it?"

"Back in the seventies, we had the option to learn Hebrew

and Aramaic while in seminary. I could still recognize it if I saw it, but I can only speak the basics. Lord's Prayer and the like."

"What does it sound like?"

The priest shifted in his seat momentarily before clearing his throat. "Well, let me think here for a second. In Aramaic I think it goes: *Abwûn d'bwaschmâja Nethkâdasch schmach...*"

Father Patrick's voice faded, but his lips continued to move, as he closed his eyes. It seemed to Maureen that he was searching his memory and trying to speak the prayer to himself before continuing out loud. After a moment he gave up and uttered a defeated laugh.

"I'm afraid I don't remember much of the middle," he said, "though I remember the last. *Metol dilachie malkutha wahaila wateschbuchta l'ahlâm almîn. Amên.*"

His last words hung in the air as Maureen felt her stomach sour. A lump formed in her throat. She looked away for a moment to hide her gulp. She realized, now that they had been said out loud, that she had heard those words before.

"Are you all right?" She heard Father Patrick's voice at her shoulder.

"Yeah, sure," she replied, smoothing her face and turning to face him with a halfhearted smile. "It was pretty."

"Many of the ancient languages are," he said.

"Do you speak any others?" she asked, hoping to distance them from the subject at hand.

"Ancient languages? No. Not Really."

"How about just regular languages?"

Father Patrick looked as if he was about to answer, but before he could, Father Preston and Detective Benitez appeared at the entrance to the nave. Maureen and Father Patrick stood up and walked over to meet them.

"I hope you found everything in order," said the old priest as he came up to stand beside the detective.

"Yes, Father," he replied. "Your associate was very helpful. I think we've got what we came for. Thank you for your assistance, Father Preston."

The younger priest bowed his head slightly and quietly excused himself, slowly making his way out of sight. The remaining three walked to the door where the detective turned around and stuck his hand out to the priest.

"Thank you as well, Father Patrick," he said as the old priest grasped his hand and shook. "I'll let you know if I need anything else."

"I'll keep you in my prayers, Detective," the priest replied, smiling warmly, before turning to Maureen. "And you as well, Ms. Allen."

The notion of a Catholic priest offering her his prayers left her with a disquieting feeling, but she nodded her head just the same. The detective began the descent down the stairs toward Main Street. Maureen stayed where she was.

"I think I'll take you up on dinner," she said quietly, as soon as she was sure that the detective was out of earshot.

"I'm glad to hear it," he said, beaming his wide smile. "How about tonight?"

That was too soon for her. A good part of her truly wanted to sit down for a meal with the old man. "How about a week from today? Next Wednesday. Around eight?" Maureen wanted to make sure she could back out if the case was cleared and she could get herself back on the road.

"A little later than I usually eat," he said with a laugh, "but I can accommodate. I'll put it on my calendar. Wait here for just a moment." Father Patrick retreated back inside the church.

Maureen turned her head to meet the detective's gaze. He stood with his hands out, mouthing for her to come along with him. Maureen shushed him, imploring him to wait. Detective Benitez rolled his eyes, but kept his feet on the sidewalk, crossing his arms and making a show of tapping his right foot. Maureen stuck her tongue out at him.

After a few moments, Father Patrick returned to the doorway. He held a folded piece of paper out to her. "The address for the rectory," he explained.

Maureen took the paper and stuffed it into her back pocket. She nodded thanks to him, turned, and headed down to the sidewalk.

"What was that about?" the detective asked as she walked up beside him.

"Nothing," she said quietly, staring ahead down Main Street. "Just something between me and Father Patrick."

Detective Benitez didn't respond.

"What did you find in the books?" Maureen asked, deciding to break the uncomfortable silence.

"Nothing of any interest," he replied. "The inventory of holy oil and all the other Eucharist supplies are all in order. Nothing has gone missing that I can see."

Their conversation was cut short as a black sedan pulled up to the curb just ahead of them. Agent Layton stepped out and stood in their path. Maureen and Detective Benitez stopped and stared at him.

"Detective," he greeted with a nod.

The detective nodded back, but the rest of his body stayed still. Maureen could feel the tension radiating off of him.

"Would you and your companion come with me, please?" The agent took a few steps to the car, keeping his eyes on the two of them, and opened the rear door.

TWENTY-FIVE

Manny felt Maureen's eyes look over at him. He turned to her and shrugged his shoulders. It was obviously not the moment to defy the FBI. They approached the sedan and got into the back seat. The agent shut the door behind them, took his place in the passenger's seat, and nodded to Agent Lorenzo in the driver's seat. Agent Lorenzo pulled away from the curb and began to drive.

"I haven't heard from you since Monday," Agent Layton began, speaking toward the windshield and not to Manny directly. "Did you get my little present?"

"I did," said Manny. "I found it very helpful."

"And yet...,"

"I wanted to make sure I had enough to give you," he said as coolly as he could, looking out the window and trying to hide his irritation. "You know, not waste your time with a thin theory or stunted research."

"I have every confidence in your investigatory skills, Detective," the agent replied. "What did you come up with?"

He was skeptical about the praise being genuine, but decided that being skeptical was good. A skeptical mind was a sharp one.

"The financial information that was gathered on both

Tom Lowes and Sandra Locke seems to indicate some kind of malfeasance," Manny said carefully. "There is evidence that during the sale of the county buildings in Glenbrook last fall, there was quite a bit of superficial work done to the properties. The county paid well over one hundred fifty thousand dollars for the work, but it definitely looks as though there was not nearly enough work done to justify that amount. I had a quick look through some of the invoices, and to me it looks like material costs were inflated by as much as a factor of six and labor costs were at least doubled."

"Indicating what?"

"Embezzlement and laundering."

"Is that a guess?"

"Agent, not to be rude," Manny said as diplomatically as his frustration would allow, "but if you're just messing with me, I find it very unprofessional."

"I would consider it unprofessional to question a superior officer," Layton replied, though with little, if any, venom in his voice. "I can tell you that we are looking at this transaction as a laundering case, but I want to know why you think embezzlement as well."

"It's what connects the two families. Sandra Locke was in massive debt due to her son's medical procedures. She took out a high-rate second mortgage on her house that she used to pay off his surgeries, but her late husband's life insurance was cashed and her savings was also completely tapped months ago. The bank had begun foreclosure proceedings. Then, after the sale of the county buildings, she suddenly paid off her mortgage in full. Seventy-five thousand dollars just like that. It can't be a coincidence."

"Very impressive," the agent said, turning around in his seat to look Manny in the eyes. "Now go further. Let's hear some theories about how the money scheme played out."

"I hadn't thought that far."

"Humor me."

"Okay," said Manny, taking a deep breath and running back through all that he'd read in the last two days. "Well, Sandra had to know what was going on. She was crucial to the plan working because she controls the county ledger. She's the money. So I would guess that in exchange for helping the laundering activity go through, she got the seventy-five grand as a payoff. So it wasn't two separate crimes, it was all part of the same crime. That would mean that she and Tom were working together. As for Lowes, it seems strange to me that he'd do something like this. He's a very successful and respected pillar of the community. Engaging in money laundering is usually an indication of desperation. So maybe he's not doing as well as he advertises. Maybe he got into some trouble, got in bed with some unsavory characters, and was forced to launder as part of his debt to them. Could be that the money they pocketed wasn't supposed to be taken, and they sent someone after their sons as a message. But there's just something about all this that doesn't scream professional hit."

"And that is?"

"The vomit at the first crime scene," Manny said. "I've been thinking that whoever killed Jacob Lowes had never killed before. I didn't see much of the report on the second crime scene, but I'm assuming that the CI team didn't find any vomit in the field?"

"No, they didn't," the agent answered.

"That says to me that he's starting to get more comfortable with killing. And in just the space of a couple days? It could indicate extreme sociopathic tendencies, though I don't know if you could call him a true psychopath, due to the initial physical reaction to the first murder. All we can say is that he's learned to suppress his empathetic side."

"Not bad, Detective," Agent Layton said, staring steadily at him and nodding his head. "Not too bad at all."

The agent turned back around and faced out of the windshield again. Several awkward minutes passed. Manny looked at Maureen as they drove along. She had her legs drawn up to her chest with her feet on the car seat, staring out at the passing buildings of the town. Her face was flushed and tense, and he could see her pulse thumping in her neck.

"Lorenzo, pull over," Agent Layton said.

As the car rolled to a stop, Manny saw that they had returned to Main Street, no less than twenty feet from where they had been picked up. Agent Layton opened his door and stepped out onto the curb. Manny took it as a cue and did the same. Maureen followed suit. The three stood on the sidewalk, with Maureen a few paces away from the two men. Agent Layton, for the first time, seemed to ignore Manny and concentrate on her.

"Ms. Allen," he said, "could you excuse us for just a moment?"

She said nothing and looked at Manny.

He pulled his keys out of his pocket and handed them to her. "Why don't you turn on the radio. I'll be there in a second."

Maureen took the keys from him and slowly backed away, turning her eyes back to the agent. Manny watched as she crossed the street and hopped into the passenger's seat of his truck and sat, watching the two men. He tried to push her gaze away and focus on the agent, curious on what he wanted to talk about that would necessitate sending Maureen out of hearing.

"So, I'm told you and Ms. Allen shook down the lab assistant at the County Coroner's Office yesterday," Agent Layton said, pulling a pack of gum out of his pocket and offering Manny a stick.

"Who told you that?" Manny asked, turning down the gum.

"Dr. Winherst," the agent said casually.

Of course. "Am I in trouble now?" Manny asked. He was ready if that was the case.

"Not at all," the agent replied, chewing his gum. "I told you to investigate. I'm just curious what made you come to that church this morning."

Manny looked down the block at St. Mary's. "You've been following us," he smiled, certain that his guess was correct.

"Only this morning," the agent replied. "I was willing to give you your space. But I was curious to find out what made you go to the lab last night, so I put a detail on you today."

"I wanted to find out what the accelerant was," Manny told him.

"And?"

"It was balsam and olive oil," he said. "It's what they use to make holy oil. I decided to talk to Father Patrick at St. Mary's and discuss their supply of holy oil and the two families."

"Why St. Mary's?"

"Both Tom Lowes and Sandra Locke are devout Catholics and members of St. Mary's. I was just running down a connection."

"What did you find?"

"Father Patrick's junior priest took me into the sacristy and we went over their inventory books. Everything is in order. Somehow, I still think the killer is connected to St. Mary's, though."

"Why do you say that?"

"The crime scenes are staged like an Old Testament sacrificial altar. We think the killer is also uber-religious, in a twisted kind of way."

"It's 'we' now? Detective, I think you need to be careful about your association with Ms. Allen. I have some serious reservations about her having inside access to your investigation."

"You should know that holy oil isn't the only thing I discovered at the lab. Her DNA doesn't match that found at the crime scene, which proves she's innocent."

"Innocent in this case, maybe," Agent Layton said. "Look, I'm just saying that you should be careful with her. Maureen Allen might not be exactly who you think she is."

Before Manny could ask him what he meant by that, the agent turned away and got back into the black sedan. Manny watched as the car drove away before heading across the street and getting into his truck. His keys were already in the ignition, and the radio was playing quietly. Manny started the truck.

"What was that all about?" Maureen asked.

"The agent just wanted to ask some follow up questions. No big deal." He looked over at her and smiled.

She returned it with her own small grin, laid her head on the window, and closed her eyes. The sun shone off her hair and created a halo of light around her. She looked beautiful. Manny pulled away from the curb and headed back to his place. He hadn't figured out their next move yet, but he did know one thing.

No matter what the agent said, he knew exactly who Maureen was.

TWENTY-SIX

Slowly, the candlelit room came into focus. She felt the knees on a hard surface. It might have been stone. In front of her was a miniature altar, covered in linen, with a small ornate crucifix. Wherever she was, she felt a certain sense of enclosure, as though the walls on either side were very close. The familiar sound of a low voice droning from the throat hit her ears. The language was unknown to her, and yet somehow, she seemed to understand exactly what was being said.

"We pray thee, Oh Christ," it intoned, "be now our guide as we strive to shape the world in your holy image. Grant us strength as soldiers in your army to continue in your name on to victory. As your perfect blood delivered us from the sin of Adam, so now shall the blood of the unblemished serve to cleanse all wickedness from this place. Receive these sacrifices as a sign of our unending devotion to you, Lord and Savior. Amen."

She watched through the eyes as the hands delicately fingered the fringes of the cloth covering the altar, tracing each intricately stitched design. She had a bizarre feeling filling her, yet she struggled to put words to it. Lust, maybe? Could a person lust for a holy object? Whatever it was, the feeling unsettled her own mind enough to begin to pull away from the trappings of the dream. The scene began to fade into inky blackness, but she did hear one last sound: the sound of a telephone ringing somewhere overhead.

Maureen's eyes flew open, and she sat bolt upright on the detective's couch, searching all around for any sign of him or his phone. When none could be found, she realized that the ringing was coming from her dream and cursed herself for pulling away when she did. If she could have stared through the killer's eyes for longer, it was possible that she could have listened in on his conversation and gotten his identity.

"Of course it couldn't be that easy," she mumbled to herself as she clambered off the couch and slunk down the hall toward the bathroom. She rubbed the fog out of her eyes as she went, tiptoeing as softly as she could so as not to wake the detective. His bedroom door was closed as she passed it. She stopped briefly, listening for any sound of him sleeping; maybe he was a snorer. His room was as silent as the hall that surrounded her.

Maureen began to wonder if he'd gone out, maybe on some errand for the FBI. She eased the bedroom door open and crept inside, overcome by a strange curiosity. She'd been in the room before to change, of course, but she had never done any proper snooping. The idea of finding something that would help her know him better—or make fun of him—was too tantalizing to resist.

The bed was empty, the sheets were mussed up, and the pillows were strewn about. The outfit the detective wore the previous day was lying on the floor near the corner, next to the hamper, which was nearly full itself. Aside from that, the detective's room was relatively tidy.

Maureen carefully walked over to the dresser opposite the bed. She slowly opened the top drawer. It was full of neatly folded T-shirts, some printed with sports teams and some embroidered with raised designs that looked like the tattoos she'd seen on the arms of juiced-up meatheads at the gym. She could picture the detective wearing the shirts as a college student, doing bicep curls in front of a mirror. He looked like an idiot in her mind, and the faces she imagined him making made her laugh out loud.

She continued to rummage through his drawers, though she had no clue what she was looking for. She knew it was an invasion of privacy, and if she stopped to think, that was probably the reason she was doing it. He knew so much about her, and now it was time for her to know about him.

Maureen was looking through the detective's sock drawer, hoping she'd find his porn collection or something else to throw a shadow over his squeaky-clean persona, when she lifted a pair of wool socks in the back to reveal a pistol. It didn't look like the standard issue service weapon that she had seen him wearing day after day. She reasoned that it must be his backup weapon. She had heard most cops had them.

She stared at the gun for several moments, transfixed by it. Before she knew what she was doing, she grabbed it out of the drawer and ran out into the living room, stuffing it in the bottom of her pillowcase and covering it with the rest of her dirty clothes. She rationalized her actions by telling herself that before she was through in this town, she might need it.

And if she ever needed to fire a gun, it might go better for her if it was one registered to an officer.

Maureen stood up and paced around the living room. She still could not detect any sound of movement in the house, and it was making her feel uneasy. She decided that a little television would take the edge off, so she stuffed her pillowcase underneath the couch, sat down, and grabbed the remote. After flipping through the channel guide for a minute, she decided on one of the home improvement and craft shows she'd heard talked about by patrons at any number of the bars and restaurants she'd worked at. She didn't understand why people liked watching things like that, but figured that she could at least turn her brain off for a while. It would be the closest thing to therapeutic she could get at the moment.

She was in the middle of her third episode of the same show and wondering why the couple on the television would worry about something as trivial as the color of the kitchen counter tops when they could afford a half-million-dollar home, when the front door opened and the detective walked in. He was wearing a pair of jeans with his badge clipped on the belt, a shirt and tie, and a sport coat. He had shaved and put gel in his hair. He was probably trying to look impressive. In his hand was a thin booklet of papers bound with a plastic ring.

"Where did you go all dressed up?" Maureen asked. She tried to make her question sound as sarcastic as possible, to hide the fact that she was glad he was back and it was no longer just her in the house.

"Getting this," he said holding up the packet.

"And what is that?"

"It's the directory for St. Mary's," he replied, stepping over to the couch and sitting down next to her. She could smell his deodorant and a hint of aftershave. She was loath to admit that she liked it.

"You went back without me?"

"I met with the FBI, would you really have wanted to come?"

Maureen closed her mouth tight.

Manny shrugged and told his story. "I got a call from Agent Layton early this morning. He asked me to meet him for breakfast and when I got there, he handed this to me. He must have gotten it from the church after we left yesterday. Anyway, it seems that the Feds are going to be pretty busy keeping surveillance on the known drug traffickers in the area, and they don't seem to hold other local law enforcement in high regard, so he asked me to run through the directory here and see if anyone knows any more about the dealings of Tom Lowes and Sandra Locke."

"Why doesn't he just ask the two of them himself?" she asked.

"We're apparently going to leave them be for a bit. Until we've got something a little more concrete on the laundering theory. They've been through enough for now."

The detective leaned back, put his palms over his eyes and let out a loud sigh. "I gotta say, I'm not exactly looking forward to doing this rundown. Talking to some three hundred people who probably don't know anything isn't my idea of a fun time."

"So, don't do it," Maureen said.

"I can't just dump an assignment. How would that look?"

"Why are you trying to impress Layton so much?"

Now it was Manny's turn to avoid answering. He leaned forward and began to leaf through the directory, making sure he didn't make eye contact.

"And I suppose I'll have to go with you?" Maureen sighed, flopping back on the couch and folding her hands on her stomach.

"If you don't mind," he said.

"Why would you even want me there?"

"I like having you with me."

Maureen's heart fluttered, but she ignored her desire to press forward. She wasn't sure how she would proceed if she opened that box, and that scared her more than anything.

The detective picked up the directory and pushed himself to his feet. "You hungry?" he asked, turning to her.

"I could eat," she replied.

"How about we head to the burger stand? We can have a sit-down and decide what order we want to hit these folks in."

She got up and pulled her hair back into a ponytail, fastening it with the hair tie she kept on her wrist. Manny opened the front door for her. Begrudgingly, she accepted his act of chivalry and walked through in front of him.

"Thank you, Detective," she mumbled as she passed him.

"Any time," he said.

As she began to walk down the walkway toward the truck, Maureen felt her head look back and past the detective to the living room. Her pillowcase containing the detective's gun was just poking out from under the couch. She felt a pang of guilt that she was stealing from him. But, deep in the recesses of her mind, she knew that rather than put it back in its place, she'd act counter to decency and find a way to hide it further when she had a chance.

And even if he found out what she had done, she was certain that she could make the detective forgive her.

TWENTY-SEVEN

"I'm out of clean clothes," Maureen said as they sat on the couch reviewing the interview notes that they had gathered over the past three days.

Manny slurped up the mouthful of spaghetti he'd just shoved into his mouth. He chewed quickly and swallowed, not wanting to talk to her with his mouth full.

"You could just wash them here," he said, surprised that the prospect hadn't occurred to her.

"All right, you got me," she said, sticking her tongue out. "I'm just homesick."

"We'll see," he told her. "For now, let's focus on making some sense out of these notes."

They had a lot of work to do on that front. As the days went by, they had interviewed more and more members of the church, and it became apparent that gossip within the community clouded the truth that they were seeking, and hearsay sent them in circles. They had decided that afternoon that they needed to regroup and reorganize their priorities going forward.

Older women, especially those that had been a part of the church for decades, were particularly eager to dish on any perceived unsavoriness that existed among their fellow parishioners. Digging through what was real and what was imaginary would be crucial to prevent them from going on any more wild-goose chases.

"Jim Donaughy's obviously got a thing for Annie Brogden," he recalled one octogenarian named Virginia Stanton saying during their interview with her on Thursday afternoon. "You can see how he hangs on to their handshakes just a bit longer during the peace. And he always makes sure that his family sits right by the Brogdens so he can look at Annie during the service. Of course that Annie isn't any better. Her parents moved into the neighborhood thirty years ago when she was just a little girl. When she hit her teens and blossomed, my goodness, the outfits she used to wear. She looked like a streetwalker. And do you think she moderated herself when she married Andy? Oh, no! That woman still packs on the makeup and walks into the church in those low-cut tops of hers. And after having two babies as well! There's no place for that among decent, God-fearing people."

His notebook was filled with interviews like this. It had been impossible for Manny to keep up with the pace at which many of these women talked, but their voices stuck in his memory, so he was able to fill in whatever gaps he found as he read his notes. He heard the thin, nasal voice of seventy-one-year-old Sharon Easton as she told him and Maureen about a dispute between two neighbors who each attended the church, which revolved around a fence being erected over the property line. Oliva Graves complained in her husky, cigarette-scarred voice about her son wanting to put her in a nursing home, failing to grasp the concept of what the detective was asking.

The interviews contributed very little to the investigation on the surface, but even still, Manny was intrigued by the multitude of underlying feelings that bubbled beneath the surface of the church community. True, whether or not Jim really had a thing for Annie almost certainly had nothing to do with the deaths of two young boys, but there still seemed to be quite a few grievances among the people of St. Mary's that, put simply, no one ever talked about out loud. Of those grievances, only one seemed to be connected in any way to Tom Lowes and Sandra Locke.

Paris Meintz and her husband, friends of the Lowes family, revealed that a former member of the church by the name of Steven Hanson had a very public falling out with Tom Lowes about three years prior. The rumor was that Tom had listed Steven's house on the edge of town for sale, and things hadn't quite gone according to plan. Tom had brought an inspector to the property to check out some work that Hanson had done in the basement, only to find a variety of code violations. Tom had reported these to the county, as most were electrical in nature and posed a significant safety risk.

"He got hit with some serious fines," Paris had said, "and I know Hanson blamed Tom. He said he had no right to report him and was just supposed to sell his home and not ask questions. Steve actually lost money on the sale, refused to pay Tom his commission, and left a threatening message on Tom's phone. He played it for us at dinner once. Steve said that Tom had screwed with the wrong person, and that he better watch his back.

"Then we heard that he tried to sue the county so that he didn't have to pay the fines. I'm pretty sure he barged into the county offices and yelled at Sandra, since it was her name on the notice. The courts threw out his case and he left the city, but I wouldn't put it past a guy like that to make good on his threats. He was never charged, but we're all pretty sure that his first wife left him because he hit her on a regular basis."

Unfortunately, the lead didn't go anywhere. Manny had given the name to Agent Layton, but it turned out that this Steven Hanson guy had apparently cleaned up his act, remarried, and was living north of Kansas City. Friends and family in the area confirmed that he, his new wife, and stepson had been on an end-of-summer vacation in Yellowstone for two weeks and had returned two days after the second murder. A cursory check by the Feds into their financial activity confirmed the dates of the plane tickets, rental car, and cabin they had stayed in.

"No one in this town is who they say they are," Manny mused aloud as he paged through his notebook. He turned to look at Maureen, and she was focusing on mopping up the remaining sauce on her plate with her last meatball. He found the way she ate adorable, and Manny couldn't help but stare at her as she let out a sated sigh and put her plate on the coffee table. It was then that she noticed him ogling her and turned to stare back, raising her eyebrows to silently question what he was looking at. Manny tried to speak but found only empty air coming from his throat. Maureen said nothing either, and the two simply sat for countless agonizing moments.

The hanging silence was broken by Manny's ringtone. He picked up his phone and checked the caller ID. It was his mother.

"Hi, Ma," he said as he got to his feet. "I'm kind of in the middle of something. Can I call you back?"

"I'll be quick, Cariño," his mother's voice sang through the phone. "Me and Papa just wanted to know if you're free for brunch tomorrow morning. We haven't seen you in so long."

"Um, yeah sure, Mama," he said, shifting uncomfortably on his feet and looking at Maureen seated on the couch. "I'll call you later tonight to firm it up. Love you."

Manny hung up the phone, cutting off his mother's farewell. He felt guilty that he didn't want Maureen to hear him speaking with his mother. He cleared his throat and put his phone in his pocket.

"Looks like you might get to spend some time at home after all," he said to her. "I got a brunch date with my parents. Unless, of course, you want to come with?"

"No chance," she replied.

"I'll drop you off at your place tomorrow morning then, and pick you up after I'm done?"

"Sure, that sounds fine."

Manny grabbed up the empty plates from the coffee table and took them into the kitchen, depositing them into the sink. He was about to head back into the living room when his phone began to vibrate in his pocket and its muffled ringtone hit his ears. A smile hit his face as he thought it was his mother calling him again. The smile faded when he looked at the caller ID. It was definitely not his mother.

"Agent Layton," he said quietly as he put the phone to his ear, "what can I do for you?"

"I hope I'm not interrupting anything, Detective," Layton's voice said.

"Not at all."

"I'm calling to inform you that we're planning on bringing

in Tom Lowes and Sandra Locke in tandem this week Thursday."

"Why so late?" Manny asked.

"We've decided to sit on the St. Louis cartels a little longer to see if we can find some more leverage. I'd like to have a few days to see if there's any suspicious activity before we go at a couple of grieving parents."

"Not to be rude, Sir, but why call me on this? Last I checked, I'm just your errand boy. I mean, that *is* why you stuck me with the directory assignment, isn't it?"

"I'm calling you, Detective, because I want you there when we interview Mr. Lowes and Mrs. Locke."

His stomach turned a somersault. "You want me there for what?"

"I'll let you know when I see you," came the reply. "In the meantime, keep going on the church angle just to be thorough and be at the Sheriff's Department at 10:00 a.m. on Thursday. If I need to speak to you beforehand, I'll call you."

The line clicked and Manny stood for a moment staring at his phone. An invite from the Bureau to help break the case. It was the chance he'd been looking for. He slid his phone back into his pocket and headed into the living room.

"I've noticed that you like your baseball," Maureen said, pointing at the television as he sat down on the couch. "Thought you might want to watch. Should I grab some beers?"

"Yeah, sure," Manny said, surprised at her offer.

Maureen jumped off the couch, ran into the kitchen, and was back in a moment with four beer bottles stuck between her fingers. She popped the top off two of them and handed one to him.

"So which team are the good guys?" she asked as she sat down and curled her feet under her. "The ones in red or the other ones in red?"

Her ignorance of the game made him laugh. Manny had no clue why Maureen was being so friendly all of a sudden, but she was putting him at ease. He leaned back on the couch and decided to put his assignment out of his mind until the game was over.

"The good guys are winning," he said, and it was true. It was already the seventh inning and the Cardinals were well ahead of Cincinnati.

They watched the rest of the game in silence and after it was over, Manny got up. "I should probably get to bed."

"But it's still early," she said.

"I know, but I still need to call my mom back about tomorrow, and I know she'll want to meet earlier for brunch than I would like. I'll see you in the morning. Goodnight, Maureen." Manny turned and began to walk to his bedroom. He was just turning the corner to enter the back hall when he heard her voice.

"Goodnight, Manny," it called softly.

The sound of his name finally coming from her lips almost made him turn back.

✝ƜƐ∩✝Ɏ-ƐIǪ∀✝

"In times of tragedy, it is easy to ask why," Father Patrick's voice boomed throughout the church. "It's easy to question God's plan for us. But, as difficult as it is, sometimes it is necessary for us to face forward and allow His plan to unfold. We cannot hope to understand the mysteries of God. But what we can do is hold our brothers and sisters close and enfold them with Christian love. For love is the true weapon against evil. Love is what can give us all the courage to go forth into the world and change it for the better. So I encourage all of you, before you allow these horrific occurrences to lure you into anger or hate, please reach for love instead.

"Thank you, Father Preston, for allowing me these few moments to speak to our congregation before your sermon this morning. I want to conclude by letting all of you know that if anyone is in need of council or special prayer, we are extending office hours tomorrow, Tuesday, and Thursday for an extra two hours in the evening. No need to ask for an appointment, simply come to the church office, and we will be happy to meet with you and offer whatever assistance you require."

The old priest stepped down and yielded the pulpit to his younger counterpart. Maureen looked on from the rear of the church where she leaned against the frame of the large double doors that provided the main access to the nave. She felt incredibly conspicuous, but she didn't have the stomach to enter the church and sit in one of the pews while the actual Sunday Mass was going on. The last time she had done that was a lifetime ago, and she had been forced by medieval means to do it. There wasn't a power on earth that could make her participate in a service again.

So, then, why was she there? After Manny dropped her off at her apartment that morning, she felt a compelling need to walk down to Main Street when she heard the bell tolling from the steeple of the church, signaling the beginning of 10:00 a.m. worship. Maureen had come with the crowd, taken up her place standing in the entryway, and watched. That was that.

Father Preston, now at the pulpit, was droning on about the Gospel reading they had just heard. She could tell that he didn't have the oration skills that Father Patrick clearly had. His tone was almost businesslike, as if focused more on the accuracy of the words than on inspiring any kind of spiritual awakening in his audience. Maureen couldn't even zero in on a central message. It seemed to her like he was just restating the chapter they had read. Mark, if she heard correctly. Something about an argument with the Pharisees over hand washing. She had no mind for biblical details.

Father Preston finished his sermon and stepped down from the pulpit as she continued to stand in her place and observe the holy display in front of her. The crowd's constant shift from standing to sitting to kneeling and back brought to mind the physical urgings of her mother when she was a small child to comply when all she wanted to do was sit in the pew and color. She shuddered with the memory. Four-year-olds shouldn't be held to the standards of adults. She found herself searching through the heads of the crowd, looking for families with small children to see if these people subscribed to the same method of spiritual enforcement. She didn't see any, though she heard a sharp shush from a mother near the back.

"And now at the Savior's command," Father Patrick's voice shook her from her thoughts, "and formed by divine teaching, we dare to say…,"

At this, the congregation joined in with their monotone chant, "Our Father, who art in heaven, hallowed be thy name. Thy Kingdom come, thy will be done…."

Maureen knew the prayer well enough. She followed along with her own inner monologue, but didn't allow her lips to move. She folded her arms across her chest, stared behind the altar at the crucifix, and reflected on all the shit that was allowed to happen in the name of that man hanging on the cross.

"The peace of the Lord be always with you," Father Patrick intoned to the crowd.

"And with your spirit," they responded and began to walk about, shaking hands and greeting their neighbors.

No one gave Maureen a second look, though some may have recognized her as the woman who accompanied the detective. She was fine with that. She didn't want to be noticed. And yet, she still couldn't bring herself to walk away. She was, yet again, rooted to the floor.

The throng began to assemble in the aisle for the Eucharist. She watched them line up to receive a wafer from Father

Patrick and then a sip of wine from either Father Preston or another similarly dressed man on the opposite side of the altar. It was an efficient assembly-line type of system that had the whole mass through in only a few minutes. Organ music from the balcony above her played until everyone was sitting again. Maureen knew the end of the Mass would be coming soon. Father Patrick stood at the foot of the altar and for the first time, made direct eye contact with her. Maureen froze.

"May Almighty God bless you," he said, holding her with his gaze as she felt the color drain from her face, "in the name of the Father, Son, and Holy Spirit."

"Amen," the congregation cried out.

Maureen swallowed hard and turned away from the oncoming procession out of the church. She pushed through the outer doors and, as calmly as she could, descended the outside steps, taking a seat on one of the last ones before the sidewalk. She kept herself off to the side and stared out at Main Street while the crowds of people began to trickle past her.

"I didn't think I'd ever see you here on a Sunday, Ms. Allen," Father Patrick said over her shoulder.

Maureen turned and looked up at him. She scrambled to her feet to stand in front of the priest, surprising herself with her knee-jerk reaction to the sight of a robed authority figure after all these years. "Well, uh, I was walking around and got curious."

"About?" he said, breaking into his familiar soft grin.

"I wanted to know if your Mass is as boring as I remember mine being when I was a girl."

"And?"

"Worse."

Father Patrick actually laughed out loud at this, longer than she thought was necessary. He even put a finger to his eye to wipe a tear as he calmed himself. "Thank you for keeping me humble, Maureen."

Maureen shifted her weight uncomfortably, unsure if he was purposely laying it on thick.

"So, you spent the entire Mass standing in the entryway. Any reason for that?"

"I like to stand?"

"And you didn't want to come up for communion?"

Maureen sneered at the question. "Look, Father, I can appreciate the pageantry and symbolism of what you do here, but it's not my thing. Besides, I may be able to set foot in a church without bursting into flames, contrary to what some might think, but what would your little flock do if they saw a woman get burned from the inside out after taking a sip of the Blood of Christ?"

"I don't believe such a thing would actually happen," the priest chuckled.

"Yeah, well, you're just too taken with my sparkling personality to be objective." This banter with the priest was actually beginning to annoy her. She turned and began to leave.

"I've heard whisperings around the church that the detective from the police department has been questioning our parishioners," he called after her.

Maureen turned around to face him.

"There's been quite a bit of tongue wagging as well about the mysterious woman he brings with him."

"Are you trying to piss me off?" she growled at him.

"Not at all," Father Patrick told her, breaking into a sly

grin once again. "But I needed you to turn around so I could firm up our dinner plans for Wednesday."

Maureen let out a frustrated groan. He had played her like a fiddle. "You could have just asked."

"You're a very difficult person to gauge, my dear." He took both of her hands in his. "I feel the need to throw the occasional curve ball with you. Just to ensure that your responses are, how do I put this, less guarded? A snappy response to an unexpected question is usually the most honest one in my experience. So, dinner?"

"Yeah, fine, I guess," Maureen said, giving in. "It's a nice thing you're doing, by the way. Offering extra time to talk to people and all. Do you think it'll help any?"

"I wouldn't offer services that I didn't think I could provide," Father Patrick said. "Very often, people who are struck by some sort of tragedy, even if only by proximity, find comfort in speaking to a trusted adviser."

"What if someone spills something about the case?" she asked. "Like, say someone knows something about what happened, and they tell you. Do you have some sort of confidentiality thing with your congregation, or would you call Manny and tell him?"

"You know, that's the first time I've heard you call the detective by his first name."

Maureen responded with an eye roll.

"I believe it would be my duty to lead them on the righteous course," he answered.

"And by that, you mean make them go to the police with the information?"

"I can only lead. I can't force them to follow."

"You're a priest. Don't people usually do what you tell them to? Aren't they afraid they'll go to Hell if they don't?"

"My view of the priesthood is not to dictate. Every sheep in a flock requires something different. For some, they need their shepherd to be a hard-handed disciplinarian. Others seek to unburden themselves in the confessional, and that is enough for them. Still more just need the love and understanding that our Lord can provide. But, if pressed, yes, in that specific situation you have just described to me, I would indeed encourage them to take their information to the authorities. And if I believe they do not intend to, you may rest assured that I will personally speak with your young Mr. Benitez."

"He's not *mine*!" she blurted out before she could stop herself.

"Maureen," he said softly, "take it from an old man who knows. The worst thing one can do is throw away something that could be wonderful simply because of fear."

Maureen didn't have any words. Her and Manny? Sure, she'd come around to the idea that he was her friend, but any more than that? Impossible.

"It looks like you have some other people who want to talk to you," she said to the priest, nodding in the direction of a man and woman standing behind him.

"I got the address, I'll see you Wednesday," she said as she walked down the steps.

Maureen ambled down Main Street back toward her apartment, her thoughts consumed by the old man's words. What did he see between herself and the detective? Whenever the priest spoke to her, it always seemed like he could peer right through her into the parts that she kept from the world.

She didn't understand how he did it, and why it bothered her and made her feel safe in equal measure. She admitted to herself, as she turned off Main and headed south toward her building, that she was most likely going to have to go through with having dinner with the man.

Manny was sitting on the tailgate of his truck waiting for her as she walked up. He had a half-finished bottle of soda in his hand and another unopened one next to him.

"I came back around 10:30 and you weren't here," he said, standing and handing her the unopened bottle. "What were you doing?"

"I just needed to go for a walk," she said. "You know, clear my head a little."

"Well I was banging on your door for ages," he replied. "So here." He reached into his pocket and brought out a small, red flip phone. He grabbed her free hand and pressed the phone into it.

"What's this?" she asked, surprised.

"Well, if I'm going to start letting you out of my sight from time to time, I'm going to need to be able to get a hold of you. So I went home quickly and got my personal phone. I mainly use my work cell anyway, so there probably won't be anyone but me calling you on this one. And you can get a hold of me, too, if you need. My work cell is speed dial two."

"Uh, thanks, I guess?" She didn't know what else to say, so she gave him her best approximation of a grateful smile and slipped the phone into her jeans. Then, to drive the point home, she cracked open the bottle he'd given her and took a big sip of cola.

"And sorry," he said. "About the soda, I mean. I was so

full after brunch that I didn't think to grab you any actual food."

"Don't worry about it," she told him. "I can hold out until dinner."

"Well, good news there, my ma gave us a heaping plate of her famous empanadas."

"That was nice of her, I guess."

"Yeah, she gets really into cooking when she thinks I have a girlfriend."

"But you told her you don't, right?" She was taken aback by how much her heart rate had climbed at the mention of that word.

"Take it easy, I just told her a little bit about you on the phone the other day, and she got carried away. Don't worry, I set her straight this morning."

Maureen stared at him for a moment. His posture mirrored the awkward conversation and she assumed she looked no better. "So, I'll just pop up and get myself some clean clothes?"

"Right. And I'll just wait here."

Not daring to say another word, Maureen turned and dashed inside and up the flight of stairs to her apartment. She felt her face flush, and her heart was still pounding as she entered. Tossing her empty cola bottle onto the couch, she made her way over to her bed. The pillowcase with her clothes inside was lying at its foot, where she had left it that morning. She knelt down and pulled a duffel bag out and rummaged around for more clean clothes, placing them on the bed. She then pulled out the dirty clothes from the pillowcase and shoved them into the duffel.

Last of all, she pulled out Manny's pistol. For the first

time since she had taken it from his dresser, she examined it closely. The manufacturer's name was etched into the coal-colored barrel. *Browning.* The grip was the standard brown, cross-etched style. She'd fired several guns like this one over the years at shooting ranges in the backwoods of some hick town. She'd never owned a gun in her own right, but she knew how to handle one, even if she wasn't a proficient marksman.

Besides, you don't have to be accurate if it's your own head you're firing at.

The glum thought overtook her as she tucked the pistol into the bottom of her duffel and slid the bag back under the bed. If things took a bad turn as she continued to stay in this town, she had to know she had at least one sure way out.

"But," she said aloud as she scooped her clean clothes into the now empty pillowcase and headed back down to meet Manny, "we'll just keep that as a last resort."

Twenty-Nine

"You'll call me as soon as you're done, right?" Manny asked as they sat in his truck in front of the red-brick Cape Cod that served as St. Mary's rectory.

Maureen sat in the passenger's seat, staring at the house and wondering why she had ever agreed to have dinner with Father Patrick. The days had passed uneventfully since she had last seen him on the steps of the church. She and Manny had continued to run down the church parishioners day in and day out with no success. She hadn't had a chance to think about tonight until just before leaving the detective's home less than half an hour before. Now that she could reflect on her position, she was sure she was in for an evening of the priest's ceaseless positivity and friendly conversation. She honestly didn't feel in the mood for that, but she had made a promise, and for some reason, she couldn't go back on it.

"Yeah, we've been over it. I'll call."

"And you have the phone, right?"

Forget the damn thing on the coffee table once, and the guy can't let it go. Refusing to reply, Maureen simply gave him a sideways look, pushed her door open, and hopped out, smoothing her shirt as she walked up the sidewalk toward the front door. She turned around to see Manny watching from the car. She shooed him with her hand, and he drove off down the street. She turned back to the house, walked the last few steps to the door, gathered herself, and rang the bell.

The door opened almost immediately. As usual, Father Patrick wore his friendly smile, along with dark slacks and a button-down shirt with a sweater vest over it. Maureen felt instantly underdressed in her jeans and flannel shirt, but she tried to push away the thought.

"Right on time," the priest chirped as he held the door open for her and motioned with his hand for her to enter. "Please come on in."

The dark wood of the crown molding and baseboards swallowed some of the light from the two antique lamps that were in the front room, causing the house to have a dim glow. Maureen could smell what she thought was furniture polish mixed with the certain smell that told her a person over the age of sixty lived there. It reminded her of her grandmother's home in Massachusetts when she was a child. She was actually relieved, thinking that maybe the inside of priests' homes smelled like their church office, and that smell would uncover memories she couldn't handle while sober.

Father Patrick led her past the staircase and through a hallway toward the rear of the house. Though she couldn't see it, she judged by the smell of hot oil and rich spices that the kitchen lay to her right. The priest opened a door at the end of the hall. It opened into a carpeted den that was decorated like a reading room or library. One full wall was taken up by an enormous bookshelf, filled to capacity with an array of leather-bound tomes, paperbacks of contrasting size, and other hardcovers placed on the shelves in whatever order they would fit. On the wall opposite this, there was a drink cart with several glasses and several decanters holding various liquids. Whiskey, wine, and either vodka or gin, Maureen guessed. Either Father Patrick liked his liquor, or he was eager to impress his guest.

A round card table draped with a plain, white tablecloth took up the middle of the room. Upon it was a basket filled with a loaf of bread wrapped in a linen napkin, a tray of butter, two plates with another napkin folded on each, and two sets of silverware. It looked like the type of setup she imagined a fancy restaurant would have. She began to wonder if the old priest saw this as some kind of date. It was an uncomfortable thought.

"Would you like a drink?" Father Patrick asked.

"Uh, sure, what do you have?" said Maureen, turning to find him standing next to the drink cart.

"Plenty of choices," he replied indicating each bottle with his hand. "I've got vodka, gin, and vermouth if you'd like a martini. I've got a nice port, though I might recommend that as a dessert drink. If you're a wine drinker, there's other wine, both red and white. I've got scotch, and there's beer in the refrigerator."

"Scotch, I guess," she said. He sounded like a man who actually knew a thing or two about the finer things. Maureen felt out of her depth, but scotch was whiskey and whiskey was always her choice, so she went for that.

Father Patrick nodded and pulled out the stopper from the decanter and grabbed a short glass. "Do you like it on the rocks or neat?"

"What do you recommend?" she asked.

"It's a fair scotch, but I like this particular one better on the rocks."

Maureen waved her hand at him, indicating that he should go ahead and pour.

Father Patrick plunked a few cubes into the glass and poured the liquor halfway up. He swirled it and handed it to Maureen.

She tried not to frown at the stingy pour and took a small sip. "Smooth," she said, giving the priest her best smile.

Father Patrick fixed himself his own drink, a gin martini by the looks of it, and set it on the table next to one of the plates.

"I have to excuse myself for a few minutes," he said to her. "The main course is ready to go whenever, but I decided I wanted to make some lumpia for an appetizer, and it's best served hot, right out of the oil. I'll be back shortly, and then we can eat. In the meantime, make yourself at home." The old man retreated out of the den and around the corner.

Maureen could hear him humming in the kitchen, along with the periodic sound of hissing and sizzling. She resisted the urge to walk over to the door and watch him work. She'd never heard of lumpia before and wondered what it was and if she would even like it. Instead, however, she grabbed a piece of bread from the table, filled her glass up, went over to the bookshelf, and began to stare at the titles, wondering what kind of books a Catholic priest kept in his home. She expected nothing but religious and Christian titles to fill the shelves. There were some of these, of course, gathered together on the very corner of the top shelf, almost out of eyeline. The more accessible shelves were filled with history books and even some works of fiction. Maureen traced her finger over the titles. *A Comprehensive History of French Indochina. 1968: The Year the War Was Lost. Kamikaze: The Divine Wind. The Tao Te Ching. Miyamoto Musashi and the Book of Five Rings. The Art of Happiness.*

It struck Maureen as an oddity that a man like Father Patrick had shelves full of books on Eastern thought and history. The Catholic religion, as she understood it, was supposed to look down on things like that. But then again, she could see from the start that the priest was in no way like most of the other men of God that she had known. It was probably for that reason that she had even agreed to this dinner with him. She had a feeling in the pit of her stomach that the evening would eventually turn into another one of his attempted therapy sessions.

She was staring at the section of the bookshelf that contained Father Patrick's fantasy novel collection, many written by novelists that she actually recognized, when the priest returned, carrying a platter of golden brown rolls. They looked to Maureen like the egg rolls that she was familiar with from Chinese takeout, only thinner. The smell of their fried shells filled her nose.

Father Patrick set the platter on the table and motioned to Maureen that she should sit down. She eased herself into the leather chair opposite him. He smiled, folded his hands, and closed his eyes. Maureen placed her hands in her lap and tried to be polite. She kept her eyes on the priest as he intoned the blessing.

"We thank you, O merciful Father, for the gifts of food we

are about to receive. May it nourish our bodies as your Holy Spirit nourishes our souls. In the name of Christ Jesus, our Lord. Amen."

Father Patrick crossed himself and opened his eyes. He picked up the platter of food and held it out to Maureen. She gingerly picked one of the rolls from the top of the pile. The priest nodded and kept the food in front of her, encouraging her to take more. Maureen obliged and took three more. Father Patrick placed three rolls on his own plate, put down the platter, and picked up his martini. He held it out to her for a toast.

"I want to thank you for having dinner with me," he said. "I know it's something that's a bit outside your comfort zone."

Maureen raised her glass in a toast, took a sip, and took a bite of one of the rolls. It really did taste like an egg roll, only the vegetables inside were crisper, the meat—whatever it was—was juicier, and the shell was thinner. She took another big bite and looked up at Father Patrick. The old man was looking at her with an amused look on his face, holding a knife and fork, having cut his own roll into bite-size pieces. Maureen covered her mouth in embarrassment, but the priest let out a short chuckle, put down his silverware, picked up a roll, and stuffed it into his mouth.

"I appreciate the trouble you went through to make dinner," she said, swallowing her food, "but I'm not sure where you're expecting this night to end."

"Oh, my dear," he replied, shaking his head, "I've been celibate for nearly thirty years."

"Have you ever had sex?"

"I wasn't always a priest."

"So that's a yes?"

"That's a yes," he said and took another sip of his drink, casting his eyes to the side.

"I hope she was special," she said, trying to cut the tension.

"Oh, she was," he said warmly. "But that was another life."

Maureen knew she shouldn't pry any further. She reached out, grabbed two more rolls from the platter, and took a bite of one before setting them on her plate.

"So what were you before?" she asked, trying to appear casual.

She swallowed her food and took another sip of her drink. The scotch was getting low in her glass again, and she began to wonder how appropriate it might be to get up and pour herself more so early in the meal. There was no need, it turned out. Father Patrick seemed to sense her thoughts. He wiped his face with his napkin and went to the drink cart, retrieved the decanter of scotch, and filled her glass. Maureen couldn't tell if he was being polite or didn't want to answer her question.

"You said you weren't always a priest," she said, deciding that she really wanted to know, "so what were you before?"

Father Patrick sat down in his chair and sighed. "To tell the whole story would take a very long time, so I'll give you the short version. After high school, I was in the military, serving my country in Vietnam. It was those experiences that woke me to the evils of this world and made me decide that becoming a priest and serving God and my fellow man would be my life's work from then on."

Maureen hadn't expected that to be the answer. She had pictured him as a college-educated man, maybe the president of a fraternity at a high-end university. There was little about the old priest that said *soldier* to her eyes. Father Patrick took a sip of his drink, shook off whatever malaise had come over him, and smiled.

"I think I'll grab the main course," he said. "Please excuse me for a moment."

He left the room and returned shortly with another tray with two steaming bowls filled with a fragrant broth, noodles, an assortment of vegetables, and what looked to Maureen like beef. Father Patrick set one bowl in front of her, along with a large ceramic spoon and a pair of chopsticks. He sat back down in his own place and gestured to her.

"Please eat," he said.

"What is it?" Maureen eyed the dish.

"Ah, one of my favorite dishes. It's called *pho*. A Vietnamese noodle soup. Very good, very comforting."

Father Patrick picked up his chopsticks and deftly scooped some of the noodles into his mouth, slurping them down. Then he picked up the ceramic spoon, filled it with the broth, and sipped it, smiling with contentment as he swallowed. Maureen tried to copy him, but she had never been good with chopsticks, and so she abandoned them for her fork. The dish was tasty, just as the priest had promised, with hints of ginger and garlic. They sat in relative silence as they finished the meal.

As Father Patrick cleared away the dishes, Maureen sat at the table, staring into her glass. She wasn't keeping count of her drinks, but she was feeling warm in the face. She promised herself that she would keep on her guard, though, being determined that no amount of drink would allow her to reveal anything to the priest that she didn't want to.

"Can I pour you another scotch?" Father Patrick's voice

startled her. He was standing at her elbow, holding the half empty decanter and a glass of scotch and ice of his own.

"I don't want you to think I'm a drunk," she said, though she knew she could go on drinking all night. Manny wouldn't come get her until she called, though, knowing him, he was probably sitting in a parking lot around the corner.

"I don't begrudge anyone their vices," he said, settling down opposite her. "I believe that we manifest our broken nature into certain behaviors. It's only natural. Facing the truth about oneself is exceedingly difficult without a crutch. No matter who you are."

At this, he raised his glass to her and took a sip. Maureen thought for a moment he looked as broken as she felt all the time. She shrugged her shoulders and decided that if the remainder of the night was going to be spent wallowing in a bottle, she wasn't going to let him outdo her.

"Well then, fill me up," she said, sliding her glass to the middle of the table.

He did, and they sat in uncomfortable silence for another few moments. Finally, Father Patrick leaned back in his chair and looked intently at her. "Maureen, I'm aware that you know that my reason for asking you to have dinner with me is to learn more of your story. I want you to know that it's okay if you don't want to speak to me about these things, but I believe it will help you. And that's all I want to do, I promise you."

"I believe you. I just don't know if I agree that it will help me. What more do you want to know? You already know me better than anyone else. Except for—"

"Detective Benitez," he finished for her. "Yes, he seems like a good man. Maybe too good?"

"I can't give him what he really needs," she said, echoing the thought that she had repeated to herself for days. She pushed the thought away and took an aggressive sip of scotch. "Can we just talk about something else?"

"As you wish," Father Patrick said. "Tell me something. You seem to have a certain discomfort with religion and God in general. Your abilities to see, at least to me, seem to suggest something that should be embraced as a gift from the Lord. Why don't you?"

"Are you sure you want to know?"

"I really do," he said.

Maureen pressed her lips together hard and debated about how much to tell him.

"You can trust me," he prodded.

"Fine," she sighed and took a long sip of her drink. "It started when my brother died. I was eight, he was five. He disappeared from our house one afternoon. My mother went insane, looked everywhere for him. The cops were in and out of the house for days. No one was coming up with anything.

"A few nights later, I had the first dream that I can remember. I was driving along the road, and I stopped at a mile marker. I can still see it as clearly today as I did then. Highway 3, mile marker twenty-five. Facing north. I went to the back of the car, opened the trunk, and pulled Braden out. His body was limp and cold, and I was carrying him from the side of the road into the woods. The whole time, even though I was young, I could tell it wasn't really me. The hands were covered with gloves, but I could tell they were too big to be mine. And Braden felt light in my arms. I knew I could never carry him like that. The arms dug out a little grave off a pine-needle-covered path, put Braden in, and covered him with leaves. It was fall so there were plenty of leaves to hide the body.

"I'm told that I sleepwalked downstairs that night. I remember waking up standing next to my mother in the living room and trying to tell her where Braden was. She told me that I just had a nightmare, that it meant nothing, and that I should go back to bed. I knew from school that to talk to the police you needed to dial 9-1-1. So I snuck into my mother's room to use her phone, and I called them and told them about the mile marker, and that Braden was buried off a path in the leaves.

"I know they found him quickly the next day, and they took my mother out to the crime scene. I was left behind. I found out soon enough that it was because I was to talk to an FBI psychologist. I didn't know any better at the time, so I told her everything that I had dreamed—seeing the mile marker, the arms and hands carrying Braden into the woods, everything. I really thought that they believed me, but a few days later, I was sent to the hospital with a bunch of other children. Apparently, they concluded that I had an emotional instability or something like that, and they said they wanted to remove me from the environment that caused me to make up these stories. What they were really doing was trying to observe me to find out if I had something to do with killing my brother.

"While I was there, I had more dreams. As I look back on it now, I'm fairly certain that one of the orderlies, I still don't know which one, was a kid fucker. The sicko would sneak into the other kids' rooms at night and touch them under the sheets. And I watched it all through his eyes. I tried to tell someone in charge, but they just said I was making it up for attention and did nothing. When we were in the common room, I would go find the kids that I had seen him abusing and tell them that I knew what was happening. One girl denied it, another boy yelled at me for telling, and we got into a fistfight and were put in isolation for a day. I had weekly therapy sessions with a shrink. They told me that if I accepted that I wasn't seeing the things I was, that the dreams didn't mean what I said they did, and that I was lying about the things I was saying, then I could go home. To this day, I don't know why I stuck so hard to my guns. Childish willfulness, I suppose."

Maureen paused for a sip of her drink and looked up at Father Patrick. The old man hadn't taken his eyes off her and sat as still as a statue.

"I was there for about three weeks before my mother bothered to come and see me. I hadn't even been allowed out to go to my brother's funeral. When she came to the hospital, she was accompanied by a very stern priest, and I was told that I would be going away to a special school where they would help purge me of the evil that was inside me. I was to stay there until I was clean. And that's how I ended up in Maine at Saint Dymphna's."

At the mention of the name of the school, the priest blinked.

"You've heard the name," Maureen said and Father Patrick nodded. "Then you know its reputation."

"I do," he confirmed.

Maureen polished off the rest of her scotch and filled her glass again before continuing. "All that stuff that came out in the press after it was closed down, it's not even a tenth of the story. The first thing they make you do when you get there is strip naked, put on a cotton robe, and kneel in this little chapel, praying to their statue of the patron saint. You have to stay like that for twelve hours, and if they come in and find you've fallen asleep or gotten up or done anything rather than kneel, they hit you with a rod and make you start over. I had to start over twice and was in there for something like twenty hours when it was all said and done. After you finish with that, you get sent to an isolation room with nothing in it but a picture of Jesus for you to reflect over. You have to stay in there for two days with no food, only holy water. They call it 'the purification period' and it was supposed to make you receptive to their interventions.

"I was one of the youngest there when I arrived. In all, I would say there were around one hundred girls at any one time. The older girls who had been there longer and were indoctrinated into the way things were done formed a kind of self-policing coalition and sometimes even helped the priests and nuns in dispensing punishments. Most of the girls paired up or collected in little groups to look after each other. The exceptions were the girls who had devils or demons in them like I did. There were only a few of us and, because of the severity of our conditions, we were the outcasts. Our education was also more specialized. We were placed on a regimen of regular exorcisms along with the usual Catholic education curriculum. I lost count of how many exorcisms I went through over the years, but it's probably somewhere in the mid-hundreds. The methods they used escalated until I'd grown big enough to be whipped."

Maureen stood up and turned around, lifting up her shirt a little so that the priest could see what she meant. "Ugly, isn't it?" she said, hoping he'd be shocked.

"Maureen," she heard him say gently, "I have to look very hard to see the physical marks on your body. But I do mourn for the toll they've taken on your soul. The people who did this were not working in the name of God. Please continue, if you can."

Maureen felt a tear begin to form in her eye as she listened to his words. She angrily brushed it aside and yanked her shirt back down, turning back and flopping down in her chair.

"I still had the dreams there," she went on. "You have no idea how true what you just said is. At least one of the priests was a predator. The school was like a hunting ground for him. For years, in my sleep, I was forced to watch him rape countless girls. I tried to do something about it once when I was fourteen. There was a sixteen-year-old girl named Stephanie who had been sent there by her parents because she'd gotten pregnant. She was maybe four or five months along when she got there. Despite their willingness to beat the shit out of people like me, the priests and nuns wouldn't do anything to hurt a pregnant girl physically. They'd emotionally abuse her, for sure, telling her that she was a whore and that she should repent. They were going to make her go through with childbirth—with no doctors—and if the baby lived, it was going to be taken and she would never see it again.

"Stephanie was the first person in five years who I had some sort of friendship with. She was really scared and confused as to why she was there, and I guess I just felt like I needed to protect her. I couldn't, though. She had a daughter, and after she'd recovered from childbirth, one of the priests started to visit her at night. I had to look through his eyes as she was raped and told that this was what whores deserved. She fought back at first, but after a couple of times, she began to simply accept it. She'd repeat the things he'd say, that this was how whores were baptized, and when he came on her face, she'd thank him for the blessing. It made me sick to watch her shrink and get brainwashed like that, so I went to the headmaster and told him what my dreams were telling me. He summoned the other three priests to his office, and the four of them began to berate me for making false accusations. They gave me a chance to take back what I had said and admit that I was lying. I refused. They broke both of my big toes before I told them what they wanted to hear. After they had finished with me, one of them, Father Michael, leaned over and told me that I was fortunate that a good fucking wasn't the method necessary to cure me.

"For the next three years, I kept out of the way of the priests and nuns as much as possible. When it became obvious to the adults that I was a lost cause, they started putting me on medication to numb me up and keep me quiet, figuring I was never going to be well enough to leave the compound ever again. I began stashing the pills. Some of the girls came from wealthy families and had a good amount of money with them, so I started selling them my drugs. By the time I was seventeen, I had enough cash to hit the road. I broke out, caught a bus down to Connecticut, and hid out in a little college town for a while. I got a waitressing job, and eventually I got connected with the right people who taught me to make fake IDs and such.

"From there I just kept moving. I never stayed in one place for too long. The nightmares always followed me. It never took more than a few months for them to catch up, but there were some periods of peace, I suppose. I tried to keep out of the way of the law, but it didn't always work out. I got arrested in Ohio when I got pulled over and had a half an ounce of weed on me. I spent three nights in jail since I didn't have enough money for bail, and I had to ditch my car. I knew I'd never be able to pay the fine, so I invented a new identity and split town."

"So Maureen Allen isn't your real name?"

"Closest I've used in a while," Maureen said, taking the opportunity to take another sip from her glass. "My birth name, if it makes any difference, is Maureen Allerton."

"What about your family?"

"My mom's from Ireland, married my dad after they met while he was on a business trip. They were in the process of divorcing when my brother died. I haven't seen my dad since. I'm pretty sure he married his secretary. Ma wasn't very shy about making it known that they were humping while he was still married to her. Mom came up to the school a few times for the first few years I was there, but they were short visits and were never pleasant, to say the least. I thought about dropping in on her after I busted out, but I decided there would be no point."

"Maybe one day," the priest said.

"I doubt it," she scoffed. "But, sure, maybe. Anyway, there's not much else to say, I suppose. I've seen most of this country in the last seventeen years. And seen too much in my dreams. But I deal with it."

"How?"

Maureen held up her glass. "This helps. Blacking out makes sure you don't dream, you know? I got numb to just the booze though, so in recent years, I've needed the help of pain killers every now and then."

"You don't buy them from dealers on the street or something like that, I hope."

"It's pretty amazing what you can do when you make the right contacts and learn how to forge prescription pads."

"Can't say I approve of that. I'm sure there are better ways."

"Yeah, but in this case, I prefer easy to better."

"So tell me, then," Father Patrick said, "have you ever taken the hard way and used this ability of yours to help others since you left the school?"

"I don't like cops."

"That wasn't the question," he said with a sternness that surprised her.

"A few years ago, I was in Chicago, living in a pretty shitty slum. It was a real shady building, you know? Cash only rents, no background checks or leases, and I'm pretty sure if anyone were to call the city inspector, the whole place would end up condemned. It was a perfect place for me, though. I got a couple of evictions on my record along with the other stuff, and even though I was using a different name, it was nice not to risk anything. Anyway, one night I was asleep, and I had one of my nightmares. I saw a young, black kid tied to a chair, his face was covered in blood, and I felt the shock run through my hand and arm as whoever I was seeing through punched him. Then I saw the hands hold a pillow up to the kid's head, press a gun to it, and pull the trigger. Poor kid's brains were all over the wall behind him.

"I looked on as the killer stalked out of the apartment and walked through the halls. The conscious part of my brain, the part that was me, recognized the doors of the apartment building as the one I was living in. The guy was on the second floor. He walked up the back staircase one floor and went into apartment 309. That was across the hall from me. That's when I woke up. I didn't really think, I just grabbed my things, left the key to the apartment behind, and got out. I stopped off at a pay phone, called the cops, and left them the tip. Then I took the L to the bus station and got out of town."

"And did they catch the man?"

"I don't know. I made a clean break, and I wasn't going to look back. I made the choice to get involved, but it cost me in the long run. That apartment may have been a stink hole, but I was making some of the best money I'd made in my life in the big city. Why does it matter anyway?"

"It might not," he said quietly, "but I believe that God is calling you to something. And it may be, that He will continue to send you these dreams until you accept your role and use this power to help your fellow man."

Maureen actually laughed at his assertion. She finished her drink and slammed her glass down on the table so hard that one of the ice cubes nearly jumped out.

"That's a good one, Father," she said. "What about that makes any sense?"

"Faith doesn't always make sense," he said, holding eye contact. "I don't presume to understand the mysteries of God, but I do know it is important to answer when called. And I do believe the old proverb that He never sets anything before someone that they can't handle. You've had something very great placed on your shoulders, so He must know that you can handle it. It's a profound thing to be offered an opportunity to change lives. You shouldn't take it lightly."

"You think I'm some sort of saint?" she scoffed. "How would me catching this guy change anything?"

"It'll give two grieving families closure. One can never discount how large of an impact a small thing can make. And perhaps more importantly, it just might change you. It just might be, that it's here where you find a true path to tread and leave behind your years of wandering."

"Well, I still think He could do better," Maureen said. The scotch was beginning to go to her head, and she was getting tired and didn't feel in the mood to fight his interpretation of her situation any further. "Maybe find someone who actually believes in Him."

"He found Paul on the road to Damascus." His smile returned. "Look at what that 'non-believer' accomplished."

"Well, we'll have to see, won't we?" she said, pushing herself up out of the chair. "Personally, no matter what happens here, I'm pretty sure my immediate future includes a nice stretch behind bars."

"Saint Paul, again," he answered, smiling wider.

"Whatever. Thank you for the meal, Father. It was delicious. Really. But if I'm going to go forth and conquer in the name of your God, I'm going to need some sleep first."

"Are you going to call your detective friend to pick you up?"

"Yeah, I'll call him from the street. Probably meet him up by Main Street."

"I'd feel better if you'd wait here," he said. "You've had quite a bit to drink."

"I can handle my liquor, Father," she scoffed.

Father Patrick looked intently at her. His stare made her feel like a child.

"Fine, I'll wait on the stoop. Alone."

Her answer seemed good enough for Father Patrick. He accompanied her to the door and opened it for her. Maureen stood on the front stoop, breathing in the night air. The smell of fresh-cut grass and the flowers in the gardens filled her nostrils, and she closed her eyes for a moment, briefly imagining an alternate life where she could actually live in a quiet neighborhood like this.

"Maureen." Father Patrick's voice made her turn around. "Thank you for allowing me to understand you. And I want you to remember that you don't have to let your past define who you are."

Maureen opened her mouth but found no words. She simply nodded at him as he closed the door. Then she turned away and sank down to sit on the cement, slipping her hand in her pocket to remove Manny's phone. She found his work phone number in the contacts list and hit the dial button.

"Hey, it's me," she said after he'd answered. "You can pick me up. All right, bye."

She continued to stare out into the night. Her eyelids felt heavy, and the world swayed on the edges of her vision. She couldn't wait to lie down. Hopefully she'd managed to drink enough for her night's sleep to be uninterrupted. What she had said to Father Patrick as they parted wasn't entirely in jest. She wasn't sure that bringing this child killer to justice would purge the nightmares from her life, but nothing else she'd ever done had worked either. So, if there was a chance that the old priest was right, then she'd have to play the role that she had been given.

†HIR†Y

Manny sat on a bench in the hallway of the Sheriff's Department, leaning his elbows on his knees and tenting his fingers to his lips. His eyes were fixed on a single tile on the floor in front of him, his vision occasionally broken by a pair of feet going by. He should have been thinking about his purpose for being there. Instead, he was thinking of Maureen. She seemed different ever since her dinner with the priest—more serious, determined. He told himself to let it go for the time being. The continual mystery of that woman needed to wait.

Manny jerked his head up at the sound of a slamming door across the hall. Agent Layton stood opposite him as if he had materialized out of thin air. The older man looked at him for a moment before stepping over and taking a seat next to him.

"Sandra Locke broke pretty quickly," he said. "We only needed to sweat her for about half an hour. It was just like we figured. She helped doctor the books and got the payoff to clear her mortgage. Unfortunately, she wasn't involved so far as to know who was behind the laundering. The LLC that purchased the building is routed through a couple dozen shell companies and bank accounts, and it's nearly impossible even for our forensic accountants to unravel it. So we need to get Tom Lowes to roll on his business partners. You ready?"

Manny let out a sigh and slowly rose to his feet. He straightened his tie and buttoned the top button of his jacket.

"Let's go," he said as he began to start up the hallway.

"Hang on, kid," the agent said, holding his arm in front of Manny. "Slow yourself. You can't go head-on at Lowes and expect him to just give it all up."

"So what are we going to do?"

"Not 'we'," the agent said. "You."

"Come again?"

"I've read all your notes on the case," Layton replied. "I was particularly drawn to your early ones, where you detailed how you decided to follow our good Ms. Allen the night you caught her at the Lowes house. You caught a small throwaway comment from a bartender, who you had never met, and you followed your instincts. So follow your instincts now. How would you suggest we go about handling our situation here?"

Manny thought for a moment, pacing the hall. Suddenly he realized that he hadn't seen anyone come out of the interview room since the agent's exit. A smile came to his face.

"Does Tom Lowes know that Sandra is here right now?" he asked Layton.

"He does not," the agent replied, grinning.

"And Tom is still out in the waiting room, correct?"

Layton nodded.

"Then I think I have an idea. We're going to take her out, right past him, and make him paranoid about what she might have told us."

"Bravo," said the agent.

A few minutes later, Manny and Agent Layton were silently escorting Sandra Locke through the halls toward the waiting room. The agent had made sure that the woman's hands were not cuffed and remained visible in front of her. After all, they could only charge her as an accessory to fraud, and she was technically a free woman. Whether the county courts wanted to charge her, was their business.

They rounded the last corner and came into the waiting room. Tom Lowes was sitting in a chair next to his wife, an uneasy look threatening to break through on his face. Manny and Layton slowed their pace, making sure that the broker had ample time to see Mrs. Locke with them. Sandra's eyes remained cast down at the floor, but as they neared, Manny saw them raise the slightest bit and find Tom. He saw that the man had caught her look and was now making a concerted effort not to continue looking in their direction.

Gotcha.

Manny turned his head to hide his satisfied look and led Sandra to the front doors and then mimed a quick conversation with the agent. Layton headed in the opposite direction, and Manny waived over one of the deputies and asked him to escort Mr. Lowes to interview room three.

Following the plan that he and Agent Layton had formed, Manny went to the break room for a cup of coffee and waited a good twenty minutes before he headed over to the interview room himself. He made sure he was carrying a manila folder with several papers inside. Several blank papers. He entered the room where Tom Lowes sat, leafed through the folder without looking at him, then excused himself, stating that he had the wrong file. He exited, marched around to the viewing area and exchanged his manila folder with a forest green one that the deputy was holding. In a few moments, Layton came around the corner and stood by the window. He nodded at Manny.

That was Manny's cue to enter. The agent was going to watch from behind the glass, and he would conduct the interview. Between the strategy that they had mapped out and Tom Lowes' guilty conscience, they would get what they needed.

"Mr. Lowes," he said as he walked into the room and took a seat at the table opposite the broker, "you're not under arrest, but I would appreciate it if you would answer my questions."

"Must I? I mean, I've heard that you're no longer with the investigation."

"That is technically true," Manny replied turning and nodding toward the mirror, "but would you rather have me or a federal agent sitting across the table from you right now? Sandra already talked. You might as well help us out. Help yourself out. And if not for you, for the memory of your son."

"You don't understand," Lowes said, looking down at the table. "I can't. More lives will get destroyed."

"Only if you don't talk," Manny said, allowing his voice to build to a crescendo. He and Layton had worked out his act: first he'd play on the emotions of a father, then he'd bring the thunder.

"That deal you did for the county building," he continued. "We took a hard look at the numbers. Over a hundred fifty grand for work that should cost no more than thirty? Awfully suspicious. And then there's the seventy-five thousand dollar payoff to Sandra to go along with it. Tell me how it is, Tom. You got in bed with some shady businessmen, laundered money for them, and then decided that, hey, why not get yourself and Sandra some profit, too? Problem is, when you steal from these people, they tend to retaliate in violent ways. Your son is dead because of what you did!" Manny felt a pang of guilt for coming down so hard as the man buried his head in his hands.

"My wife, Kristin, has a brother, Darren," Tom finally began. "He owns a construction business outside St. Louis and about a year ago, he got into some financial trouble and was going to lose his company. One of the drug cartels came to him and offered to invest, and in exchange they used his business to help in their money laundering. He came to me when I put the Glenbrook buildings on the market and told me that he would pay above list price for it. I knew what he— they—wanted it for, but it was a cash deal, quick close. All we had to do was agree to the work they wanted to do and get the county treasurer to go along with the billing.

"It wasn't easy to convince her, but when the bank began foreclosure procedure, one of their lenders called me for a valuation of the property. I knew that was my in, so I got him to let me know how much she needed in order to keep her house. I promised her the money in exchange for going along with the plan. I filtered the money out of the project up front. I wasn't thinking, though. I figured the bosses would never notice it since they make so much, but they did, right away. I panicked and made a deal. I said I'd pay them back double what I took. I figured I could do it within two months. But, we didn't make our sales goals and I was short.

"Darren was the go-between. He told me that I had to either give them my brokerage, or something bad would happen to me. Darren begged me to give up my company to them, but I couldn't do something like that to my employees. I told him to tell them I'd pay quadruple, and they'd have their money in sixty days. He told me guys like this don't mess around, that I was being stupid, and to punish both of us, they might make *him* do something. But, I paid the money on time, and I never heard anything from them since. I thought that was it. And now..."

Tom's voice wavered, and he bit into his clenched fist, stifling a whimper. No father deserved what Lowes had been through, but he reminded himself that it was of the man's own making. And now he had a suspect.

"I'm going to have someone come in," he told Lowes, standing up from the table, "and have you make a written statement. And we'll need your brother-in-law's address." Manny strode out of the room. It was a terrible story that he had just confirmed, and he couldn't help but feel for all involved. However, he was about as satisfied as he could be.

"What do you think?" Agent Layton said as Manny came into view.

"Sad," he replied. "But it does tie everything up nicely. If Darren was forced to kill those kids by the cartel, it would fit the evidence."

"How so?"

"The vomit at the first crime scene. He got queasy cutting up and burning his nephew and puked. He wasn't emotionally connected to the second victim, so he wasn't affected as much. I'd also bet that he was given the blueprint of how to carry out the hits. Cartels are mostly made up of Latinos, and most Latinos are Catholic. They'd know the Bible as well as anyone, they'd just pervert the written word and use the bloody parts as a message. What do you think?"

"I think it all fits," the agent affirmed. "We'll track down the brother-in-law and bring him in. He'll talk."

"Maybe you'll get to put another dent into the St. Louis cartel."

"It would be a nice silver lining, and as much of a win as we can hope for in all of this. Nice work, Benitez. We'll take it from here, but you'll feature prominently in our report just like I promised. You can head on home." Layton slapped him on the shoulder and smiled.

Manny nodded and headed in the opposite direction, handing his file to the deputy standing along the wall. He blew out a deep breath of relief. He may not get to complete the arrest of the man responsible, but he had been a key component in the investigation. And that was enough for him.

Wasn't it?

Manny walked through the waiting room on the way out the door. As he went, he saw Tom and Kristin Lowes in the corner. He couldn't hear what was being said, but Tom was doing the pleading and his wife was crying and pushing him in the chest. She must not have known what was actually going on until now. Manny shook his head and pushed open the door.

Tom Lowes was right. Two boys were dead, but these murders were going to destroy so many more lives.

THIRTY-ONE

Manny came back with a giant pizza in his hands and a giant smile on his face. He was as genuinely excited as Maureen had seen him in a week. He told her all about his interview with Tom Lowes, and how they had finally caught the break in the case that they had been looking for.

"The Feds are going to bring in the brother-in-law," he said as they stood in the kitchen. He was grabbing two plates out of the cupboard and barely pausing for breath. She could hardly keep up with him.

"I couldn't have done it without you," he said as he handed her one of the plates with two slices of pepperoni on it. "I want you to know that."

Maureen's relief that the ordeal was finally over was mixed with trepidation over what was to come. Now that she had fulfilled her purpose, what would become of her? Once the killer was in custody, would Layton come back for her and force her to serve time for her other crimes? Could she parlay her cooperation into leniency? Or would she have to go on the run again? Part of her wanted to stay and make a more permanent home, maybe even with Manny. But deep inside she knew that it would never work. Even though her feelings for him had begun to deepen, it would never last. But that was something for the next day. For tonight, there was only one thing to do.

Maureen went to the cabinet and pulled out two of Manny's double-shot glasses and set them on the counter. She then grabbed the premium bottle of silver tequila that she had been saving for something special. This seemed like as good a time as any, so she filled both to the top and handed one to him.

"A little toast," she said, grabbing her own glass and raising it to him. "To the best detective I've ever known, and the only cop I've ever trusted."

"Salud," he said, smiling and tipping the shot into his mouth.

"Sláinte," she said, before draining her own glass.

Maureen filled both glasses again before capping the bottle, tucking it under her arm, and carrying it and her food into the living room. She plopped the bottle and her plate on the coffee table and took a big bite of her pizza. Manny sat down next to her and turned on the television, clicking through the channels until he found the sports show he was looking for.

"So, Irish, huh?" he said as he put down the remote and picked up his own plate.

"What's that?"

"That toast of yours. It's Irish, right?"

"Yeah, so?"

"I didn't know you were Irish, that's all. I don't think Allen is an Irish name."

"I'm pretty sure I told you that."

"You said 'old country' when you told me about your mom. Never said that meant Irish."

Maureen took a swallow of her tequila. She didn't know how she felt about telling another man in Sycamore Hills about her past, even if that man was Manny. She decided, since he obviously liked her and she didn't think he was so bad either, that she could give him a little. But he'd have to reciprocate.

"Half Irish. Mom's a Keane from Donoughmore in Cork. Dad's American. He's older, liked younger women. My mom caught his eye while he was on a business trip, whirlwind romance, better life for her, blah blah blah, you get it."

"But they obviously broke up. Did it have something to do with your brother's murder?"

Maureen nearly choked on her pizza. "I know I didn't tell you that!"

"Layton," he said. "It's in his case notes. I shouldn't have brought it up. I'm sorry."

"Just forget about it," she replied, shaking her head and finishing her drink before pouring another. "But yeah, you're right, they broke up. Though they were already separated when my brother died."

"I'm guessing you don't see them often, judging by your nomadic existence."

"Haven't seen my dad since I was eight. Mom, maybe around thirteen."

"No desire to reconnect?"

"My dad left me and my brother with our conservative, superstitious Irish Catholic of a mother to screw his secretary. Why would I want to have anything to do with either of them?"

"We all need family."

"Not all of us."

Manny took a drink of tequila and finished off his first slice. Maureen sat quiet for a moment before deciding she wanted her reciprocity.

"What about you?" she asked the detective.

"What about me?" he replied.

"You've had me here basically as your hostage for more than a week," she said, putting as much honey in her voice as possible, "and yet, you haven't told me anything about yourself. I've told you stuff about me. It's only fair."

"What do you wanna know?"

"You're a smart guy, obviously. Why be a detective?"

"I wanted to give back to my hometown."

She took a hard look at him and their eyes met. The detective held her stare for only a moment before he blinked and looked to the side. "You're lying," she said triumphantly.

"How can you tell?" he asked with a grin.

"I'm psychic."

Manny looked as if he was trying to hold back his laughter at her on-the-nose joke, but it trickled out regardless. Maureen smiled too.

"I've got an idea," she said.

Maureen jumped off the couch and dashed into the kitchen. She grabbed another plate and piled a few more slices onto it before shoving the box with the remaining pizza into the fridge. Out of the fridge, she pulled out a six-pack of beer and then returned to the living room. She set the fresh provisions on the table and filled both their glasses up with tequila again.

"I've got a game we can play," she said to Manny, sitting down and tucking a leg under her. "You've been trying to get to know me, but you haven't told me much about yourself, so I've got a way we can do both. We take turns asking each other questions. If you answer, the other person has to drink. If you don't answer, then you have to drink. You can play with beer or tequila, your choice."

"I'm game."

"Opening shot first," she said and grabbed her shot glass and drank it down.

The detective hesitated for a second, then followed suit. She reached for the bottle again, but he beat her to it and poured two more shots for them and pulled two beers out of the case, opening them and setting one in front of each of them.

"All right," he said, "who's gonna start?"

"Where did you go to school?" Maureen asked, not daring to give him the first question.

"Truman High here in town. Then I studied criminal justice at Saint Anselm in New Hampshire."

Maureen drank half of the tequila in her glass.

"What about you?" he asked. "What was your school?"

"School of hard knocks," she said.

Manny gave her a sideways look.

"Fine," she said, rolling her eyes. "It was called Saint Dymphna's. And that's all you're gonna get out of me."

He took the entire shot of tequila in front of him.

Trying to show off for me, huh? "I don't even think I know how old you are," Maureen said, taking a sip of her beer to chase down her second slice.

"Twenty-nine. Would it be rude to ask you the same?"

"I don't care," Maureen said. "I'm cradle robbing at the ripe old age of thirty-four."

275

They clinked glasses and downed their shots again.

"How many times have you been arrested?" Manny asked.

"I thought it was my turn, but whatever. I'd say at least half a dozen times, but it might be a couple more."

"What was the worst offense?"

"Uh-uh, you don't get two in a row." She waited for him as he took a heavy swallow of beer. "Who was your first kiss?"

"Leslie Wynn, eighth grade."

They continued their back and forth with the bottle of tequila slowly draining down and the beers falling along with it. Craziest place she'd ever had sex (truck stop bathroom). First time he got drunk (third week of college, puked in the bushes of the house where the party was). Maureen avoided the questions about her family but answered the rest. And she learned more about him tha she ever thought she would. Some was boring. He played on the junior varsity football team in high school but quit after his junior year when it became obvious he wasn't going to be good enough for varsity. His mother was the first member of her family born in America, and his father was a naturalized citizen from Mexico. He'd only been out of the country once to visit his mother's family in Puerto Rico. Some was actually a bit interesting. When he was a kid, he had a pet snake named Chavez who got out once and ate the family guinea pig. He tried out for the cheerleading team in college to meet girls and ended up being the mascot for the basketball team for two years. Eventually, Manny's speech was starting to slur enough for Maureen to ask her first question over again.

"Why be a detective?" she asked.

Manny paused, blinking, as if trying to decide something.

After a moment, he reached for his half full shot glass and slowly began to raise it to his lips. Maureen placed her palm over the top before he could drink it. His mouth brushed the back of her hand. Maureen felt her heart jump, but she kept her face neutral. With a tiny smile and raising of his eyebrows, Manny acknowledged that she wasn't going to allow him to not answer the question. He sighed and put his glass down.

"It wasn't easy growing up as a Hispanic kid in a lily-white town," he said, leaning back and looking up at the ceiling. "I mean, I'm as American as they come—both my parents are legal citizens and Spanish is actually my second language—but all people see is this brown skin, and they listen to all that bullshit on TV about Latinos sneaking into the country and stealing jobs. I guess I let it affect me more than I thought. And it doesn't help now, when all my coworkers were the king-jock seniors while I was still in grade school.

"Anyway, all I wanted to do was get out of here when I graduated. Saint Anselm had a full-ride scholarship available for a minority student who wanted to study criminology. I was third in my class, and my SATs were thirteen-seventy, so I went for it. I'd always liked detective stories, and I'm good at solving puzzles, so I thought I might be able to make a difference by solving crimes. And wouldn't you know it, I got it. And I gotta tell you, I really liked it, and I was good at it. But no matter how many friends I made, it was a small private school, and the kids who went there had money—and lots of it. They didn't let me forget that I was there on charity because of my ethnic background.

"During my senior year, the FBI put out a call for the country's top criminology students for an early recruitment interview. My student adviser sent in an application on my behalf. I didn't even know. But I said I would do the interview. I went down to DC, but on the day of the interview, I just couldn't make myself go. I caught a bus out and rode all the way back up north. I never told anyone that I bailed, I just said I didn't get accepted.

"I ended up at the New Hampshire Justice Department as an aide, and I was pretty good at that too. Learned more about the inner workings of the law and saw firsthand how the DAs used police evidence to build cases. My bosses recommended me for a couple promotions over the next five years, but I never could pull the trigger. I don't know, afraid I guess.

"I decided to just come home. It seemed easier to settle into mediocrity down in Missouri than up in New England. I applied here at the police department. They didn't even have a detective before I came, but Captain Wellner decided to bring me on board. That was a little over eighteen months ago."

"Something tells me that you haven't been solving murders this whole time," Maureen said, leaning on her elbow and watching him.

"This is my first, and I gotta tell you, I wanted to be the one to solve it. I wanted it bad. Maybe too much." Manny shrugged and leaned forward to grab his glass. He swirled the liquor around before tipping it back into his mouth and slamming the glass back on the table.

Maureen had about half a beer left in front of her. Deciding that he shouldn't drink alone, she drained it in two swallows.

"You did a good job," she told him. "You got that Lowes guy to give up his brother-in-law."

"Yeah, but let's be honest, I was only in that room on

278

the charity of Layton. He could have done it himself just as easily."

"But you've already proved that you're really good in the interrogation room."

"I couldn't crack you," he said with a cynical laugh.

"You got closer than anyone."

Manny turned his eyes toward her. They were beginning to shimmer, and the effects of the booze were slowly eroding his mask of self-confidence. He stared at her for a long, unwavering moment. Then slowly, he lifted himself off the couch and pivoted to face her. His mouth twitched, looking as if it wanted to pucker. He moved closer, but slowly. Maureen could tell he was waiting for a sign. She froze in her seat, but she didn't put up any resistance. Instead, she closed her eyes and waited.

His kiss was soft and wet. He tasted like tequila and pepperoni, of course, but his lips were smooth, and Maureen couldn't help but kiss back, allowing herself to grasp his face in her hands and pull him into her. Almost immediately, she found herself lying back on the couch and pulling him on top of her. She felt Manny's hands glide up her leg before he rested one behind her head and the other cupped her breast, causing her nipples to harden and press on the padding of her bra. She thrust her chest upward as he ran his lips down her neck and began to kiss her collarbone.

After a moment, Maureen's brain snapped back to reality. She wanted this for sure, wanted him, but her need to be in control overwhelmed her other senses. She gently pushed him in the chest and guided him to a seated position on the couch. He offered no resistance, and ever so slowly, she ran her hand between his legs and felt him begin to get hard. She straddled his lap and clasped both hands behind his neck. She leaned forward, grinding her hips into him and gently ran her tongue around his ear before trailing it down his neck. He let out a gasp of pleasure and reached his hands under her shirt. Maureen felt her heart jump as his fingers began to caress her back.

"No," she gasped in a barely audible whisper and stopped his hands.

Manny froze for just a moment and looked at her. He seemed puzzled and startled by her reaction. She wanted to warn him about her scars and explain why she didn't want him to touch them, but she couldn't get a word out. Manny seemed to realize why she stopped him as he gently began to run his hand back and forth on either side of her spine, his fingers tracing the crisscrossing path that each of the pale, white marks made. He stared deep into her eyes and despite the liquor, his own were full of a saddened sympathy that showed her he understood. It was a look that she had never seen a man give her in her entire life.

Maureen stared back at him, bit her lip, and slowly moved her hands to the hem of her shirt. She drew it over her head, threw it to one side, and immediately reached back to unhook her bra. She did her best to tell herself that the only desire she was feeling for him was a physical need for sex, but it was impossible to deny the emotional connection to Manny she was feeling in that moment. The look he had given her made her feel truly seen. It was frightening and thrilling at the same time, and she decided to satisfy herself to the fullest.

Maureen cupped Manny's face and threw every ounce of lust that was building inside into her kiss, probing his mouth with her tongue and grinding her hips even harder against his bulge. Then she grabbed him by the back of his head, and shoved his face into her chest, forcing a rock hard nipple into his mouth. She closed her eyes and allowed herself to give in to pleasure, if only just for one night.

THIRTY-TWO

Ra'ah's knife glinted in the candlelight as he drew it across the whetstone in his left hand, pleased with the work that it had already done and eager for the next task. His mission had gone far from perfectly thus far, but he had at last found his next soul to save. She would be easy to follow, and her weakness would give him ample opportunity to acquire his sacrifice. It would need to be purified first, a complication in his plans that he had not foreseen, but that was of little matter. Ra'ah had the perfect place for the ceremony. He was glad that he had made sure it stayed under his control.

Ra'ah set his knife on the table and pulled out a piece of parchment. His report to the Urim was late. The success of his mission was paramount to their plans, being the litmus test for the greater work that would soon begin. Once he proved that they could accomplish their goals, their ranks would swell, and the real battle would begin. He was a servant of a greater power, a cause beyond human understanding. Their order, hidden long in the shadows, could soon step into the light of day and lead the world to paradise.

Ra'ah began to write, detailing all his work, the good and the bad. He lamented his weakness in the yard of the first sacrifice, where his body betrayed him and he vomited after removing the child's intestines from his body. He thanked God for forgiving him and allowing him to complete his second sacrifice in a much stronger fashion. He chronicled his brilliance that allowed him to sit and wait for the sinners to come to him, rather than having to hunt them down. He advised on how to effectively evade detection by the federal agents.

And of course, he warned them of the meddling detective and his companion—the bewitched whore who called herself Maureen.

THIRTY-THREE

Manny opened his eyes to the sunlight glaring in through the window. As he yawned, the dull ache in the back of his head and the cotton in his mouth reminded him of how much he had drunk the night before. The light stung his eyes. His stomach bubbled. He was lying naked in bed and felt amazing.

The memories of the night before played out like a movie in his mind. The moment his lips met Maureen's was a revelation. He'd never been with a woman who did the things that she did. She'd finished him so quickly on the couch that he almost felt ashamed. But she'd taken him by the hand back to his bedroom, brought him back to life, and proceeded to continue blowing his mind with how she made love. The way she took his bottom lip between her teeth and used her hand on the small of his back to guide him into her. The way her breasts heaved as she rode him furiously just to the point of a second completion and then backed off to tease him some more. To his mind, it was the best he'd ever had, and by the time he and Maureen had finally curled up in each other's arms, he had begun to think he might actually be falling in love with her.

Manny rolled over to throw his arm around Maureen and found her side of the bed empty. The shock of sitting up as quickly as he did sent a jolt of pain through his head. He steadied himself for a moment before he could focus his vision on any one thing. Around his room were the signs of their night together. His jeans and shirt were crumpled on the floor by the door. His boxers were at the foot of his bed. He found Maureen's satin thong lying next to them. He picked them up and twirled them around his finger like some kind of immature college student before he carefully laid them on top of his comforter on the bed. Her jeans were still on the floor where she had stepped out of them after pushing him onto the bed. He knew that her tank top and bra were likely still in the living room where she had taken them off. What he didn't know was where she was.

Manny pulled on a pair of shorts and tiptoed out of his room and into the hallway. He moved slowly, trying to keep the dizziness at bay. The first place he looked was the bathroom across the hall. The door was closed so Manny tapped on it softly and whispered her name. There was no answer, and he could not hear any water running in the shower so he tried the knob. It was unlocked, and the door swung open with a push. The bathroom was dark and empty. Manny flipped on the light and the florescent glow of the fixture in the ceiling hit his eyes like an ice pick. The stab in his brain brought to him an awareness of his own body that reminded him that hangovers weren't the only aftermath of a night of drinking. He stepped over to the toilet to relieve the pressure in his bladder and was almost amused to notice two condoms sitting atop the refuse in the wastebasket. He didn't remember going through two—or going into the bathroom to throw them away afterward—but then, he wouldn't have been surprised if there were gaps in his memory. He hadn't drunk the way they had in years.

Manny flushed the toilet, washed his hands quickly, and went back out to continue his search for Maureen. He poked his head into the two other bedrooms on the way down the hall toward the living area. They were empty as well. He came to the end of the hall where he had partial views of both the living room and the kitchen. He went to his right when he caught a glimpse of movement in the corner of his eye. Manny moved toward it, rubbing his eyes to clear them a bit more and was met with a startling sight.

Maureen was sitting on the floor of the kitchen, her back against the cabinets below the sink, rocking slowly back and forth. Her eyes stared through the wall opposite her. She was naked, and her lips were parted, moving ever so slightly as if a silent dialogue were being carried out. In her right hand was a kitchen knife that she was lightly gliding across the floor.

Manny carefully stepped around her and sat down on her left, away from the blade. He slowly put his arm around her and gently reached for the knife. To his surprise, she handed it to him with no objection and turned her head to him. Despite the desperation deep in her eyes, her face was even.

"He took another one," she said softly. "It just happened. Maybe less than half an hour ago."

Her eyes moved back to the floor where she had been dragging the knife. He followed them with his own and saw that she had carved the now familiar Aramaic characters. אורים *Urim*. Light.

Manny couldn't be totally sure whether the churning in his stomach was due to Maureen's chilling revelation, or the remnants of the previous night, but he forced himself to his feet, sticking the knife back in the block. Maureen continued to sit, seemingly lost in thought. Her breathing returned to normal and, aside from having her legs drawn up to her chest, she made little effort to conceal her nudity. Manny cast an eye around her. Something was missing beside clothes.

"You didn't vomit," he said.

"I didn't feel nauseous," she said, looking up and shrugging. "Maybe I'm getting more desensitized to this. I don't often have this many dreams looking through the same person's eyes. I haven't thrown up since that night in the jail. I don't know. I feel like I'm getting deeper into his mind."

"You said he took someone. You mean he killed again?" Manny asked.

"No. I mean took, as in abducted."

"Okay, tell me *exactly* what you saw."

"I'll try." Maureen got to her feet and began to pace around the kitchen, running her hands through her hair, as if trying to massage the memories out of her scalp.

In spite of the gravity of the situation, Manny couldn't help himself from being distracted by her body. He did his best to focus.

"It was another boy," she began slowly. "I'm sure about that. He was younger than the other two, and he was taken right out of a car. A black car, four doors. I don't remember much more about the surroundings than that; there's always a blur on the edge of my vision when I'm in the dream. Maybe there were some trees, but I can't be sure. I remember more about how I felt—he felt. It was the first time I could discern which emotions were mine and which were his. He felt a rush of... justification is the only way I can really describe it. But it was like the feelings weren't directed at the kid. They were directed somewhere else. And he said something, too. What was it...? It's on the tip of my tongue."

"What?" Manny asked eagerly. "What did he say?"

"Give me a second!" she shot back. Maureen closed her eyes and turned her head side to side.

Manny looked on, hoping whatever she could come up with would break the case for them.

"'Rebirth first,'" she said. "That's all I can remember. Rebirth first."

"Well that certainly doesn't help," said Manny, crestfallen at the meaninglessness of it. The frustration didn't help his hangover, either. "What does that even mean?"

"I don't know, it's not like they were my words!"

"I didn't mean to snap at you, I apologize." Manny moved over to Maureen, put his arms around her, and held her tight.

She returned the hug, though it seemed that she pushed away awfully quickly. "I should throw some clothes on, and we should hit the road and try and figure out what this is all about." She turned and headed toward his bedroom.

"I can barely move after all that drinking," Manny said, taken aback by the fact that the previous night had seemed to leave no ill effect on her. "Maybe I should make us something to eat first."

"You call that drinking?" she said mockingly over her shoulder. "I'm gonna jump in the shower, so get something to eat and pull yourself together. I'll drive. Ten minutes."

With that, Maureen disappeared around the corner. Manny stood still in the kitchen, dumbfounded for a moment.

From the moment he had grabbed her from the bar, she had acted as though the investigation was an imposition on her life. Now she was taking the lead. *What had changed?*

Manny moved over to the refrigerator. Three pieces of pizza from the previous night were left. He grabbed the box, tossed the cold slices onto a plate, and put them in the microwave. He punched in forty-five seconds and flipped on the sink faucet to pour himself some water while he waited. Mindlessly, he drank down half a glass and filled it up again. He sipped his water slowly while staring out the window into the yard, continuing to ponder the enigma that was Maureen.

The beep of the timer snapped him back, and he headed over to the microwave. The pizza's cheese was still cold, but Manny didn't care. The crust was warmed up enough, and the sensation of food in his mouth and stomach was easing his nausea. His headache, however, was getting worse, and he couldn't believe that Maureen wasn't hungover. Moreover, she hadn't complained of any pain following her dream. Perhaps she was right and something was changing the more she saw through this psychopath's eyes. Anything was possible.

Manny was chewing on the crust of the final piece when Maureen came back in, wearing her jeans from the night before, a clean T-shirt she had stolen out of his dresser, and her flannel shirt tied around her waist as usual. She let her hair hang wet, but he knew that eventually, it would be put up in a ponytail. She walked over to him, grabbed the half-full glass of water out of his hand, and drank it down.

"You need a good roll of deodorant and some mouthwash," she said, as if he were a child. And yet, there was something off about her tone. It was too somber for her to be playfully chiding him. "And you should try to wear something professional. Maybe even a tie."

"Why?" he asked, puzzled by her words. "Where are we going?"

Maureen didn't say anything. Instead, she slowly made her way into the living room, leaned over the couch, and picked up her bra. She turned her back to him, hoisted up the T-shirt she was wearing, and quickly clasped it on. She smoothed the shirt back down over her torso and walked to the window, pulling a curtain aside to stare out.

"Maureen," Manny said, taking a few steps toward her, "you're acting odd. What's going on?"

"I didn't want to tell you until we were on the road," she said, shaking her head before turning back toward him. "I was thinking about my dream in the shower, and I realized that I recognized the kid."

Manny felt a shiver go down his spine and felt all of his joints lock in unison.

Maureen took a deep breath. "You know your friend? The one that brought her boy to the crime scene last week?"

"Tasha?"

Maureen nodded her head, walked over to him and laid both of her hands on his chest while looking steadily into his eyes. "Do you know where she lives?"

There was pity in her eyes. Manny felt himself involuntarily swallow. The sour taste of vomit filled the back of his throat.

†HIR†Y-FOUR

"How can you not have her number?" Maureen shouted as Manny pulled on his sport coat, stuffed his cell phone into the pocket, and searched for his keys. He'd obviously forgotten that she had picked them up just a moment before and was holding them in plain sight. Some people just couldn't handle their liquor. Her own head was pounding, but she had swallowed down half a pill, so she was confident she'd be fine in short order.

"I thought you were supposed to be friends," she said.

"We knew each other in high school," he said defensively, wincing with the effort of talking. "I don't know. I got back in touch when I moved back to town, but we never exchanged phone numbers."

"Do you have her husband's number?"

"Ben? No, I don't have his either."

"Then what good are you?" Her frustration with him made her want to hit him in his stupid face.

"What do you want from me? Like I said, we aren't close. I've only ever had dinner at their house once," he said.

"Jesus, why didn't you say so?" she replied. "Let's go."

Maureen looked over at Manny as they made their way to

his truck. His face wore a frown. He was obviously hurt by her henpecking. She reached into her pocket and grabbed the other half of the pill that she had taken earlier, which she was saving for after they had spoken to the kid's parents.

"Here, take this," she said, offering it to him with an open hand.

"What is it?"

"Just a pain killer. It helps."

He took the pill and swallowed it down. "I don't suppose that was aspirin," he said with a weak smile.

"It's a prescription."

"Yours?"

"More or less," she replied, looking over again only to be met with his side-eyed, disapproving stare. She rolled her eyes at him. "Okay, so the prescription is forged. But I only get enough for myself. I don't sell them or anything. It's the only thing that helps the migraines. A half a pill, though? It'll knock out any pain in less than half an hour and it won't make you too drowsy, unless you drink with it. Get a cup of coffee in you, and you should be good for hours."

"Well, in that case," he said, allowing his amused smirk to break out on his face, "thank you very much."

Whether it was the effects of the pill, or a psychosomatic reaction to her suggestions, Manny perked up ever so slightly as they took off down the road. He directed her south along the county highway then back east. Maureen soon found herself on a tree-lined street of mid-century ranch homes, each one looking like the last with the exception of brick or paint color.

"Slow down a little," said Manny as he scrutinized each house in turn.

"You don't know the address, do you?" Maureen said, easing her foot off the accelerator and tapping the brake.

"I'll know it when I see it. I'm pretty sure it's another block down, and I know it's on my side."

The homes crawled by, and just when Maureen began to think that he didn't actually know which one they were looking for, Manny let out a sharp cry.

"That's it. It's the one with the railing on the steps."

All of the houses were situated on a little hill above the street with four or five concrete steps leading to the front stoop. Maureen quickly picked out the only one with an iron railing fastened to the steps and pulled over to the curb. She slammed the truck into park and stared up at the square, red-brick house before turning to look at Manny.

"There's no cop cars or anything around here," she said. "Do you think they don't know yet?"

"I'm not sure, honestly," Manny said. "Does this street look familiar?"

"It's a neighborhood street with trees. They all look the same to me."

They got out of the truck and paced up and down the street. Maureen swung her head from side to side searching for something from her dream to flash inside her mind. Nothing came, but something was definitely missing.

"I don't see the car," she said to Manny, who was leaning against his truck, watching her.

Manny turned and labored up the steps to the front door of the house. Maureen looked on as he rang the doorbell and waited. The door remained shut, and after a moment, Manny peered into the large window to the right of the door. When that apparently didn't yield anything, he quickly went around the side of the house and disappeared into the backyard. He emerged a minute or so later around the other side and came back down the hill.

"There's no one home," he said, leaning on the truck next to Maureen and staring back at the house. "And there's no sign of fire or anything."

"Well, maybe we should drive further into town and see if there's something going on," she suggested, not knowing what else they could do. She knew they needed to find the Naismiths, but if they weren't home, they could be anywhere.

"All right, let's get going," Manny said.

"You good to drive?" she asked, holding out his keys. His speech was already much clearer, but he was still carrying himself as if he was in pain.

"Go ahead," he said. "I still feel like shit."

Maureen jumped back behind the wheel and turned the truck around, heading north. Within a few minutes, they came to the county highway and Maureen turned right, back to Main Street. Manny stayed silent, and Maureen could tell that he was wrestling with something.

"What is it?" she asked.

"I was just thinking," he said slowly, "and don't think I mean anything by this, but, what if you didn't see Benny in your dream? What if it's another kid that just looked similar?"

"I don't know why I know. I just know."

Her interactions over the last ten days with the little boy and his mother had left a definite imprint in her mind. She didn't doubt what she had seen this time. Manny's explanation would have been easier for her to accept, but she couldn't.

Main Street came into view. Maureen slowed down to the new speed limit and they continued east. Nothing seemed out of place. There were the usual number of cars parked at the meters, along with a few people walking the sidewalks. It was all normal. All too normal. She felt her stomach begin to churn. It wasn't the drink from the previous night or hunger. It was the foreboding feeling that told her they were going to find what they were looking for, and very soon.

"Nothing going on here," Manny said. "Maybe we should try Tasha's job. She teaches aerobics and spin classes at the gym over on the east side. In that little strip mall off the grocery store on Glenbrook Avenue. You know where that is?"

"Yeah kinda," she replied. She walked there once for groceries during her first week in Sycamore Hills, before resigning herself to do her shopping at the drug store on Main Street, since it was much closer to her apartment.

"Three lights up and take a right," he said.

"Got it."

Turning right at the third stop light, Maureen would have thought he was the one with the psychic ability. Two blocks up, there was a mob scene in the parking lot of the strip mall. She counted six police vehicles, including the black sedan that belonged to the Feds. As she pulled into the lot and scanned the crowd, she could see the boy's mother with Agent Lorenzo, hand over her mouth, nodding along with whatever the female agent was saying. Reading back a statement, she decided. The crime scene investigator she recognized from the previous Saturday was inspecting the back seat of a black sedan, in which she could just make out a child's car seat. Even at the distance she was, Maureen could recognize it as the one from her dream. Of the surroundings, she had no idea, but something gnawed at the back of her head, telling her that something was still missing.

"Wait here," Manny said as the truck stopped. "I'll be back in a minute."

He opened the door and quickly hopped out of the passenger's seat, crossing the parking lot while adjusting his tie and smoothing his jacket. Maureen could tell that he was making a beeline for Agent Layton, who stood slightly apart from the rest of the crowd, silently monitoring the scene.

"Oh, like hell!" Maureen shouted out loud after a moment. She was not going to be left behind. She got out of the truck to jog after Manny. He had been intercepted by the officer that she knew as the captain of the Sycamore Hills Police Department, and it looked like the two men were arguing.

"Captain, don't tell me where I can and can't be," Manny was saying as she walked up behind him. He sounded like he was trying to keep the volume of his voice in check, but the edge that he got when he was about to explode was certainly present.

"Why don't you just tell me what you're doing here," the captain growled back, "and I'll tell you if you can continue on."

It was like watching two dogs arching their backs at one another. Maureen just hoped that neither of them would bite. Fortunately, the two men were rescued from themselves, though not necessarily in a way that made her any more comfortable.

"Gentlemen, what seems to be the trouble here?" came the voice of Agent Layton. He strode up to the two men and settled himself between them.

"Captain," he continued keeping his eyes on Manny, "why don't you let me speak to the detective here."

"Sir, I don't think that—"

"Alone."

The captain backed up a few steps before sighing and turning his back on them. Agent Layton motioned with his head, and he and Manny moved onto the sidewalk in front of the storefronts of the strip mall. Maureen joined them, but stood just far enough away from Manny to prevent any sense of intimacy from being detected. The agent stared at her for an uncomfortable moment, before turning to talk to Manny.

"So, Detective," he said, "the captain raises a good question. What does bring you here?"

"We came to grab a few things at the grocery store," Maureen jumped in quickly.

"That's right," Manny said. "Just stopping by the store."

"I'm sure," the agent said.

He clearly didn't believe them, but she knew enough about the man from Manny's talks of him and her own interactions to understand that he would turn his head to certain things if it meant he could use them to get the job done.

"So what happened here?" Manny asked the agent.

"Tasha Naismith called the police about an hour and a half ago to report her son as abducted. According to her statement, she had stopped in at the grocery store here and left her son in the car with the window cracked while she ran in for a power bar. She estimates that she was only gone for two minutes, and when she came out, the back door of her car was open and her son was gone. She ran back into the grocery store in a frenzy, begging for someone to call the police. Apparently, she was so distraught that she forgot she had a cell phone. The clerk and manager at the store have backed up her story."

"Is there any security footage?" Manny asked.

"We've reviewed it already. It doesn't show the parking lot, unfortunately, just the front door of the store. It shows her walking in and out, and then running back in a few moments later."

"I see," Manny said.

Maureen felt for him. She could see that he felt useless at the scene and was searching for something that the rest of the authorities hadn't thought of that would reclaim some of his worth.

"Maybe we could go talk to Tasha?" Maureen suggested. She was looking at Manny, but speaking to Layton.

The agent clearly sensed that and gave a resigned nod.

Maureen and Manny walked over to where Agent Lorenzo was finishing with Tasha. She had since been joined by her husband, still wearing his firefighter's shirt. He was clearly in a state of shock, saying nothing and rubbing the base of Tasha's neck, trying to comfort her. Lorenzo looked over their shoulders as they approached, raised her eyebrows, and nodded. She must have gotten confirmation from Layton that they were allowed to approach. She closed her notebook and stood to one side.

"Tasha, Ben," Manny began as they came to stand in front of the couple, "I'm so sorry for what's happened. Can we talk to you for a minute?"

"I'm not saying a word with her here," the woman said pointing at Maureen. "Whatever's going on, I know she has something to do with it!"

"Tasha, I can assure you," said Manny, "Maureen has been with me all morning."

"Didn't know you liked slumming it," Tasha scoffed, rubbing the tears from her eyes with the palm of her hand.

Maureen knew that the woman was simply projecting her grief onto her. She tried not to take it personally, to pretend it didn't bother her. It did, of course, but she knew she had to bury it down with the rest of her baggage.

"Look, I'm not going to lie to you," Manny said, appearing to speak to the husband. "I'm not strictly a part of this investigation, but I still want to do whatever I can to help. And Maureen here is helping me, so you can trust her too."

"You can't help!" Tasha shouted. "Either of you! Just leave us alone, Manny! You haven't helped the other families, so get lost!" She turned and buried her head in her husband's chest and began to cry again.

Maureen watched as Manny reached into his pocket and pulled out a business card. He maintained a stoic look on his face, but Maureen could sense tension in his body that meant the woman's words had hurt him very deeply. "Just in case," Manny said softly, handing the card to the woman's husband.

The man reached out with one hand, took it from him, and nodded.

"What now?" Maureen asked him when they had gotten back into his truck.

Manny sat in the passenger's seat with his chin resting on one fist, staring out of the window. "I don't know. Our theory of the victims being related is out the window, though."

"How so?"

"Ben Jr. is only three," he said wearily. "The kids wouldn't know each other from school. Tasha has been an agnostic for as long as I can remember—and pretty outspoken about it, too—so the church is out. And she's a fitness instructor. I don't remember any gym memberships showing up in either Tom Lowes' or Sandra Locke's financials. We're back to square one."

"Well then, we'll just have to find another thing that ties them together."

"I don't see how," he said, pulling out his phone and looking at the display. "It's almost noon. We've got twelve, fourteen hours tops before the kid is dead, and we're not going to be any help to the Feds. Everything we've given them hasn't helped at all. Let's just go home."

Maureen turned the key and looked over at him. He was probably correct, but it didn't seem right for some reason. Her giving up was to be expected, but she couldn't fathom Manny giving up like this. It wasn't right.

Somehow, Maureen decided, it was up to her to make him fight.

THIRTY-FIVE

Manny paced in front of his couch while Maureen sat in silence with her legs curled under her. The morning had dawned, and no fire had been reported anywhere in the area. There was no sign whatsoever that the killer had struck again. The pervasive thought in the community became that the child was not taken by the same ghoul, and that they would need to expand the search parameters to include the more standard kidnapping fare. He, of course, knew from Maureen's dream that they were looking for the same person, but they decided to keep that to themselves and help out as much as they were allowed, in the hopes that a mass search would flush out the guilty party. The prospect that he could still prevent the boy's death had reinvigorated him, and he was now ashamed that he had even considered giving up the previous day.

Being a Saturday, it hadn't been hard for the police to round up enough volunteers to search the surrounding area for any sign of little Ben Naismith. They had combed fields, searched along the river, and even sent the county K-9 unit through the woods into the next county. Hundreds of residents were interviewed, and the Amber Alert was sent out. No word came back from the surrounding counties, and nobody who was interviewed was of any help. Now that the sun was setting, the possibility of the boy only being found once he was set upon a pyre was becoming a firmer reality in his mind. And to Manny, that was unacceptable.

"We're doing enough, right?" he asked Maureen, desperately hoping she could provide him with some kind of satisfaction. "I mean, there's nothing we're missing, right?"

"I don't know," came her stoic answer. It was not what he wanted to hear.

"C'mon, Maureen help me out a little," he said, his voice beginning to rise. "Please. We've got to be missing something! We know this person is religious to the point of zealotry. We know he's setting these crime scenes up as sacrificial altars. We know he's been killing just after midnight or early in the morning. This sick bastard lights up a signal beacon every time he kills someone, so why not now? The kid's alive, that's why." Manny felt his whole body shaking. He was losing control. He felt himself slump on the couch next to Maureen and bury his face in his hands.

"Why can't you just see who it is?" he lamented, throwing himself back and staring at the ceiling. He could feel his cheeks begin to flush and tears blurred his vision. "What good is being psychic if you can't save people? If this kid dies, it'll be our fault! How do I live with something like that?"

The pain of what he was saying hit him all at once, and Manny closed his eyes and lowered his head into her lap, seeking some kind of comfort. He couldn't hear anything except for the soft whimpers coming out of his throat.

Manny felt her hands slide under his chin and lift his head up to look into her eyes. Their deep pools, usually protected from betraying the emotion underneath, now held endless depths of pity and understanding. She ran her hand down his face, drying the tears that held on to his skin.

"I've been asking myself those same questions all my life," she whispered. "And in all that time, I've never managed to find the answers. I've lived with this torment from my earliest memories, and I've never been able to save anyone or at least turn this curse into something that does good. I've told you that it's always easier to walk away." Her eyes narrowed. "But not this time," she said through gritted teeth. "I don't know if we can save the kid, but I swear, even if it kills us, we're gonna find a way to bring this fucker down!"

Manny's heart rose at her words. He sat up, took both her hands in his, and kissed them. Then he got to his feet and stalked over to the window. The sun was already setting behind the river banks. Time was getting short. They needed to get to work.

"All right," he said, turning back toward Maureen, "maybe we should take another look through the evidence box. Look again for something we mi—"

The sound of his cell phone vibrating on the coffee table cut him short. Maureen reached over and picked it up, staring at the display.

"Who is it?" he asked.

"No name, just a number." She tossed the phone to him. It was a local number.

He hit the button to answer. "This is Detective Benitez."

"Manny," a woman's whispered, tentative voice on the other end said, "I need to talk to you."

"Who is this?"

"It's Tasha. Is there some place we can meet? It's important. I don't want to talk over the phone."

"Okay," he said, trying to sound calm. "Why don't you head down to the police station, and I'll meet you there in ten minutes."

"Isn't there some place else we could meet? Somewhere private?"

"The station will be private enough at this hour," he replied. It was the truth; there would only be one officer there. Manny would have to come up with a reason he was talking to the kidnapped child's mother when he wasn't officially on the case, but he had the car ride to figure that out.

"All right," Tasha said tentatively. "Ten minutes."

"Okay, I'll see you and Ben there."

"Ben won't be there."

The line clicked dead before Manny could respond.

"That was Tasha Naismith," he told Maureen. "She's got something she wants to talk to us about. Let's go."

Maureen nodded and got to her feet, tying her flannel shirt around her waist.

"Don't forget your phone," he reminded her.

Maureen smirked slightly and bent to pick up the old flip phone he'd given her. "Still can't get used to having this thing."

They ran out of the house and jumped into the truck. Manny felt his stomach tighten as he pondered Tasha's last words. She was coming to meet them alone. What could that mean? Where was Ben, and why wasn't he coming? Did he even know she was doing this? The questions would drive him mad, so he gripped both hands on the steering wheel, stared ahead into the growing darkness, and focused on the road instead.

The truck's lights splashed across the figure of Tasha Naismith and silhouetted her against the building as Manny pulled into the parking lot of the police station. He swung his truck into his usual parking spot and let out a long sigh.

"You don't have to come in if you don't want to," he told Maureen as he shifted the truck into park.

"I'm coming in," she replied stoically, still staring straight ahead.

Manny tilted his head toward her but said nothing. She had been silent throughout the whole drive, just staring off into the night. He wanted badly to ask her what she was thinking about, but there wasn't time. He pushed his door open and stepped out of the truck. Maureen followed suit.

"Why am I not surprised that she's with you?" Tasha said sourly, pointing at Maureen as they approached.

"Knock it off, Tasha," Manny said. "I already told you yesterday, Maureen is helping me with this investigation. So anything you say to me, you can say to her."

Tasha eyed Maureen for another moment before nodding in agreement. Manny nodded back and motioned for them to head into the station. As they approached the door, he looked back to Maureen, who was shuffling along half a step behind him. Unsurprisingly, her face didn't betray whether or not Tasha's cold reception had troubled her.

"What the hell do you think you're doing?" Officer Collins shouted, springing to his feet as the group walked through the door. Clearly, he had not expected any company tonight.

"Trying to catch a killer," Manny said, calmly walking past the befuddled officer. "Is there coffee?"

"Wh—ye—no," Collins stammered. "Hang on! You can't be here!"

"The hell I can't," Manny shot back, rounding on the young man and bringing his face in close. "Mrs. Naismith has something to add to her statement, and I'm going to hear it. Now, if you have something against solving this case and getting a child back to his mother, please let me know, and I'll be glad to stop what I'm doing."

Collins' lip quivered. He said nothing.

"Thank you, Jack," said Manny, patting Officer Collins on the shoulder. "Head back to the desk and keep an ear out for the phone. You never know if you're gonna get an important call."

He kept his eye on Collins as the officer headed back to the main desk, pleased that his gamble had payed off. It was probably a fortunate thing that it was Jack who had been assigned to the overnight shift and not one of the more senior of the officers. He could be relatively sure that his power play would not have worked on any of them.

"You should probably stay out here," he whispered to Maureen as they walked down the hall.

Maureen said nothing, but stopped after a few paces and leaned against the wall. He nodded to her and continued forward, hoping he didn't hurt her feelings by not letting her join. It was for the best, though. He would get more out of Tasha if they were alone in the room. Manny opened the door to the interview room and ushered the other woman in. He pulled out one of the chairs at the table for her to sit in and took his own familiar seat on the opposite side.

"All right Tasha," he began, pulling his notepad out of his

pocket, "what's got you so worked up that you had to call me? You do remember I'm not working on this case in any official capacity, right?"

"I trust you," she shrugged back. "I don't know, we go back a long way, you know? And when I tell you that I lied in my statement to the cops yesterday, I trust that you won't say anything."

Manny felt his heart jump at her admission. Whatever came next, it had to be bad.

"Go on," he urged her as gently as he could.

"Before I start, I just want you to know that I love Ben more than anything." Her eyes were wide with sincerity. Whatever else she said, at least Manny knew he could believe that.

"Tasha, does Ben know more about your son's disappearance?" he asked. "Are you protecting him?"

"No, no, nothing like that! It's just that . . . oh God." She buried her head in her hands.

Manny turned his head to look at Maureen, who was standing like a statue by the door. Her eyes barely blinked as she stared at Tasha. She didn't even seem to notice him.

"Tasha," he said firmly, turning back and prying her hands off her eyes, "time isn't something we have a lot of."

"I know, I know," she replied, composing herself and looking back up at him. "This is just really hard." She took a deep breath. "Okay, I'm just going to say it. I've said it out loud before, I can do it again. I haven't been faithful to Ben."

In spite of himself, he dropped his head and shook it sadly. He couldn't believe that someone who seemed so in love with her husband could be with another man.

"I'm sorry," she sniffled, trying to hold back the tears. "It's just been hard with his work schedule lately, and we got together so young, and I'd never really been with anyone else. There's this guy at the gym, Rod, one of the personal trainers. It started out as just some innocent flirting. But one thing led to another, and before I knew what was going on, we were sleeping together." She grabbed for his hand earnestly. "You have to believe me, I never meant for it to go so far."

Manny patted her hand briefly before releasing it and setting it gently on the table. He did feel bad for her, but in that moment, he knew he had to be a cop and not a friend.

"How long has this been going on?" he asked, putting on his most professional tone.

"About four or five months," she whispered. "I've tried to break it off so many times. But every time I see him . . ." She trailed off for a moment, a tiny smile nearly breaking through on her face.

Manny sighed, hoping his growing disappointment wasn't showing through. "So, why is this important, Tasha? Do you think this Rod guy has something to do with Benny's kidnapping?"

"Oh, God, no! Rod doesn't want to have anything to do with kids. Which is ironic, considering—" Tasha's eyes widened as she cut herself off and clasped a hand over her mouth.

"Oh, no," Manny said quickly. "You don't get to drop something like this on me and clam up now. Spit it out—every word. And come to the point of why this has anything to do with the investigation."

"I . . ." Tasha began, seeming to force every word out of her mouth. "I'm pregnant."

Manny couldn't even form a sentence. Was she insinuating what he thought she was? He stared at Tasha, silently compelling her to keep talking so he didn't have to be the next to speak.

"It might be Ben's," she said defensively. "I'm just not sure."

"So again," Manny said impatiently, "what does this have to do with your son?"

"I wasn't at the grocery store when Benny got taken," she said, looking down at the table. "I did go there that day, just like I said, only before that, I had called Rod and went over to his place. I left Benny in the car with the window cracked. I was just going to be gone for a minute. I went there to tell him that I was pregnant, and that I wanted a paternity test from him, and that if it was his, I wasn't going to keep it. I was going to tell him that it was over between us, that I loved my husband, and I couldn't keep lying to him. I was so confident that I could get in, say what I needed to, and get out. But he just kissed me, and I completely lost my head. It was almost a half an hour before I was back at the car, and Benny was gone."

Tasha's head fell back into her hands, and she began to sob uncontrollably. "I was so scared for people to find out. I just remember thinking, no one could know that I had lost my son while I was with another man. So I drove over to the grocery store, ran in to get a protein bar, went outside, ran back in like I did, and begged them to call the police. You know, so people would think it really happened there."

Manny couldn't believe what he was hearing. He knew he should try to be sympathetic, but all he could think of was that every step taken to find the boy since yesterday was taken from the wrong place. Despite his best efforts, the fury of it erupted from him all at once.

"So basically, you're telling me that the last day and a half of investigation was a waste, because you couldn't tell the cops the truth? And why? Because you were too afraid your husband would find out?"

"You think I don't know all of that?" she shouted back, jumping up from her chair and frantically pacing back and forth in front of him. "You think it doesn't make me sick? You think I haven't punished myself over this every minute of the day? And not just because Benny got taken and I let it happen! No! I've been killing myself over this since it started!" Tasha turned her back to Manny and began to sob again.

He stood firm, waiting patiently for her to stop. He could sense she was going to continue talking as soon as she had mastered herself. The dam had broken in her mind, and there was more that she was going to say, if he could be patient.

"I've done everything I could think of to try and deal with this," she said. Her breath came shakily as she continued to stare at the wall. Then, suddenly, she laughed bitterly. "You know, I even started taking Benny to St. Mary's on the Sundays that Ben had to work. Hell, I even went to confession a few days ago to try and make myself feel better about all this. You know, maybe, if I knew God would forgive me, then I could get Ben to forgive me, or something."

The sound of her words struck Manny in the chest. "What did you just say?"

"I know, it's stupid," she said, turning around and wiping her eyes. "I mean, me, for fuck's sake. At church! Can you imagine? Almost thirty years on this planet, and the only thing that can get me through those doors is banging another man. You think there's anything that I can do to make this better?"

"For your marriage," he said, "I don't know. For Benny, you might have just given me what I need to find him."

"I don't understand."

"Just answer me this, no matter how odd it sounds. Did you have Benny baptized?"

Tasha shook her head slowly.

"Right, stay here for a minute. I'll have Collins come grab you and walk you to your car."

Manny left the room and walked down the hallway. He turned the corner, looking for Maureen. All he found was Collins sitting at the front desk.

"Where is she?" Manny asked the young officer.

"She came through about a minute ago," he said pointing to the front door. "Said you'd be working late, and that she was going to head out to get you guys a snack."

Manny stood for a moment, deciding on his next move. "Jack," he said, motioning Officer Collins closer. "Do you have the front desk computer up and running?"

"Yeah."

"All right, I'm going to borrow it for a few minutes. Can you go into the interview room and walk Mrs. Naismith to her car? Please?"

Collins nodded.

Manny could tell that his orders were keeping the kid on his toes but at the moment, that was to his advantage. It prevented him from questioning why he could get away with commandeering a department computer when he was technically not working the case.

As Collins walked off toward the interview room, Manny took a seat behind the front desk and found the website he was looking for. It had all come together in the interview room. He now knew how the killer was choosing his victims, and that told him who was responsible. But now he needed to find the man.

Manny scrolled through his own phone and found the number he needed. *The son-of-a-bitch had better answer*, he thought as he hit the dial button. He'd call all night if he had to.

✝HIR✝ᴜ-SIX

Maureen felt as though her heart would leap out of her chest at any moment as she approached the rectory. From the moment she'd silently poked her head into the interview room and heard the end of Tasha Naismith's confession, her mind had been nothing but a blur. She had run home as fast as she could, grabbed Manny's backup service pistol from where she had hidden it, and came here. The church now was the only thing that tied it all together, which meant all signs pointed to its priest as the perpetrator. The one clear thought in her head was that if she somehow could stop Father Patrick, maybe she would draw even with the universe, and the nightmares, the hallucinations—everything—would stop. She reached around her back to make sure the old Browning was secure in her waistband and covered by her shirt.

The old priest was painfully slow in coming to the door. It seemed like an eternity had passed since she rang the doorbell. She stood, fidgeting and unsure of what she would say when the door opened. Would she pull the gun and shoot him right there on the doorstep? Would she force him to take her to wherever little Ben was being held? Did she really have it in her to be the hero of this story? She wasn't sure of anything, but she felt her hand reach behind her back once again while she was pondering all her options.

The front door opened, and Maureen jerked her hand back to her side and stood rigid as the outline of Father Patrick filled the opening. He was barefoot and dressed in shorts and a button-up, short-sleeved shirt, which he hadn't quite finished buttoning. He wore his glasses and had a thick, leather book in his hand. His face was even; he only appeared to be marginally surprised to see her. His eyes made her stomach drop.

"Maureen, it's awfully late for a visit, isn't it?" he asked, his lips widening into a grin to show that he didn't mean it.

"Well, you know me," she replied, trying to sound like her usual self, "it's barely suppertime by my clock. Sorry if I woke you up, there was just something that couldn't wait until morning."

"Oh, I was up reading. Perhaps you'd like to come in for a drink?"

Maureen shifted uncomfortably from side to side, hesitating. "Sure, why not?"

Father Patrick nodded and stood to the side, motioning her to enter. She stepped across the threshold, keeping her face to him and stood to one side while he closed the door. She tilted her head in silent indication that he should lead the way.

They walked through the house into the back den where they had had dinner just a few nights before. As then, the two leather chairs sat in their place on the far end of the room, the small bar cart standing nearby. The larger table they had eaten at had since been removed.

"What can I fix for you, Maureen?" Father Patrick's voice roused her out of her thoughts.

She stared at him for a moment before finding her voice. "I'll do some of that scotch. Rocks."

As he nodded and turned to the small bar cart, Maureen saw her chance. She eased the pistol out of the back of her jeans as quietly as she could, took off the safety, flinching at its click, and pointed the barrel at the priest's back. Father Patrick seemed to take no notice and continued to busy himself with the ice and crystal glassware.

"Father," she said, her voice shaking a bit, "I need you to turn around slowly."

The old man turned to face her, not too slowly, and almost too calmly for a man who had a gun pointed at him. He held in his right hand one of the glasses, filled with three ice cubes and scotch. He glanced at the gun for only a brief moment, almost as if he expected it to be there, before raising his gaze to meet hers. A thin smile creased his lips, but his eyes remained solemn as he raised both hands slightly.

"I know what you're doing, Father," Maureen said as sternly as she could, using her anger toward the man she thought was her friend to steady her hands. "Now where is the kid?"

"I don't think you know as much as you think you do. Why don't you put that down, and let's talk like civilized people." He took a step forward, lowering his hands slightly.

Maureen jumped back a pace and stiffened, tightening her grip on the pistol and pushing it forward. "Stay right where you are, you bastard! I swear to Christ, I will shoot you where you stand if you move again!" Her heart was beating even faster and she felt her hands begin to shake. Whether it was out of fear or rage, she couldn't tell.

Father Patrick froze and raised his hands back up again. The room was silent for an agonizing moment before he spoke again. "Maureen, you might think you're capable of this because of the other things you've done in your life, but trust me, you're not a killer."

"You don't think so? You don't think I'll put a bullet in your head if it'll stop all of this?" She felt a tear begin to well up in her eye, but she pushed on. "I'd shoot my best friend if I had one. I'd shoot my own father—wherever the hell he is—if it stopped all this! If I can do that, what makes you think I can't shoot you? You mean less to me than anyone right now!"

"I'm sorry, Maureen. I'm sorry that you feel this way. I'm sorry that you think this all has to end with more death. And I'm sorry for this."

With lightning speed, Father Patrick tossed the contents of the glass in the air. Maureen felt her eyes instinctively rise to follow the liquid and ice, and before she recognized it as a distraction, he had crossed the distance between them, twisting her wrist awkwardly and planting a leg behind her to use his momentum to trip her to the ground. She regained her awareness almost instantly, only to find him standing over her with the gun now in his hand, barrel pointed at her chest.

"Once a soldier, always a soldier," he said grimly, almost to himself, as he raised the gun away from her and nimbly removed the clip and the chambered bullet. He put both of these in his front pocket and then, to her astonishment, reached down, grasped her hand, pulled her almost effortlessly to her feet, and handed the empty weapon back to her.

"A gesture of good faith," he said as he moved back

toward the drink cart. "I'm sorry to have ruined your drink. Would you like me to fix you another one?"

"No," she found herself answering before she knew what she was doing.

"No? Well then, if it's all the same to you, I'll pour myself a little port instead. I never drink scotch alone."

He selected a small, dessert-wine glass, poured the dark wine from an old bottle, and quickly drank it down in one gulp before refilling the glass a second time.

"Had to calm the nerves a bit," he said with a grim smile. "It's been a while since I've had to do something like that. Is your wrist okay?"

Maureen looked down at her wrist and shook it for a moment. There was no pain. Still too astonished to answer, she simply nodded.

"That's a relief." Father Patrick smiled. "I tried to be careful not to hurt you."

He moved over to the brown leather chairs in the corner and set his drink on the small oak table between them. He sat himself down in one and gestured to her that she should do likewise.

Maureen didn't move.

"Maureen," he said a bit more sternly, "I think I've proven that I'm not going to hurt you. But I think you at least owe me a bit of an explanation as to what you're doing bringing a gun into my home and threatening to shoot me. Now please, sit."

"I don't understand," Maureen mumbled as she made her way over to the chair. "It has to be you."

"What? It has to be me? Maureen, what are you talking about?"

"I've been inside the man's head, Father. He's religious. He thinks he's cleansing the world. These children aren't just victims, they're sacrifices." She sat down and stared at Father Patrick intently. "All you ever seem to talk about is the need to change the world for the better. Maybe somewhere in your crazy head, you think making these sacrifices to your God will bring about this 'paradise on earth' you're looking for."

"I see," he nodded and took a small sip of his drink. "Well, you've trusted me with secrets of your past, so I guess it's only fair to share mine."

He set his half-finished drink on the table and leaned forward in his chair, staring straight ahead, like a man looking deep into his past to a memory that he'd rather forget. "You know that I was a soldier when I was young. What you don't know—what nobody knows, actually—is what I did in Vietnam during my time there. I was a Marine. I rose incredibly quickly through the ranks. The senior DI in basic singled me out early on as having a certain something, and when I completed my eight weeks of camp, I was placed in a separate company from my classmates. I was to be part of a group of counterintelligence agents. The unit was made up mostly of veteran soldiers pulled from different branches. At the time, mixing the branches was an anomaly, but we were more so, because all our unit's activities were to be completely confidential. Officially, we didn't exist.

"We shipped over in the spring of 1969 after five months of jungle training and briefing. Our missions were going to all be behind enemy lines, all geared toward cutting supply lines, POW rescues if they were possible, that sort of thing. At least, that's what they told us. It all started that way, but as the missions started to pile up, we found ourselves doing less and less subversion and more and more—what they called—extreme interrogation. Soon, all we were doing was kidnapping suspected Vietcong and torturing them for information. It didn't even seem to matter how credible our intel was.

"We'd been in country for about a year, and around this time, word came to us about a pro-North terrorist cell across the border in Laos. This was one of those tips that didn't actually come from our military intelligence, just some vague rumors among the locals, but our Sergeant decided to pursue it. A lot of us felt it was a little thin, and we debated the ethics of entering that country, but we had our orders. It was a long, two-day slog through the jungle, up around the peak of Rao Co, and over the border. Our Vietnamese guides left us at this point, and we continued toward the village for another half a day. We circled it just before nightfall. It was as small of a jungle settlement as you could imagine, a collection of less than a dozen thatched huts. A few small fires were still lit, but we saw no one moving around. No insurgents, nothing. It was decided that we'd proceed at dawn.

"The next morning, we rounded up everyone in the village. We were surprised at the lack of resistance. There wasn't a single weapon fired by anyone in their defense. A search of the village and surrounding area didn't yield anything to show the rumors that brought us there were true. No guns, no explosives. They must have been dealing in information, our officers thought, helping the Vietcong by spying, by playing the innocent villagers. A few members of our team were well versed in interrogation tactics and spoke Vietnamese. Of course, that was useless, as the villagers were Laotian, but that didn't seem to matter to them. They screamed at the villagers— at a mother clutching her crying baby, at an old man cowering on the ground—trying to extract any information they could. Each villager had the same response: a wide-eyed look of horror, a ferocious shaking of the head, and tears. Hardly the behavior of hardened agents for the North.

"Finally, our sergeant called a stop and told the company to line up the villagers and execute them for aiding the enemy. And we did. Seventeen women, fourteen men, and nine children, all their lives snuffed out in a burst of machine gun fire. Afterwards, we followed orders to set fire to the village and left.

"A few days after we returned, I went to see the unit's chaplain to talk about the morality of what we had just done. The chaplain assured me that we, and by extension America, were doing God's work by defeating the evils of Communism and bringing light to a dark world. He assured me that the villagers did not know the light of Christ, and therefore what I had done was just: no different from the Children of Israel cleansing the Promised Land of the Canaanites. Needless to say, I was disillusioned by this. How could a God of love condone this type of atrocity? Wars are fought, true, and people die in them, that is unavoidable. But the intentional murder of innocent civilians based on very thin and questionable intel? That couldn't be right. The God I knew would never condone that. I resolved to leave it all behind.

"The counterintelligence training I'd been through taught me well, so slipping out of the unit and through the jungle was not a problem. I lived off the land for a good six months, always making my way south, until I came to a fishing village and was able to barter some of my tools to get river passage down to the southern tip of Vietnam. From there, I made my way across the South China Sea to the Philippines and stayed there for a few years before managing to get myself onto a transpacific ship and eventually back to the United States. The whole time, I was searching for answers—in churches, in shrines, in the streets among the poor—and at last, I came to the conclusion that my life—the life of Corporal Mullen—had to be put to an end, and a new life must rise in its place. And so, when I finally made it home nearly eight years after my desertion and a full three years after the war had ended, I enrolled in Seminary. And on that day, Corporal Patrick Mullen died, and Father Patrick McGill was born."

Father Patrick finished speaking and sat up again, leaning back in his chair. He reached out to the table, picked up his glass, and drank down the rest of the port. He had yet to look at her since beginning to tell his story, and all Maureen could do was stare at him. She could obviously tell that the effort of relating the story had taken a toll on him emotionally. There was even the stain of a single tear tracing its path down his face. She detected a feeling in him that she knew all too well herself. Shame.

"Is that all true?" she asked quietly. "That's your whole story?"

"That's two different questions," Father Patrick said, turning and smiling sadly at her. "Yes, everything I've just told you is true. No, I have not told you everything, but I have told you enough to make you understand. I've seen enough violence to last me more than one lifetime, and I've done more than any man should. I have just as many demons to fight as you do, likely more, which is probably why I am able to speak of these things to you. My nightmares might not tell me the things that yours tell you, but they haunt me nonetheless. Another way you and I are a lot alike."

"How do you handle it?" Maureen found herself almost forgetting why she had come in the first place. The anger she'd felt toward the man had almost turned to pity. If this all was an act, she was certainly convinced.

"Prayer, lots and lots of prayer. Seems like a fairly obvious and standard thing for a priest to say, but it's the truth. I know that God knows what I have done, and I know that I'll be judged justly when my time comes. I'm not one who necessarily believes that I can erase my sins with a string of good deeds, but I do believe in atoning for them as best I can. When I pray, I acknowledge to the Lord that I am mortal—I am flawed— but I really am trying to be better and to serve others because it's right, not because I'm hoping for some reward."

"Not very Catholic of you," Maureen chided. It wasn't a very tasteful thing to say, she knew, but she had to break this tension somehow.

Father Patrick let out a short, soft laugh then paused for a moment while staring down at his empty glass and passing it from hand to hand, once again deep in thought. "Maureen," he said finally, "there are more than half a dozen churches and even more church leaders in this town. How is it that I became your prime suspect?"

"It seemed to fit so perfectly. It became pretty obvious to me and Manny after the second murder that whoever was doing this was targeting people who had sinned. Lying, stealing, and now Tasha Naismith just admitted to adultery. This guy is killing the children of commandment breakers as a sacrifice of atonement. It's straight out of the Old Testament. Leviticus is practically a how-to manual for the crimes. All the families of the victims go to St. Mary's, and at least one of each of the sets of the parents has been to confession within the last ten days, so I just assumed that…"

Maureen's voice trailed off as Father Patrick got up from his chair and, almost trance-like, slowly made his way over to the bookshelf on the opposite wall.

"Father, what is it?" she asked.

"I haven't told anyone this yet, but I was planning on retiring at the end of the year. Because of that, I've been handling less of the day-to-day responsibilities of the church." He turned and looked steadily at her, his unblinking eyes burning with an earnest horror. "Maureen, I haven't taken a confession in nearly two months."

Maureen opened her mouth, but the words got lost on their way out. The final piece hit her all at once. She quickly shot her gaze over to the clock on the wall. 11:16. If he was going to kill the boy tonight, it would be soon. There wasn't much time.

"Father, I have to go! Right now!"

Father Patrick began to protest, but she had run through the house and was out the door and out of hearing range before she heard what he had to say. She was running as fast as she could, stopping only to stuff the pistol back in her waistband. She ran another block and was now within view of Main Street when she remembered the mobile phone in her front pocket. She pulled it out and saw that she had missed six calls from Manny in the last forty-five minutes. She flipped it open, hit re-dial, and continued to run.

"Manny, it's me," she panted as she went along, not slowing to talk. "What? Yeah, I know, I'm sorry. Long story, but listen. Meet me in front of the courthouse as quick as you can. I think I've got it all figured out. No. No time to talk now, just get your butt over there with your truck, and I'll explain everything!"

THIRTY-SEVEN

Father Patrick shook his head sadly as he reached into his pocket, pulling out the clip and the bullet. The haste of youth. Of course, he had figured out the answer as soon as she had mentioned the confessions. It was still a shock, and he could hardly believe it himself, but ever since his dinner conversation with Maureen, her descriptions of the crime scenes, and the symbols and writings in her dreams, he too had been suspecting someone whom he knew well. Now a choice was before him, but in truth, he knew what he was going to do, though it was with no small reluctance.

He stuffed the clip and bullet back into his pocket and returned one more time to the bar cart. He set down his glass and picked up the bottle of port. He pulled out the cork and was about to pour when he froze. Going back to the bottle wouldn't give him any more courage, and in fact would prove detrimental if he were to go into action. The momentary sadness of the thought shook him. *Back to action. I hope you have it in you, old man.* Quickly, he put down the bottle and went upstairs to his bedroom with as much speed as his old bones could muster.

Father Patrick turned on the small lamp on his nightstand and knelt down to reach under his bed. His hand found the small metal box that he had been searching for, and he slowly pulled it out and placed it on the bed. His fingers ran over the olive green lid, and he closed his eyes for a moment before unlatching it and pushing it open.

"I was hoping you'd never see the light of day again."

Whether he was speaking to the contents of the box or to Corporal Patrick Mullen, he did not know.

THIRTY-EIGHT

Maureen paced back and forth along the sidewalk in front of the steps of the courthouse, shifting in and out of the glow of the streetlight. It had taken her no more than five minutes to run from the rectory to Main Street, and she wondered what was taking Manny so long. After all, it should have only taken the same amount of time for him to drive over from the police station, and that included the time it would probably take him to run out to his truck.

As afraid as she was that they might not be able to save the Naismith boy, she was very much relieved that Father Patrick wasn't involved. She couldn't have forgiven herself for revealing so many of her most intimate thoughts and feelings to someone who could do this type of thing to a child. Another child might die tonight, but at least she now knew who was to blame. *No, I can't think like that! Ben Naismith won't die!* She surprised even herself with that thought, but it galvanized her reserve. Just once—just *once*—the dreams were going to help prevent tragedy rather than just allow her to helplessly look on as it unfolded.

The headlights from Manny's truck hit her square in the face as he turned the corner onto Main Street. She shielded her eyes from the beams as the truck pulled up to the curb. Manny reached over from the driver's seat and pushed open the passenger's side door for her.

"What the hell took you so long?" she shouted as she jumped into the seat and slammed the door. "It's almost midnight. The kid is going to be dead any minute."

"You're yelling at me?" he shouted back as he pulled the truck into the street and sped away. "I should be asking you the same thing. What the hell were you thinking running off like that?"

Maureen cast her eyes down for a moment, feeling her cheeks warm. "I thought it was Father Patrick, and I went to his house to stop him before he could kill the kid." She swallowed hard, remembering her anger and hatred as she pointed the gun at her friend, and her shame and heartache after she had learned the rest of his story. "Only it's not him. I'm sure it's—"

"Father Preston? Yeah, I came to the same conclusion."

Maureen's eyes shot up and stared at him. "How in the hell did you figure that one out?"

The smirk that came to Manny's face had no real levity behind it. "I did a little more digging after you ran out on me. See, after what Tasha told us, I thought it might be Father Patrick as well. But, unlike you, I didn't think he'd be stupid enough to be holding the kid at the rectory or St. Mary's. That's when I remembered something."

"What?" she shouted earnestly. "Time's running out!"

"We might have a little more time than you think, if I'm right," he replied coolly. "I remembered the old St. Mary's church along the river. When I was growing up, people would use it for summer weddings every now and then. They built the current one on Main Street in the early sixties because the town had grown, and the original church became too small to hold the congregation. But the Diocese never wanted to close it down because it was one of the first buildings ever built in Sycamore Hills, and they wanted to honor the history of the town.

"Here's the thing, though. When I first came back to town, I remember driving by there and noticing a for sale sign on the property. Sure enough, it was Tom Lowes who was the agent. Then I remembered, a little less than a year ago, the sign disappeared from the property. I didn't think much of it at the time, just figured it was sold. But when I started to think about places that a priest could take a child where no one would find them, it jumped back to my mind. I did a quick check of the public records at the station and saw that the owner hadn't changed, and that the Catholic Diocese still owned the property. So, I tried Tom Lowes on his cell phone. Took me three tries, but I finally got him to wake up and discuss the property.

"It seems that the Diocese was selling it because St. Mary's was short on money, and they figured that someone might want to buy the historic building. Well, the property sat for nearly two years until they pulled it from the market. I asked Tom why, and he said that the finances of St. Mary's had been rectified, and there were some among the clergy who voiced the opinion that it was important to hang on to the property.

"What put me onto Preston's trail was the fact that it's no secret that Father Patrick has never had a head for money or financing and has been really vocal in the community about his desire for most of the church's funds to go to charitable endeavors. The timeline also fit that the property was pulled off the market no more than two months after Father Preston arrived in Sycamore Hills. That, and the one time I met him, there was just something that felt off about him. It was his eyes. No matter what else was going on with the rest of his face, they always seemed expressionless. When in doubt, I trust my instincts about people."

"So that's where we're going?" Maureen asked, admittedly impressed that Manny had made such a conclusion. If it were up to her, they'd be heading to Father Preston's house instead.

"That's where we're going," Manny affirmed. "We should be there in a little more than five minutes."

Maureen grabbed her cell phone out of her pocket and checked the time. "That's gonna be tight. It's almost quarter to midnight. If our guess has been right on his patterns, he kills them as close to midnight as possible."

"Yes, but there's one more thing," Manny said calmly.

"What?"

"Ben Naismith hasn't been baptized yet," he replied, turning his head slightly to meet her gaze.

"He's had the kid for over a day and a half. You don't think that's enough time to baptize him?"

"From what I know of the guy, and from what your dreams seem to tell you, he's a stickler for the traditional ways. I can't be sure, but I'm betting he won't baptize the boy until it is officially Sunday morning. And that's the other reason I think he'll be at the old church. If I remember right from a wedding I went to there in high school, there's an old fount that he can use. No reason to think it wouldn't still be there.

Also, and I know it's a bit of a gamble, but I'm banking on the fact that he'll use the full rite. He wouldn't think he needs to hurry like with some of the other ones. Which reminds me." He reached for his radio. "I doubt the Feds are looking at this guy. I should call Agent Layton about this. We should have some backup anyway."

Maureen's hand shot out and pulled his away from the radio. He eyed her with sudden surprise.

"Maureen, what the hell?"

"What if you're wrong?" she asked. She actually felt confident in his deductive abilities, but she needed a reason for him to listen to her. "You said the Feds aren't looking at him. Maybe there's a reason for that. Maybe we're jumping to too many conclusions. Maybe they're going after someone else tonight that you don't know about. Or, maybe he isn't at this old church after all, and we'd just be wasting resources. We shouldn't call anyone until we know for sure that we're right."

"We need backup," Manny insisted.

"I'll be your backup," she said, pulling his service pistol out of her jeans to show him.

"Is that my backup gun?"

Maureen shrugged her shoulders.

Manny turned the pistol over to reveal the empty clip. He made a face at her.

"Father Patrick is faster than he looks," she explained, embarrassed that it only took a few minutes for her to forget how easily the old man had disarmed her. "Besides, it doesn't matter that it's not loaded. Preston won't know. Yours is. I'll just point this one at him and hold him while you cuff him."

"Maureen—"

"I just need to be the one to finish this." There was no point in playing it close to the vest anymore. "I can't explain it, but something inside me is screaming that it needs to be me who brings him down. If I do that, I'll have used these visions and dreams for good, and maybe—just maybe—they'll go away. Please, Manny."

Manny's eyebrows furrowed with skepticism, but he nodded, said nothing, and put his hand back on the steering wheel. The lights of the town were dimming behind them and in the ambient glow, she could see the river glistening ahead. Within moments, a small, sand-colored brick building loomed up out of the darkness on their right. Manny pulled the truck over on the side of the road fifty yards from the front door.

"I'm only going to give us a few minutes to get this done," he said, reaching for the radio and holding it up to his mouth. "Base this is Benitez."

"This is Collins," came the reply.

"Jack, I'm checking a lead on a potential suspect in the Naismith abduction. It might be nothing, but if you don't hear back from me in fifteen minutes, send a backup unit to the old St. Mary's west of town, by the river."

"Shouldn't you be calling the Feds on this one?" Collins asked.

Manny paused and stared at Maureen, tilting his head before continuing. "Looks like I hit a dead spot and don't have any service for my phone. You'll have to pass it along for me if you need to call in that backup. I'm clear." He hung up the radio and said to her, "We'll go the rest of the way on foot."

The night hung close around them, and without the truck's headlights to guide them, they had to feel their way along the

332

grass and gravel with their feet. The shadow of the church greeted them as they ran the last few yards to its side. There were few windows in the old building, and those that were there were leaded. They couldn't see in. Maureen took a step back and scanned the entire building. Now adjusted to the dark, she could detect a faint flickering light emanating from one of the square windows near the back of the church.

Candles, she thought.

Manny must have seen them too, because he laid a hand on her elbow and guided her in the direction of the rear of the church. "There's got to be a back door," he whispered. "It's probably our best way in."

Maureen nodded and followed along silently, keeping as low as he did to avoid their heads casting any shadows across the window. They rounded the corner and continued to creep along the back side of the church, searching for a rear door. They didn't find one on the back of the building, but as they rounded the opposite corner, they were confronted with three concrete steps leading up to a landing and their way in.

Manny was first to the door, holding Maureen back with one hand as they took to the stairs. He stepped up and quietly tried the knob. Nothing.

"Locked," he hissed, stepping back and appearing to contemplate for a moment. After a breath, he shrugged and reached into his holster to pull out his gun.

Maureen stepped to his side and put a hand on his, making him lower the weapon. "Let me have a look."

In the dark she couldn't make out his eyes very well, but was able to detect the movement of his head nodding his agreement. She moved in close to examine the door. It was a hollow, metal door, probably thirty years old or more. Her hand moved to the knob. It, too, was old, without an exterior keyhole that she could pick. She jiggled it as quietly as she could, noting how loose the latch bolt felt inside the plate.

"I think I can get this door open," she said reaching behind her and opening her hand to him. "Hand me a credit card."

There was a pause before Manny spoke. "How about my library card? It's easier to replace."

She felt the plastic rectangle hit her hand and tested it with both hands. It seemed strong enough. She slipped the card into the jamb above the bolt and felt her way down, working the knob as she did. It only took a few moments before the old lock gave way, and she was able to push the door open. The hallway that the door opened to was dark except for the dimmest of lights showing around a corner some thirty feet away. Maureen recognized the flicker. Candlelight. She edged forward but felt herself suddenly jerked back by the shoulder.

"Let me go first," Manny's voice rasped. He had his gun raised and moved past her into the hall, reaching back to grab her wrist and lead her. "Stay behind me and keep close."

The candlelight they were heading toward offered no real light to go by, so they went slow, taking all the care they could not to let their footsteps fall too hard.

"You couldn't have brought a flashlight?" Maureen grumbled in a low whisper as they felt their way along.

"Shush," came Manny's response from the darkness ahead.

They came to a doorway that led to the side of the altar. Manny stuck his head around just far enough to see out, but Maureen could not wait behind him any longer. The drive to finish it all overwhelmed her, and she bolted past Manny, around the corner, and into the candlelight. His surprised exclamation broke the eerie silence and resonated off the walls of the empty church. The sound made her freeze as she realized the foolishness of her action. To her surprise, there was no movement within the church. They were alone.

Maureen turned to Manny and beckoned him to join her. He cautiously crept to her side, and they continued forward into the nave. The lacquered, wooden altar ahead, on which the largest candle she had ever seen burned and served as the sole source of illumination, was surrounded by a pile of sticks and logs. Maureen's eyes scanned the rest of the room in the dim light. From what she could make out, it was modestly decorated—as far as Catholic churches went. The pews were set in two rows and were made of the same wood as the altar. The altar itself was set on a short, raised platform of stone, surrounded by a simple wooden rail. The baptismal fount that Manny had mentioned sat off to their right. Even from the twelve or so paces that she stood from it, Maureen could see the candlelight flickering on the water inside of it.

She took two more steps toward the altar and looked to her left at the only visible sign of ostentatious décor in the place. A golden crucifix hung on the wall behind the altar with an ornately carved and polished image of Christ hanging from it in his familiar position. Maureen walked closer to it and stopped to stare into the eyes of the Christian Savior. The artist responsible had done their work. The face was so lifelike and detailed that Maureen, herself, could almost feel the anguish of crucifixion that was being portrayed, just like the one in the newer St. Mary's. She followed the eyes down to the altar and felt her breath catch in her throat at the sight that confronted her.

Little Ben Naismith was lying, shirtless, on top of the altar. His body had been obscured by the wood that was no doubt meant to be set alight as soon as the sacrificial ritual was finished. But now, Maureen could observe the child's serene features. His eyes were closed, and his face was without any trace of pain. She was relieved at the absence of a wound on the child's neck and of blood on the altar. Still, she was concerned by the raspy and ragged sound of his breathing, likely the result of whatever had been used to drug him into his current unconscious state.

Maureen reached out to try to gently shake the boy awake. As her hand brushed his hair, she felt something wet and oily on his forehead. It glistened in the candlelight as she brought her fingers closer to her face. The oil gave off a faint odor of incense that she recalled as a child, seated next to her mother on a hard, wooden pew in Massachusetts all those years ago. Now that it was in her nose, the odor seemed to get stronger around her. She allowed her eyes to dart around the altar at the rest of the wood piled up. Now that she was looking for it, the glistening, wet appearance of the oil on the logs became apparent. So, too, did the presence of the long, curved knife with the carved, wooden handle that she had seen in her dreams. It now appeared in the flesh, lying next to the Naismith child on the altar, ready to do its work.

Maureen's skin began to crawl. Something wasn't right. Father Preston had apparently finished the baptism of the boy and was preparing to begin the sacrifice. Where was he? Did he forget something and leave the boy, trusting that the chemicals he used would keep him knocked out? Did he hear Manny and Maureen break in the back door and flee? Or were the eyes of the crucified Jesus behind her not the only eyes looking at her right now?

Her eyes darted around the church looking for Manny. She saw his form at the edge of the candlelight, pistol cradled in both hands at the ready, checking up and down the rows of pews. Clearly he, too, was looking for the missing priest.

"Manny," she called out, not bothering to adhere to stealth anymore, "get up here. We gotta get the kid out of here."

Maureen saw him turn and begin to make his way toward her. She looked back down at Ben Naismith, closed her eyes, and put her hand on his chest. It gently and slowly rose up and down, and she could feel his heart beating behind his tiny rib cage. She didn't know much about kids or medicine, but to her touch, his skin felt too cold and his heartbeat too slow.

"You're going to be fine," she whispered, "you're going to be just fine."

Manny's footsteps were getting close, but just as they reached the foot of the altar, they stopped abruptly, and a loud thud replaced them in the silent air. Maureen heard Manny let out a sharp groan and opened her eyes just in time to see him limply fall sideways, sending his pistol sliding across the stone floor and coming to rest in front of the front pew.

Maureen's eyes left Manny lying on the ground and moved up to the figure looming over his body.

"You will not stop my work," its cold voice said.

†HIR†Y-NINE

Maureen drew a deep breath and slowly circled around the altar to confront her would-be attacker. She kept her hands near her sides, waiting for the opportunity to reach around her back, grab the pistol from its hiding place, and force the man to his knees. She gritted her teeth, trying to keep her jaw from quivering and betraying her nerves.

Poker face. You can do this.

She inhaled deeply and exhaled. The sound of her breath seemed to rattle off the stone walls. Maureen tried to keep her face smooth. She stopped in front of the altar and planted her feet firmly, facing down the priest as an Old West gunslinger would have. She stood as straight and confidently as she could, trying to look as strong as possible.

Father Preston came forward a couple of steps, allowing the candlelight to fully illuminate him. He wore a white alb over his priest's collar and a purple stole with elaborate stitching near its ends draped over his shoulders. His lips were creased in a bemused grin, but his eyes, like Manny had described, seemed emotionless. He carried a large, tubular object in his hand that glinted gold in the flickering light. Maureen stared closer at it and then cast her eyes up to the altar at the holder that held the candle. They were a match.

So that's why there was only one, she thought grimly.

It was clear now, despite their best efforts, that Father Preston had heard her and Manny break in, grabbed the candlestick, and hid in the shadows, waiting for the right time to strike. Manny had given him that opportunity when he rushed heedlessly to her call. She pushed away the thought that she was to blame for him being blindsided and hurt. She looked down at him lying on the stone floor at the priest's feet. Thankfully, she couldn't see any blood on the ground, and as she looked on, he began to stir and try to get up onto his hands and knees.

It would have been better for him if he had stayed down. As she looked back at Father Preston, she could see that his eyes also had shifted behind him to the fallen detective. He looked back at her and, almost arrogantly and without breaking eye contact, stepped back two paces, turned and unleashed a savage kick to the side of Manny's head. Manny flopped down on his side and lay still once again.

Maureen wasn't sure if this was the chance she had been waiting for, but as soon as the priest's eyes shifted to a different prey, her body took over. Her right hand flew behind her and grabbed the pistol from her waistband. She swept it around in front of her and held it, aiming it at his chest and trying to look as threatening as she could. She cocked back the hammer of the pistol to make the message sink in.

Maureen locked eyes with Father Preston once more. For the first time, she felt as though she could detect the slightest hint of emotion in them. Was it indignation that she was seeing? Was it scorn at her audacity to pull a gun and attempt to kill him? Maybe amusement at her feeble threat? Maybe a perverse assurance that his faith would protect him from a bullet? Whatever it was, it was clear to her that he was silently daring her to pull the trigger. She was caught. Maureen felt her face twitch as she uncocked the hammer. Her heart sank into her stomach further as she let her arms fall and dropped the gun.

At that moment, another image flashed into her head. Manny's gun. She had a vague idea of where it had come to rest. If she could just get by the priest and get to it before he had a chance to react, she might still have a chance to end this. She tensed her muscles, getting ready to spring to her left. As she did so, she broke eye contact with Father Preston and shifted her gaze toward the area in front of the front pew where she knew the pistol lay. Its barrel caught the candlelight and glinted just enough for her to mark its position.

It took less than a second for her to realize she had made a mistake. As she glanced back toward the priest, she noticed how his eyes had followed hers and now, as they again made eye contact, a sickening, knowing grin broke on his lips. As if he had read her thoughts, he darted in the direction of the gun, and, despite his long priest's garb, hurdled the railing surrounding the altar.

The move threw Maureen's timing off, and she darted around the railing as fast as she could in a desperate attempt to reach the weapon before her opponent. She was a split second too late as Father Preston made a baseball slide in front of her. Maureen leaped on his back. Her momentum betrayed her, though, and Father Preston managed with stunning ease to throw her over his shoulder and send her crashing painfully into the hard wood of the pew.

The shock wave of pain that radiated to all the extremities of her body shut down Maureen's thoughts for a brief moment. She recovered to find herself lying on her side, back still against the pew, with Father Preston hovering a few paces away. He was facing her, obviously pleased with himself, and holding her last hope firmly in his right hand.

"It seems God is on my side," he said triumphantly.

"You actually believe that," she snorted back. The wild light in his eyes had slowly begun to grow, as if the madness inside his mind had at last begun to seep through the cracks.

"I know it, Ms. Allen," he shouted, spreading his arms wide in emulation of the pose of the carved Christ behind him and looking up to the ceiling rafters.

Maureen bristled at his use of her name.

"Oh, you didn't know that I knew who you were?" he continued, looking back down at her. His voice was rising to a manic tone. "Of course I know you. That old fool Father Patrick won't stop talking about you. The mystery woman with the visions. I found it very interesting that you and he believe that you can see inside my mind. Well if it is true, tell me, do you understand the great work that I am undertaking?"

"I understand that you're insane and you think sacrificing children like they were a cow or a lamb is what it will take to gain your God's favor."

Father Preston's chuckle froze her blood. "You understand nothing," he growled, gliding a half dozen paces away from her and placing himself in front of the altar. He then began to pace, as if he were giving a sermon to a full congregation seated in the shadows before him.

"The world has descended into chaos," he intoned in his

most priestly voice. "The enemies of God are closing in on all sides. The faithful, those who truly understand the Bible's teachings, are scarce. The end times are approaching faster than you realize. This war in the Middle East is the prelude to Armageddon, and we have to choose the side we will serve. Will we join with the armies of Gog and Magog and be destroyed, or will we join the enlightened and the faithful and achieve paradise? That is the choice that lies before us.

"But we must be ready, for those who would count themselves among the chosen must prove themselves obedient. I'm no monster, Ms. Allen. I am a shepherd. I am the Ra'ah! I do not sacrifice these children for perverse pleasure. I do it to wipe away the sins of their families, and in so doing, to bring them back into favor with God. Only when one loses something pure and precious to them, can one find atonement. They will not do it for themselves. These lip service believers will go to confession, and I will tell them that they are absolved, but I know the truth. This is the only way to build the Lord's army for the coming war with darkness. The signs are clear; the enemy will be here soon. We must all be pure in the eyes of God in order to swell his ranks! Now do you start to understand?"

"I understand that people like you are why I tend to avoid church," Maureen hissed through clenched teeth. She had managed to pull herself up to one knee but still kept one hand on the ground for support. "I don't see any reason your God would want you to do something like this."

"Then you are blind! Priests are specifically selected to carry out these duties!" Father Preston tightened his grip on Manny's gun and continued to wave it about as he spoke. "Was it not the job of the Kohanim in ancient Israel to carry out these sacrifices? A sacrifice of atonement is not valid unless it is done by a priest! The priests of the Tribe of Levi were not only the most holy of men, they were warriors. Was it not they alone who could carry the Ark into battle and drive back the hosts rallied against the Army of God? All of this has been forgotten by the modern day clergy. They preach tolerance of those who set themselves against the teachings of the scriptures. Your own dear Father Patrick would take sinners like Tom Lowes and Tasha Naismith to his side and coddle them and console them if they came asking to be forgiven.

"And then there's you!" He leveled the pistol at her. "Poor little Maureen Allen. You think that the men of God who tried to drive that evil out of you mistreated you. So you live on the road, living as other people, surviving through thievery, medicating yourself with ill-gotten drugs, and drowning yourself in alcohol. He wants so badly to save you, you know. He wants to bring you back to God because he believes your visions are divinely sent!" Father Preston let out a single, scornful laugh. "He can't see you for what you really are: a despicable whore whose abilities come from the Devil himself. Your mother was right about you!"

Maureen felt her face twist in anger at the mention of her mother. She pushed herself to her feet and stood rigid, fists clenched. She had no plan for getting past the gun, but she almost didn't care. Almost. That minute amount of fear and uncertainty kept her feet rooted to the floor in front of the priest.

"Did I hit a soft spot?" he said with mock sympathy. "Well, your reaction just proves that you know what I say is true. You are a child of evil and beyond redemption. Fortunately," he grinned as he spoke, "I can put you out of your misery."

Maureen eyed the gun pointed at her chest. "Go ahead," she replied coldly, trying her best to remain defiant to the end.

"I shall, but first, I think I'd prefer you on your knees before me."

No chance in hell, Maureen thought. She didn't move a muscle.

"Do it, or I'll shoot the cop first and make you watch!" he shouted as he swung the pistol to the side and pointed it at Manny. He was still lying face down on the floor, breathing, but nothing else.

At least he's not going to have to watch me die. Defeated, Maureen bowed her head, gritted her teeth, took a step forward, and knelt in front of Father Preston.

The priest re-aimed the gun at her head and began to chant the prayer that she had felt come from her own throat in her dreams:

Abwûn
d'bwaschmâja
Nethkâdasch schmach
Têtê malkuthach.
Nehwê tzevjânach aikâna d'bwaschmâja af b'arha.
Hawvlân lachma d'sûnkanân jaomâna.
Waschboklân chaubên wachtahên aikâna daf chnân schwoken
l'chaijabên.
Wela tachlân l'nesjuna
ela patzân min bischa.
Metol dilachie malkutha wahaila wateschbuchta l'ahlâm almîn.
Amên.

Maureen closed her eyes. The gunshot shattered the air.

FORTY

The silence of the church swallowed up the echo of the muzzle blast. She couldn't count the seconds that she knelt there in the darkness behind her closed eyes, waiting for the pain of hot, burning lead to engulf her body. The sensation never came. Her chest continued to inflate and deflate, and the sound of her own breath returned to her ears.

I'm alive, she told herself.

Maureen opened her eyes and was met with the sight of Father Preston's body sprawled out at the base of the altar. His eyes were open, unblinking. A stream of blood was oozing from a gaping wound in his chest and collecting in a dark pool on the floor. Maureen slowly got to her feet and tiptoed to the body. Her eyes immediately found Manny's pistol lying some five feet from the priest's outstretched hand. She picked it up as quickly as she could and pointed it down at Father Preston, waiting for a twitch, a muscle spasm—any sign of life. When none came, she nervously kicked one of his feet. Nothing. Father Preston was dead.

Maureen let out a sigh, but her relief quickly turned to confusion as she turned around to see Manny only now beginning to pull himself off the floor and into a seated position, rubbing the back of his head and jaw with both hands. He didn't have another backup firearm, as far as she could see anyway, so it couldn't have been him that fired the shot. But then who did?

As she scanned around the shadows of the church, her eyes fell upon a dark mass in the back corner. As she looked on, it began to move toward the candlelight, its footsteps clattering on the stone floor. Maureen raised Manny's gun.

"That's the second time tonight you've pointed a gun at me, Maureen," an all-too-familiar voice rang out in the darkness.

Father Patrick stepped into the light. His eyes were somber as he slowly made his way over to her. His right arm hung at his side, weighed down with his own pistol that looked much like Manny's backup service weapon. He gave her a weak smile as he reached into his pocket. "You ran out before I could stop you," he said, handing her the clip he had taken from her. "I was worried you wouldn't be able to properly defend yourself if Father Preston got the jump on you." He looked over her shoulder at the body of his junior priest and shook his head sadly.

"You followed us here?" Maureen said, still in shock to see the old man, let alone wrap her mind around the fact that he had just saved her life.

Father Patrick nodded. "I felt a certain responsibility to you and the children. Once I had all the facts, I realized I should have seen Preston for what he was. All that time, I ignored that gut feeling that you get when you first meet someone and they seem a little off, you know? I thought he was just a very buttoned-up, young priest who held too strictly to the old Catholic ways. He laid his true soul bare though, didn't he? Is the boy all right?"

"Yes, it looks like he's knocked out by the same chemical that Father Preston used on the others, but he's breathing," Maureen responded before she had fully processed what he had just said. "Wait, you mean you heard that entire speech and waited that long to shoot him? I should kill you for that!"

"I'm not as young as I used to be," the old priest replied, his voice full of sadness. "I needed time to make a clean shot."

Maureen opened her mouth to say something, but there were no words. As angry as she wanted to be at him, she couldn't do anything except hug him. "Don't get used to it," she said as she released her embrace.

The old priest smiled at her.

Maureen went over to pick up the second pistol, and Manny, now moving a little steadier on his feet, came up to them. His eyes were still blinking rapidly to push away the pain, but his voice was strong.

"Is everyone all right?" he asked.

Maureen and Father Patrick assured him that both they and Ben Naismith were all right. He wore his relief like a badge and gathered her in his arms, holding her close. Maureen placed her head to his chest. His heart was beating fast as he kissed the top of her head.

"All right," said Manny, releasing her and taking his sidearm back, "I admit, I got knocked around pretty hard there, and I was in and out for most of it. So, let's go over what happened."

Before Maureen could say anything, Father Patrick spoke up. "I'm afraid I was forced to kill Father Preston. It was, of course, in defense of Maureen and the young boy, but nevertheless, I believe you'll have to take me in."

He placed both his hands in front of him while offering Manny his gun. Manny looked apologetically at Maureen before turning to the priest and nodding his head in agreement. He put his pistol in its holster and began reaching around his back for his handcuffs.

"Wait!" Maureen broke in and turned quickly to Manny. "Am I correct in assuming you have to account for every discharge of your service weapon?"

Manny nodded slowly, a suspicious look breaking on his face.

Maureen didn't let him get any questions out. She ripped his gun from his belt and ran out the side door into the night air. She stopped several paces from the edge of the river and fired a single shot out into the water. A small geyser erupted from the surface, but her eyes stayed on the casing that flew away from the weapon. She picked it up and ran back inside with it.

Father Patrick and Manny had begun to run out behind her and were just reaching the door when she came back. She pushed past them without a word and rushed back to the altar to complete her plan. She rubbed the spent bullet casing on her shirt and let it fall on the ground near Father Preston's body. Manny and Father Patrick came up behind her a moment later.

"Maureen, what the hell are you doing?" shouted Manny.

"Completing the story," Maureen said, her eyes still down on the fallen priest.

"What story?" asked Manny.

"The story we're going to tell to the police."

"Oh I see," he said, "and what story would that be?"

"We're going to tell them everything that happened,"

Maureen asserted, "except for one thing. I struggled with Father Preston for your gun, and it went off and killed him. Father Patrick was never here."

"Maureen, I don't think—" Manny began.

"He was never here!"

Father Patrick laid a hand on her shoulder. "Maureen, what I've done, I was compelled to do by my conscience. But that same conscience also compels me to face the repercussions of my actions. I hoped never to have to take another life for the rest of mine, and now I have. Even though the cause would seem just, I don't have any divine right to exact this type of punishment, even on someone as far gone as Father Preston. The heavenly court will judge me one day, but the earthly courts should handle my fate now. It would be best if I turned myself in."

Maureen stared into his eyes. They were unwavering in their resolve. She looked to Manny. He crossed to her and put his hand on her shoulder, taking back his gun from her.

"Father Patrick is right," he said gently. "Response teams will be here any minute. He's not going to be able to leave without being seen. It'll be fine. Father Patrick shot Father Preston to keep him from killing you. Nobody would bring charges against him."

Maureen turned her head to the priest, who smiled solemnly and nodded his head. He handed his weapon to Manny and took Maureen by the hand. She could think of nothing better to do than squeeze it with all the reassurance she could muster. It was only then that she became aware of a single tear that had begun to well up in her eye. She hadn't realized how much, but in the short time she'd known him, she'd come to care for Father Patrick. The feeling was clearly mutual, and it saddened her to think that it might be the last time she'd see him. After all, once this whole mess was cleaned up, she could hardly stay in Sycamore Hills, even if she was now cleared of suspicion. There was too much of a stain on her name. And besides, she couldn't be sure the dreams wouldn't return.

Manny went up at the altar to check on little Ben Naismith. His eyes were still closed but his breathing seemed a little stronger. Manny picked him up, and together they walked through the darkened nave toward the front door. They left Father Preston where he lay, the single candle keeping vigil over his body.

They were greeted by the sight of two Sycamore Hills police cars pulling up with lights flashing. Manny carefully handed Ben to Maureen and walked with the priest to greet them. As she hoisted the boy up, she felt his little head nestle onto her shoulder. He let out a soft coo and almost instantly, a tiny pair of arms were clasped around her neck. Maureen realized in that moment that she'd never held a child before. She was surprised at how easy it was.

Before she stepped out into the night air, a strange sensation overcame her. She turned and stepped just to the threshold of the nave and stared up at the altar to meet the gaze of the statuesque Christ. Closing her eyes, she began her silent conversation.

All right, I used whatever this thing is in my head for good. I don't know if You gave it to me, but I've done what Father Patrick said I needed to do. So, can You please, PLEASE take it away now? I've never asked for anything, so, maybe You kind of owe me this?

She felt a bit silly. She didn't really know how a person was supposed to talk to God. And so, she did what only seemed appropriate if the Almighty were actually listening.

There, in the dark, Maureen Allerton prayed—for the first time since her brother died—the only prayer she still remembered:

Our Father, who art in Heaven
Hallowed be thy name...

FORTY-ONE

"Well, Ms. Allen," Agent Layton said as he slammed his briefcase on the table in front of her and pulled out a manila folder stuffed with papers, "it's a pleasure to see you again."

Maureen had been waiting for over three hours for him to come and release her. She had given her statement to the officers who arrived on the scene. Their explanation of the priest's plan, and the fantastical nature of the events that had occurred, had been met with skepticism to be sure, but she had been certain Manny had convinced his coworkers that their account was indeed the truth. That was, of course, until Agent Layton had arrived and ordered her and Father Patrick taken into custody. Her neck was still sore from trying to sleep on that jail cell bed. She wondered how the priest had fared. Manny had advocated for their release, but to no avail. His reward was being banished to the hallway bench outside the interrogation room of the Sheriff's Department, presumably waiting for Agent Lorenzo to take him to another room in an attempt to poke a hole in their story. If she moved her head to the right, Maureen could see his face through the half-drawn blinds.

"Ms. Allen," Agent Layton's voice rousted her from her

thoughts, "I've gone over your file, and I'd like to go over a few things with you."

"Don't know what I can add, Agent," she said matter-of-factly. "I know it all sounds a little crazy, but it's the truth."

"Oh, no doubt there," he replied. "We have plenty of evidence to support that from the search of Preston's home. It's just like you and Detective Benitez said. We found an excess of holy oil, purchased via account book manipulation. We found the bibles with his scribblings in them and a small, basement altar and shrine. We've got a supply of chloroform and some black gloves that we're testing for the murdered boys' DNA. There's little doubt that you found and killed the man we were looking for. But it's not the case file I'd like to go over with you."

He picked up the manila folder and began leafing through it, almost too casually for Maureen's liking. "Lots of great stuff in this file, Ms. Allerton. Oh! I mean, Ms. Allen. Or do I mean Ms. Anderson? Or is it *Mary* Allen? Or maybe I should call you Maria Adams?"

Maureen frowned. She'd been waiting for the hammer to fall, and now the time had come. He knew he had her, and she could see he was reveling in it.

"You've been quite a few people in your life, haven't you?" he pressed. "I have to wonder, though, why you've never used Keane as one of your identities."

"If you knew my mother, you'd understand," Maureen said flatly. She could see there was no point in denying anything.

"Well, for simplicity's sake," said Agent Layton, "what should we call you?"

"Allerton's fine. I've always called myself Maureen Allerton in my own mind."

"Very good then, Ms. Allerton! Let's talk about your friend, Father Patrick."

"What about him?"

"I won't beat around the bush," he said, folding his hands on the table and staring earnestly at her. "We took notice of your relationship pretty early on. It wasn't too hard for us to find the FBI file on one Corporal Patrick Mullen, a former Green Beret who deserted in Vietnam thirty-seven years ago. And it took us even less time to determine the good Father and the Corporal were one in the same. The man's been left unmolested by the FBI for all these years for the simple reason that we've never seen him as much of a security threat. Especially given his choice to enter the priesthood. But now, who knows? It's a hard thing for a soldier to completely forget who he used to be, and he's now shown his willingness to take a life in what he believes is a just cause. What's to stop him from doing it again? Would the community be safer if he were behind bars?"

That was too much for Maureen. "You can't do that! Manny promised that he wouldn't be prosecuted."

"Since when does the word of a local detective take precedence over the FBI? So I'll ask you, Maureen. What are we going to do about this situation of ours?"

"Oh, we're on a first name basis now? Fine. What do you want from me, Howard?"

Agent Layton chuckled softly and shook his head. "You're right, Ms. Allerton, I do want something, but it's likely not what you think." He closed the folder in front of him, put it back into his briefcase, and pulled out another folder. This one was a dark green color and held only two pages inside of it. He opened it and slid it across the table. "I can send you away for a decent clip with the sheet I've got on you for your identity and fraud crimes. And if I felt so inclined, I could drag our good Father Patrick before a federal prosecutor. And I'm friends with one, so if I really wanted to, I could get something to stick and ruin that old man's life. But instead, I called her and got this little deal worked out. You sign that paper in front of you, agreeing to six months in a female, minimum-security federal prison plus three years' probation, during which time the FBI can call you in to utilize your—let's call them—less-than-conventional techniques, and your original statement becomes part of a closed file. Patrick Mullen can go on being Father McGill, undisturbed by law enforcement, and his involvement in this case will be kept out of the public record. So what do you say, do we have a deal?"

Maureen felt her stomach drop. "What do you mean by 'less-than-conventional techniques'?"

Agent Layton's eyebrows raised slightly. "I'm not usually a man who believes in anything but the physical evidence presented to me, Ms. Allerton. Nevertheless, I am familiar with certain FBI, shall we say, legends? And this past week has brought to mind one that apparently happened in Massachusetts, oh, a little more than twenty-five years ago. Apparently, there was a little girl whose dream led to the discovery of her murdered brother's body. Darndest thing. It was the perfect crime, too. No apparent motive, all of the people closest to the family had tight alibis, no clear direction to move the investigation in, and then a thirty-second phone call, a child's hysterical voice on the other end, and lo and behold, the body was found the next day. It really defies explanation!" Agent Layton tilted his head and gave Maureen a long, knowing look.

Maureen couldn't hold his gaze for long. She simply looked down at her feet. "I didn't ask to be like this," she mumbled.

"I believe it," said Agent Layton, his tone suddenly softening. "I can't imagine anyone who would ask to be able to do what you seem to be able to do. I'm still not one hundred percent sure I believe it myself. But, I do know a useful resource when I see one. So, let's just call your position a 'consulting profiler'. It's pretty simple, really. We find ourselves stumped on a case, we bring you in, you sleep a little for us and see if whatever you see in your dreams can give us the missing pieces. Doesn't come with much in the way of monetary benefit, I'm afraid, but look at it this way, you'll be able to balance the karmic scales a bit, and what's more, you'll be allowed to start fresh without all those warrants hanging over your head. And as for the prison time, judging from what I've seen in the paper trail of your various identities over the last decade or so, Waseca will be an improvement over quite a few of the places you've called home. So what do you say, do we have a deal?"

Maureen could see she had very little choice. The out that she was being given was probably more than she deserved. The prospect of being treated like a performing monkey for the FBI for three years was less than appealing, but she had six months to figure out how to wriggle off that hook. She raised her head and looked steadily into Agent Layton's eyes. "Do you have a pen?"

Agent Layton got up as soon as she had signed the paper and quickly walked out of the room without saying another word to her. Maureen followed him with her eyes and watched intently, shifting her head so that she could again see through the blinds as he stopped in front of Manny. He got to his feet and stood in front of the agent for a few brief moments. Agent Layton was clearly doing the talking, and after he had finished, he reached into his pocket and handed Manny a small, white card before turning and heading for the exit. Manny stood in the hall for a moment before rushing in the opposite direction to come around to the door to the interrogation room. There was a look on his face that seemed to her to be equal parts confusion and elation.

"What was that all about?" she asked, not wanting him to have the first word. It would probably just have been something sappy.

"What? Oh, that? Agent Layton just congratulated me on a job well done and gave me his card. Seems there might be an opening in the criminal profiling department at the St. Louis branch, and he thinks I should apply."

"Yeah, absolutely, why not?" She had no doubt he'd do fine and anyway, after all that had happened here, why would he want to stay in Sycamore Hills just to go back to what he was doing before? She knew that if he joined the FBI, a relationship would be nearly impossible for them, given what had just happened to her with regards to Agent Layton, but maybe that was for the best. After all, she wasn't really the type to settle down the way she sensed he would want her to.

"Well, it's been a long day for us," he said. "Can I take you out for a drink or three?"

"No," she said firmly. His face fell but she put on her best smile to comfort him. "No drinks for me tonight. You can take me to dinner though. And, who knows, maybe we can go to your place afterwards?"

She moved in close to him and put her arms around his neck. *Poor man,* she thought, *the least I can do is give him one more night before I go.*

"I have to warn you up front though, I can't stay," she said. "I have some place that I have to be in the morning, and there will be hell to pay if I'm not there."

EPILOGUE

Father Patrick flipped the car into park, sighed, and stretched, his hand brushing against the rosary beads hanging from the rearview mirror. It had been a twelve-hour drive up from Missouri, and he had only stopped for gas; he wanted to be sure he was here on time. He kept the old Volvo running so the heat stayed on. Back home in Sycamore Hills, the winter hadn't been all that bad, but it had seemed there was going to be another cold snap and dusting of snow before spring really settled in. It didn't look like spring was anywhere near up here in Minnesota. He checked the clock on the dashboard. 8:58.

Glancing in the rearview mirror again, Father Patrick noted a black sedan pulling into the lot and parking about two hundred yards down. No one got out. *Obviously doesn't think he's been made,* he thought to himself, but Father Patrick had been tracking his tail since the Highway 14 exit. The black sedan had been fairly conspicuous on the side of the roundabout exit off I-35. He even caught a glimpse of the driver, a very young-looking man in a black suit. Agent Layton hadn't even given him the courtesy of sending out a veteran! The rookie had done everything by the book: pulled up to the rear of the Volvo to identify the license plate, then dropped two car lengths back and one lane over, and maintained pace with him the rest of the way. Father Patrick had made no attempt to shake his pursuit. It wasn't yet time.

The loud horn signaling the opening of the security gate shook him out of his thoughts. Father Patrick turned his eyes to the passenger's seat where a bulky manila envelope sat. He wondered how this would all be received. He'd held the debate in his head over and over for six months, wondering if he was overstepping his bounds, even resolving less than a week ago to not even drive up. In the end, though, his sense of duty had prevailed, and even promises made to oneself were promises that needed to be kept.

He turned back toward the gate, which was now beginning to slowly crawl open. A small, flannel-clad figure had appeared, waiting to cross over the threshold to freedom. She had a large duffel bag slung over her shoulder, and her honey-blonde hair was pulled back in that familiar ponytail. Father Patrick wondered how she could stand the cold with no jacket. He honked the horn once, loud and sharp, and flashed the high beams. The woman turned her head and began to make her way over to the vehicle. Father Patrick leaned over to the passenger's side door and pushed it open as she approached the car.

"Well, Father," said Maureen as she stuck her head into the car, "fancy meeting you here."

"Yep," he replied, "even though you didn't answer any of my letters, I had a feeling you were going to need a ride when you got out of this place." He reached over to the passenger's seat and removed the manila envelope, using it to wave her into the car. "Get in before you freeze."

Maureen stood for a moment before shoving her bag over the headrest into the back seat and climbing in herself. She looked the same as the day the Feds had taken her out of Sycamore Hills. There had been many questions among the locals as to where she had gone and, though Father Patrick had insisted to all who had asked him personally that she was safe, he didn't divulge anything else as to her whereabouts. The town had eventually settled into quiet gossip, most of it inaccurate, about the strange young lady who had only been a part of the community for a few short weeks, and her ties to the unsettling events that were now, thankfully, behind them.

Father Patrick backed the car out of the parking space, turned, and headed toward the long entrance road that led back to the highway. Looking in the rearview mirror, he could see the black sedan pulling out of its spot, giving him a short lead, and heading down the same road. He smiled to himself and switched on the radio, turning the sound down low so he could talk with Maureen.

"So how was it inside?"

"I've been in worse places," she responded casually. "It's pretty low security as far as those things go. I even had a cell to myself. Little present from Agent Layton, I guess. Did you know the Enron guy was here before they turned it into a chick jail?" Father Patrick shook his head. "Yeah me neither. One of the guards told me. I didn't have his cell, though."

"So, does that mean you got my letters?"

Maureen looked over at him. "Now look, Father, I know you meant well and everything, but I was just trying to make a clean break. Don't get me wrong, I appreciate everything you've done for me, but me being a part of your life...well, you're just going to end up in a bad spot. I'm not worth it, believe me." She turned her head back to the window.

"Then why did you take the ride?" he asked. She made no answer so Father Patrick removed the envelope from his lap and slapped it down into hers. "Why don't you let me decide what's worth it," he said firmly.

"What's this?" she asked quietly.

"Five grand to get you started."

She pulled out the tightly banded brick of cash. "I can't take this!"

"You're going to have to, because I'm not taking it back." He had come to the end of the entrance road and paused for a minute. The black sedan would need to catch up a bit to be able to take his bait. Smiling to himself, he turned the car right and headed west.

"Now listen to me, Maureen," he continued. "Don't worry about the money, I've got a lot more stowed away in case I ever had to disappear. I made up my mind to stay with you for a little while and help you find your way. I got a visit from Agent Layton over the winter, and he told me why I was never questioned after Father Preston's death. Probably trying to rattle me, make sure I knew I was free on the back of his charity, in case he ever needed some leverage. Whatever the case, he told me what you agreed to."

"Yeah, well, he can think again if he thinks I'm going to be his little dancing monkey!"

"Maureen, you have been given a gift, and I truly believe that it comes from God as a means to do good in this world. But—"

"Oh, cram it with your God crap! Whatever the hell is in my head, it hasn't ever done me one bit of good! I did what you said and used it to help, and I still got screwed! And don't you dare start in with your whole 'God afflicts those he loves' bullshit, either!"

"It's not supposed to do *you* good, but it made all the difference in the world to a little boy in Sycamore Hills and his family!" Father Patrick was beginning to feel the blood rush to his face. He paused for a minute, took a deep breath and regained control of his voice. "But if you had let me finish, I was going to say that it's not up to me to convince you of what you're meant to do. I know you're not truly ready to receive God back into your life and embrace the role He's given you. Yet. So I'm going to help you disappear for a while. I've got a little place in eastern Wyoming with a few trustworthy people I know close by. I'll take you out there and get you settled, and I'll stay as long as you feel you need me to. I gotta warn you though, I'm going to have to take you on a very roundabout way, and so it'll take us a week or more to get there. And I don't want any questions."

"Guess that means we'll be spending some time in some seedy little motels on the way?" she asked in a mocking-seductive tone. "You wouldn't want to go breaking your stupid celibacy vows now, would you?"

"Trust me, child," he replied, putting on his most priestly tone, "if I wanted to break my vows, you would not be high on the list of people I would call."

"Too young and hot for you?"

Too Anglo, he thought to himself, while out loud, he dryly replied, "Something like that."

They rode in silence for a few minutes before Maureen reached into her pocket and pulled out a small, black flip phone.

"They gave this to me as I was leaving this morning. Another little gift from Agent Layton," she said, showing it to him. "I guess this is supposed to be their line to me. Cheap bastards could have at least gotten me one of those Blackberry phones or something. Well, here's what I think of this." She began to roll down her window.

"No!" Father Patrick yelled sharply, surprising even himself.

Maureen stopped and stared back at him, a stunned look on her face. "Why not? I'm getting out of this deal somehow, and you can't stop me!"

Father Patrick glanced again into the rearview mirror. The black sedan had taken its place about five hundred yards behind. There were no other cars within sight at the moment.

"I'm not going to stop you, but you can't throw it out the window right now, trust me. Give it here." He put his hand out, and she hesitantly put the phone in his palm.

He inspected the phone as best he could while keeping one eye on the road. It was three-year-old technology at least, but that didn't mean there couldn't be a bug or tracker in it. In fact, he was almost positive there was. They'd have to dispose of it very carefully.

"I have a couple of ideas about this," he said finally, "but we'll need to take a couple extra days."

"Whatever you say, Father," Maureen said. It seemed to him that she'd resigned herself for the time being. "But you're paying for gas and food, right?"

Father Patrick smirked at her. Prison hadn't mellowed her at all. "I'll pay. I've brought plenty of cash."

Maureen let out a soft chuckle and turned back toward the window, letting her eyes close as she leaned her head to rest it on the seat, finally letting some of the tension release from her body. Father Patrick settled himself back in his seat. This trip would be trying on the patience, but he had made a vow. He had killed a man and, as evil as that man was and even in the defense of another, the taking of that life would not sit quietly on his conscience. The debt had to be paid, and he was now even further in the red than he had been. He would see this journey through to the end, wherever that might lead him. He flipped his blinker on and took the next exit off the highway.

The black sedan followed.

author notes and acknowledgments

The core concept of *Unholy Shepherd*—what I call The Demon Sight—is, in its presentation in this book, a creation of my own mind. However, it does draw from its share of real-world phenomena and documented research. Government projects, such as Stargate in the 1970s (which will be touched on in later books), tested multiple purported "psychics" and reportedly documented their share of evidence supporting the idea as true (or, at least, plausible), especially in cases of remote viewing. Additionally, fringe theories also exist— occasionally promoted on certain entertainment shows— regarding the idea of prophetic dreaming potentially being genetic. Little true scientific evidence exists to support this theory—more a loose collection of anecdotes—but it's fun to think about nonetheless.

I would tend to call myself a "skeptical believer." I am willing to believe in almost anything as long as good evidence can be presented. As it pertains to the idea of true psychics, I would say that the overwhelming majority of those who hold themselves out as such are simply selling something and can be easily debunked by vigilant observers who can see through the various cold reading and other techniques that they use. As a man who was raised in the Christian faith and—while no longer affiliated with any hard religion—still considers himself a spiritual person, I do believe there is a higher power and energy that binds all of existence and directs our lives. It is this force that I believe a few select people can tap into, for reasons beyond human understanding, and it is that which gives Maureen her ability. The assertion that The Demon Sight is an Irish superstition is nothing more than an inside nod to my honeymoon in Ireland, from which my wife and I had recently returned when I began to write this novel.

While the people and places in the novel are fictional, I did want the world of The Demon Sight to be able to fit itself snugly into our world. Sycamore Hills is not a real town, but it was modeled on a real-world town in Madison County, Missouri which research told me mirrored everything I wanted in the novel's setting. The reform school Maureen is sent to in her formative years, Saint Dymphna's—named for the patron saint of mental illness and anxiety—was based largely on the Élan School, a therapeutic boarding school in Maine that employed a controversial behavior modification and attack therapy program. The school closed its doors in 2011 amid multiple investigations into allegations of abuses ranging from sleep deprivation to physical restraint to the policy of having students fight one another in a boxing ring, allegedly leading to the death of a student in 1982.

Additionally, I would be remiss if I did not thank those who allowed me to pick their brains regarding the scientific side of things, namely my good friends Dr. Carrie Gray and

Dr. Abby Rothstein, who gave me invaluable insight into the world of pharmaceuticals, surgery, and human anatomy. I hope I got the details right. And finally, I need to thank the team at Ten16 Press for taking a chance on this quirky concept and, most of all, my talented editor, Leslie Stradinger. Thank you for helping me make this book what it is and helping me refine my writing technique. I look forward to our continued partnership. Maureen's story is far from over, and she has several adventures and a lot of growing to do before the end.

CPSIA information can be obtained
at www.ICGtesting.com
Printed in the USA
LVHW100911290321
682811LV00006B/12/J